Starlight on Willow Lake

Center Point
Large Print

Also by Susan Wiggs and available from Center Point Large Print:

Candlelight Christmas
The Beekeeper's Ball

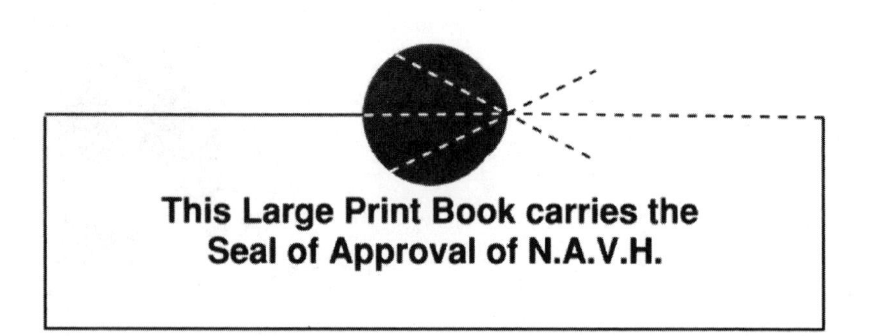

Starlight on Willow Lake

SUSAN WIGGS

CENTER POINT LARGE PRINT
THORNDIKE, MAINE

This Center Point Large Print edition is published
in the year 2015 by arrangement with Harlequin Books S.A..

The text of this Large Print edition is unabridged.
In other aspects, this book may vary
from the original edition.
Printed in the United States of America
on permanent paper.
Set in 16-point Times New Roman type.

ISBN: 978-1-62899-710-1

Library of Congress Cataloging-in-Publication Data

Wiggs, Susan.
Starlight on Willow Lake / Susan Wiggs. — Center Point
Large Print edition.
pages cm
ISBN 978-1-62899-710-1 (library binding : alk. paper)
1. Large type books. I. Title.
PS3573.I38616S73 2015
813′.54—dc23

2015028955

For my parents, Nick and Lou Klist,
my first and best readers.
Your love, wisdom and courage
are my inspiration.

Part One

✵ ✵ ✵ ✵ ✵

"Of all things visible, the highest
is the heaven of the fixed stars."
—Nicolaus Copernicus

✵ 1 ✵

Mason Bellamy stared up at the face of the mountain that had killed his father. The mountain's name was innocent enough—Cloud Piercer. The rich afternoon light of the New Zealand winter cast a spell over the moment. Snow-clad slopes glowed with the impossible pink and amethyst of a rare jewel. The stunning backdrop of the Southern Alps created a panorama of craggy peaks, veined with granite and glacial ice, against a sky so clear it caused the eyes to smart.

The bony, white structure of a cell phone tower, its discs grabbing signals from outer space, rose from a nearby peak. The only other intrusions into the natural beauty were located at the top of the slope—a black-and-yellow gate marked Experts Only and a round dial designating Avalanche Danger: Moderate.

He wondered if someone came all the way up here each day to move the needle on the dial. Maybe his father had wondered the same thing last year. Maybe it had been the last thought to go through his head before he was buried by two hundred thousand cubic meters of snow.

According to witnesses in the town near the base of the mountain, it had been a dry snow avalanche with a powder cloud that had been visible to any resident of Hillside Township who happened to look up. The incident report stated that there had been a delay before the noise came. Then everyone for miles around had heard the sonic boom.

The Maori in the region had legends about this mountain. The natives respected its threatening beauty as well as its lethal nature, their myths filled with cautionary tales of humans being swallowed to appease the gods. For generations, the lofty crag, with its year-round cloak of snow, had challenged the world's most adventurous skiers, and its gleaming north face had been Trevor Bellamy's favorite run. It had also been his final run.

Trevor's final wish, spelled out in his last will and testament, had brought Mason halfway around the world, and down into the Southern Hemisphere's winter. At the moment he felt anything but cold. He unzipped his parka, having worked up a major sweat climbing to the peak. This run was accessible only to those willing to be helicoptered to a landing pad at three thousand meters, and then to climb another few hundred meters on all-terrain skis outfitted with nonslip skins. He removed his skis and peeled the Velcro-like skins from the underside, carefully stowing the gear in his backpack. Then he studied the mountain's face again and felt a sweet rush of adrenaline.

When it came to skiing in dangerous places, he was his father's son.

A rhythmic sliding sound drew Mason's attention to the trail he'd just climbed. He glanced over and lifted his ski pole in a wave. "Over here, bro."

Adam Bellamy came over the crest of the trail, shading his eyes against the afternoon light. "You said you'd kick my ass, and you did," he called. His voice echoed across the empty, frozen terrain.

Mason grinned at his younger brother. "I'm a man of my word. But look at you. You haven't even broken a sweat."

"Mets. We get tested for metabolic conditioning every three months for work." Adam was a firefighter, built to haul eighty pounds of gear up multiple flights of stairs.

"Cool. My only conditioning program involves running to catch the subway."

"The tough life of an international financier," said Adam. "Hold everything while I get out my tiny violin."

"Who says I'm complaining?" Mason took off his goggles to apply some defogger. "Is Ivy close? Or did our little sister stop to hire a team of mountain guides to carry her up the hill so she doesn't have to climb it on her skis?"

"She's close enough to hear you," said Ivy, appearing at the top of the ridge. "And aren't the guides on strike?" She wore a dazzling turquoise parka and white ski pants, Gucci sunglasses and white leather gloves. Her blond hair was wild and wind-tossed, streaming from beneath her helmet.

Mason flashed on an image of their mother. Ivy looked so much like her. He felt a lurch of guilt when he thought about Alice Bellamy. Her last ski run had been right here on this mountain face, too. But unlike Trevor, she had survived. Although some would say that what had happened to her was worse than dying.

Ivy slogged over to her brothers on her AT skis. “Listen, you two. I want to go on record to say that when I leave these earthly bonds, I will not require my adult children to risk their lives in order to scatter my remains. Just leave my ashes on the jewelry counter at Neiman Marcus. I’d be fine with that.”

“Make sure you put your request in writing,” Mason said.

“How do you know I haven’t already?” She gestured at Adam. “Help me get these skins off, will you?” She lifted each ski in turn, planting them upright in the snow.

Adam expertly peeled the fabric skins from the bottoms of her skis, then removed his own, stuffing them into his backpack. “It’s crazy steep, just the way Dad used to describe it.”

“Chicken?” asked Ivy, fastening the chin strap of her crash helmet.

“Have you ever known me to shy away from a

ski run?" Adam asked. "I'm going to take it easy, though. No crazy tricks."

The three of them stood gazing at the beautiful slope, now a perfect picture of serenity in the late-afternoon glow. It was the first time any of them had come to this particular spot. As a family, they had skied together in many places, but not here. This particular mountain had been the special domain of their father and mother alone.

They were lined up in birth order—Mason, the firstborn, the one who knew their father best. Adam, three years younger, had been closest to Trevor. Ivy, still in her twenties, was the quintessential baby of the family—adored, entitled, seemingly fragile, yet with the heart of a lioness. She had owned their father's affections as surely as the sun owns the dawn, in the way only a daughter can.

Mason wondered if his siblings would ever learn the things about their father that he knew. And if they did, would it change the way they felt about him?

They stood together, their collective silence as powerful as any conversation they might have had.

"It's incredible," Ivy said after a long pause. "The pictures didn't do it justice. Maybe Dad's last request wasn't so nutty, after all. This might be the prettiest mountain ever, and I get to see it with my two best guys." Then she sighed. "I wish Mom could be here."

“I’ll get the whole thing on camera,” Adam said. “We can all watch it together when we get back to Avalon next week.”

A year after the accident, their mother was adjusting to a new life in a new place—a small Catskills town on the shores of Willow Lake. Mason was pretty sure it wasn’t the life Alice Bellamy had imagined for herself.

“Do you have him?” Adam asked.

Mason slapped his forehead. “Damn, I forgot. Why don’t the two of you wait right here while I ski to the bottom, grab the ashes, helicopter back up to the rendezvous and make the final climb again?”

“Very funny,” said Adam.

“Of course I have him.” Mason shrugged out of his backpack and dug inside. He pulled out an object bundled in a navy blue bandanna. He unwrapped it and handed the bandanna to Adam.

“A beer stein?” asked Ivy.

“It was all I could find,” said Mason. The stein was classic kitsch, acquired at a frat party during Mason’s college days. There was a scene with a laughing Falstaff painted on the sides, and the mug had a hinged lid made of pewter. “The damned urn they delivered him in was huge. No way would it fit in my luggage.”

He didn’t explain to his sister and brother that a good half of the ashes had ended up on the living room floor of his Manhattan apartment. Getting

Trevor Bellamy from the urn to the beer stein had been trickier than Mason had thought. Slightly freaked out by the idea of his father embedded in his carpet fibers, he had vacuumed up the spilled ashes, wincing at the sound of the larger bits being sucked into the bag.

Then he'd felt bad about emptying the vacuum bag down the garbage chute, so he'd gone out on the balcony and sprinkled the remains over Avenue of the Americas. There had been a breeze that day, and his fussiest neighbor in the high-rise co-op had stuck her head out, shaking her fist and threatening to call the super to report the transgression. Most of the ashes blew back onto the balcony, and Mason ended up waiting until the wind died down; then he'd swept the area with a broom.

So only half of Trevor Bellamy had made it into the beer stein. That was appropriate, Mason decided. Their father had been only half there while he was alive, too.

"This is cool with me," said Adam. "Dad always did like his beer."

Mason held the mug high, its silhouette stark against the deepening light of the afternoon sky.

"*Ein prosit*," said Adam.

"*Salut*," Mason said, in the French their father had spoken like a native.

"*Cin cin*." Ivy, the artist in the family, favored Italian.

"Take your protein pills and put your helmet on," Mason said, riffing on the David Bowie song. "Let's do this thing."

Ivy lowered her sunglasses over her eyes. "Mom loves skiing so much. It's so sad that she'll never ski again."

"I'll film it so she can watch." Adam took off one glove with his teeth and reached up to switch on the GoPro camera affixed to the top of his helmet.

"Should we say a few words?" asked Ivy.

"If I say no, will that stop you?" Mason removed the duct tape from the lid of the beer stein.

Ivy stuck out her tongue at him, shifting into bratty-sister mode. Then she looked up at Adam and spoke to the camera. "Hey, Mom. We were just wishing you could be here with us to say goodbye to Daddy. We all made it to the summit of Cloud Piercer, just like he wanted. It's kind of surreal, finding winter here when the summer is just beginning where you are, at Willow Lake. It feels somehow like . . . I don't know . . . like we're unstuck in time."

Ivy's voice wavered with emotion. "Anyway, so here I am with my two big brothers. Daddy always loved it when the three of us were together, skiing and having fun."

Adam moved his head to let the camera record the majestic scenery all around them. The sculpted crags of the Southern Alps, which ran the entire length of New Zealand's south island, were sharply silhouetted against the sky. Mason wondered what the day had been like when his parents had skied this mountain, their last run together. Was the sky so blue that it hurt the eyes? Did the sharp cold air stab their lungs? Was the silence this deep? Had there been any inkling that the entire face of the mountain was about to bury them?

"Are we ready?" he asked.

Adam and Ivy nodded. He studied his little sister's face, now soft with the sadness of missing her father. She'd had a special closeness with him, and she'd taken his death hard—maybe even harder than their mother had.

"Who's going first?" asked Adam.

"It can't be me," said Mason. "You, um, don't want to get caught in the blowback, if you know what I mean." He gestured with the beer stein.

"Oh, right," said Ivy. "You go last, then."

Adam twisted the camera so it faced uphill. "Let's take it one at a time, okay? So we don't cause another avalanche."

It was a known safety procedure that in an avalanche zone, only one person at a time should go down the mountain. Mason wondered if his father had been aware of the precaution. He wondered if his father had violated the rule. He doubted he would ever ask his mother for a detail like that. Whatever had happened on this mountain a year ago couldn't be changed now.

Ivy took off her shades, leaned over and kissed the beer stein. "Bye, Daddy. Fly into eternity, okay? But don't forget how much you were loved here on earth. I'll keep you safe in my heart." She started to cry. "I thought I'd used up all my tears, but I guess not. I'll always shed a tear for you, Daddy."

Adam waggled his gloved fingers in front of the camera. "Yo, Dad. You were the best. I couldn't have asked for anything more. Except for more time with you. Later, dude."

Each one of them had known a different Trevor Bellamy. Mason could only wish the father he'd known was the one who had inspired Ivy's tenderness and loyalty or Adam's hero worship. Mason knew another side to their father, but he would never be the one to shatter his siblings' memories.

Adam pushed through the warning gate and started down the mountain, the camera on his helmet rolling.

Ivy waited, then followed at a safe distance behind. Thanks to Adam, the cautious one of the three, each of them wore gear equipped with beacons and avalanche airbags, designed to detonate automatically in the event of a slide.

Their mother had been wearing one the day of the incident. Their father had not.

Adam skied with competence and control,

navigating the steep slope with ease and carving a sinuous curve in the untouched powder. Ivy followed gracefully, turning his S-curves into a double-helix pattern.

The lightest of breezes stirred the icy air. Mason decided he had worked too hard to climb the damned mountain only to take the conservative route down. Always the most reckless of the three, he decided to take the slope the way his father probably had, with joyous abandon.

"Here goes," he said to the clear, empty air, and he thumbed open the lid of the beer stein. The cold air must have weakened the pottery, because a shard broke loose, cutting through his glove and slicing into his thumb. *Ouch.* He ignored the cut and focused on the task at hand.

Did any essence of their father remain? Was Trevor Bellamy's spirit somehow trapped within the humble-looking detritus, waiting to be set free on the mountaintop?

He had lived his life. Left a legacy of secrets behind. He'd paid the ultimate price for his freedom, leaving his burden on someone else's shoulders—Mason's.

"Godspeed, Dad," he said. With his ski poles in one hand and the beer stein in the other, he raised his arm high and plunged down the steep slope, leaning into a controlled fall. Just for a moment, he heard his father's voice: *Lean into the fear, son. That's where the power comes from.* The words drifted to him from a long-ago time when everything had been simple, when his dad had simply been Dad, coaching him down the mountain, shouting with unabashed joy when Mason conquered a steep slope. That was probably why Mason favored adrenaline-fueled sports that involved teetering on the edge between terror and triumph.

The ashes created a cloud in his wake, rising on an updraft of wind and dispersing across the face of Trevor's beloved, deadly mountain.

The things we love most can kill us. Mason might have heard the saying somewhere. Or he had just made it up.

The faster Mason went, the less he was bothered by something so inconvenient as a thought. That was the beauty of skiing in dangerous places. Filled with the thrill of the ride, he was only vaguely aware of Adam pointing the camera at him. He couldn't resist showing off, making a trail in a fresh expanse of untouched powder, like a snake slithering down the mountain. Spotting a rugged granite cliff, its cornice perfectly formed for jumping, he raced toward it. *Lean into the fear, son.* He aimed his skis straight down the fall line and launched himself off the edge. For several seconds he was airborne, the wind flapping through his parka, turning him momentarily into a human kite. The steep pitch of the landing raced up to meet him with breathtaking speed.

He wobbled on contact but didn't wipe out, managing to come out of the landing with the mug still held aloft.

He gave a short laugh. *How's that, Dad? How'd I do?* In one way or another, his whole life had been a performance for his father—in sports, in school, in business. He'd lost his audience, and it was liberating as hell. Which made him wonder why tears were fogging up his goggles. Then, as the slope flattened and his speed naturally slowed, he realized Ivy was waving her arms frantically.

Now what?

He raced toward them and saw that Adam had his mobile phone out.

"What's up?" he asked. "Was my epic run not pretty enough? Or are you posting a Tweet about it already?"

Despite the chill air, Ivy's face was pale. "It's Mom."

"On the phone? Tell her I said hi."

"No, dipshit, something happened to Mom."

2

For Mason, money was a tool, not a goal. And when he had to get from a remote mountain town to an international airport, he was glad he had plenty of it. Within a few hours of the aborted ash-sprinkling, the three of them were in the first-class lounge at Christchurch Airport, booked on a flight to New York. From there, they'd take a private plane up to Avalon, north toward Albany, along the Hudson. He'd instructed his assistant to find an amphibious plane so they could land on Willow Lake and tie up at the dock in front of their mother's place.

The entire journey would take about twenty-four hours. Thanks to the time zone change, they would arrive the same day they left. The journey cost in the neighborhood of thirty grand, which he paid without batting an eye. It was only money. Mason had a knack for making money the way some guys made wooden birdhouses in their garages over the weekend.

Adam was on the phone with someone in Avalon. "We're on our way," he said. Then he checked the clock in the lounge. "We'll get there when we get there. Yeah, okay, just sit tight."

"Did you get more details out of them?" Mason asked.

"She fell down the stairs and broke her collarbone," Adam said, and zipped the mobile phone into his pocket. "It's a miracle she didn't crack open her head or get crushed by her motorized chair."

"I can't believe she fell," Ivy said, her voice trembling.

"And what the hell was she doing at the top of a flight of stairs?" Mason asked. "The entire downstairs of the house has been adapted for her."

"If you bothered to go see her more than once in a blue moon, you'd know they finished installing the elevator," Adam stated. He was in charge of her day-to-day care, living on the premises of the lakeside estate. Mason had taken the role of looking after provisions, finance and logistics for their mother, a role more suited to his comfort zone.

Mason batted aside his brother's criticism. "Screw that. I don't get how the hell she managed to fall down the stairs. She's a quadriplegic in a wheelchair. She's incapable of moving."

"She can move her mouth and drive the chair with her breath," Ivy pointed out. "She's been working with her physical therapist on extending her arms at the elbow, so that can help with her mobility, too."

"I don't get why she was upstairs, either," Mason said. His heart was pounding so hard that his chest hurt. He and his mother had their differences, but when it came down to moments like this, he felt nothing but love and sorrow. And now a surge of panic.

"You're sure she's all right?" Ivy asked, bringing a tray of cappuccinos and croissants to the seating area where they were waiting.

"Other than her usual state of rage and bitterness, yeah," said Adam. "She's okay."

"Jesus." Mason raked his splayed hand through his hair.

"No, the caregiver on duty was named José." Adam consulted the email displayed on his phone.

"Fire the son of a bitch," Mason ordered.

"I didn't have to," Adam said. "He quit. They all quit. None of her home health aides have lasted more than a few weeks."

"He couldn't have stopped it," Ivy pointed out. "According to Mrs. Armentrout, Mom took the elevator upstairs without telling anyone."

"Armentrout? The housekeeper?" asked Mason. "Then she should be fired, too."

"You're the one who hired her," Adam pointed out.

"My assistant hired her. With my approval."

"And she's terrific. Besides, it's the caregiver's job to look after Mom. Not the housekeeper."

"She needs assistance, not to be under surveillance," Ivy said.

"Maybe she does, if she's sneaking upstairs." Mason spent more time than anyone imagined thinking about their mother. On that day a year ago, their father had suffered the ultimate tragedy. Everyone—himself included—said their mother was lucky to be alive.

She didn't consider herself lucky, though. From the moment she had been told the spinal injury meant she would never walk again—much less ski, salsa dance, cliff dive, run a triathlon or even drive a car—she had raged against her fate. Anyone who dared to mention to her face that she was lucky to be alive risked a tongue-lashing.

After multiple surgeries, drug therapies and intensive rehab, Alice had agreed to move to Avalon to settle into her new life as a widow and a quadriplegic, determined to find what independence she could. Avalon was the town where Adam lived, on the shores of the prettiest lake in Ulster County, just a couple of hours by train from New York City.

Each of the three Bellamy offspring played their part. Adam, a firefighter with training as an EMT, now lived over the boathouse on the property Mason had bought for their mother after the accident. Adam was hands-on when it came to caring for people, and it was a relief to have a family member on the premises for their mom.

Mason was responsible for making sure their mother had everything she needed to create her new life in Avalon. He had provided her with a sprawling lakeside estate, the house and grounds adapted to her needs and large enough to accommodate a staff. The historic compound, on the sun-drenched shores of Willow Lake, had been remodeled and retrofitted for his mother's motorized wheelchair, with ramps, wide doorways and an elevator, an intercom system and a network of graded pathways outdoors. There was a private gym equipped for physical therapy, a heated pool, sauna and spa, and a dock and boathouse with ramps and hoists. She had a full staff, including a Balinese chef with Cordon Bleu credentials, a driver, and living quarters for a resident home health aide.

Everybody had a role. Mason thought it was working. But apparently, there was now no resident caregiver.

"What did you mean when you said they all quit?" he asked Adam.

"Like I told you before, you'd understand if you'd go see her. Ivy lives on the West Coast and she manages to visit more often than you do, and you're just down in the city."

Ivy's role was more amorphous, but just as vital. Sometimes it seemed to Mason that she did her part by simply being adorable and loving and supportive. Ten years younger than her brother, she was the kind of person who could walk into a room and fill it with light. During the early days after the accident, Ivy was as vital to their mother as pure oxygen.

"Mom doesn't need my company," Mason pointed out. "I set her up in the best house we could find, hired a full staff, had the place retrofitted for her and the chair. I don't know what the hell else I can do."

"Sometimes you don't have to *do* anything," said Ivy. "Sometimes just being there is all she needs."

"Not from me." He checked the calendar on his phone. "So she's already had the surgery to fix her collarbone. How long will she have to stay in the hospital?"

"Probably not long," Adam said. "We'll know more when we meet with the doctors." He sat forward in his chair, resting his forearms on his knees. "Listen, I was going to tell you this over dinner tonight. You're going to be in charge of Mom for the next few months—maybe longer."

Mason dismissed the notion with a wave of his hand. "I can't even stay a few hours. I'm supposed to go to LA with Regina the day after tomorrow," he said. "She set up a meeting with a major new client."

He didn't deem it prudent to mention at this time that he and Regina—his colleague as well as his girlfriend—had built a few days of surfing in Malibu into their work schedule.

"You're going to have to cancel it," Adam said simply. "You need to stay with Mom."

"What the hell do you mean, stay with her?"

"Live at the lake house. Make the place your base of operations."

Mason recoiled. "What's this about?"

"I have to go away for a while," Adam said. "Special training. For work."

Mason immediately turned to Ivy.

She put up both hands, palms out. "My fellowship in Paris, remember? The one I've been working toward for the past five years? It starts next month."

"Postpone it."

"Right. I'll just tell the director of the Institut de Paume to keep a slot open for me." Ivy raised her sunglasses and fixed him with an intense glare. "You're up, bro."

"Okay, fine, but I'm not moving up to the Catskills. I'll have my assistant find another live-in aide."

"Damn it," Adam said. "Mom needs family. She needs *you*."

Mason had provided a lengthy roster of hired help, material things and creature comforts for their mother. He had spared no expense—elevators, adaptive devices—nothing was too good for Alice Bellamy.

Thanks to Mason, she wanted for nothing.

Except the one thing no one could give her, and all of Mason's millions could never provide.

Some troubles could not be solved by throwing money at them.

Yet he couldn't imagine anything worse than being trapped in a small town with his bitter, wounded mother with whom—unlike his brother and sister—he'd had a rocky relationship since he was a teenager.

And now he was expected to move in with her.

Oh, hell, no, he thought.

"What kind of special training?" he asked Adam.

"I'm getting certified in arson investigation. I'll be up in Albany for twelve to sixteen weeks."

"Seriously?"

"He's having girl trouble," Ivy said. "It's the geographic cure."

"Shut up, brat. I am not having girl trouble."

"Okay, let's call it *lack* of girl trouble."

"What? Come on." To Mason's surprise, Adam's face turned red. "It's complicated. And speaking of complicated, exactly how many frogs have you kissed this year alone?"

Ivy often bemoaned the state of her love life, and Mason had no idea why. She was gorgeous, a total sweetheart, a little bit nutty, and everyone loved her. Just not the right guy, he supposed.

"*You* shut up," she retorted, and Mason heard loud echoes of their childhood years seeping into the exchange.

"Both of you shut up," he said. "Let's focus on what to do about Mom."

"Ivy's going to Paris to get laid—"

"Hey." She punched him in the arm.

"And I can't change the dates of the training course to suit your travel schedule. You're up, Mason."

"But—"

"But nothing. It's your turn to step up."

Mason scowled at his brother and sister. It was hard to believe the three of them shared the same DNA, they were all so different. "Not a chance in hell. There's nothing my being there can help. No damn way I'm moving to Willow Lake."

✵ 3 ✵

"I'd kill the fatted calf for you, but I'm a bit indisposed at the moment," Alice Bellamy said when Mason arrived at the estate on Willow Lake.

"That's okay. I'm a vegetarian anyway." Mason wondered if his mother realized that he had not eaten meat since the age of twelve.

Crossing the elegant room to where she sat near a window, he bent down and brushed his lips against her cheek. Soap and lotion, a freshly laundered blouse, the smells he had always associated with her. Except in the past, she'd been able to offer the briefest of hugs, to reach out with her hand and smooth the hair back from his brow, a gesture that had persisted since his childhood.

Concealing a wrenching sense of sorrow, he took a seat across from her. He studied her face, startled at how little she had changed—from the neck up. Shiny blond hair, lovely skin, cornflower blue eyes. He'd always been proud to have such a youthful, good-looking mom. "You broke your collarbone," he said.

"So I'm told."

"I thought you'd be in a cast or a sling or something."

She pursed her lips. "It's not as if I need to keep my arm immobilized."

"Uh, yeah." Since the accident, he didn't know how to deal with his mother. Who was he kidding? He'd *never* known how to deal with her. "Are you in . . . Does it hurt?"

"Darling boy, I can't feel anything below my chest. Not pain or pleasure. Nothing."

He let several seconds tick past while he tried to think of a reply that didn't sound phony or patronizing or flat-out ignorant. "I'm glad you're all right. You gave us a scare."

More silence echoed through the room, an open lounge with a massive river-rock fireplace, fine furnishings and floor-to-ceiling shelves crammed with books. Everything was spaced and arranged to accommodate his mother's chair. There was a corner study with a big post office writing desk and another corner with a powerful brass telescope set on a tripod. The baby grand piano, which had occupied every house the family had ever lived in, was now a resting place for a collection of photos.

The ever-present view of Willow Lake was framed by French doors, which could be operated by a switch. "So anyway," he said, "we'll get you fixed up with a new helper right away. My assistant is working with a couple of agencies already." He checked his watch. "I've got plenty to keep us busy for the day. The lawyer is coming in half an hour. Are you up for that?"

"Lawyer?" She frowned, then took a sip through

a straw from the coffee mug affixed to the tray on her chair.

"My attorney in the city recommended someone local, from here in Ulster County—"

"Whatever for?"

"To deal with the negligence suit against the caregiver who let you fall down the stairs, and the outfit he works for."

"Oh, no, you don't. It was just a stupid accident," she said. "Nobody's fault."

"Mom, you fell down a flight of stairs with a three-hundred-pound motorized chair. It's a miracle you weren't crushed. Somebody was negligent—"

"That would be me," she stated. "I leaned on the control and drove myself off the rails."

"Then the chair manufacturer is at fault."

"No lawyers," she said. "What I—What happened was no one's fault. There will be no lawsuit. End of story."

"Mom, you're entitled to a settlement." If there was one thing Mason couldn't stand, it was people failing to take responsibility for their actions.

"Absolutely not," she said. "I won't hear another word about it."

He sent Brenda a text message to cancel the lawyer. "Whatever you say. That gives us more time to meet with potential new caregivers."

"Lovely."

"Adam warned me that you were going to be a sourpuss."

"I bet he didn't say *sourpuss*. He's a firefighter. I'm sure he has a more colorful term for me, like *hell-bitch*."

Adam is a saint, thought Mason. St. Adam. He silently cursed the saint for having left already. Adam and Ivy had stuck around until their mom was discharged, then they both had to leave; Adam to his training and Ivy back to Santa Barbara to prepare for her move to Europe.

"I printed out the résumés of the candidates we're meeting with," he said. "You want to go over them now, or—"

"I think I'd like to go out into the garden now."

He gritted his teeth, looking away so she wouldn't see his annoyance.

"You're annoyed," she said. "You can't wait to leave. You've got one foot out the door."

Damn. Busted. He schooled his face into a pleasant expression. "Don't be silly. I'm glad I'm here to spend some time with you."

"Right." She nudged a lever on her chair and rolled toward the French doors. "Let's go inspect the property you bought. You've never even seen it in the summer."

He stood aside, impressed by how nimbly she used her chair to operate the switch plate, which opened the doors. When he stepped out on the deck, the view and the cool clarity of the air stole his breath. "Wow," he said.

"You did well," she told him. "I do appreciate everything you've done for me—moving me to Avalon, getting this house adapted for my needs, hiring a staff. If I'm going to be a cripple the rest of my life, I might as well do it in style."

"I thought we weren't going to say *cripple*."

"Not when I'm being polite. I don't feel terribly polite these days."

"Let me savor the view for a few minutes, okay?" The last time he'd seen the property, it had been blanketed in snow. The estate had been known as the Webster House, having been built in the 1920s by descendants of Daniel Webster himself. For Mason, the decision to acquire and restore the house had not been based on historical significance, prestige or even investment value. He wanted his mother to have a nice place to live, near Adam—aka her favorite—that could be quickly adapted for her special needs.

During that process, he had come to appreciate the benefit of having a big extended family living in a small town. His cousin Olivia was married to the contractor who had restored the fanciful timber-and-stone mansion to its original gloss as a grand summer residence from days gone by. His cousin Ross was married to a nurse who specialized in adaptive living. Another cousin, Greg, was a landscape architect. Olivia was a talented designer in her own right, so in a matter of months, the place was ready for his mother and Adam, and their staff of live-in help.

Mason had spared no expense. In his position, there was no need to. For the past decade, he had run his own private equities-and-lending firm, and business was good. He had all the money in the world. But of course, wealth had its limits. He couldn't buy his mother her mobility. He couldn't buy a way to make her smile again.

He took a deep breath of the morning air. "It's sweet," he said.

"I beg your pardon."

"The air here. It's sweet."

"I suppose it is."

"The landscaping looks great. Are you happy with it?"

"Your cousin Greg sent a crew to take care of the mowing and gardening," she said, nodding in the direction of a long swath of grass sloping down to the water's edge. There was a dock and a timber-and-stone boathouse, home to kayaks, a catboat and a 1940s Chris-Craft. When not on duty at the fire station, Adam lived in the upstairs quarters.

A fringe of ancient willow trees dipped their budding branches into the placid, sunlit water. The word that came immediately to mind was *unspoiled.* Willow Lake was one of the prettiest lakes in a landscape full of pretty lakes. The green-clad hills, with a few puffy clouds riding on their shoulders, rose gently upward from the shore. On the north end of the lake was a grand old summer camp, a hundred years in the making—Camp Kioga.

At the south end was the town called Avalon, as picture-perfect as a storybook setting, with its whistle-stop train station, old-fashioned town square, stone-built Greek revival library and shady shoreline parks. Its outskirts were equally attractive—a mountain road leading to a ski resort, a ball field for the local bush-league baseball team, white-steepled churches, their spires seeming to thrust through the new-leafed trees. The cliffs of the Shawangunks attracted climbers from all over the world. Somewhere not so far away, there was probably suburban blight—shotgun shacks and mobile homes, ramshackle farms and big-box stores. But he couldn't see any of that from here. And more important, neither could his mother.

The place he'd acquired for her was on the western shore of the lake, so it caught the sunrise every morning, something his real-estate agent had pointed out when he had bought the property. The agent had babbled on about the attributes of the historic mansion, not knowing Mason was already sold on getting the place. He was looking for security for his mother, not for a return on investment.

"Why do they keep quitting?" he asked her, paging through the printouts of the candidates for the job of primary caregiver. "Is it the living quarters?"

"Have you *seen* the living quarters?"

He'd looked at pictures after the remodel was done. The living quarters, located in a private wing of the house, featured a suite of rooms with a view of the lake, new furnishings and luxurious fixtures. "Okay, good point. So?"

"I haven't been conducting exit interviews. I'm sure Adam gave you an earful. Nobody wants to live with a miserable old woman who can barely change the channel on *The Price Is Right*."

Oh, boy. "You're not old," he said. "Your parents would freak out if they heard you say that. And being miserable is optional. So is watching *The Price Is Right*."

"Thank you, Sigmund Freud. I'll remember that next time I'm lying in bed, pissing into a plastic tube—"

"Mom."

"Oh, sorry. I don't mean to trouble you with the reality of my body functions."

Now he understood why they all quit.

"Where should I put your things, Mr. Bellamy?" asked the housekeeper.

Mason stood glaring out the window at an impossibly serene and beautiful view of Willow

Lake. Although he'd arrived late the day before, his luggage had been delayed—some mix-up at an airport between here and New Zealand.

Now Mrs. Armentrout rolled the two large bags into the room. The suitcases wore tags marked Unattended Baggage.

He hadn't seen the luggage since dashing to the airport in New Zealand after getting the call about his mother's accident. Now he realized he didn't need the bags at all, since they were packed with winter clothes.

"Right there is fine, thanks," he said.

"Would you like some help unpacking?"

"Sure, when you can get to it."

"I can do that right now."

The housekeeper worked with brisk efficiency, hanging his bespoke suit in the antique armoire, carefully folding cashmere sweaters away in a cedar-lined drawer. She lifted a dress shirt out of the suitcase and put it on a wooden hanger, her hand moving appreciatively over the fabric.

Philomena Armentrout actually looked more like a supermodel than a housekeeper. A native of South Africa, she was tall and slender, with creamy café au lait skin, wearing chic black slacks and a white blouse, shining dark hair and subtle makeup. Only the closest of inspections would reveal the tiny scars where the jaw wires had been surgically anchored after her husband had assaulted her. Mason had committed himself and all his resources to staffing the household with the best personnel available, and Mrs. Armentrout was definitely the best. That wasn't the only reason Mason had hired her, though. Broken and battered, she had needed a new start in life, and Mason was taking care of her immigration process. According to Adam, she ran the place like a high-end boutique hotel, supervising every aspect of the household.

His phone in the charging station on the desk murmured insistently, signaling another text message from Regina. She had not taken the news of his change of plans well. She'd peppered him with all the questions he'd already run through with his brother and sister: Why did he need to come here in person? Couldn't a staffer take care of hiring the new caregiver? Couldn't Adam or Ivy change their plans and step in?

No, they couldn't. Both had commitments that couldn't be broken—Adam's training in arson investigation, Ivy's art fellowship at the Institut de Paume. But Mason didn't feel like getting into a big debate with Regina at the moment, and so he ignored the message.

Last night he'd slept like a corpse in the comfortable guest room. It was so damned quiet here, and the air was sweet and the jet lag had finally caught up with him.

"Is my mother up yet?" he asked.

She glanced at the clock on the mantelpiece.

"In a bit. Lena, the morning aide, will bring her to the lounge room for coffee at nine. You can go see her in her room right away if you want."

He did want to see his mother. Just not . . . before she was ready for the day.

One of the hardest things Alice Bellamy was having to adjust to was the loss of privacy. Needing another person to look after all her personal needs was a constant source of irritation. "I'll wait," he said. "The coffee is great, by the way. Thanks for sending it up."

"Wayan roasts his own. He gets the green coffee beans from his family in Bali. It's got a funny name, tupac or leewalk, something like that."

"Luwak," said Mason. "No wonder it's so good. You should look this stuff up sometime. You won't believe where it comes from."

"Right. That's the stuff that comes from a civet cat's arse or something, yes?"

"It's organic."

Like Mrs. Armentrout, the personal chef had been selected for his unique excellence as well as his urgent need to escape his dire circumstances. Wayan had been attending cruise ship school in the Philippines. The Balinese native had abruptly been cut from that program, leaving him stranded and nearly penniless in a foreign land. Mason had found him through a sponsorship program and brought Wayan—along with his wife and son—halfway around the world. The family lived above the old carriage house, now a four-car garage and workshop. His wife, Banni, served as an evening aide and personal assistant, and their son, Donno, was Alice's driver, mechanic and general fix-it guy. Mason hadn't met Wayan yet, but Adam sang rhapsodies about his cooking.

Mrs. Armentrout held up a rash guard shirt. "It's a shame you had to cut your vacation short," she said. "I've heard the surfing in Malibu is the best in the world."

"It will keep," he said simply.

"And the skiing was good?" she inquired.

"You bet." It occurred to him to explain the trip wasn't strictly a vacation, but a journey to fulfill his father's last wish, followed by a work trip. He knew the explanation would make him sound less like a selfish prick who was avoiding his wounded mother.

But it didn't actually bother him to be regarded as a selfish prick. It just made things simpler.

"How is she doing?" he asked Mrs. Armentrout. "She didn't have much to say about her fall."

"The doctor said the collarbone will heal nicely. There was a surgery to repair it with plates and screws, and she was able to come home the very next day."

"I've spoken to the surgeon about her collarbone already. That's not what I'm asking."

"She's . . . It's terribly hard, Mr. Bellamy. She is bearing up."

“Were you around when she fell?”

“No one was around. You can look over the report from the EMTs.”

“I’m sure Adam went over that with a fine-tooth comb,” Mason said.

The mantel clock chimed nine. He felt Mrs. Armentrout watching him. He could practically hear her thoughts. She was wondering why he didn’t seem so eager to settle in. “I’ll let you finish here,” he said, wishing he could be a million miles away. “I’m going to see my mother. We’re starting the interviewing process today.”

As he descended the wide, curving staircase, he wondered if this was where his mother had fallen in her chair. Had she called out in terror? Had she felt pain?

He trailed his fingers over the silky walnut hand-rail. She couldn’t feel the texture of the wood with her fingertips. Physical sensation below the spinal cord injury was gone. Yet when he thought of the expression he’d seen on her face last night, he knew that she still felt the deepest kind of pain.

“Mrs. Bellamy?” Mrs. Armentrout came out on the veranda. “Your first appointment is here.”

“Lucky him,” she said.

“We’ll meet in there.” Mason gestured at the great room through the French doors.

Thus began the work of finding the right individual to make life bearable for an angry, disabled woman with a major attitude problem. They met with the first group of candidates in quick succession.

The back-to-back meetings were brief and businesslike. Mason watched his mother closely as she questioned the visitors. She gave up nothing, holding her face in a benign, neutral expression, speaking in controlled, icy tones that highlighted her crisp diction. Alice Bellamy had been educated at Harvard, and although she claimed she had spent most of her college years skiing, she'd graduated with honors. She'd had a successful career as an adventure travel specialist and guide, which had nicely complemented her husband's job in international finance.

Mason listened carefully to each applicant, wondering how the hell a person would go about helping someone like Alice Bellamy remake her life. Which candidate was up to the task? The military nurse built like a sumo wrestler? The motherly woman with a master's degree in nutrition and food science? The spandex-clad personal trainer? The registered nurse with a rack Mason couldn't stop staring at? The tough-as-nails Brooklyn woman whose last client had written a glowing three-page letter of reference?

He was glad Brenda had provided photographs along with the résumés, because the interviewees were all starting to blend together. Each one of them had outstanding qualities.

Mason was sure they'd met the right person. They just had to pinpoint which one.

Afterward, he placed the résumés on the table and offered his mother an encouraging smile. "Brenda did a great job," he said. "They were all excellent. Did you have a favorite?"

She stared out the window, her face unreadable.

He picked up the résumé on top—Chandler Darrow. "So this guy was great. He's got an impressive list of credentials—top of his class at SUNY New Paltz, with references from grateful families for the past ten years."

"No," said Alice, glaring at the photo attached to the résumé.

"He's perfect. Single, good personality, seemed really caring."

"He had shifty eyes."

"What?"

"His eyes—they look shifty. You can see it in the picture."

"Mom—"

"No."

Gritting his teeth, Mason arranged his face into a smile as he picked up the next one—Marianne Phillips, who also had flawless references, including the fact that she had worked for the Rockefeller family.

"She smelled like garlic," his mother said.

"No, she didn't." Shit, thought Mason. This was not going well.

"I've lost most of my abilities, but not my sense of smell. I can't stand garlic. You know that."

"Okay, next. Darryl Smits—"

"Don't even bother. I can't stand the name Darryl."

"I don't even know what to say to that."

"I just said it—*no*."

"Casey Halberg."

"She was the one wearing Crocs. Who wears Crocs to an interview? They look like hooves."

"Jesus—"

"I didn't like him, either. Jesús Garza. In fact, you can cross all the men off the list right now and save us a lot of trouble." She paused to gaze thoughtfully at the display of family photos on the baby grand. "I've never had much luck with men," she added softly.

"What?" He had no idea what she was talking about. "Never mind," Mason added, not wanting to get distracted. "Let's go back over the female candidates."

She sighed impatiently, then glared again at the photo display. There were pictures of her parents—Mason's grandparents—who lived in Florida. Immediately following his mother's accident, they had worn themselves out trying to take care of her. Then her dad had been diagnosed with Parkinson's, and Mason had stepped in. His mom's brothers, who ran a seaplane service in Alaska, were too far away to pitch in.

"Why is there a piano in here?" his mother demanded.

"You've owned that piano all your life. You love piano music," Mason pointed out. "Everybody in the family plays." He'd taken lessons as a kid and used to be really good, but he hadn't played in years. Why was that? He liked making music, but he just didn't bother anymore.

"Every time I look at that thing," his mother said, "it reminds me that I used to be able to play a dozen Chopin nocturnes from memory. Now my piano is nothing but a display area for old photos."

"We thought you might like having someone in to play for you every once in a while."

"Like you?"

Touché. "I'm pretty rusty, but I'll try to play for you whenever I'm around, Mom."

"That's just it, you're never around."

"Hey, check it out," he said, brandishing one of the résumés, "the woman named Dodie Wechsler says she plays piano and put herself through school giving lessons."

"She was the chatty one," said his mother. "She talked too much."

"Mom, I get that you've lost your independence. We all wish you didn't need a single soul to take care of you. But the reality is, you do. So we damn well better pick somebody, and soon."

"All the people we met today are unacceptable. There's not a single one in the bunch I can stand."

"Mabel Roberts."

"Too churchy."

"What?"

"She kept mentioning what a blessing everything is—this house, the lake, the beginning of summer. I'd feel as if she were judging me all the time."

"She had a positive attitude. That's a good thing."

Alice sniffed and looked away.

"I get it, Mom. The person you need doesn't exist. Because the person you need is a freaking saint. Just not a *churchy* one."

They had run through all the candidates his assistant had found, except one—a last-minute addition of someone named Faith McCallum. Her profile on a jobs website looked promising, though Brenda hadn't scheduled a meeting with her yet.

What were the chances that she could be the one? Could she be strong enough to handle Alice Bellamy?

Though there was no photograph attached, Mason liked this candidate already. He liked the name—Faith McCallum. It was a sturdy name, even though his mother might think it sounded churchy. It was the name of a person who was organized, in control and classy. The name of a person whose life ran as smoothly as a Tesla motor, and whose saintly qualities would bring peace to the household.

✵ 4 ✵

"Shit." Faith McCallum stabbed a finger at the keyboard of the ancient hand-me-down laptop. "Come on, you son of a bitch, work for me one last time."

The job posting had finally brought results. As her email had flashed past, she'd seen the subject line: "Response to your posting." But the moment she'd clicked on it, the damn thing had gone into blue-screen meltdown.

She had rebooted, but now the computer screen was frozen on its opening page—daily devotions for diabetics. Today's thought was particularly annoying. *Leap, and the net will appear.*

Faith had done her share of leaping, but so far, she hadn't accomplished anything but a bumpy landing. Leap of faith. Ha-ha.

She got up in frustration, went outside and refilled the cat's water dish. It wasn't her cat. It wasn't even her dish, for that matter. The stray had started coming around a few weeks ago; it wouldn't let anyone near it, so Faith named it Fraidy and put out food and water under the stoop.

Returning to the computer, she stared for a moment at the still-frozen screen, then tried clicking the link to the job-posting site she had been checking three times a day, without fail. Her search for a new position was getting desperate. The home health care agency she had been working for hadn't sent anything her way in three months. Even when they did find work for her, the outfit didn't pay her enough to sustain a pet gerbil, let alone two growing daughters. Faith was already two months behind on the rent, and the place was under new management.

In desperation, she had posted her résumé on every home health aide job site she could find, hoping to negotiate a living wage on her own rather than going through yet another agency that helped itself to a hefty percentage of her wages.

Finally, the sluggish browser responded. The mobile home park's "free" Wi-Fi unfurled at leaden speed. She usually got several chores done while waiting for a page to load.

"Mo-oo-om!" Faith's younger daughter, Ruby, stretched the word to several whiny syllables. The little girl stomped inside, slamming the door open wide. The impact caused the rented double-wide to shudder. "Cara forgot to wait for me at the bus. And she stole my lunch ticket—again."

"Did not," said Cara, following her younger sister into the room and flopping down on the tiny swaybacked sofa. With elaborate nonchalance, she opened her AP biology textbook.

"Did so."

"Did not."

"Then where did my lunch ticket go, huh?"

Ruby demanded. She shrugged out of her back-pack, depositing it on the built-in table.

"Who knows?" Cara asked without looking up. She twisted a strand of purple-dyed hair around her index finger.

"You know," Ruby said, "because you stold it."

"Stole," Cara corrected her sister. "And I didn't."

"You're the one who took it last time."

"That was a month ago, and you were sick that day."

"Yeah, but—"

"Did you eat anything for lunch?" Faith broke in, exasperated.

Ruby pulled her mouth into a pout that somehow made her look even more adorable than usual. Sometimes Faith believed Ruby's cuteness was the only thing that kept her alive, she was so fragile. "Mrs. Geiger gave me half of her tuna fish sandwich and a carton of milk. And those yucky dried apple chips. I hate tuna fish. But then after school, Charlie O'Donnell gave me Bugles during soccer practice."

Ruby had a little-girl crush on Charlie O'Donnell, an eighth-grader who helped coach the primary school soccer team.

"Get some water and sit down," Faith said. "We'll check your levels in a little bit." A familiar knot of tension tightened inside her. Every day, Ruby's type 1 diabetes brought a new worry, and a new challenge. She turned to Cara. “You’re supposed to wait for her at the bus stop.”

“I forgot.”

“How can you forget something you’re supposed to do every day?”

“She knows the way home.”

Faith suspected the real reason was that Cara didn’t want people to see where they lived. Lakeside Estates Motor Court wasn’t all bad, but no kid wanted to admit she lived in a trailer park. Despite its name, the place was not beside the lake, and it was far from an estate, but it was safe and close to the girls’ schools.

The page finally loaded, and Faith turned her attention to navigating her way to the job-posting response. Outside, the Guptas’ dog went crazy barking, heralding the daily arrival of the mailman in the central courtyard. Ruby, who was scared of dogs, cringed at the sound.

“I’ll go.” Cara shoved aside her homework and went to check the mail.

The response to Faith’s carefully worded posting, offering her services as a skilled caregiver, looked promising. She leaned toward the screen, her interest piqued. “We’re looking for an experienced individual to supervise all aspects of in-home care for a wheelchair-bound lady with a spinal cord injury. Salary and benefits package to include on-site living quarters.”

Okay, so maybe not. Faith and her girls couldn’t

all fit into a closet-sized guest room in some woman's house. Still, the position was right here in Avalon, which made it worth looking into, because the girls hated the idea of changing schools at the very end of the school year.

She wrote down the contact information in case the laptop crapped out again. Then she replied to the interview request, suggesting a meeting the following morning. Tomorrow was Saturday, so Cara would have to miss work at the bakery to watch Ruby, which meant squabbling, but that was too bad. Desperate times called for desperate measures.

Cara came in from the motor court, sorting through the mail. "Bills and junk," she said.

"You were expecting maybe we'd won the Publishers Clearing House?"

Cara dropped the bills on the counter next to Faith and put the rest in the recycle bin at her feet.

Faith picked up a glossy brochure. "What is this from Johns Hopkins? It's addressed to you."

Cara shrugged and turned away. "Like I said, junk mail."

Faith regarded the beautiful photograph of a college campus. A letter on university letterhead slipped out. There was a personal note at the bottom—"Cara, you have a bright future ahead of you"—and it appeared to be signed by hand from the director of admissions. "It says here that based on your test scores, you're invited to apply early, and the admission fee will be waived."

Another shrug. "Not interested."

"You didn't tell me you got your scores back."

"Oh. So I got my scores back."

Cara drove Faith crazy as if it were her job to do so. Daily.

"And?" Faith demanded.

"And I did okay."

"Cara Rose McCallum."

Heaving a long-suffering sigh, Cara dug in her backpack and came up with a printout.

Faith scanned the numbers, assessing her elder daughter's verbal and quantitative achievements. If she was reading it right, her daughter had crushed the hardest standardized test given at Avalon High. "And you were going to show me this . . . when?"

"It's just a bunch of numbers." She flopped down again and went back to her homework.

"Numbers that tell us you're in the ninety-ninth percentile of students who took the test."

"Does that mean she's really smart?" Ruby asked.

"Really, really smart," said Faith. Pride, exasperation and frustration mingled together. When a girl was as smart as Cara, she should be proud of her own potential, not blasé or, worse, defeated. Faith wanted to give her the world. She wanted to give both girls the world. Instead, she had them living in a trailer park while she held on by the tips of her fingernails.

"If she's so smart," Ruby mused, "why does she keep forgetting me after school?"

Faith ignored the question as she looked through the bills—two ominously thick packets from St. Francis Hospital and Diabetes Center. She had been paying a dead man's bills for six years. The vows said "until death do us part," but clearly the hospital billing system still believed that even in death, the bills didn't have to end.

The next envelope gave her a jolt. She opened it, read the single page. "Oh, come on," she muttered under her breath. "Really?"

"What now?" asked Cara.

Faith sent her a warning look. "E-V-I-C—"

"T-I-O-N. You don't have to spell it in front of me," said Ruby. "I know how to spell it, and I know what it means." She got up and crossed the room, leaning over Faith's shoulder. "And I know what *final notice* means."

The new management company gave her no quarter. She had tried reasoning with them and had held them at bay for several weeks, but apparently they were done waiting. She hated the tone of the letter. Did they think she actually had the money and was holding out on them?

Cara slammed her book shut. "It means we're moving again," she snapped. "That's great. Just great. Two weeks before school lets out. Maybe we could go for a record—how many times do we have to change schools in one year?"

"Cara, I'm not doing this on purpose." Faith felt sick. "I know you like Avalon High. I'll try my best to see if you can stay in the district."

Cara yanked her bike helmet from a closet by the door. "I'm going to work. I guess I'll have to give notice at the bakery."

"Come on, Cara—"

"It says we've got twenty-four hours." Cara snatched up the letter and shoved it under Faith's nose.

"I'll figure something out," said Faith. "I always do."

"She always does," Ruby said loyally.

Faith gave her a hug, drawing Cara into it. "What did I do to deserve you two? You're not in the ninety-ninth percentile. You're in the one hundred and tenth percentile. A hundred and ten percent awesome."

"Right," said Cara, stepping back and cracking a smile for the first time just before she went out the door. "That's us. A hundred and ten percent pure, unadulterated awesome. I've got to go."

"Bring me a kolache," Ruby piped up.

"Sure thing." The Sky River Bakery, where Cara worked, made delicious sugar-free kolaches. Faith's daughter liked working there. She liked her school.

She hated being broke all the time.

But not nearly as much as Faith hated it. She watched her elder daughter ride away on a bike she'd snatched from the donation pile at Helpline House, a local charity. Other kids had cars, but Cara didn't even have her license yet, because the driver's ed fees were too high, not to mention insurance for a teenage driver.

She sat down and drew Ruby onto her knees, holding her close. Then she tightened her arms around the child in her lap, feeling her younger daughter's impossibly small frame. Ruby felt as fragile as a baby bird. "Let's check on your sugar bugs," she said. The endless routine of testing her levels, administering insulin and managing her diet and exercise was always at the forefront of their lives.

"My meds cost the moon," Ruby said.

"Where did you hear that?"

"The school nurse. I wasn't supposed to hear, but I heard. So I asked her what the moon costs and she said it's just an expression, but I know it means it costs a lot of money. Which we don't have."

"We have exactly what we need," said Faith.

When the girls were asleep, that was when the demons came to visit. The ones that promised Faith she was drowning and taking the girls down with her. Sometimes in her more lunatic moments, she silently raged at Dennis, as if all this were his fault. And it wasn't, of course. It wasn't his fault for having a severe form of diabetes with fatal complications, any more than it was Faith's fault for loving him.

It wasn't his fault their younger daughter had the same disease.

No one's fault, but Faith was left to deal with it.

Late that night—their last night in Unit 12 of Lakeside Estates—Faith realized it was preferable to stay awake with her own thoughts than to sleep with demons, so she got up and finished the last of the packing. It wasn't much. The unit had come fully furnished, so it was really just their clothing and personal belongings, which fit easily into the paratransit van.

The van was from Dennis's final year, when he'd been in a wheelchair that had to be raised and lowered by the van elevator. He had known he was terminal and had made the rash decision to spend the last of their savings traveling across the country from LA to New York, seeing the sights of America in the midst of a long, sad farewell. Faith had known it was a reckless move on his part, but how did you say no to a dying man?

Most of their mementos were digital photos, but there was one framed shot Faith cherished, showing the four of them lying on a hill of grass somewhere in Kentucky. A friendly local had gamely climbed a tree to take the unusual shot. They were laughing in that moment, their faces full of love. The joy in Dennis's eyes was palpable. On their unforgettable family trip, they had learned to steal moments like this, to wring every drop of happiness from them.

She carefully wrapped the framed photo in her favorite Dennis artifact—an impossibly soft woven blanket in the traditional McCallum tartan from his native Scotland. For months after his death, the blanket had held his scent, but by now it was faded, and she couldn't even remember what he'd smelled like.

She placed the wrapped photograph in an old duffel bag. The useless laptop emitted a soft chime, signaling an incoming email.

Faith jumped up to check it.

She had a job interview, first thing in the morning.

✵ 5 ✵

"She's a no-show." Mason's mother glared at the clock on the mantel.

"That means she's out. Fired before she's hired. If she can't show up on time for her first appointment, then Faith McCallum is not the one we're looking for." Mason raked a hand through his hair. "Damn. She was the last one on the list." He glanced over the printed résumé, which he'd found so impressive when Brenda sent it to him. "Hasta la vista, Miz McCallum." He crumpled the page in his fist and tossed it in the wastebasket.

Regina, who had arrived on the late train from the city the night before, got up and walked over to him, trailing her hand across the back of his shoulders. Her high heels clicked on the hardwood floor. She always dressed in expensive suits, as if she had an executive board meeting on her calendar. He found it sexy, but a bit much for a lake house.

"That's too bad," Regina said. "She seemed promising on paper." Gorgeous, accomplished and smart, she was eager to help Mason find someone so they could get back to the city.

He nodded. "Yeah, now what?" He grabbed his phone and tapped out a message for Brenda to cast a wider net as she trolled for the ideal caregiver. "Hey, Reg, how about *you* stay with Mom? The two of you make a great pair."

The two women regarded him with such horror and disbelief that he laughed aloud. His mother and Regina got along all right, but the idea of both of them living under the same roof clearly made them both mental.

"To be honest," Regina said, "I wish I did have the skill set to help you, Alice."

"If you had the skill set to help me, I'd force my prodigal son to set a wedding date immediately," said Alice.

Mason kept a poker face, knowing his mother was trying to get a rise out of him.

"We're in no hurry," Regina said soothingly. "I always knew I wanted a long engagement."

"When did you become such an adept liar?" asked Alice. "No woman ever born wants a long engagement."

"Mom—"

"She's right," Regina agreed. "I don't want that." She genuflected in front of the wheelchair. "It would be lovely to have the wedding right away, but Mason and I want to make sure the timing is perfect for everyone involved. Now, what can I bring you from the kitchen?"

"A vodka martini. Dirty, three olives."

"Very funny."

"Oh. Too early? Make it a Bloody Mary, then."

"I'm on it." Regina went toward the kitchen.

"She's too good to be true," Alice said once she was gone.

"You think?"

"Yep. That's how I know she's a big fat phony."

"Why do you assume any woman who wants to be with me is a phony?"

"That's not what I said."

Mason eyed the crumpled résumé in the basket, wishing Faith McCallum had worked out. As Regina had pointed out, the candidate had looked great on paper—midthirties, years of experience as a home health aide, glowing references, able to start immediately, willing to live on the premises. He shouldn't be surprised that she was a no-show. People were never what they presented them-selves to be.

"Ever think maybe I'm just lucky?" That was what everyone said when they met Regina. He was a lucky stiff. They had been introduced by Mason's father. When Mason had taken charge of the New York office of Bellamy Strategic Capital, his father had brought Regina on board, presenting her like a rare delicacy acquired at great expense. Mason couldn't argue with his father's taste. She was every guy's dream—beautiful, sharp, successful, exuding a WASP-y, private-school self-confidence. Best of all, she didn't have that nesting thing going on, that persistent need to set up housekeeping, spend hours decorating the place with fragile things and have three babies. In some respects, she was the female version of Mason—with one notable exception. He wished she liked sex as much as he did. Sometimes trying to convince her to have sex felt like talking her into attending an insurance seminar.

"You still haven't told me about your trip," Alice said, regarding him with narrowed eyes.

He read the challenge in her gaze. "Oh, you mean the trip to scatter Dad's ashes? The one where we had to make a pilgrimage to the same avalanche zone that killed him? The one that was cut short when we got a phone call about you falling down the stairs? Is that the trip you mean?"

"Yes. That is the trip I mean." She glowered at him.

"It was great, Mom. Fantastic."

"You know what I'm asking."

"Yeah, we did it exactly as instructed. They're scattered to the four winds, just like he wanted." He left out the part about breaking the beer stein.

She gazed out the window at the pretty spring day. "He's really gone, then."

Mason didn't reply. How could someone be gone when the memories were burned into your mind? There were moments when he felt as if his father—his funny, charming, flawed, maddening father—was right in the next room, mixing drinks.

"Ivy said it was rather beautiful."

"Then why did you ask me?"

"Because I'm interested in your take on it. For God's sake, Mason, can't we ever just have a normal conversation?"

"We have them all the time, Mom." It was true. He placed a video call to her several times a week. But deep down, he knew what she meant. There was always that distance between them, a sense of matters neither would ever bring up directly.

No, not always, he conceded, remembering. When he was a little kid, his mom and dad had been his whole world. He and his mother had been great together, the dynamic duo. She'd been more playmate than parent, taking him along on adventures all over the world. One summer, they might be building houses for displaced people in Cambodia, followed by snorkeling off the coast of Bali. Another year, it would be camping in Siberia at an arts program for homeless children. She'd had a unique flair for combining humanitarian work with family fun, and she'd ingrained in her son the same urge to do good in the world.

It wasn't until later—his seventeenth summer—that the gulf had appeared. That was the year his discovery of a family secret had caused him to keep his distance from both of his parents. He couldn't talk about it with one parent without betraying the other. Forced into an untenable position, he had simply turned away from them both, forging his own path through life. They thought his sudden change in attitude was the result of teenage rebellion, and maybe it was in part, but he had also felt the need to wall himself off, in order to avoid those intimate ties.

Sometimes he thought that was the reason he was addicted to the rush of risk-taking—in sports, in finance, in anything but emotional entanglements. It was a way to escape the pressure of family expectations. Truth be told, he was more comfortable cave-diving or making risky business deals than he was getting emotionally involved.

He regarded his mother thoughtfully. A little more than a year ago, she had completed a triathlon. Her photo had appeared in the *New York Times* as she crossed the finish line, first in her age group, her muscular legs gracefully outstretched, sweat-streaked blond hair flying out behind her, an expression of triumph on her face. The ski trip to New Zealand had been a reward to herself for a job well-done.

Now her life had veered along a horrific and unanticipated path. She was confined to this house, where she struggled through every day, and eating her breakfast had become more challenging than any grueling race.

She had responded to the trauma and its aftermath by vacillating between grimness and outright rage. Did she know he ached for her every moment? Did she know he wished there was some magical way to take away the emotional pain he saw in her face and heard in her voice?

Maybe this was their moment. Maybe it was a chance for them to make a new start. "Listen, Mom—"

"Where the hell is Regina with that Bloody Mary?" his mother snapped. "I need a better intercom system. The one you chose never seems to work."

"I'll have someone check it out."

"See that you do."

And just like that, the moment for reaching out to her was past.

"Excuse me, Mrs. Bellamy." The housekeeper hurried in, wringing her hands. "I'm sorry to interrupt, but there's a young woman at the door."

"She's not at the door." The young—very young—woman barged into the sitting room. She looked like a character from a comic book, in shorts with torn-off leg holes, dark stockings laddered with runs, lace-up army boots, a striped shirt that resembled a cast-off from the janitor's closet. Her hair was a crazy shade of purple. She wore thick, horn-rimmed glasses that gave her an owlish look. "I need a phone, quick," she stated.

"Ms. McCallum?" She didn't jibe with the crumpled résumé.

"Yeah, so listen, I need you to call 911. Like, *now*."

"What the hell?"

"It's a fucking emergency, okay? There's been a wreck. My mom needs help."

Faith kept her crumpled-up jacket pressed against the spurting artery. She glanced across the ditch at the van, parked half on and half off the road. "Hurry, Cara," she said through gritted teeth. *"Hurry."* Faith didn't know how much longer she could last like this.

"How you doing, honey?" she called to Ruby. She couldn't see the little girl, but had ordered her to stay in the van, several yards away. There was so much blood. Oceans of it. Not to mention an apparent impalement in the lower thigh. Even Faith, with her medical training, was freaking out.

"I'm scared, Mom. What if nobody comes?"

"Cara went to get help," Faith said, injecting into her voice a confidence she didn't actually feel.

"She's a fast runner, right?"

"A really fast runner. Remember her winning time at that track meet last fall?"

"Yep. She set a school record in the four hundred."

Ruby would know. Despite her complaints, she idolized her sister. Faith wished Cara could have driven for help, but Cara couldn't drive. The van had a stick shift and was a clunker even for an experienced driver.

The mobile phone—the only one they had—didn't work. The battery was dead or they had run out of minutes on their pay-as-you-go plan; it was always something with that piece of garbage. Fortunately, the Bellamy place, where they'd been headed for Faith's job interview, was just around a bend in the road.

Only moments ago, they'd been full of hope, spying the house in the distance. There was a long, winding private road leading to a stone-and-timber mansion, which crowned a green knoll overlooking the lake. By cutting across a broad, empty meadow from the road, Cara had probably managed to get there in a matter of minutes.

Now Faith wondered if such a fancy-looking place was surrounded by security fencing or protected by slavering guard dogs. Cara was resourceful, though. And, unlike her sister, fearless. It would take more than a slavering guard dog to intimidate Cara.

The wadded-up jacket Faith was holding on the wound had nearly soaked through. *Damn.* "Ruby, honey, I need a favor. Can you find a towel or something in the van? Something I can use as a really big bandage."

"I don't see anything, Mom."

"Keep looking."

"I'm scared."

"Look anyway." Faith gritted her teeth. How had she ended up in a mess like this? She had used her own jacket to staunch the blood. So much for her best outfit for the job interview. But oh, well.

An involuntary spasm caused the victim's back to arch and contort.

"Easy," Faith said to the stranger, even though he appeared to be unconscious. "You don't want to move. Trust me, you don't." She eyed the piece of metal in his thigh with concern. If it cut the femoral artery, he could die in minutes.

The victim was lucky she'd come across him, probably seconds after the crash. The lakeshore road was deserted, and his motorcycle had ended up deep in a ditch. If she and the girls hadn't happened by, he would have bled out by now.

It had been Cara, jiggling her leg and watching out the window, who had spotted a flurry of dust and exhaust in the ditch. Her yell—*Mom, pull over, I mean it, Mom, pull over right now*—had been delivered with an urgent imperative Faith hadn't questioned. She and Cara had their differences, but the girl wasn't one to cry wolf.

Ruby appeared at the edge of the ditch. "I brought you my bathrobe." A gasp escaped her. "Mommy—"

"It looks like a mess, but we need to help this man," Faith said. She could see Ruby starting to sway. "Don't pass out on me, kiddo. I can only handle one crisis at a time. Just toss me the robe and go back to the van and wait for me, okay?"

Ruby didn't hesitate. She threw the wadded-up robe to Faith and rushed to the van. Faith pressed the freshly laundered fabric on top of the soaked jacket. The hot, coppery scent of his blood filled her senses.

Where the hell were the EMTs?

As crucial moments ticked by, Faith did her best to assess the injuries of the unknown victim. She'd checked his airway immediately—all clear, though he was unconscious—and then wrapped her jacket around the big bleed from the arm, the bright rose-red of arterial blood pulsing out in spurts. In addition to the metal protruding from his thigh, he almost certainly had a compound fracture of the lower leg. A bloody bone, like a branch of stained and broken driftwood, was poking through the torn denim of his jeans.

There were probably other issues, as well, but

she couldn't let up on the bleeding in order to examine him in detail. She yearned to stabilize the piece of metal, but that was too risky. He was male, in his forties or fifties, perhaps, judging by the face framed by the now-battered helmet. He seemed to be about six feet tall, two hundred pounds. It was probably best he was unconscious, because that fracture was one of the most painful-looking things she'd ever seen.

Her mind, trained by instinct, flashed again to Ruby, who had obediently returned to the van. What time was it? When your kid was diabetic, you always needed to know what time it was. When did she last eat? When did she have her insulin? Were her levels okay?

"Ruby, I want you to speak up if your alarm even thinks of going off."

"I will," said the little girl.

The blood-smeared face of Faith's discount-store watch showed nine-twenty. It was past time for the job interview.

Ah, well, the position had sounded too good to be true, anyway. The invitation that had popped up in her inbox late last night had been an interview with a Mrs. Alice Bellamy, who lived in a fully staffed estate on the western shore of Willow Lake. Finding a client who could accommodate Faith and her two girls was a long shot, but Faith had run out of options.

After what seemed like an eternity, she heard

the crunch of tires on gravel. No sirens, but at this point she would take whatever help she could get.

She glanced up and saw a shiny dark blue car that was eerily silent in its approach. One of those new electric things that made no noise. The door opened and a guy in a crisply pressed three-piece suit with a white shirt and tie jumped out and rushed toward her.

“Do you have a phone?” Faith yelled. “Call 911.”

“Already done,” he said. “They’re on the way.”

She could tell the moment he spotted the victim, because his gasp was audible. He looked a bit as Ruby had, regarding the sea of blood.

“Hey, get a grip,” she said. As she spoke, the victim made an involuntary spasm. She really needed to check his pulse. “I could use some help here.”

“Okay. What do you need me to do?” She could feel his gaze moving over the blood that covered her.

“He’s bleeding from the brachial artery. That’s why there’s so much blood. We have to keep applying pressure. This robe I used is soaked through already,” she said.

“Then should I . . . Okay.” She could see his shadow on the road as he removed his jacket and bent down beside her. “Now what?”

“I need you to keep compression right here.” She could barely see her own hands.

"I'm ready," he said.

She caught a glimpse of the label on his jacket —Bond Street Tailors, London. It sounded very posh. It was about to be ruined, though.

"What do I do? Should we wait for help?"

"We hope he doesn't bleed out or stroke out before they get here."

This guy clearly needed very specific guidance. "Listen carefully. This is important. Don't move the compress that's already there, because that'll only make it worse. Put the jacket directly over the bleed and press down hard. It's an arterial pressure point. Don't worry about hurting the guy. He's unconscious. The only thing that's going to keep him from bleeding out is the pressure you apply."

"Jesus. I can't—"

"Just do it. Now. I need to check his pulse. I think he's seizing, and that's bad."

Before the guy could protest again, she grabbed the jacket from him, clapping it over the wound.

"Press down hard," she said.

He turned an even whiter shade of pale, and his eyes rolled upward.

"Don't you pass out on me," she said. "Don't you dare."

She carefully removed the helmet. The victim was gray-faced, his features slack now, his pupils dilated. She checked his airway again. Still clear, but there was almost no pulse. The whole time, she was inwardly urging the EMTs to hurry up and get here.

The useless guy swayed, then struggled to rally. Okay, he wasn't totally useless. Just . . . out of his element. And definitely overdressed. Still, she was grateful he'd happened by.

"Is he going to be all right?"

"I can't answer that. His breathing's not right. He's got multiple injuries and almost no pulse. Do yourself a favor and don't look at his left leg."

And then of course he looked. "Oh, Jesus."

"Keep pressing and don't let up. And don't disturb his upper thigh."

This was bad. Faith knew she was way out of her depth. She had plenty of training in trauma situations, but hadn't put those skills into practice since Dennis. Pulling her mind away from her late husband, she stayed focused on the victim. "I'm losing his pulse," she said, unbuttoning his shirt. "I need to begin chest compressions."

"Losing . . . what? Ah, Christ . . ."

"You sure the EMTs are on their way?" she asked the guy.

"Positive." He spoke through gritted teeth.

"Did they give you an ETA?"

"The dispatcher said they're ten minutes out. That was almost ten minutes ago, so—"

"Okay, I need to concentrate here." Faith knew it was better to perform a few unnecessary chest compressions for someone with a beating heart, rather than withhold compressions from someone in cardiac arrest. Holding her hands one over the other, she leaned over his bare chest and got started. Everything else fell away as she pushed hard and fast, counting out thirty compressions at a hundred beats per minute. She visualized the heart, such a fragile organ beneath her hands, being forced to pump again and again, oxygenating the victim's blood.

"Ma'am, are you sure—"

The rest of his words were drowned out by the welcome *yip* of a siren.

"They're here," the guy said.

"Don't let up," she ordered him. She was covered with sweat and blood, keeping up the rhythm of the chest compressions.

"Not letting up," he said.

The EMTs swarmed from the truck. "I'm Joseph Kowalski," one of them said, putting on protective gear. "Did you see what—*Christ*."

"A male in his forties," Faith rapped out, knowing they needed information fast. "I came upon him about fifteen minutes ago. He's bleeding from the right brachial artery. Compound fracture of the left leg and there's an impalement in his upper right leg. Possible trauma to the head, pupils dilated. I started chest compressions as soon as this guy showed up."

The team of EMTs got down to work, draped, shielded and protected—a reminder that Faith and the other guy were not. The medical team took over the CPR and bleeding control with swift efficiency. One of the guys radioed in the incident, repeating essentially the information Faith had relayed.

"Who was the first responder?"

"That would be me," she said, trembling from the rush of adrenaline. "I just happened by. I've got training. LPN," she explained.

The well-dressed guy swayed a little on his feet, regarding his bloodstained clothes. "Deep breath," she told him. "You'll be all right."

"Ma'am, are you familiar with BBF exposure protocol?" One of the guys handed Faith a wad of antiseptic wipes. He offered the same to the guy in the suit.

"BBF exposure?" asked the guy in the suit.

"Blood and body fluids," she translated. "We're going to have to get a post-exposure evaluation."

He swallowed visibly and swayed a little on his feet. "For . . . ?"

"Blood-borne pathogens."

His face turned an even paler shade of gray. "Oh. Damn."

"We'll go in as soon as we can," she said as the EMTs finished their work. She used the antiseptic wipes to scrub her hands, getting the worst of the blood off.

The local police showed up after that, two squad cars forming a parentheses around the wreck.

Faith moved toward the van, eager to check on Ruby.

"Good work," an EMT said to her as the team secured the backboard. "The guy'll live to ride another day. He probably would have bled out if you hadn't stopped."

Cara showed up, out of breath from running. Her gaze flicked from her mother to the stranger in the suit, eyes widening at the sight of all the blood. "Oh, *man.*"

"Ma'am," said a police officer, eyeing the blood. "I'll need to get a statement from you."

"I don't have time at the moment," she said, speaking over the wail of the departing ambulance siren. "My name is Faith McCallum." She dictated her phone number.

He wrote it down. "But, ma'am—"

"Sorry. I need to check on my younger daughter, I have to get to the ER for BBF exposure and I'm already late for an appointment," she said. Maybe, just maybe, Mrs. Bellamy would understand. "I've got a job interview."

"Actually," said the guy in the suit, "you don't."

She paused, checking the area for her belongings. "I beg your pardon."

At the same time, Cara glared at the man. "What the hell?"

"The job interview." He still looked shell-shocked as he turned to Faith. "It's not going to be necessary."

"And why would that be?" she asked in annoyance.

He loosened his collar, further smearing himself with the motorcyclist's blood. "Because you're already hired."

✵ 6 ✵

It turned out the useless guy was actually Mr. Mason Bellamy, the son of her potential client and the person in charge of hiring Alice's caregiver. And clearly he'd seen something he liked in Faith at the scene of the bloodbath.

The van backfired three times as she followed his sleek, silent car down a long, winding drive toward the house, where he said they could get cleaned up before the ER. Slender poplar trees lined the winding lane, the spring-green leaves filtering the late-morning sunlight and dappling the beautiful landscape.

As they rounded a curve in the private drive, the historic mansion came into full view in all its glory. The house was a breathtaking vintage Adirondack lodge of timber and stone, with a wraparound porch, a turret on one end, mullioned windows and walkways draped in blooming vine pergolas. Surrounding the main house was a broad lawn featuring a grass tennis court and swimming pool, a gazebo on a knoll and a boathouse with a long dock jutting out into Willow Lake.

"We're not in Kansas anymore," Faith murmured, studying the place over the shiny roof of Mr. Bellamy's car. One of the EMTs had given her sterile draping for the car seat and a micro-fiber cloth for her hands, so she didn't slime the steering wheel with the stranger's blood. She was going to need buckets of soap and water to get cleaned up. Mason Bellamy had promised there were ample facilities at the house.

"I knew you'd say that." Cara propped her feet on the dashboard. "You always say that."

"It's from *The Wizard of Oz*," Ruby informed her.

"Duh."

"I say that whenever we enter a new world that's nothing like the place we came from," Faith explained to her younger daughter.

"I know, Mom," Ruby said.

"The driveway's a quarter mile long," Cara said. "I ran the whole way."

"How do you know it's a quarter mile?" asked Ruby.

"Old lady Bellamy said."

"You met her?" Faith glanced over at Cara. "What's she like?"

"Cranky."

"Cara—"

"You asked. So are you going to take the job?"

"We'll see."

"You always say that, too," Ruby pointed out.

"Because we *will* see. I need to meet with Mrs. Bellamy—who, by the way, should never be called old lady Bellamy—and see if we're a good match."

"That guy already said you're hired," Cara pointed out. "I heard him."

"The client is his mother, so she gets final say," Faith explained. "Frankly, I'd pay *them* just for the chance to scrub this blood off me."

"It's really gross," said Ruby. "But this place is like a castle," she added softly, leaning forward in her seat. "If you take the job, do we get to live here?"

"That's what the job description said—that it's a live-in position." When she had replied to the posting, Faith had been open about her situation. She had explained that she had two girls, and that the younger one had special needs. The reply, which had come from a woman named Brenda—"Assistant to Mr. Bellamy"—had stated that they would still like her to interview for the position. To Faith, that meant the Bellamys were either very open-minded or very desperate.

"I want to live here," Ruby said, scanning the arched entrance at the end of the driveway.

"If we did, then we wouldn't have to change schools," Cara pointed out.

Faith caught the note of yearning in her elder

daughter's voice. She was just finishing her junior year at Avalon High School and longed to graduate with her friends. Since Dennis had died, they had moved at least six or seven times; Faith had lost count. It was rough on the girls, always being the new kid and having to start over at a new school every time their mom changed jobs.

Cara coped with the situation by adopting an edgy, rebellious attitude. She had a mouth on her that sometimes reminded Faith of Dennis—sarcastic, but never truly mean. Cara was a lot like her late father in other ways, too. She was scrappy and smart, cautious about whom she let in. Dennis's doctors said he had outlived his prognosis by several years simply because he was such a tough guy, and Faith could see this trait in her elder daughter.

Ruby, by contrast, went the opposite direction, retreating into her books and toys, hiding behind a bashful facade. Even as a toddler, she'd been far more cautious and fearful than Cara ever was.

It would be nice to offer the girls a sense of security. From the looks of this place, security was assured. The compound looked as if it had sat here forever at the water's edge. Large enough to billet a small army, it seemed like a lot of real estate for one woman.

That was Faith's first clue to the high-maintenance quality of Alice Bellamy.

She parked in front of a multibay garage with an

upper story that ran the entire length of the building. Mr. Bellamy's car glided silently into one of the bays, and the door automatically rolled shut. A few seconds later, he joined them.

"Welcome to Casa Bellamy," he said as they got out of the van. He'd removed his tie and opened his shirt, and the cuffs were rolled back, but he still looked decidedly uncomfortable in his blood-spattered clothes.

"This is Ruby," said Faith, gesturing at the little girl.

"Hiya," he said affably. "I'm Mason. I'd shake your hand, but I'm a mess."

"That's okay." She pressed herself against Faith's side. "Mom, you're a mess, too."

"And you've already met my other daughter, Cara."

"I did. Between you and your mom, you saved that guy's life."

Cara merely stood back with her arms folded across her middle. She'd never been the type to be easily won.

"Tell you what," said Mason. "We've got some major cleaning up to do." He eyed her skirt and top, which were covered in blood, sweat, dirt and grass stains. It was her one decent job interview ensemble. She'd forgotten the ruined jacket at the scene of the accident.

"I have a change of clothes in the van," she said.

"Okay, the girls can go inside for a snack or

something while you and I use the showers in the pool house."

There was a pool house. With showers. Definitely not Kansas anymore.

"You remember the way in?" he asked Cara.

She nodded.

"Tell Regina we're back, everything's going to be okay with the guy and that your mom and I will be in after we get cleaned up."

"Sure. Okay. Come on, Ruby."

Ruby towed her Gruffalo along. She clung to the threadbare plush toy in times of stress.

Faith grabbed a bag with a clean dress in it.

Mason briefly checked out the van. "This a paratransit vehicle?"

She nodded. "It's pretty old, but the lift still works." Noting his inquisitive expression, she said, "It hasn't been used for paratransport in quite a while."

"Is it for clients?" he asked.

"My late husband was in a wheelchair."

"Oh. I'm . . . I see."

She could sense him processing the information. People didn't expect a woman in her midthirties to be a widow, so that always came as a surprise.

"He passed away six years ago," she said.

"I'm sorry." Awkward silence. No one ever knew what to say to that.

Faith gave a brisk nod. "Let's get cleaned up."

The pool house had separate showers, the space

divided by weathered cedar boards in a louver pattern.

Faith scrubbed her hands and arms with a cake of soap that smelled of lemon and herbs.

"I have to admit, that's a first for me," Mason called from the adjacent shower stall.

Even though they couldn't see each other, Faith felt awkward and exposed while she showered within earshot of a man she'd just met. "I wish I could say the same." She watched a thin stream of watered-down blood drain into the river-stone bed of the shower. "In my line of work, things sometimes get messy."

"How long have you been a nurse?"

"All my life, pretty much. I was raised by a single mom. She was sick—congestive heart failure—and I was her caregiver until she passed away when I was about Cara's age."

"Damn. That's rough. I'm sorry to hear it, Faith."

"I went to school but couldn't afford to get my RN degree. I trained in a work-study program and I've worked in the field ever since."

She dried off with a big bath towel, which was as thick and luxurious as a robe at a Turkish spa—not that she'd ever been to a Turkish spa. But she'd imagined one, many times.

Then she put on a clean dress, hoping it wasn't too wrinkled from packing. It was a blue cotton wrap dress, not her first choice for meeting a potential client, but it would do in a pinch.

"All set," she said, finger combing her wet hair as she stepped out of the cabana. "I just need to —*Oh.*"

Words failed her as Mason Bellamy came out of the shower stall wearing nothing but a towel and a smile. Time seemed to stop as she had a swift, heated reaction to the sight of his body, a reminder of just how much time had passed since she'd had a boyfriend—or even a date. He was built like a men's underwear model, perfectly proportioned, with sculpted arms and legs, shoulders and abs not found in nature. His towel-dried hair lay in damp waves, framing his face. His lips curved upward at the corners even when he wasn't smiling, and she detected both kindness and wariness in his eyes. A small, upside-down crescent scar at the top of his cheekbone kept him from being too handsome. She gave herself a stern, silent reminder that a guy who looked like this undoubtedly spent too much time at the gym. He was probably obsessed with himself.

Or maybe he might just be the kind of guy who took care of himself, said another little voice in her head. In her profession, she saw too little of that. Might as well enjoy a little eye candy.

"Guess I need to find some clean clothes, too," he said. "Getting drenched in a stranger's blood wasn't on the agenda today."

"I need to check you out."

He raised one eyebrow, looking intrigued. "Yeah?"

She flushed, wondering if he'd read her mind. "What I mean is, I should check your hands, see if you have any open wounds. When we follow up at the hospital, they'll need to check again."

Mason blanched and stuck out both hands toward her. Immediately, the towel hit the ground. "Whoops," he said, bending to pick it up. He tucked the towel in more securely around his waist. "Didn't mean to flash you."

"Don't worry about it." She felt a bit light-headed, because of course she'd peeked. His body was amazing.

"I'm not worried. Just don't want to seem rude." He held out his hands again. "So you mentioned blood-borne pathogens. Like HIV?"

"It's extremely rare, but yes. Also, HBV, hepatitis, malaria—all very unlikely, though it's best to rule them out."

"How will we find out if the guy is okay? Will the hospital tell us?"

"There are privacy issues. The victim doesn't have to share the results of his panel if he doesn't want to. Most people are pretty reasonable about it." She bit her lip, deciding not to postulate what might happen if the guy never regained consciousness, or died. "The hospital will help us figure out if there's a serious risk. You can also be tested every few months just to make sure you're in the clear."

"Lovely."

"Hazard of the trade."

"Not my trade," he murmured.

She took hold of one hand at a time, inspecting every detail—nail beds, cuticles, palms, wrists. She could tell a lot about a person just by checking out his hands. Thick calluses meant manual labor, or hours at the gym, handling body-sculpting equipment. He didn't have any calluses to speak of.

Ill-kept nails meant poor grooming. Bitten nails were a sign of issues.

His hands were well-shaped and well-groomed, no surprise. His skin was warm and damp, and he smelled heavenly. She turned his hands over in hers again. As a nurse, she did a lot of touching, but usually with more clinical detachment than she currently felt. Maybe it would seem more professional if he didn't happen to be standing there in a towel. Smelling heavenly.

He wore no wedding ring, but there wasn't a chance in hell that he wasn't taken. She ran her fingers over a recently healed cut at the base of his thumb.

"Cut it on a beer stein," he said.

Was he a wild party animal, smashing beer steins while drinking with his buddies? If that were the case, it would be easier to crush this funny feeling inside her. She pushed his hand aside and stepped back. "A beer stein. Like a pottery mug?"

He nodded. "This is probably going to sound weird to you, but my dad's ashes were in the stein. My brother and sister and I were scattering them according to his wishes."

"Where, out on the lake?"

"No. The three of us were on a mountain in New Zealand. It's kind of a long story."

"New Zealand. Wow, that's a long way to go for . . ." She stopped herself. "I'm sorry about your dad." Then she turned his hands over in hers and was surprised to discover he was trembling. Delayed reaction to the emergency? She looked up and studied his eyes, her gaze flicking to the faint crescent scar. "Hey, are you feeling all right?" she asked.

He flexed his hands, giving hers a brief squeeze. "Yes, sure."

The hesitation in his voice snagged her attention. "You don't sound so sure."

"I'm not good with stuff like this. Traumatic injuries and blood. I'm fine now." He looked down at their joined hands, then gently let go. "Thanks for asking."

There was a spot of blood on the side of his neck. "Hold still, you missed something," she said, dabbing at it with the corner of a towel. She stood close enough to feel his body warmth, to catch the soap-and-water smell of them both, mingling together. In her work, she got close to people; in her personal life, not so much. It occurred to her that this was the most intimate she'd been with a man in . . . forever, it seemed. She needed to get out more. Maybe after she was no longer homeless and broke, she would give it some thought.

"You're most likely okay," she told him, finishing up the exam quickly. "Are you free to go to the hospital tomorrow?"

"Sure. Guess I won't worry until there's something to worry about," he said. "Tell you what. I'll send someone to help you move your things into the house." He spoke like a man used to taking charge.

"That's getting ahead of things," she said. She hadn't even set foot in the house or met the client.

"You mentioned in your email that you'd be able to start right away."

"That's assuming your mother and I agree that this is a good match. I need to learn more about the job. It might not be the right thing for me."

As if she had a choice.

"I'll do whatever it takes to make it right."

She couldn't decide whether his can-do attitude was annoying or attractive. "First things first. Your mother and I need to meet and have a nice long chat."

"She'll agree. She'd be crazy not to."

"Why do you say that?"

He held open the door and stood aside to let her pass. "Because you're awesome. See you inside."

✵ 7 ✵

Cara tried her best to act totally chill about sitting in the fanciest living room she'd ever seen. She leaned her elbow on the arm of the cushy leather sofa, crossed her legs at the ankles and stared out the French doors at an amazing view of Willow Lake. Every few seconds she surreptitiously checked out some detail of the room—a tall grandfather clock that softly ticked into the silence, a rustic chandelier perfectly centered over the middle of the room, an oil painting that looked exactly like a Renoir. It probably *was* a Renoir.

On the opposite end of the sofa, Ruby sat twirling her feet in small circles, her brown eyes like saucers and her fingers twisting into the fur of her Gruffalo. New situations always intimidated the hell out of Ruby.

The woman named Regina was acting all flustered as they waited for Cara's mom and the Bellamy guy to get cleaned up and join them. After a few minutes of awkward silence, Regina jumped up, smoothing her hands down the front of her expensive-looking beige slacks, and said,

"I'm going to get some refreshments from the kitchen. Alice, what sounds good to you?"

"A sloe gin fizz, but it's too early in the day for that." Old Mrs. Bellamy didn't crack a smile.

"How about you, Cara? Lemonade? Iced tea?"

"I'm fine," said Cara. "Thanks."

"Ruby?" Regina's voice went up an octave, the way some people's did when they talked to little kids. Everybody assumed Ruby was younger than she looked, because she was so puny. "I bet I can talk Wayan—he's the chef—into bringing you a plate of his special frosted sugar cookies."

"No, thank you." Ruby's eyes widened in terror. She was so damned bashful all the time.

"Well, then." Regina grinned with phony brightness. "I'll go ask for a tray of lemonade and snacks. In case you change your mind." She practically ran out of the room, as uncomfortable as Cara felt inside.

Cara wasn't sure who Regina was or how she fit into the Bellamy household. She seemed way too stylish to be a housekeeper or whatever. She looked totally polished, with shiny, straight hair, expertly applied makeup and nails, and an outfit a TV news anchor might wear. She was attractive, but Cara couldn't be sure if that was due to the hair and makeup, or if she *really* was attractive.

Cara's mom was pretty, but it was a tired kind of pretty that just happened naturally, because she was slender and had light brown hair, kind eyes and a nice smile. Cara sometimes wished her mom would find time to get a makeover or whatever, but of course there was never time. Or money.

Throughout high school, Cara had given herself several makeovers. One of the few—very few—perks of having to move all the time was that she got to reinvent herself, and no one thought it was odd. Yet despite all her experiments with different looks, nothing seemed to work. She had tried going boho, with layers of organic cotton and weird footwear, but that kind of made her look like a homeless person. Which technically she had been off and on ever since Dad had died. Last year she tried to go preppy with stuff from thrift shops, but it had made her look like a total poseur. Knee socks had gone away for a reason. Her current look was her version of steampunk. It wasn't working, either, but at the moment she couldn't decide what to pursue next. Besides, she didn't have the dough.

She sneaked a glance at Mrs. Bellamy, but the old lady caught her.

"So this accident," said Mrs. Bellamy. "You simply happened to come upon it."

"Yep." Cara nodded. "Just like that."

"And it was at the end of the driveway."

"Across the road from the driveway. Motorcycle versus ditch."

"It was Cara who saw him first," Ruby ventured in a tiny voice.

"I spotted him out the window," said Cara. "A puff of smoke and the sun glinting off a piece of metal. He must have just crashed."

"I see."

At least Mrs. Bellamy didn't say something patronizing like it was a good thing Cara had come running for help and all that crap. It was kind of a no-brainer. It would've been simpler if Mom had let her drive the van, but Cara didn't know how to drive. Mom had shown her the basics, but the stick shift was way too challenging. It was embarrassing. All the kids in her school drove or were currently in driver's ed. Cara just went to study hall during that block and wished with all her heart she could join the class. Most days the only other kid in study hall was Milo Waxman, an oddball who thought the whole world should ride bicycles or dogsleds or something that didn't pollute the environment. Cara secretly found him interesting, but it would be social suicide to hang out with him.

She yearned to be normal, whatever normal was. Driving a car and living in one place for more than a few months at a time. But she didn't like asking her mom for anything, because she knew damn well that Mom would give her and Ruby *everything* if she could afford it. And she couldn't afford it.

Cara remembered the day she finally understood that they were poor. And not just ordinary, having-to-clip-coupons poor, but poor like we-don't-have-a-place-to-live poor. Not long after Dad had died, the three of them had spent several nights "camping" in the van. Mom had acted as if it was a fun adventure, even when the mornings were so cold that the van's windows were etched with frost. Cara had pretended to be asleep when a park ranger had come along, telling Mom it was time to check and see if the county housing agency had found a place for them yet.

"You're seventeen, according to the letter your mother sent last night," said Mrs. Bellamy, interrupting her thoughts.

It wasn't a question, so Cara simply nodded, happy enough to quit thinking about the past.

"And you're eight," the old lady said to Ruby.

The woman wasn't really old, Cara observed. She just looked that way because she was a sourpuss, and she wore her blond hair in a granny bun.

"Yes," Ruby replied in a soft, shaky voice.

"What grade are you in?"

"Second grade. My teacher's name is Ms. Iversen."

"Your mother said you have special needs. What's that supposed to mean?"

Ruby trembled as if the old lady were breathing fire. "I . . . I . . ."

Mrs. Bellamy blew into a tube on her wheelchair and the thing moved closer to Ruby.

"Speak up. I can't hear you. What did you say?"

"Nothing." Ruby looked as if she were about to pee her pants.

Just then Regina came back with a fancy tray loaded with frosted cookies and icy glasses of lemonade. "I brought extra, in case you changed your mind," she chirped. "Once you taste Wayan's treats, you won't be able to resist."

"Well?" demanded Mrs. Bellamy, glaring at Ruby. "I was asking about your needs. Your *special* needs."

Ruby's mouth moved, forming the words, *I'm diabetic,* but no sound came out. Cara always hated when Ruby acted ashamed, as if the disease were somehow her own failing.

"She's diabetic," Cara snapped. "And no, thank you," she added as Regina set down the tray. "We both totally appreciate the offer, but she can't have any of Wayan's damn cookies."

Ruby's hands came up to her cheeks, and her eyes got even rounder. At the same time, Mason Bellamy and Mom walked into the room.

"Well," said Mom, surveying the situation, "I see everyone is getting along just fine."

Cara shut her stupid mouth, but she didn't see any reason to apologize to the dragon lady or to Regina. Her outburst might have cost Mom the job, in which case she owed her mother an apology, not anyone else.

Mom walked right over to Mrs. Bellamy and sat

down in the wingback chair beside her. “I’m Faith McCallum,” she said. “I’m glad to meet you.”

“Likewise, I suppose,” said old lady Bellamy. Cara could tell already that she had a way of sizing people up with her eyes.

“This is Regina Jeffries,” said the guy named Mason. He had changed out of his bloody clothes and now wore clean jeans and a white shirt, open at the collar, the cuffs turned back. He was super good-looking for a guy in his thirties. Now Cara understood how Regina fit into the picture—she was his girlfriend. It was obvious by the way she stared at him.

Mom stood up briefly and shook hands with Regina. There was an obvious contrast between the two of them. Regina had every hair in place, while Mom looked . . . well, just kind of ordinary in a dress with pockets and flat shoes, her damp brown hair pulled back in a ponytail. No makeup. Ever.

“That was more drama than we expected this morning,” said Mason. “How about we start over?”

“Lemonade?” asked Regina. “Cookie?”

“I’m fine,” said Mom. She shifted her focus to Mrs. Bellamy. “I’d love to hear about you—what you need, what you want. Your expectations.”

Mrs. Bellamy narrowed her eyes. “You are to be in charge of assisting me, including the supervision of the two other home health aides who cover the evening and early-morning shifts.”

Mom nodded. "All right."

"The compensation package includes parking, room and board for one person. I hadn't anticipated two extra children."

"I did bring it up in my reply," Mom said. "Obviously, it's nonnegotiable."

Cara's mother had this thing she did. She usually seemed all meek and mild because she was quiet and small. But when something came up involving the family or people she cared about, there was a subtle shift, and Mom became a rock. She was doing it now, regarding Mrs. Bellamy with a perfectly pleasant expression on her face, but anyone in the room could see that the balance of power had shifted.

Which was funny, Cara reflected, seeing how Mom didn't have any bargaining power, none at all. She was out of options. Then again, she had nothing to lose, because they had already lost everything. If old lady Bellamy said no deal, Mom would be scrambling for a place in line at the county housing office.

This was not a new situation for the McCallum family. This was the norm, thought Cara, slumping back on the sofa and tucking her chin into her chest.

"You're slumping." Suddenly Mrs. Bellamy was talking to Cara. "Sit up straight."

Cara shot her a look.

"Don't give me that look. I'm your elder."

"You sure are," Cara murmured, then sat up as instructed, all innocence. "Just agreeing with you."

Then Mrs. Bellamy turned to Ruby. "You're a beautiful child, but too scrawny. You need to eat something. Now that I realize you can't have sugar, I'm going to have to consult with the kitchen staff. We'll make sure there are plenty of sugar-free options for you."

Holy crap, thought Cara. The woman was schizoid, barking like a mad dog one moment and then catering to everybody the next.

"What's that disreputable-looking thing you're dragging around with you?" the woman asked Ruby.

"My Gruffalo."

"What is a Gruffalo?"

"It's from a book called *The Gruffalo*," Ruby patiently explained. "When I was younger, it was my favorite. My mom made me my very own. She sewed it herself out of a sock and some yarn and buttons. He's one of a kind. Did you ever make stuff for your kids when they were little?"

"I made trips to FAO Schwarz, but that's about it."

"What's FAO Schwarz?"

"It's a very large toy store in New York City. You should visit there sometime."

"Will you take me?"

"Don't be ridiculous. I'm not capable of taking you anywhere." She swiveled the chair to face

Mom. "Where's their father? He's not going to come barging in uninvited, is he?"

Mom regarded her steadily. "I can guarantee he will not."

"Are they noisy?" asked Mrs. Bellamy.

"They're kids. They make noise."

"I imagine they're messy, as well."

Ruby walked over to their mother and looked Mrs. Bellamy in the eye. She was still acting scared, but intensely determined as she faced the old woman. "Last year at the end of first grade, I got the Neat as a Pin award."

The old lady returned the steady gaze. "What about this year?"

"I'm working on it. But Shelley Romano is in my class, and she's giving me a run for my money."

Mrs. Bellamy glared at the kid with dragon eyes. Yet buried beneath the fierce glare was something Cara recognized—a glimmer of humor.

"I suppose you'll be wanting your own room."

"That would be nice, thank you."

"And your own bathroom?"

Ruby relented. "We could share."

"Why don't you finish telling us about your expectations," Mom suggested gently.

"I expect each day to be no different from the last. My schedule is quite simple." She rattled everything off in a brusque, bitter tone. "I wake up at nine each morning and have coffee. Then I'm bathed and dressed for a late breakfast. Lunch is at one o'clock and dinner at seven-thirty. I'm in bed by ten. Any questions?" She seemed to be daring them.

No one spoke. Then, to Cara's surprise, Ruby raised a tentative hand.

"Yes?" demanded Mrs. Bellamy. "What is it?"

"You asked if there were any questions," Ruby said. "I have a question."

"You have a question. And what might that be?"

"I was wondering . . . What do you do?"

Aw, jeez, thought Cara, watching the old lady's face.

"I beg your pardon," the old lady fired back. "What do you mean, what do I *do?*"

"I mean like, do you go to a job, or have meetings, or run errands? Stuff like that."

It was a good thing Ruby was tiny and super-cute, because it made people more tolerant of her.

But maybe not Mrs. Bellamy. She had the look of a fire-breathing dragon again. "Child, can't you see I'm confined to this chair?"

"Yes, ma'am. I can see that."

"Then you must understand that I can't *do* anything. I can sit, and on a good day, I might have the tiniest bit of function in my arms. But I don't actually have any good days, because I can't *do* anything."

"Oh." Ruby simply stared at her, unperturbed. After the initial scare, the kid was showing some backbone.

"I'm open to suggestions, if you happen to have any."

"You could sing," Ruby said without missing a beat. "Or if you don't like singing—"

"How did you guess?"

"You could listen to music. Or audiobooks—I used to listen to them before I learned to read. You could also tell jokes and talk on the phone if you put it on speakerphone. You could tell me all your favorite flowers, and I would plant them in the garden so you can have a bouquet whenever you want one." She shrugged matter-of-factly. "I can think up more stuff and make you a list if you want."

The silence in the room felt like a storm about to descend. Mom looked mortified. If Cara's rudeness had put the job in jeopardy, Ruby had finished it off. Poor Mom.

Then Mrs. Bellamy blew into her tube, and the chair glided toward an arched doorway leading to a long hallway.

No one moved. Mrs. Bellamy stopped, and the chair swung back. "Well?" she asked, eyeballing Ruby. "Are you coming?"

Ruby blanched. "Coming where?"

"To see where you'll be living."

The job posting had simply stated that the offer included "ample living quarters." Cara thought she knew what was meant by ample, but this was definitely more than ample.

Mrs. Bellamy led the procession down the hallway and through the house. Each room they passed was pretty and sparkling with the light reflecting off Willow Lake. The rooms had old-fashioned names like the conservatory, the library, the card room, the solarium. The place at the end of the hallway was known as the quarters.

The quarters turned out to be bigger than most apartments they had lived in. It was a sunlit suite of two bedrooms, separated by a fancy bathroom with black-and-white tile, a deep claw-foot tub and a separate shower surrounded by clear glass. There was an antique-looking desk and, best of all, a deck on the outside, with a view of the lake. Everything was as elegant as a set on *Masterpiece Theatre*.

Ruby acted as if she had entered the Magic Kingdom, not that anyone in the McCallum family could afford to go to Disneyland.

"This reminds me of Mary Lennox's house," Ruby exclaimed. She turned to Mrs. Bellamy. "Mary Lennox is the girl in—"

"*The Secret Garden*," said Mrs. Bellamy. "I'm a cripple, not an ignoramus."

Cara wondered if it was politically incorrect to say *cripple* when you were the one in the wheelchair.

"Do you like books?" Ruby asked her. "I love books, and I can already read chapter books all by myself. I still like reading aloud, though."

"So do I. We will have to begin reading together," said Mrs. B.

"It's beautiful, Mom," said Ruby. "Do we get to stay?"

Mrs. Bellamy swiveled to face Mom. For the first time, the old lady seemed to smile. It wasn't an actual smile but almost. A lightness in her eyes, like the sun reflecting off the lake. And Cara realized old Mrs. Bellamy really wasn't actually old, and she wasn't a total sourpuss, after all.

"I was just about to ask you the same question."

8

Mrs. Bellamy promised to be a difficult, angry patient, but Faith had dealt with difficult and angry before. The emotional roller coaster was part of the job.

The house and grounds were expansive, like something out of a magazine fantasy. Ruby made no attempt to suppress her delight in the situation. The beautiful gardens were just starting to bloom, ducks were nesting along the shore and the spectacular setting offered dozens of places for a little girl to play, hide, imagine . . . escape. They wouldn't have to change schools, after all. Cara could keep her job at the bakery, and Ruby was looking forward to the long, lazy days of summer by Willow Lake.

The household ran like a precision clock, thanks in large part to Mrs. Philomena Armentrout, the exotic housekeeper. The Balinese family—Wayan, Banni and Donno—kept the kitchen running, and Banni was the evening aide. The weekly schedule included a physical therapist, psychological counseling and a sports trainer.

It was late at night by the time Faith finally found time to put away the last of her things—a few books and keepsakes, memorabilia of life before it got so complicated. It was interesting how little one actually needed on a day-to-day basis—a few changes of clothes, a decent bar of soap, toothpaste and toothbrush. It was hard to believe there had been a time when she'd daydreamed of having a house of her own, maybe one with a garden and a tree where she could hang a swing for Ruby, and sending Cara off to any college she chose. The future Faith had once imagined for herself was a distant memory from another life, a life she'd nearly forgotten. These days she didn't have time for hoping and planning. She'd nearly forgotten what that was like. Lately, all she had time for was the daily juggling act of trying not to drop all the balls she had to keep in the air.

But things were looking up. Instead of standing in line and filling out humiliating forms at the

Ulster County Housing Authority, she stood in an opulent bedroom with an antique poster bed, with the French doors open to a view of the starlight on the lake. The girls were fast asleep in the adjacent room, and the only sound Faith could hear was the pleasant chirping of frogs outside.

She finished arranging a small stack of folded clothes in a drawer. Then she drew herself a bath in the big claw-foot tub. She couldn't remember the last time she'd had a proper bath. As she settled back into a cloud of scented bubbles, the sense of indulgence was so intense, it brought on a vague feeling of guilt.

Don't be stupid, she told herself. *This is where you live now. You have a bathtub. There's no shame in using it.* She noticed a bit of blood still caked under her fingernails. She found a brush and scrubbed away the last of it.

After the bath she slipped on an old jersey nightshirt and checked on the girls. Their room adjoined to hers through the bathroom and dressing area, and at the moment it was a minefield of their belongings, hastily hauled in from the van. As usual, Ruby's bedside lamp was on, because she was afraid of the dark.

Cara had fallen asleep the way she always did, with a book still open to the page she was on. Faith picked it up and angled it toward the light—a novel called *Saving Juliet.* Cara was always interested in saving things that were doomed.

Faith bent down and quietly switched off the lamp. Moonlight streamed in through two dormer windows, and the shadows outlined the twin beds against the opposite wall. Ruby slept with her Gruffalo clutched in the crook of her arm, her sweet face pale in the bluish glow. Faith reached down and, with the lightest of touches, brushed the hair away from Ruby's forehead and placed a kiss there.

Look at our girls, Dennis, she thought. *Look how beautiful they are.*

Studying Ruby's face, she could still see him in the shape of the little girl's mouth and the tilt of her eyebrows. *You're still here,* Faith said to Dennis. *Then why do I feel you slipping away?* Time, said the widows in the grief group she'd attended for a while. It was both a healer and a thief. As the months and then the years passed, the pain of missing him faded—but so did the memories.

She returned to her own room, but she was too keyed up to sleep just yet. She walked outside, her bare feet soundless on the cool surface of the deck. Taking a deep breath, she gazed up at the stars and then broke down and wept with relief.

It wasn't like her to cry; she wasn't by nature a crier, but the pent-up tension of her past struggles had been sitting inside her like a time bomb waiting to go off. And now that the waterworks had been unleashed, she found she had no power to turn off the flood of relief.

After a few moments, or maybe it was an eternity, she heard a door open and shut; someone cleared his throat.

"Oh, hey . . ." She stood and turned, seeing Mason Bellamy silhouetted against the lights coming from the main house. She quickly wiped her cheeks with her bare hands. "Is everything all right? Does your mother need something?"

"No," he said. "Everything is great. How about yourself? Is there something in your eye? Or are you just glad to see me?"

"I'm okay." She knew she didn't sound okay. Her voice shook. "These are tears of relief."

He gestured at the glider placed at the edge of the deck, positioned for a view of the lake. "Have a seat. Stay there, and don't move. I'll be back in a minute. Ninety seconds, tops."

She complied, pleased that he didn't seem too freaked out to find a woman in a state of meltdown. Dennis hadn't been good with meltdowns, so she had learned to control them, keeping her emotions in a tightly wrapped box and enduring her darkest moments in private.

The beauty of the moon and the stars reflected on the lake was so intense that she nearly cried again. Instead, she inhaled deeply, tasting the fresh sweetness of the air and listening to the chirping of frogs down by the water's edge.

True to his word, Mason returned a moment later with two short glasses, clinking with ice. "Are you a whiskey drinker?" he asked.

"Not often enough. What are you pouring?"

"Scotch. I figure with a name like McCallum, you'd have a taste for it."

"That's my married name. But I'll try the Scotch."

"This one is called Lagavulin. I found a bottle that's been waiting sixteen years for someone to open it." With the dexterity of a seasoned bartender, he poured a shot into each glass. "Cheers," he said, touching the rim of his glass to hers.

The whiskey was remarkably smooth, its flavor unexpected. "Oh," she said. "I've never tasted anything quite like it."

"Essence of peat smoke. They use peat to roast the barley." He stirred the wooden glider with his foot, and they sat together in the nighttime quiet, savoring the whiskey.

"Well, thanks. I like it . . . I think. Warms my chest."

"So about those tears." He shifted around to face her.

She wondered if he actually cared about her tears. Unlikely. He was simply trying to make sure he hadn't engaged an unstable person as his mother's caregiver.

"Like I said, it was a rare meltdown. Nothing to worry about. You didn't hire a wacko."

"I'm already convinced of that. You said you were feeling relief. Because . . . ?"

"The past few months have been a tough spell for us. I wasn't getting anywhere with the placement agency I'd been working for. Just before you got in touch with me, I was looking at having to move right at the end of the school year. The idea of uprooting the girls yet again was awful."

"Your daughters like it here in Avalon, then."

"We all do. Small town, good schools, beautiful area. But I think they would like anywhere that feels stable to them. We've had a lot of upheaval since their dad died. Sometimes I think most of my life has been spent in some sort of upheaval or other."

"Sorry to hear that." He added a tiny splash more Scotch to her glass. "Care to talk about it?"

She smiled shakily into the glass and took another sip. "Depends on which upheaval you're talking about." She fell silent, traveling back through the years to the first big shock of her life. When she was just a schoolgirl, her grandparents both died in a single, tragic moment, leaving behind their only daughter—Faith's mother. The tragedy had occurred in Lockerbie, Scotland. They had not been on the tragic Pan Am flight that day in 1988, but on the ground, visiting friends in the town, on a tiny loop of a street called Sherwood Crescent.

Faith's grandparents had saved for months for

their overseas visit, planning to spend Christmas with the Henrys, whom they knew through an international church group.

It would have been long dark when they sat down for dinner on that dreary December eve, but inside, there would have been a cheery fire in the grate and probably something warm and comforting to eat. Surely they never knew what hit them, but the investigation determined that it was a giant Pratt & Whitney engine, and the impact was so enormous that some of the Henrys' blue garden paving stones flew three blocks away, landing on the roof of the police station.

Faith came home from school the following day, flush with excitement for the upcoming holidays, to find her mother sitting in the dim afternoon light, twisting tissue after tissue in her hands as she stared at the breaking news on TV. For months afterward, Faith always felt a chill of horror when a plane passed overhead.

Between sips of whiskey, she related this to Mason, who sat motionless, not even blinking. "So I guess," she concluded, "it's not surprising I have a strange connection to things from Scotland."

Mason moved at last, tossing back his drink. "That's . . . Man, that's incredible, Faith. I'm really sorry. A shock like that. It can turn your life upside down. It's like you can't escape the memories. They're always there, intruding whether you're asleep or awake."

She nodded, startled by his insight. "You're right. Even now, walking into a dark house with nothing but the TV on takes me back to that day. I never told the girls. I figure they've been through enough in their own lives."

"What sort of things? If you don't mind saying."

"I don't mind." She had no use for deception. Never had. Secrets and lies had never done anyone any good, least of all her. "Dennis was sick for a number of years. He was diabetic, and there were complications. Including the fact that he was foreign—Scottish—and had never bothered to get a green card. He was facing deportation, and we couldn't afford to fight it. The medical debt from his treatment is a hole so deep, I doubt I'll ever dig my way out. And now there's Ruby's care and her meds . . . I won't bore you with all the details."

"You're not boring me."

She smiled, had another sip of the strange-tasting whiskey. "I must be. I'm boring myself."

"Come on."

"We should be talking about your mom, not about me. I'd like to talk more about your mother's situation," she said. "The more I know about her, the better I can help her."

"Oh, sure." Something in his reply told her he wasn't expecting that. "Mom will tell you everything you need to know—implicitly if not explicitly. She had an amazing, vibrant life as an athlete and a world traveler. Now she has to figure out how to live with quadriplegia. There's really nothing I can add. Except that she doesn't seem to be doing so hot in the attitude department. I totally get why she's so pissed off all the time. You and I can't imagine what it's like, living with this level of disability."

"That's true. We grow up hearing we have to play the hand we're dealt, but we are always looking for a way around that."

They sat quietly for a few minutes, sipping the whiskey and watching the reflection of the stars on the lake. "We really have no idea what it's like to be paralyzed," said Faith. "The loss of privacy and independence are huge. Your mother might still be going through a grieving process for the loss of her old life."

"Yes. You're right. I feel so damned bad for her, and then it pisses me off, because there's nothing I can do about it."

"There is. You can't fix her spinal cord injury. You can't give her back her physical abilities. But there's plenty to be done."

A silence ticked slowly between them, but it was a comfortable silence. A thoughtful one.

He tipped his head back to look at the sky. "I'm not used to it being so dark at night," he said.

"I like the dark," she said. "It lets you see more stars."

He nodded. After a while, he said, "I want you to know, you can always call me or ask me anything. I'm here to help, as limited as I am in the nursing skills department."

"Good to know." She felt a pleasant warm buzz from the whiskey. "That's powerful stuff."

His smile—a little crooked, eyes crinkling at the corners—was way too charming. She could look at him all night. "It coats the nerves with happiness," he said.

"Well put. So I do have a question. You said I could ask you anything. Where does your mind go when it wanders?"

"I wasn't expecting that kind of question." He finished his drink and rattled the ice in his glass. "My mind never wanders," he stated. "I have laser focus."

She couldn't tell whether or not he was joking. "Must be a gift."

"How about you? Where does your mind go?"

"My girls. Their well-being. Their future. See? I'm boring myself again."

"But you're not boring me."

Faith was surprised by all these flickers of attraction toward Mason, but she quickly and systematically extinguished each one. They came from different worlds. He was born with a silver spoon in his mouth, while Faith's background was unequivocally blue-collar. Or pink-collar, as it was known. Her mother had worked when she could, selling sewing notions and quilting supplies at a small fabric shop, but most days, she was too sick to go out. As a girl, Faith used to dream of growing up and becoming a doctor and finding a way to cure her mom's congestive heart failure. As she grew older and truly grasped their dire financial situation and the enormous cost of education, she had surrendered that dream. She just wished Cara didn't have to surrender it, too.

She watched the play of the moon and the stars on the lake. "It's so beautiful here. Did you grow up in Avalon?"

"No. We have family in the area, and my brother, Adam, lives here. He's the reason we brought Mom here after the accident."

"Will I meet Adam?"

"Sure. He lives in the quarters above the boathouse. But he's away now, attending special training for his job. He's a firefighter, going for his certification in arson investigation. You'll meet our sister, Ivy, too, one of these days. She lives in California, but she's moving to Paris for a two-year art fellowship."

"Paris. How exciting to be in Paris. Have you been?"

There was a beat of hesitation; then he said, "Yeah. I've been to Paris."

"And?" She wanted him to elaborate. One of the

things she loved about her job was the people aspect. You could live a lot of lives just listening to other people's stories.

"And what?" he asked.

"City of light? Movable feast? Everything it's cracked up to be?"

His hand twitched around the whiskey glass; then he tossed back the rest. "A big, busy city. A place to get lost."

He didn't seem interested in talking about Paris.

"Tell me more about your mother's accident," she said. "How did you get word?"

"I was at work—a Thursday just after the closing bell of the stock market. It was last summer, so that meant it was winter where they were, in New Zealand. My brother, Adam, called. Mom and Dad were on a ski trip to their favorite place. They're both—They were both expert skiers. But something went wrong that day. There was an avalanche. Dad died on the mountain. Mom survived, probably thanks to an airbag device in her jacket. There was a scramble to get to her. Adam and I landed just before she went into surgery, then Ivy a few hours later."

Faith could too easily picture the frantic journey. He'd just been going about his business, when the news had dropped on him like a bomb. "I'm sorry. It must have been like a nightmare." Without thinking, she reached out and gave his shoulder a squeeze. She felt his muscles contract under her hand and quickly took it away. "Sorry," she said. "It's the nurse in me. It's a very hands-on profes-sion."

"I don't mind, Faith." He rested his elbows on his knees, steepled his fingers together and stared into the darkness. "Yeah, it was surreal, especially at first. We didn't tell our mom that Dad was dead, but she knew. They were prepping her for surgery. And she just said something like, 'He's gone, isn't he?' "

"Oh, my gosh. What an awful time for your family."

"I told her yes. She didn't go into hysterics or anything. I kind of expected her to, because she was completely . . . I mean, Dad was pretty much her whole world."

"I'm sorry. He must've been wonderful."

"She thought so."

Faith was bemused by that statement. *But you didn't.*

"The emergency treatment was top-notch as far as we can tell. She was given a drug—a kind of steroid in the ER—methyl . . ."

"Methylprednisolone?"

"I think that's it."

"It can reduce the damage to nerve cells if it's given right away."

"That was the idea. There were a lot of meetings and consultations. Surgeons and specialists. Decisions to be made. It was crazy, the way the world changed in a split second. The most important thing was to get Mom stable enough to travel, and then settled in a place where she could figure out her new, completely unexpected life. Of the three of us, Adam is the most settled. He wanted her in Avalon."

"It's lovely here. She's lucky you all rallied around to help."

"Yeah, just don't tell her she's lucky, or you'll get an earful. Since she moved here, she's been getting all the treatment that's available. You have the list, right?"

She nodded. Mrs. Bellamy was getting physical therapy, which included muscle movement, respiratory exercise, massage, electrical stimulation of nerves by neural prosthetic device—anything that would keep her as healthy as possible. "I haven't seen all her medical history, but it sounds as if everyone's working toward the goal for her to regain as much function as possible." She paused. "What about emotional support?"

"She has a shrink."

"That's her support?" Faith sensed that Mason didn't seem too eager to stick around for his mom. Faith missed her mother every day. It was hard to relate to a guy who kept his distance like this. "So do you come up on the weekends?"

"Not very often. Do you think I need to?"

She hesitated, determined not to judge. "That's up to you."

"My mom's got an entire staff, and now she has you. I don't think she needs me hanging around, too."

She took a moment to digest that. Coming in cold to a family situation was always challenging, because she had to scramble to figure things out. She had the impression that Mason loved his mother, was devoted to her, even. But he was holding himself back, and she hadn't yet figured out why.

"Anyway," he said, "I'm glad you're on board to help her."

"I'll make it my daily mission."

"Good. Thanks. So are your girls settling in?"

"Sleeping soundly. Ruby's already in love with the place. And Cara . . . She likes it as well as a teenager can like any place. I'm just relieved to have a roof over their heads." She glanced over at him but couldn't see his face in the darkness.

She finished the whiskey, enjoying the sleepy warmth it imparted. "I should get to bed. I've got to get up early with the girls. Their school buses don't come out this far, so they will have to hike a half a mile to make the first pickup on the route."

"They don't have to take the bus," he said. "Donno can drive them."

A driver? "That's not necessary."

"But totally doable."

She pictured her girls getting into the shiny

black SUV and being chauffeured like foreign dignitaries to their schools. “I don’t think—”

“Donno is on call whether he’s driving or not. You might as well use his service.”

It would mean the girls could sleep in an extra forty minutes. “All right,” she said. “I’m sure they would love it.”

“Good. I want you to be comfortable here. I want this to work, Mrs. McCallum.”

“So do I. And please call me Faith.”

“Okay. Faith it is. But only if you call me Mason.” They both stood to go inside.

She was surprised to feel so comfortable around a guy like this. He was obviously crazy rich, like Bruce Wayne in the Batman series, the kind of guy who took it for granted that a staff of servants and workers would look after things. Yet for no reason she could fathom, she felt completely at ease in his company.

“What’s a good time to go to the hospital for the blood tests?” she asked him.

“Early is better for me. I was planning to get an early start to the city,” he said. “Regina needs to get back to the city for work. So do I, for that matter.”

“Yes, of course,” she said, feeling like an idiot for forgetting the perfect girlfriend. “Thanks again for the whiskey. Good night, Mason.”

“Good night, Faith.” He hesitated. “It’s good to have you here. Really. I hope you enjoy the peace and quiet of Willow Lake.”

• • •

In the morning Faith waited for Mason in the foyer, wanting to get the hospital visit over with before Mrs. Bellamy was up for the day. Regina appeared, heels clicking, Chanel briefcase in hand, smartphone held to her ear as she spoke about some kind of marketing strategy. She looked so polished and stylish that Faith wondered if they were on hidden camera. How did some women do that? How did they get every hair and stroke of makeup in place?

Faith shuffled her feet and fished out her wallet, checking to see that she had her ID, her ACA card, a tiny amount of cash.

"Sorry," Regina said, ending her call but keeping her attention on the phone screen. "My business day starts early."

"Oh. Um, I see." Faith offered a smile.

"I need to be on that early train." Regina thumbed through several screens.

One of the browser windows showed a display of wedding gowns. Faith saw it scroll by.

Regina tapped her foot. "Punctuality is not Donno's strong suit. Maybe it's a cultural thing. We have a different understanding of time than they do in Bali." With an audible sigh, she put her phone away and offered Faith a brief smile. "Anyway, I'm glad you're here to help out. What was your name again?"

"Faith. Faith McCallum."

"That's right. And your girls are Cara and Ruby. The little one is just adorable."

"Thanks."

"And the older one . . ." Regina's expression turned sympathetic. "I suppose some girls go through that phase."

"What phase would that be?"

"Adolescence." Regina hesitated, studying Faith for a moment. "You seem awfully young to have a teenager."

"I was young when I had Cara."

"So what did he rescue you from?"

"I beg your pardon."

"Mason. It's kind of a thing with him. Everyone he hires seems to have some hard-luck story, and he gives people a second chance. The housekeeper had some high-profile husband who knocked her around, the chef and his family were indigent and the other aide, Lena . . . I'm not sure what her story is . . ."

In a way, thought Faith, Mason *had* rescued her. But she wasn't sure how she felt about Regina making that assumption.

Regina turned to the big mirror over the hall table and checked her lipstick. A moment later, Mason appeared, dressed in a tailored suit, his shoes shined, a conservative tie neatly knotted against his crisp white shirt.

"There you are," Regina said. "And where's Donno? I need to get to the station."

"We'll drop you there on the way to the hospital," he said easily.

She favored him with a brilliant smile. "You're a lifesaver. I was just telling Faith that."

"She saw my lifesaving skills in action," he said. "Rusty, to say the least."

Regina slipped her arm through his. "I'd never call you rusty." Groomed to the last inch of her shadow, she made Faith feel shabby and unkempt by comparison.

Normally, Faith wasn't one to compare. Her best friend, Kim, was ridiculously beautiful, the kind of woman whose style seemed effortless, but Faith never felt self-conscious around Kim. This was different. Maybe it was because Regina moved in on Mason as if she owned him.

Mason stuffed the paperwork from the hospital into his briefcase. Getting a blood and bodily fluid evaluation had been a first for him, but it had gone fine. The accident victim, a guy named Richard Sanders, had given his consent to be tested, as well, and there were no issues, thank goodness. For safety's sake, they would go back in six months to be retested.

Regina had made it clear that she wasn't happy about the idea of heading down to the city without him, but he kept thinking about his conversation with Faith the night before. She had seemed so surprised by his need to make a quick exit. He didn't have anything urgent on his agenda, so he figured he could stick around a bit longer.

Almost right away, he felt like a fifth wheel. The household ran smoothly, and now that Faith was on board, he wasn't needed at all. Still, it seemed like a good idea to make sure the new caregiver was everything they'd hoped for.

It was a beautiful morning, and out on the patio facing the lake, Faith and his mother were getting started on their day. He could hear their voices drifting through the sliding screen door. He didn't want to hover, but he was curious about how they were getting on together.

"According to this schedule, you're to spend two to four hours a day working out," said Faith.

"Does it say that?" his mother inquired with a marked lack of interest. "I suppose it does."

"Let's get started, shall we?"

"No, thank you. I don't care for working out."

"Understood. But it's necessary to preserve your muscle tone as much as possible."

"I'll pass today, thanks."

Mason sensed a note of tension in his mother's voice. In the study, where he'd gone to check his email, he craned his neck to see what was going on.

The two women sat facing each other, his mother in the electric rig and Faith on a patio bench. There was a small table with some paper-work and an iPad propped on it.

"That's not a good idea," she said to his mother. Her chin lifted, just slightly. Just enough to display a stubborn streak. She was not physically large. She was on the small side, actually. But there was a quiet power to her personality. "I'm certain your rehab team explained to you how crucial it is to maintain muscle tone. And as a gifted athlete, you surely understand that skipping a workout is only cheating yourself."

"And as my hired help, *you* understand that ultimately the decision is mine."

"Of course. Do you have something better to do?"

"That's irrelevant. I simply don't care for this boring, pointless exercise."

Faith consulted the app on his mom's iPad. "Let's start with your upper body. According to the chart, your head, neck, shoulders and upper chest can function. You have biceps function but not triceps. If we keep you strong, you'll be more comfortable and develop more independence. Let's start with the upper body."

"No. I have a broken collarbone, in case you've forgotten."

"The surgical repair has stabilized it, and the doctor's recommendation is that you begin using it normally right away, so the muscles don't atrophy. Let me do my job, Alice. Start with some deep breaths and shoulder rolls. There you go."

His mother's attempt was halfhearted.

"Use your diaphragm," Faith ordered. "Keep it strong. It's your lifeline." She helped his mother with some arm movements, manipulating her elbows and hands.

After a few minutes, she said, "I'm tired. All I feel is pain and discomfort."

"Then just say, 'Hello, pain and discomfort. I've been expecting you. You're the reason I'm doing this.' "

"When I feel pain, I stop. Simple as that. It's what any thinking person does."

"Not when you're recovering and trying to build your strength. Let's keep going."

"You're talking nonsense."

"Trust me, I'm a professional."

"Very funny."

"I'm here to help, but I can't do the work for you. Push yourself, Alice. You're the only one who can."

"This is a ridiculous and useless exercise."

Faith didn't let up working her forearm. "Keep going, Alice. You're doing great."

"I can't. It hurts."

"That's because you're working. It's a good sign. Come on, you can do it."

"Stop. Please." Her voice was thick, as though she was fighting back tears.

Mason's jaw was so tight he gave himself a headache. His heart went out to his mother. She'd been through hell, and she was still there. Faith

McCallum was driving her too hard. She was demoralizing his mother. Maybe Faith wasn't the right person, after all.

"You're fired," his mother was saying, as if she'd read his mind.

"All right, fine. You can fire me. But only after you give me eight more elbow extensions on each arm."

"Do you have any idea how excruciating this is?"

"I don't," Faith said. "But I have an idea that you can do it. You have to, Alice."

"I'm done. Leave me alone." His mother was on the verge of a breakdown.

Mason stood up. He was about to go to the patio and fire the woman himself.

"Four, three, two, one." Faith counted down the repetitions. "Good work, Alice. I know it's hard—"

"Shut up. Please, just leave me alone now." She steered the chair across the patio.

Enough already, thought Mason. He strode across the room and exited through the sliding door. His mother was nowhere in sight. Good. He could give Faith McCallum a piece of his mind.

She was seated at the patio table with the iPad and therapy documents in front of her, the pages blowing lightly in the breeze. Her head was bent, and her hands shook as she picked up the papers and carefully folded them on the table in front of her. When she looked up and saw him, the look in her eyes took him aback.

"Remind me again what you said last night," she said. "Something about enjoying the peace and quiet of this place."

His anger evaporated. Until this moment, it had not occurred to him that helping his mother was so very hard on the caregiver. "Everything all right?"

"Fine. We just finished our first exercise session."

"How'd it go?"

"Your mother is a strong-willed person. That's a good thing. She's going to need all her strength to make progress."

"I'm sure she'll come around," he assured her. "She can be really pleasant when she wants to be."

"Right. If we don't murder each other first."

9

Faith could hear Mrs. Bellamy griping all the way down the hall.

"I can't stand the smell of rosemary," she was saying to Lena, her morning aide. "If you'd been paying attention, you would know that."

Faith paused and tapped lightly at the door.

"Come in," barked Mrs. Bellamy. "I'm completely naked, but that doesn't seem to stop anyone from barging in."

"Just finishing a bath," said Lena, her smile taut.

"That rosemary soap is vile," Mrs. Bellamy said. "Find something else."

Lena said something in a low voice.

"What's that?" Mrs. Bellamy demanded. "I can't hear you."

"I said, it's not rosemary. It's lavender."

"Nonsense. I can tell the difference between lavender and rosemary."

Faith came forward, picking up the soap dispenser. "Good morning to you, too. I don't know French, but I'm guessing *huile de lavande* does not mean rosemary."

"It must be mislabeled, then," Alice snapped.

"True," Faith replied. "Because lavender is known to have natural calming properties, and you're having a hissy fit." After yesterday's disastrous therapy session, Faith knew she had to push her client. She met Lena's gaze and saw that the young woman was on the verge of tears. "Why don't you go down and check on breakfast?"

The girl practically fled.

"I should fire her. There was rosemary on the pork roast last week and I said I couldn't stand it."

"You're not going to fire her," Faith said calmly.

"No? Watch me."

"Don't be mean. It costs a small fortune to get a green card. She needs this job."

"I'm not a charitable organization. If she does poorly at her job, then she deserves to be fired."

Unwilling to enter into an argument, Faith held up a wrap skirt.

Alice scowled, but she nodded assent, and Faith helped her finish dressing. It felt good to be working again, doing what she did best. She had a deft way with patient care, and she liked the connection and healing that took place. Over the years, she had learned everyone had the capacity to heal, spiritually if not physically. Some were more challenging than others.

She brushed Alice's hair. It was long and blond with no visible gray. Its silky texture was lovely, but Alice insisted that it should all be pulled back into a bun. "I used to wear it loose," she said, "but now, if it falls forward, I can't brush it out of my face."

Faith's heart softened, and she took her time with the gentle brushing. "Have you thought about a haircut? A pixie or a bob?"

"At my age? It would look silly."

"Silly, like Jamie Lee Curtis? Sharon Stone? Ellen DeGeneres? They're all your age."

Alice sighed. "It's astonishing how much I took for granted, before all of this. Putting on lipstick . . . Oh, God, what I wouldn't give if I could just put on lipstick."

"I can help you with that." Faith's makeup-applying skills were severely limited, but she figured she could do lipstick.

"Fine. In the vanity drawer."

Faith opened the drawer. There was a nice array of expensive-looking cosmetics. Most looked untouched. "Watermelon Wine?" she said, reading the colors. "Coral Kiss?"

"Watermelon Wine, which sounds dreadful but it's a nice color."

Faith gently applied the lipstick. Mrs. Bellamy had a beautiful face—full lips and creamy skin, bright blue eyes. But she barely looked at herself when Faith held up the mirror.

"Let's begin, shall we?" She regarded her new client with bright anticipation. In her career, she had uttered the question hundreds of times to dozens of clients.

"I can hardly wait." Mrs. Bellamy's surly sneer didn't faze Faith. Many of the people she'd worked with in the past struggled with feelings of anger and outright depression. Faith knew better than to take it personally.

"Whenever you're ready," she said softly.

Mrs. Bellamy sighed. "Whatever," she said. "We might as well begin."

"I went through the therapy plan from your team. Looks like today's morning routine is supposed to be all about navigation skills."

"Indeed."

"Since I'm new here, you could start by giving me a tour of the place."

"Love to." She didn't sound as if she would love to.

"I'll follow your lead."

Alice moved forward in her chair and started the tour. They went first to the study, adjacent to the sunny main room. This was where she spent much of her time, probably because here, she was able to exert some measure of control. The desk area resembled a setting for a futuristic movie, with a big-screen monitor, a microphone for voice commands and some switches that could be activated by nudging them with the wheelchair.

Dozens of thoughtful adaptive features had been retrofitted throughout the house. Alice demonstrated the use of the elevator. It was just big enough to accommodate the chair and another person. On the second floor Faith found herself at the top of the tall, curving staircase that wound down to the marble foyer. She looked over the edge and felt a chill. "Is this where you fell?"

A beat passed. "Yes," said Alice.

"Tell me about what happened. Everything you remember."

"It was an accident," she said simply, and backed the chair into the elevator.

Faith pursed her lips, resisting the urge to question her further. She did have questions, though. Alice seemed fairly adept at operating the chair. What had she been doing at the top of the stairs by herself? Did she move about the house by herself frequently? Had there been other mishaps?

They went back downstairs together. Alice

negotiated the opening of the back door by bumping the control plate, then led the way through the automatic doors and headed down the ramp.

The housekeeper, Phil, met them in the kitchen. “You have visitors,” she said.

“I’m not up for company,” said Alice.

“Then we won’t stay long.” A tall, gorgeous redhead strode across the room, bearing a colorful bouquet of sweet peas. “Just stopping by to see two of my favorites.” Kim Crutcher, Faith’s friend, set down the bouquet and bent to give Alice a kiss. “We were just in the neighborhood.”

Kim’s mother, Penelope Fairfield, came in behind her. “My daughter’s lying,” said Penelope. “We wanted to make sure you’re all right. Are you in pain? I was so worried when I heard about your fall.”

Alice pursed her lips. “Small towns are so charming that way. Everyone knows everyone else’s business. And to answer your question, I have a broken collarbone, and I’m told it will heal.” She looked from Kim to Faith. “I take it you know each other?”

“Small town,” Kim affirmed with a nod. “A few years ago, Faith saved my babies.”

“She saved my sanity,” Penelope said.

“That’s a bit of an overstatement,” Faith said.

“You’re talking about the twins?” Alice asked.

Kim nodded. “Four years ago, Willie and Joe were born prematurely.”

“It was touch and go for weeks,” Penelope said. “Then when they were discharged, it was chaos at Kim and Bo’s house, trying to feed and look after two underweight infants.”

“I met Faith through a service,” Kim explained. “Just when Bo and I were at our wits’ end, she came along and turned everything around. Now she’s their godmother, and her girls are honorary aunties.”

“What a lovely story,” Alice said. “And now your boys are ragingly healthy. I’ve always liked a happy ending.”

Penelope reached down and squeezed her shoulder. “I’m glad the two of you are teaming up. We won’t keep you. I’m sure you have things to do.”

Alice gave her a wry smile. “My busy life.”

“We were just going out for a walk,” Faith said. “I’m still getting oriented here.”

“And we have a hair appointment at the Twisted Scissors,” said Kim. “Bo is pitching against the Kansas City Royals this coming weekend, and there’s a reception.”

“You’ll dazzle them, as usual,” said Faith. After the twins, Kim had taken a hiatus from her career in sports broadcasting, but she was slowly making her way back into the industry. As the wife of a major-league pitcher, she had a lot of options.

"Thanks," she said. "That's my plan, anyway."

The four of them went out to the courtyard together. "Don't be a stranger," Penelope said to Alice. "We miss your input at book group."

"You're in a book group together?" asked Faith.

"Our monthly excuse to get together and gossip," Penelope admitted.

"Sometimes we actually read the book," Alice said.

"You should join us at the Hilltop Tavern some Friday night," Kim said to Faith. "You, too, Alice. It's a group of women, and we don't even pretend to read books. We call it the Friday Night Drinking Club."

Faith smiled. "Thanks, but I actually like reading."

After Kim and Penelope left, Alice said, "There's something I left out of your job description."

"What's that?"

"In addition to being my live-in help, you are required to have a life."

Faith gave a little laugh. "No problem." She stooped and picked up a piece of litter. "A luggage tag from Air New Zealand. Your son is well traveled."

Alice nodded. "He couldn't wait to get out of here."

"Mason?"

"He and Regina both. They have busy careers in the city. Mason is very successful, so I shouldn't complain. I have him to thank for setting me up here." She didn't sound overly grateful. "He tends to be hands-off, but he takes care of things."

"A dispassionate problem solver," Faith said, though in her mind's eye, she could picture his face when he watched his mother.

"Yes. I instilled in him a sense of responsibility." She paused, took a breath. "Sometimes I worry about his heart." She went down an asphalt-paved pathway that wound past the pool and pool house. Faith couldn't help but think about the moment she'd had there with Mason. When he'd exited the shower, she had nearly forgotten herself. And then there was that other moment, late at night when they'd shared a glass of whiskey and probably too much information. It was just as well he wasn't planning on sticking around.

"Your girls got off to school all right?" asked Alice.

"Yes, they did, thanks. This is their first live-in situation, so it'll be an adjustment. They're very excited about living in such a beautiful spot."

"I see."

Faith couldn't tell if the woman was genuinely interested, or if she was just filling empty conversational space.

"Ruby's ready to embrace it all," Faith said. "She thinks she's moved to the Magic Kingdom."

"She didn't have much to say at dinner last night."

"She's always been tentative about new situations." Faith paused. "To be honest, she's downright fearful of a lot of things. Her condition is a factor in that, but I hope as she gets older, she'll gain confidence."

"What sorts of things does she fear?"

You, for one. Faith didn't mention it, though. "It's a long list—things like barking dogs and swimming, going to third grade next year—"

"Going to third grade? Why would she be afraid of that?"

"Some smart-alecky kid at her school said all second-grade girls had to have their ears pierced before starting third grade."

"And she believed them?"

"She's pretty gullible. Even after I explained that it's not true, she kept worrying about it."

"People who avoid doing things out of fear are missing out on the best part of life," Alice declared. "Of course, if I'd been too afraid to ski down a mountain, I wouldn't be in this chair right now, so maybe there's something to be said for cowardice."

She steered around the corner, and the landscape revealed a sunny slope with a few raised garden beds. "Mason had his cousin Greg build up the beds when he bought the place. It's for a garden, but clearly I'm in no shape to garden."

"I can help you plant some things," said Faith.

"Thank you, but I'll pass."

Faith had noticed right away that Mrs. Bellamy's focus was stuck on all the things she couldn't do instead of the things she could. Something to work on, certainly.

"And your other girl, Cara? She didn't have much to say, either, though I suspect that's due to an entirely different reason."

"Cara is a tough cookie," Faith said.

"Most tough cookies I know have something to hide."

"Are you speaking from experience?"

"Maybe. I might be."

The path wound gently down the slope to the lake. There was a sturdy ramp linking the path to the dock adjacent to the boathouse.

"I've always loved Willow Lake," said Faith. "I grew up in Kingston, and it was a special treat to come down here on a hot summer day. I never dreamed I'd have a chance to live here." She thought about the other night, her quiet conversation with Mason Bellamy and the unexpected places her mind had wandered when she was with him.

"As you can see, Mason took care of everything."

"It's very thoughtful of him. I once heard that if you wanted to determine how a man will treat his wife, you should look at the way he treats his mother."

"I've heard that, too. Best not mention it to his

fiancée," said Alice. "He goes to great lengths to avoid having to deal with me."

Faith didn't reply. She had worked with a lot of families over the years, and she'd discovered that each had its own dynamic. "People show their love and caring in different ways."

"Or not at all," Alice said sourly.

During the tour around the property, Faith noticed how adept her client was at driving the chair. She took corners and navigated smaller spaces with expert coordination.

"Is this the same chair you were in when you fell?" she asked.

"No, that one was too badly damaged, so this is a replacement. Why do you ask?"

"You're an excellent driver. So tell me again about how you fell."

Alice threw her a surly glare. "I'm sure it's in all the reports you read. I took the elevator upstairs. I can't even remember why I went there."

Faith had indeed studied the accident report. The caregiver on duty had brought the mail to Alice that day. As usual, he had opened each piece so Alice could go over it. It all seemed entirely routine, although there was one unusual piece of mail. It was a document of some sort, in French. The housekeeper had signed for it. Alice ordered the aide to go fetch something she'd forgotten, and in the few minutes that had elapsed, she had made her way upstairs, using the elevator with its switch plate that allowed her to operate it independently.

Alice scooted back toward the house. "I'm tired," she said. "I'm going to rest for a while."

Faith accompanied her to a room designated the solarium, an enclosed small porch with an abundant arrangement of potted plants, mostly aspidistra and Boston ferns. "Could you turn on the music?" Alice asked.

"Anything in particular?"

"Random selection is fine. I have thousands of hours of music, but it's not organized into playlists."

"That's something Cara can help you with. She's an expert at making playlists."

"Oh, she will love that," said Alice. "What a lucky girl."

"I'll propose it to her when she gets home from work tonight. She has a job at the Sky River Bakery in town."

"Glad to hear the girl has some employment. Fosters independence. And she'll learn that there's no excuse for being broke," Alice went on. "It's a matter of being smart about managing one's money and working hard."

"And you would know this . . . how?"

"I know you think I've been spoiled, that I don't know the meaning of poverty."

"Actually, you don't know what I think. But it's a good guess. For the record," Faith said, "I'm good at managing money, and I do work hard. But I'm still broke."

"What's the trouble, then?"

"Medical bills," she said.

"Oh. I see. Then you should have found yourself adequate health care coverage."

"Yes," Faith agreed. "I should. Silly me." She had fought. She and Dennis had both had jobs. Coverage. But his illness and legal situation had overwhelmed everything, and claims were denied.

"All right, you've made your point."

"If I comb my hair right, it won't show."

"You're cheeky. You left cheekiness off your résumé."

"So," Faith said, enjoying the way Alice's eyes gleamed when she was challenged. "What else is on the agenda today? We've already covered tantrums and bullying. There was a note in your treatment plan about doing more work in anger management."

"It can hardly be surprising that I'm angry at the world," Alice lashed out. "Anyone in my position would be."

"Being paralyzed is a condition. Being angry is a choice," said Faith.

"That's bullshit," said Alice. "Imagine not being able to walk, to comb your own damn hair—"

Faith's heart lurched. "I can't. But I can imagine letting people help me with these things."

"It's not just the disability. I lost more than my

mobility that day. My independence, my career, my privacy. And you can't even fathom what it's like to lose your husband forever."

"That's something I don't have to imagine."

"Why not?"

"I already know what it's like."

"Just because a man walked out on you doesn't mean you know what it's like to really lose him."

"I never said he walked out," Faith shot back. "He's dead. So don't tell me I can't fathom a loss like yours."

"Oh. For Lord's sake, you should've told me."

"I just did."

"I mean really told me."

Faith saw honest emotion in her face and, for the first time, something other than rage and fear. Something like empathy. She said, "It's a long story."

"You think I've got something better to do with my time?"

When Faith was seventeen, she lost her own mother to the congestive heart failure that had plagued her all her life. The day after high school graduation, Faith discovered her mother had died in her sleep. She remembered sitting in the tiny, quiet clapboard house where she'd grown up, feeling a loss so deep she could scarcely breathe. She'd sat with her mother for what seemed like a long time, with the tears running down her face and the phone in her hand, her fingers too numb with grief to dial for help.

It was a painfully young age to learn the true meaning of aloneness. With nothing more than a high school diploma and her mother's empty bank account, Faith grabbed any job that would keep even a tiny sum of money trickling in.

When you were young and alone, and struggling to survive, a guy like Dennis McCallum could definitely turn your head. He was matinee-idol handsome and spoke with a Scottish burr. He rode a shiny black-and-silver motorcycle, played guitar with a fine hand, and he lived like there was no tomorrow. Which turned out to be the case for him.

In the way of any stupid-in-love seventeen-year-old, she got pregnant. Dennis, with his insatiable appetite for everything life had to offer, was thrilled, and he married her immediately. People assumed he did so in order to get his green card, but Faith knew better. She had never felt so cherished as when she lay in Dennis's arms at the end of a long day, or listened to him strumming softly on his guitar on a Sunday afternoon, after all the week's chores were done.

Against all odds and predictions, they were wildly happy. Cara—the name was Dennis's choice, a favorite name in Scotland, where he'd been born and raised—was a magic baby, perfectly healthy, well behaved, bright and cheerful even as an infant.

They scarcely noticed or cared that there was no money. Her wages as a home health aide, and his as a motorcycle mechanic—without a green card—just managed to cover their living expenses. She got pregnant again. Things were looking up. They lived on hope and happiness, and nothing fazed them until one day, when Cara was about eight. She and Dennis were playing a madcap game of one-on-one in the schoolyard near their apartment when Cara came running in.

"Dad's on the ground, and he won't get up."

He'd had a virus that week, and later it was discovered that this was the trigger to everything that came after.

Thus began the terrible odyssey of his diagnosis and prognosis. Initially, doctors were baffled, because his symptoms were so strange. He had no family history, because he'd been a runaway in Scotland.

Eventually, however, the subtle symptoms added up. He was always thirsty. Occasionally, dark patches appeared under his arms. He couldn't keep weight on, even when he tried. He'd been known to sweat buckets.

Dennis took the diagnosis the way he took everything else in life—as a joke. Their minimal health coverage didn't allow them to pursue the most aggressive and expensive treatments. He did his best to adjust to the recommended lifestyle changes and insisted on taking "his girls," as he termed Faith and Cara, on a cross-country road trip.

Then Dennis's health took a turn, and he was beset by the worst complications of his type 1 diabetes. By the time Ruby was born, he was too sick to do anything. Faith worked day and night to care for her newborn daughter and her husband. They sank deeper into debt over his medical bills, which piled up as the insurance company denied claim after claim. She managed to work out a payment plan whenever possible. Dennis outlived his prognosis by several years. No one could explain it, but Faith suspected it was pure stubborn will and determination.

One day she spied an official-looking letter stashed in the bottom of his guitar case. It was a Notice to Appear from the US Citizenship and Immigration Service, stating that he was required to appear at a deportation hearing.

"This is dated six months ago," she said, icy fear running through her veins. "When were you going to tell me about it?"

"I'm not spending our money on lawyers, Faith," he'd told her.

"We have to. We have to fight it. We—"

"Faith." The immeasurable sadness in his eyes broke her heart. "There's no point. I'll be gone before they take action against me. Let me be with my girls. You're my reason for living."

The final blow came when Ruby was also diagnosed with type 1 diabetes.

The world stopped being fun anymore, even for Dennis. The complications of his illness piled up even faster than the bills. He was rarely able to walk, and he quickly went from cane to walker to wheelchair.

They spent the final week of his life at Camp Kioga on Willow Lake. The historic resort belonged to the Bellamy family, yes, those Bellamys, some distant great-uncle of Mason Bellamy. They were able to have a family holiday at the lake, thanks to a charitable initiative known as Cottage Dreams. The program offered a respite week in a lakeside cottage for families dealing with a devastating illness.

Faith remembered that time with a sweet ache of sadness. It was autumn, and in the final stages of his illness, Dennis summoned enough strength to get out of his wheelchair and take a short walk around the property. The two of them sat in Adirondack chairs on the deck, watching the confetti-colored leaves of autumn sprinkling down on the placid surface of the lake. Nearby, Cara and Ruby giggled and played on a swing hung from a huge, old maple tree.

There was something utterly perfect about that moment. Even now, Faith could still envision the deep autumn blue of the afternoon sky and the glance of the sun's rays on the leaf-strewn water. The dry sighing sound of the wind through the trees stirred a colorful shower of falling leaves.

She could still feel the touch of Dennis's hand as he reached over and laid it atop hers. She could still hear the smile in his voice as he said, "You were the best ride I've ever had, Faith."

And that was saying a lot, because he rode everything. Blades, skateboards, bikes, scooters. Motorcycles were his passion.

His fingers were ice-cold. His ears and the tip of his nose had lost all color. She knew what was happening and realized he did, too. He must have seen the panic in her eyes the moment she grasped the significance of the moment.

"Don't," he said. "Just, maybe tuck that blanket around me."

She did so with tears streaming down her face; then she tugged her chair up against his and laid her head on his shoulder. They sat listening to the sound of the wind through the trees and the laughter of their daughters, the sweetest music on earth.

"Should I tell them to come over?"

"No, my love." His voice was faint and thready. "There's no need. I just want to close my eyes and listen to them laughing. And if I'm being honest, I shall have to admit that in the end, I want you all to myself. Is that selfish of me?"

"No. Good God, no." It took all her strength to

resist rushing to the house, calling for help. They both knew it would only turn this inevitable moment to chaos and horror. "Take a breath, Dennis," she said. "Feel my love. Feel the sunlight on your face."

"Yes," he said. "I feel it. I feel you."

"Dennis, I can't . . ." She bit her lip to hold back words of despair. But how would she go on without him?

"Now listen to me, Faith, and listen with all your heart. I'm not leaving you. I said I'd never leave, and I won't. You have to believe that. The part of me that loves you will never die. Say you believe it, because I swear it's true."

"Yes, all right." She could barely get the words out. She did, though, because she loved him so much that she would not worry him with her terror and her grief. "And you have to believe it, too."

"Of course, love. Of course."

Everything that needed saying had already been said, again and again through the months and years of his decline. She leaned over and kissed him. His breath was extremely shallow, his features already going slack. She kissed him; his lips were warm. *Oh, my God,* she thought, *oh, my God, this is the last time I will ever kiss this man.*

She held his hand for a long time, it seemed, the fingers cold and stiff, and she never quite grasped the precise moment of his death. At some point she looked up and saw that his eyes were open, but there was no other movement. And that was the moment she knew. He'd left with the gentle grace and silence of an autumn leaf slipping from a tree and blowing away on the breeze.

When she had sat down in the Adirondack chair only moments before, she had been a young wife and mother, just twenty-eight years old and at the beginning of the best part of life.

When she got up from the chair, she'd been a widow, about to embark on the struggle of a lifetime.

"I'm sorry," said Alice, regarding Faith with new eyes. "And you and I both know that all the I'm-sorrys in the world will never make it better."

"That's true. I'm sure we both heard the same clumsy and even stupid things from well-meaning people. But it's nice to hear a caring thought." Faith discreetly dabbed a tear from Alice's cheek.

"Thank you for telling me."

"I'm glad you asked. I used to break down every time I had to explain my situation, but after a while, I started to like talking about him." In her line of work, Faith had figured out that people tended to grieve the same way they loved. For Faith, that meant deeply, intensely and with all her heart. "In the end, Dennis tried to explain to me that a person is never really gone if you still think about him. If you can close your eyes and see his face, if you can hear his voice calling your name or the sound of his laughter, it means he still lives somewhere." She paused, studying Alice's face.

Alice gave no sign of understanding. "And you have no other family?"

"No. I never knew the man who fathered me. When I was little, I'd ask, but all Mama said was that he was her biggest mistake and she didn't want to talk about it." Faith had never liked that answer, because it meant she was the result of her mother's biggest mistake. "She told me his name, but I didn't pursue it. I couldn't imagine what I would say to that person."

"And your husband's family?"

"I never met anyone from his relatives in Scotland. They weren't close. He became a runaway at age sixteen. No one came to see him when he got sick. After he died, I wrote to his mother and aunt a few times, and they replied, but that tapered off. I think they were worried I'd come to them, looking for a handout."

"Ah, that's too bad. I'm glad you have your girls. I've heard it said that daughters are life's reward for all the hard work and struggle. Do you believe that?"

"Of course. Cara has her issues, but she's smart and tough, and I adore her."

"You're an admirable woman, Faith. I'm sorry for your loss."

"And I'm sorry for yours."

Alice was quiet for a few moments. Then she

said, "I never told Mason this, but Trevor was still alive. That day, on the mountain. I couldn't move, but I could see him. He was coughing up blood. I said I was sorry. I said I loved him. But I will never know if he heard or understood. He just coughed. The blood sprayed everywhere, all over the white snow."

Faith tried not to wince at the image. At the same time, she wondered at Alice's self-control. "I hope as time passes, you'll remember all the wonderful things about your life together, not just that moment." She got the sense that the Bellamys tended to protect each other—a practice that sometimes did more harm than good, because it meant hiding things that mattered. "Tell me about your daughter, Ivy."

"I can do better than that. She's coming to visit on her way to Paris."

10

Ivy Bellamy arrived during a storm. Faith and Mrs. Armentrout watched from the window of the foyer as the car entered through the gates and came around the circular drive, where windblown petals from the blossoming trees resembled a pink blizzard.

Donno, who had collected her from the station, jumped out with an umbrella, but she waved him off and made a dash for the front door while he brought in her luggage.

She laughed as Mrs. Armentrout helped her off with her coat. "Sorry. I've brought the rain inside."

"Do you want to go to your room and freshen up?"

"Later," Ivy said, and turned to Faith, offering a bright-eyed smile. "You must be the famous Faith McCallum."

"I'm Faith. I don't know about the famous part."

"Well, your reputation precedes you. According to my brother, you're a miracle worker."

"He said that?" Faith felt a strange, little, unearned thrill, which she immediately squelched.

"Verbatim," Ivy said, holding up her right hand. "Swear."

"Let's go find your mother." Faith wondered what kind of reports Ivy had received from her.

Alice was in the solarium, where the French doors framed a view of the deck and the lake beyond. The storm came across the lake in great wind-driven gusts that bent the trees and lashed the windows. Inside, it felt cozy and warm, with a fire crackling in the big river-rock fireplace at one end of the room. Alice's face looked pensive and immeasurably sad in the silvery light through the windows. Faith often found her like this—too often.

"There's my gorgeous mother," Ivy declared, rushing across the room to embrace her.

Alice showed a rare smile, and a light danced in her eyes. The sadness vanished like a shadow chased by sunlight. "Hello, gorgeous daughter. Welcome to the wettest place on earth."

"I don't mind a bit," said Ivy. "All that Santa Barbara sunshine can get boring. I say, bring on the drama." She grinned at Faith. "I like drama."

"Your mother mentioned that. The two of you . . . look like sisters," Faith observed. They both had fair skin and honey-blond hair, cornflower blue eyes and camera-ready smiles. "I bet you get that a lot."

"Yes, we do," said Ivy, "but she's shorter."

"Not funny," said Alice.

"Okay, I'll go back to hand-wringing and beating my chest."

Faith liked her already, because of the way Alice lit up for her daughter. Faith liked Ivy even more when the girls got home from school and came in to meet her. Ivy didn't bat an eye at Cara's latest getup—slouchy pants with way too many grommets and shoelaces and straps, a Buckethead T-shirt, her hair in a messy bun—and like most people, Ivy visibly melted when she met Ruby.

"Second grade," she exclaimed, clasping her hands together as she gazed at Ruby. "I loved second grade. My teacher was Mrs. Mary Beth Smith, and she smelled like breath mints, and for the last twenty minutes of every day, she let us draw pictures."

"I like to draw," said Ruby.

"I draw and paint for my job. I'm going to Paris for a year to study and get better at it."

"You're an artist?"

"That's right. It's all I've ever wanted to be, and I'm lucky enough to get to do it every day."

"I drew the garden plan." Ruby grabbed a large sheet of paper from a drawer in the study and showed it to Ivy. "Your mom said what she wanted to plant, and I drew it all in rows. See? Sunflowers, strawberries, tomatoes . . . It's going to be awesome."

"A garden," said Ivy. "What a great idea. It'll be a first for my mom."

"She didn't want to at first, but I talked her into it," Ruby said.

"Don't boast," said Faith. "Not until we're eating your fresh berries and tomatoes."

A crash of thunder shook the house. In one swift leap, Ruby ended up in Faith's arms.

Cara rolled her eyes. Alice turned to her and said, "Let me guess. She's afraid of thunder."

"And lightning," said Cara. "Not to mention her own shadow."

"Mom," Ruby complained. "She's just mad because I know she has a secret crush on Leighton Hayes."

"Shut up, brat," said Cara, her cheeks turning red.

"Ivy just got here," said Faith. "No bickering. Go do your homework and chores."

"But—"

"Now, ladies." Faith gave them the look that needed no further explanation. They were both familiar with it, and they both knew what it meant.

After they left, Alice shook her head. "Raising a girl is challenging, isn't it?"

"I think raising any child is challenging," Faith admitted.

"True, but I do believe it's easier to raise boys."

Despite Alice's words, her bond with Ivy seemed far less tense than her relationship with Mason. Faith wondered why that was. And then she wondered if it was any of her business. Living with a client was tricky that way. The lines tended to blur.

Despite the stormy weather, it turned out to be one of Alice's best days. Ivy's presence kept her brightened up and engaged. Her usual undercurrent of sadness seemed a bit more distant. Faith and the girls had dinner with Alice and Ivy, as they did most days. Alice had decided that she didn't like eating alone. Though she was sometimes brusque with the girls, she genuinely seemed to enjoy their company. Dinner was a feast of all Ivy's favorites—macaroni and cheese, Caesar salad, fresh-caught trout from the lake and rhubarb pie for dessert.

"I'm mad for cheese," Ivy said, adding more Parmesan to her salad. "It's an addiction. Two years in France will be the death of me. The summer between my junior and senior years in high school, I worked in Paris, and I subsisted on baguettes, cheese and chocolate."

"Where'd you work?" asked Cara.

"At an NGO—a nongovernmental agency—called AIDE. That stands for *Alliance Internationale pour le Développement de l'Éducation*. Its main sponsor is a foundation run by our father's company, and we all got a chance to work there as teenagers."

"Paris has always made me nervous," Alice said. "Mason's internship didn't go so well."

"In what way?" asked Faith.

"Never mind," Alice said hastily. "He can tell you about it sometime. These days, he's in charge of the sponsorship."

"Teens come from all over to work there, and the organization provides funds for education in areas where it's most needed," Ivy said.

While Faith pondered Alice's cryptic statement, Cara listened with rapt attention. Watching her daughter, Faith knew she was yearning to see the world. She hoped one day there would be a way for Cara to do that. The girl was just so smart and full of dreams. She'd always loved seeing new places, but the opportunities were limited. *Ah, baby, I wish I could give you the world,* thought Faith. *Who am I kidding? I can barely scrape together the fee for a cap and gown.*

"My dad's company has an apartment in Paris where I lived that summer. It was near Rivoli, and to this day, it's my favorite neighborhood." She refilled her wineglass. "Who's living there now, Mom? If it's empty, maybe I could—"

"No," Alice said sharply, her voice making everyone jump. She took a sip of her wine from a straw. "It's not available."

"I know that," Ivy said. "I was just wondering who's using it."

"I don't recall offhand," said Alice. "Ruby, suppose you finish reading me *The Phantom Tollbooth* after dinner."

"Okay. We've got one chapter left." Ruby and Alice had taken to reading together in the evenings, and Faith loved it. Both Alice and Ruby shared a serious love of reading, and the little girl was delighted to have an audience.

Ivy lifted her glass. "Cheers to that. I loved *The Phantom Tollbooth*."

"We're going to read *Charlotte's Web* next," Ruby announced.

"Another classic," Ivy said. "My mom picks out the best books, doesn't she?"

"Yes, but she's bossy about it."

"Ruby," said Faith.

"I'm not bossy," Alice said. "Just opinionated."

"I'm keeping you up," Ivy said after they had bade Alice good-night, and the aide helped her to bed. “I’m still on California time and wide-awake. Sorry.”

“I don’t mind,” said Faith. “Let’s sit by the fire.”

The wind had died down, and the rain had slowed to a steady drizzle. They sat on the big leather chesterfield sofa, gazing into the flames.

“I wouldn’t blame you if you couldn’t wait to escape,” Ivy said. “Your days are long, and Mom has never been the world’s easiest person.”

“I like her. We get along. I think your mother and I are going to do all right. And she’s great with the girls.”

“I can’t tell you what a relief it is to hear that. It’s been quite an ordeal, finding someone who can take charge.” Ivy’s tears came just as the storm had earlier, in a sudden copious flood. “Sorry,” she gasped between sobs, “it’s just been so hard, seeing her struggle and not knowing what to do.”

Faith went and got a box of tissues and the wine bottle from dinner, along with two glasses. “Just enough left,” she said, setting the wine and tissues on the coffee table in front of them.

Ivy availed herself of both. “Mason said you had outstanding nursing skills. He was right.”

“It’s very technical,” said Faith. She uncovered the candy dish on the coffee table to reveal a selection of chocolate truffles. “Voilà. A trifecta of therapy.”

Ivy sighed, helping herself to a chocolate.

"What else did your brother say about me?" Faith asked. Then she winced at the way that sounded, as if she were some junior high school girl wanting to know if a guy liked her.

"He said you were amazing in an emergency, and you've got a strong enough personality to deal with Mom."

Amazing. Did he say *amazing?*

"It's just so heartbreaking. And she's getting worse, not better, in terms of attitude."

"Just before the recent fall down the stairs, did anything change?"

"Not that I know of. I thought things were improving bit by bit. My brothers and I were in New Zealand scattering Daddy's ashes when we got the call about her accident. We were horrified. She survived an avalanche, and then for her to go crashing down the stairs . . ." Her voice trailed off, and her hand trembled as she picked up her wineglass. "I couldn't stand to lose both parents."

Faith didn't say more right away. But she had questions. She had heard from the housekeeper that, prior to the fall, Alice had seemed slightly better, in the sense that she was more cooperative with her aides and perhaps less angry. The caregiver on duty had been there longer than any of his predecessors.

Alice had been working hard on her physical therapy and making the tiniest bit of progress. She'd been encouraging of all three of her children about scattering their father's ashes. Insistent, in fact. Adam hadn't wanted to go so far away, but she'd assured him she would be fine on her own with the help. But something had changed, clearly.

"What was your father like?" Faith asked Ivy.

"Ah, where do I start?" A worshipful expression came over her face. Faith was reminded, obliquely, of the way Cara looked when she talked about Dennis. Fond memories softened a person's heart, and it was nearly always reflected in their face. For some reason, she had not sensed that kind of sentiment in Alice when she spoke of Trevor. Maybe she'd missed it . . . or maybe Alice's memories were not as fond as Ivy believed.

Ivy went over to the piano and picked up a framed photo. It depicted Trevor Bellamy at a train station, running along a steam-clouded platform. The print was crisply rendered in black-and-white, so that it resembled a vintage photo in *LIFE* magazine. "I've always liked this shot. Mason took it in Paris about twenty years ago, I think. He managed to capture our dad's energy. Growing up with him was like racing to catch up with a runaway train. It was a wild ride. He just seemed to veer from one adventure to the next."

Mason would have been a teenager when he took that picture, Faith reflected. Had he liked having a runaway train for a dad?

She looked at Ivy, whose tears had dried into

white ghosts on her cheeks. "Was that fun for you?"

"Enormous fun, but then, I've always been good with spontaneity and unpredictability. It's probably not for everyone, though. Daddy's death nearly destroyed me, but in a strange way, I'm not surprised he died in an avalanche rather than growing old and fading peacefully away. Still, his death was so sudden, and so sad." She shook her head, gazing into the fire. "Sometimes I honestly don't know how Mom survived. Emotionally, I mean. They had a complicated relationship, I guess you could say. But a passionate one. She adored him. Whenever he went away, she was like a lost soul."

Complicated. Yes, Faith could sense that. "What do you mean, *went away?*"

"He had to travel a lot for work, and for the foundation. He had so much business in Paris that he got an apartment and an office there."

"She didn't join him?"

"They both had superbusy careers, and on top of that, they were both committed to the foundation. Paris was rarely in her travel plans. As kids we took turns traveling with our parents. It was so much fun, even when it was a working vacation."

"What kind of vacation is that?"

"Well, we'd go somewhere amazing, like to Machu Picchu or Alaska or Angkor Wat, and Mom would always find a way to help the local community. It's always been a priority with her. One summer Adam and I were really jealous that Mason got to go to Paris to be with Dad and to work for the foundation."

"The summer he took that picture?"

"Yes. He would have just finished his junior year in high school. I was just a youngster, but I remember when he came back from Paris, everything was different. I think maybe something happened in Paris."

"Your mom started to say something at dinner."

"I was so much younger, just six or seven, and Mason didn't seem to stay around the house for more than five minutes at a time. I do recall when he got back from Paris, he was all banged up, you know, as if he'd had an accident. Maybe he got in a fight. You could ask my brother about it sometime."

She might have to.

"So, back to your mom." Faith set the photo back on the piano. "When this kind of trauma happens, it's a huge life change, but you said she seemed to be making progress."

"I did say that, but I'm no expert. It's such a radical change for anyone. For someone like my mom, who was so active all the time, it was like a bomb going off in her life." Another tear slipped down Ivy's cheek. "I hope I'm wrong, but . . . sometimes I think she just wants to be released."

"Released. Tell me what you mean by that."

"Just that she doesn't want to go on."

Faith caught her breath. "Did she say that?"

"Not directly. This morning she said she didn't see the point of anything. And it's so not like her to give up. All her life she's met challenges, and I thought she would meet this one, but she's so angry and depressed."

Faith thought about Dennis. He had lived with passion and incaution, but in the end he had managed to find a peaceful spot within himself. His hunger for life quieted, and unexpectedly, in the midst of the storm, he found a strange kind of contentedness. The damned illness. He'd been open about his feelings, but he'd never actually said he craved release.

Ivy lightly tapped the cover over the piano keys. "Mom used to play pretty well. She did everything well. I wonder if having the piano here bothers her."

"Have you asked her?"

"Sure. She says it's here for when Mason comes."

"Your brother plays?"

"Yes. We all do, a bit, but Mason was always the best at it. Mom taught him when he was little. One of my earliest memories is of the two of them playing 'Heart and Soul.' And a Chopsticks medley that got faster and faster, and for some reason, it made them laugh themselves silly every time they played it together."

Faith tried to picture Mason and his mother laughing side by side. They were so tense around each other now. What had changed? she wondered. And had it changed before or after Alice's accident? Was something else going on between Alice and her elder son?

Ivy turned another picture toward Faith. It showed Trevor and Alice in a midair cliff dive. "Acapulco," she said. "By the time they were my age, they were married and had the two boys. I wonder sometimes why the three of us are so romantically challenged."

"You are? How so?"

"I've never had a relationship that lasted, and I don't know why. I've never had a relationship that I *wanted* to last. And Adam—I get the sense that he wants something he can't have. Or can't find. Although he'd never admit it, that's one reason he went away for his arson investigation course. Then there's Mason . . ."

"He has Regina. Aren't they engaged? That was my impression, anyway."

"I think that's Regina's impression, too. And yeah, Mason would say they're engaged, but they haven't gotten around to picking a ring. Or a date. Or even a reason that they should be together for life. I'd love it if they were really into the whole wedding thing, but they're both holding back. I have no idea why, and I suspect they don't, either." She popped another dark chocolate. "So there you have it. Our nutty family in a nutshell."

"What if you met someone in Paris?" asked Faith. "Think how romantic that would be."

"Totally. I'm worried about being so far away. I told Mom I'd postpone the fellowship, but she wouldn't hear of it."

"Sounds like something your mother would say. She told me right from the start she doesn't want to hold any of you back from doing whatever you want to do."

Faith could relate to this completely. That was one reason she felt so guilty about Cara and college. She knew her daughter yearned to go to college, and she intended to support Cara's ambition. When she looked online at all the costs involved, it practically gave her heart palpitations. But she was going to leave no stone unturned.

"I'm planning to come back for a visit at least every two or three months," said Ivy. "And I'll come more frequently if you think Mom needs me."

"I'll stay in touch," Faith promised.

"Thank you. I'm so grateful you're here for Mom."

They watched the fire die down for a while longer. Then Faith got up and stretched. "I'd better get to bed. See you in the morning."

"Yes. My flight's not until late at night, so I'll have another half day with Mom."

"Good night."

"Hey, Faith?"

Faith paused in the doorway. "Yes?"

"Did you think Mom acted weird when I asked her about the Paris apartment?"

"Weird, how?"

"She just seemed really brusque, like she didn't want to talk about it."

"Oh . . . maybe."

"And is she also weird about her tumble down the stairs?" Ivy asked. "Like maybe it scared her more than she admits?"

Faith wanted to get a few more facts about the accident before she explained her thoughts about what had happened that day. "Tell you what. You stay focused on getting settled in Paris. Your mom's going to be all right."

11

Sometimes Cara took the school bus home instead of riding with Donno. Her sister's school got out earlier than the high school, and she didn't like making him drive twice, or wait for her with Ruby squirming in the backseat.

When they'd first moved to Downton Abbey—Cara's private nickname for the Bellamy estate—it had been cool to get out of the sleek black car as if she were some kind of diplomat or VIP, but she got tired of explaining to her friends that, no, her mom hadn't won the lottery, blah, blah, blah . . .

After the school bus let her off, she hiked a sunny half mile to the long, winding drive leading to the house. She liked to pretend she actually lived at the Bellamy mansion, not as a temporary resident but as someone who belonged there. The driveway was so long it had its own street name, Webster Lane, in honor of the guy who had built the house a hundred years ago. The road was lined by rows of tall, straight trees, shedding white blossoms like snowflakes in the breeze. The grass was emerald green and perfectly cut, and at the end of the lane were two river-rock pillars and a wrought-iron gate that stood open to a glorious view of the house and lake.

Being part of this idyllic picture made Cara temporarily forget that she was only a transient visitor. Forgetting her overstuffed backpack filled with schoolbooks, she felt like a character in some *Masterpiece Theatre* drama, with nothing more pressing on the agenda than getting dressed up for a high tea of jam and cream scones.

Whatever the hell cream scones were.

She pictured herself in period costume, some frilly outfit that weirdly made her look good. She was walking beside Leighton Hayes, aka the hottest guy in the junior class, the guy who looked as if he should have his own TV series. In her mental picture, Leighton Hayes wore a shirt with a starched white collar, with a Mr. Darcy–style ruffle, his curly black hair tumbling rakishly down over his brow. He would turn to her and say something totally cheesy like, "Miss McCallum, I am entirely smitten with you. I shan't rest until you understand the depth of my emotions." And she would whirl around with her frilly skirts flying. "Why, Leighton Hayes, I am forced to tell you, I feel the same way, and I would like to know what you intend to do about it."

"Well," said a voice, "I was going to ring the bell, but then I thought it would be less intrusive if I knocked."

For a moment Cara felt as if all the wind had been knocked out of her. Milo Waxman, aka the geekiest guy in the junior class, stood just inside the main gate. His bike was propped against the garden wall, and he was regarding her with laughter in his eyes. He was skinny, and his jeans were too short and he wore horn-rimmed glasses that made him look even smarter than he actually was. His bike helmet gave his head the look of a mushroom.

"Sorry to interrupt you and your imaginary friend," he said, stripping off his helmet and hanging it on the handlebars. His rusty-brown hair was plastered to his forehead. "I was just stopping in to take care of some business." He tapped the clipboard he was carrying.

She wanted to curl up and die, right then and there. For a second she considered trying to explain herself, but she knew he would see right through her. The fact was, she had been caught red-handed being as silly and predictable as any mindless high school cheerleader, having a crush on Mr. Homecoming-King-in-waiting, who didn't even know she was alive.

And by studying her for half a second, Milo Waxman clearly had it all figured out. She could tell by the bemused, knowing look on his face. "You disappoint me, Miss McCallum. I thought you were a member of the intelligentsia."

She tossed her head. "Hit the road, Milo."

"What, you're not inviting me in? Afraid I'll make fun of your Justin Bieber posters?"

She was never going to hear the end of this. "No, I'm trying to protect you from the wrath of old lady Bellamy. She doesn't like company, even when they're invited guests. I can only imagine what she would do to a door-to-door solicitor."

"I'm working on a fund-raiser for the local animal shelter," he said, showing her the information page on his clipboard. "Puppies and kittens. Who doesn't like puppies and kittens?"

She glared at him. It would serve him right if Mrs. B tore him a new one. "This way," she said, and led him up the stairs to the grand front entryway. She caught a glimpse of herself in the giant mirror over the hall table, and the Leighton Hayes fantasy dissolved into the ether. Her reality crashed down, with the mirror reflecting the image of her with one of the few boys who bothered to speak to her—Milo Waxman. And there she was in her leggings and droopy cargo jacket, her dumb hair she'd stupidly cut in spikes and tipped in purple. It was one of her many what-was-I-thinking moments.

She tended to have a lot of those.

The house was freakishly quiet as usual. She made her way to the kitchen, finding Wayan there, methodically trimming the ends off asparagus.

"Hey, Wayan, this is Milo," said Cara. "He's here to see Mrs. B."

"I'll betcha you're looking for a snack," Wayan said with a grin. He loved feeding people. It seemed to be his passion in life. "I made some sugar-free peanut butter bars."

"Thanks." Cara and Milo each helped themselves to one. "Delicious," Cara said. "It's really nice of you to make sugar-free things for Ruby."

"No problem, only solution. I like trying new things. And that little kid, you know, she is so sweet, she doesn't need any added sugar."

Cara nodded in agreement. "No argument from me."

"You're lucky," Milo said. "My younger sister is a cross between a rat terrier and a weasel. You don't want to mess with her."

Cara resisted a smile. "Ruby has her moments, but most people are pretty crazy about her." Her little sister was like a baby kitten, adorable and cuddly, playful and probably way too skittish.

Pretty much the opposite of Cara, who was prickly and disagreeable, with a habit of saying the wrong thing at exactly the wrong moment. And she wasn't afraid of anything. If she could survive losing her dad, she could survive anything.

"Did she get home yet?" Cara asked the chef.

Before Wayan could answer, there was a plinking sound of the piano being played. Well, not so much played as played *with*. From day one, Ruby had been fascinated by the shiny black Steinway in the parlor, though she had no clue how to play.

Cara grabbed an extra cookie on a napkin and led the way. "Hey, Ruby, this is Milo Waxman. He—"

"I know you." Ruby stopped playing and regarded him with a worshipful gaze. "Your sister Wanda's in my grade."

"Oh." He pushed his glasses up his nose. "Are you friends with her?"

Ruby lowered her gaze to the floor. "She's kinda scary."

Milo nodded sagely. "Yep, that's Wanda."

"You came to my classroom last week to talk about taking care of pets." Ruby turned to Cara. "He brought a newborn baby kitten that was an orphan and had to be fed with a bottle, but we weren't allowed to touch it."

"You're scared of cats, anyway." Feeling snarky, Cara turned to Milo. "She's scared of cats."

"Maybe one day you'll come to the shelter and get to know some of the cats and kittens there."

Ruby quailed. "Maybe." She swiveled around on the piano stool and plinked out a few notes, then tried a chord. "I like how these notes go together," she said, and tried a few more, with varying success.

"What do you think you're doing?"

Ruby jumped back as if the keyboard had turned into a hungry crocodile.

Cara stepped defensively in front of her sister as Alice Bellamy glided into the room. "She was just—"

"I know what she was doing," barked Mrs. Bellamy.

Cara narrowed her eyes at the woman. "You asked."

"It was a rhetorical question." She aimed a sour look at Milo. "Who's your friend?"

"He's not—" *Far from it.* "This is Milo Waxman. He goes to my school. He says he's here about a fund-raiser."

Mrs. Bellamy pursed her lips. "I have a non-profit foundation. You can apply for a grant and go through the same evaluation process as every-one else who comes looking for a handout."

Milo regarded her placidly, seemingly unmoved

by her bullying. He turned the information sheet toward her. "Kittens and puppies?"

She glared at the display of large-eyed adorableness. "Take a card from the hall table on your way out. Blaine Hopper, my business manager. Tell him to make a fifty-dollar donation."

"We're looking for a commitment of three-fifty," Milo said. "That gets you a plaque on a cat cage at the shelter."

"I don't need a plaque. One hundred dollars."

"Two-fifty." He didn't waver. "And we'll put your name on the Happy Helpers donor wall."

"Two hundred," she snapped. "And you can find your own way out."

Milo grinned from ear to ear. For a moment he didn't look so insufferably dorky. He just looked . . . clever and smart. "That's awesome, Mrs. Bellamy. You'll be glad to know a donation at that level gets you a plaque on a dog food bin."

"Oh, for heaven's sake, I don't need—" She interrupted herself and rotated toward Ruby. "Put the child's name on the plaque."

Ruby lit up. "My name? Really? Cool."

"Will do, Mrs. B."

"Please don't call me Mrs. B. I am not Mrs. anything. My name is Alice."

"Yes, ma'am."

"Can we call you Alice, too?" asked Ruby.

Mrs. Bellamy aimed a monstrous glare at her.

"Ma'am?" Ruby added meekly.

"That would be fine. Alice it is. It's better that way. 'Mrs.' implies I'm married, which I'm not. I'm a widow, and I must say I don't happen to be fond of the designation."

"Thanks from the animals, Alice," said Milo. "And remember, there are always pets in need of homes. So if you ever—"

"Highly doubtful," said Alice.

"I understand. I'll see myself out." Milo grinned at Cara. "I guess we can look at your Justin Bieber collection later."

"Cara can't stand Justin Bieber," Ruby said.

"It's all a front. She's obsessed with the guy." And with that, Milo was gone.

"Cheeky young man," said Alice with a sniff.

"He's all right," Cara said, surprising herself by defending him. Milo was known to be a loner at school, not really a part of any group. She found herself wondering if he chose to be friendless, or if he just ended up that way. She wondered if sometimes he felt so lonely he wanted to scream. It was a feeling she could relate to, although at Avalon High and at the bakery, she had made some good friends. Thank God they were staying here another year or more.

"Are you taking piano lessons?" Alice asked Ruby.

"No," said Ruby. "I don't know how to play."

"Well, this is a fine instrument. It's not a toy."

"Then why is it called *playing?*"

That made Alice pause. Cara could see Ruby bracing herself for the dragon lady to roar. Instead, Alice remarked, "That's a good question. It's simply a manner of speaking."

"Oh." Ruby looked mystified. She dangled her feet, swinging herself back and forth on the piano stool.

Alice moved the wheelchair closer. "First things first. You have to sit at the proper height. You're too low. Cara, help your sister adjust the seat. It needs to be about four inches higher."

Cara was as startled as Ruby looked. Neither asked questions, though. She used the lever under the seat to raise it.

"Your arms should form an L shape when you rest your hands on the keyboard," Alice explained.

Ruby placed both hands on the shiny keys. "Like this?"

"Yes. Now, think about your posture. Sit up straight, shoulders back and down. Good. The way you hold your hands is very important, too. Pretend you're picking up a tennis ball with a loose grip. Roll your thumbs over just a bit—yes. And there you have it."

Ruby looked delighted to be sitting there, poised to begin playing. "Now what?" she asked. "When do I get to make music?"

"How about now?" asked Alice. "I started all my children with a simple little song. Touch that white key, right there. No, the one next to it.

That's middle C. Memorize it. That key is your home base."

Ruby played the note. Cara moved quietly away, gobsmacked by what she was seeing. This was the longest Alice had ever gone without getting cranky or having a hissy fit about something or other. She wasn't smiling or anything like that, but she was acting kind of . . . well, almost pleasant. Maybe she was coming around.

She explained to Ruby how to play three simple two-note intervals. After a few false starts, Ruby got the hang of it, and before long, the notes came together in a simple song that actually sounded like music. The first time she got through it smoothly, she looked over at Alice with her eyes full of wonder.

"Can you show me more?" she asked softly.

"Of course I can. But not yet. You must practice this piece until it's automatic. It's based on a simple theme by Mozart, but we'll keep adding to it until you have the whole piece down."

They worked together on some other things. Cara stuck around, fascinated by the shift in dynamics. She picked up a coffee-table book, a heavy, oversize one with crisp photos, and started paging through it. She could understand the appeal of coffee-table books. They were colorful and didn't require you to think or judge or read too many words. You just had to flip through the pages and enjoy the show.

Cara herself didn't care for coffee-table books. They were big and unwieldy and they took up space. Besides, they portrayed everything in such a totally unrealistic bullshit way. The books always seemed to display things like food a regular person would never be able to prepare, clothes no real-shaped woman would ever actually wear and beautiful places in the world she would never be able to travel.

The one she was paging through now had a beautifully formed ocean wave on the cover, with a tiny figure of a girl on a surfboard in the tunnel of the wave. Inside, there were photos of a sun-gold young couple, holding hands and racing into the surf, looking impossibly flawless. They were lean and blond, laughing with abandon, as though they hadn't a care in the world. The next few pages showed off the same couple in equally exciting settings—diving off a cliff into a pristine waterfall, skiing down a mountain with the distinctive crag of the Matterhorn in the background, riding horses in an emerald forest, walking through an ancient castle at sunset.

They looked like the most perfect couple ever created, but Cara reminded herself they were models or actors. That was their job, to look perfect.

She browsed through a few more pages of the book called *Journey*, noting the captions here and there—Cap d'Antibes, France. Bora Bora. Mount

Rainier. There was a close-up of the perfect couple under the Arc de Triomphe in Paris, and that was when Cara finally realized what she was looking at.

"These are pictures of you," she said loudly.

Alice's chair careened away from the piano. The dragon lady stare was back. "I beg your pardon."

"These pictures in this book. They're pictures of you." She held up the cover. "I thought it was a celebrity thing."

"Oh," said Alice, "that. My children had it made while I was in the hospital. A pictorial memoir of all the things I'll never be able to do again."

Cara smoothed her hand down a double-page spread of Alice poised atop a mountain, draped in climbing gear, a grin of triumph on her face. "Yeah, but at least you got to do it."

"I want to see." Ruby jumped up and came to peer over her shoulder. "Wow, look at you, Alice. You know how to do lots of cool stuff."

"Not anymore," she stated.

"But you still know how."

"And what possible good can that do for me?"

One thing Alice might not know yet about Ruby—she had an answer for everything. Now she looked the woman in the eye and said, "You get to remember what it was like. You get to tell people about it, if you want. Or you could teach us, like you're teaching me piano. If you want," she repeated emphatically.

Alice looked as if she was going to spit out galvanized nails. "You're very precocious, aren't you?"

Ruby ignored the look and the comment as she pointed out a picture of Alice swimming in the middle of a lake. "Do you get scared when your feet can't touch the bottom?"

"Of course not. That's the whole point of swimming." Alice drilled her with a stare. "Isn't it?"

Ruby shrugged her narrow shoulders. "I don't know how to swim."

"That's ridiculous. You're eight years old. You should know how to swim."

Ruby folded her arms. "Well, I don't."

Alice glared at Cara. "And you?"

"Sure. I learned when I was little. My dad taught me. Ruby hasn't learned because she's scared of the water."

"You live next to a lake now, and there's a pool on the property," Alice said to Ruby. "You have to learn to swim, for safety's sake."

"Will you teach me?" Ruby asked.

"I can't possibly—" Alice stopped. She stared fiercely at the kid. "I'll see what I can arrange."

"I'm afraid."

"Young lady, I don't even have the use of my arms and legs anymore. If I can get in the water without fear, then so can you."

"But—"

"No more buts. I said I would see what I can arrange. I'm through talking about it."

Mrs. Armentrout came in with the day's mail. "Would you like to look through it now, or shall I put it in the study?"

"These young ladies can help me go through it."

Cara tried not to feel annoyed by Alice's assumption that she and Ruby had nothing better to do. But then again, they didn't. Now that the school year was winding down, Cara barely had any homework; the teachers just seemed to be marking time until summer arrived in all its glory. She'd put in for more hours at the bakery, but at the moment, she had nothing better to do than to help out here.

She took the stack of mail and held up each piece so Alice could see it. Most of it went to the recycle pile—catalogs and brochures, envelopes stuffed with coupons, special offers from credit card companies and postcards from grinning real-estate agents.

The bills, bank statements and financial documents went into a stack for the bookkeeper, who came every Friday. There was some stuff for Cara's mom—mostly bills, it looked like—and the other live-in help.

"Look, it's a postcard from Ivy." Ruby held it up. "It's a picture of the . . ." She frowned at the words. "Jar . . . din des . . ."

"Jardin des Tuileries," said Alice, the words

rolling off her tongue. "That's how the French say it." She had Ruby repeat the pronunciation a few times. "There. You sound like a French girl." She didn't smile but there was a happy-sounding note in her voice. She said it in both French and English.

"You're really good at French," Cara remarked. She had been taking it as an elective for the past three years, and it had become one of her favorite subjects in school.

Alice's expression turned sour. "Yes. Well. Not nearly as good as my late husband, as it happens."

"Why do you say late?" Ruby asked bluntly. "When he's dead."

Cara was appalled. "Rube—"

"That's a fair question," Alice said, and she didn't seem mad anymore. "He's not late, is he? He's dead."

Cara diverted their attention to the rest of the mail, sorting it into stacks for the household. Bored, Ruby wandered off to play in the yard. Watching her through the window, Alice said, "The child needs a swing."

"That'd be fun, assuming it doesn't scare her."

"I'll have one hung from that nice big hickory tree over there."

"Sounds good." The bottom two envelopes in the mail delivery were thick ones. When Cara saw what they were, her heart skipped a beat. A blush lit her cheeks on fire.

"What's that?" asked Alice. The woman didn't miss much.

"These two are addressed to me." Apparently, Cara didn't hide them quickly enough.

"You have a letter from MIT?" asked Alice. "And is that one from Harvard?"

Cara tossed them unopened into the recycle pile. Her heart seemed to go with them, hitting bottom with a paper *thud*. "Junk mail," she stated. "I don't need to open them."

"What do you suppose they say?"

"Just the same as all the other junk mail. Computer-generated marketing."

"There have been others?"

Cara nodded. She didn't really want to talk about it.

"What others?"

"Columbia, Cornell, Rensselaer, NYU, Rutgers." She counted them off on her fingers.

"And what sort of marketing is this?"

Cara shrugged her shoulders, wishing Alice would quit with the nosy questions. "I started getting stuff after we took a test at school. Waste of trees."

"Why do you say that? Aren't you interested in going to college?"

"No."

"Why not? You strike me as a bright girl."

"Bright enough to know these colleges aren't for people like me."

"And what sort of person might that be?"

"People who can't afford to spend four years studying stuff like 'Zombies in Popular Culture' and endlessly discussing 'The Rape of the Lock.' "

"I've always thought 'The Rape of the Lock' was a very good poem. Thank you for trivializing the entire academic experience." Alice sniffed. "May I see one of those letters?"

Cara shrugged again. "Which one?"

"What about Harvard? That's my alma mater."

"You went there?"

"Don't look so surprised. I think I'm insulted."

"You speak French, play the piano, have a bronze medal . . . *and* a Harvard degree? Most people would be satisfied just accomplishing one of those things."

"I've always liked a challenge."

Cara decided to be blunt. She nodded at the wheelchair. "Just not that challenge."

"You're a smart aleck."

"So are you."

"Read the letter to me."

"They're all starting to sound the same." Cara heaved a sigh and tore open the envelope. She'd been over this several times with her mom. She didn't need to go through it again with Alice. It was nice and flattering that the top colleges in the country had noticed her test scores. But she knew better than to believe a test score wrapped in wishful thinking could actually turn into a future.

Still, the letterhead made her heart beat faster. She took the cover letter from the envelope. Even the thick, creamy stationery felt rich in her hands. She read the now-familiar text. The dean of the College of Arts and Sciences was interested in receiving her application, blah, blah, blah, and she was invited to attend an informational evening with alumni, learning what her life would be like as a student at the nation's oldest and most venerated university . . .

It was a marketing ploy. Nothing more. Still, she felt the most intense urge as she read the magic words. She wanted to go to college, wanted it so much that she felt a lump in her throat. Though she tried to keep a poker face while sharing the letter, she couldn't quite manage, because Alice stared at her with a knowing light in her eyes.

"This isn't just something to be tossed aside," Alice said. "They are seriously interested in you."

"Hello? Dirt-poor here. We were one day away from being homeless when we came here."

"What?"

Oops. "Nothing. Please don't tell my mom I said anything."

"Now that you've said it, you'll need to explain."

Cara set down the letter. "She ended up with massive bills after my dad died. Do you have any idea how much it costs to die of diabetes-related complications? And on top of that, he was being deported because he was Scottish and his time ran out and he didn't have a green card. There's probably more to the story, which my mom won't tell me because she doesn't want to worry me, but what the hell. I worry." Tears pushed at the backs of her eyes, burning them. "After high school, I'm going to work. I'll go part-time to community college at night or whatever and work my way through a degree program. But this stuff—this Harvard and MIT stuff—isn't for me. I won't waste my time even pretending it could happen."

"I'm sorry. But there's something you should ask yourself."

"What's that?"

"Are you using your lack of financial resources as a legitimate roadblock, or is it an excuse to avoid doing something that scares you?"

12

Sometimes, Mason reflected as he sat at the head of the boardroom table in his Manhattan office, making a business deal was as satisfying as really good sex. Well, almost, he amended, checking out the rack on the woman who leaned over his shoulder to sign the agreement. Lisa Dorfman, his firm's legal counsel, was the only person he knew who could make solar storage cells look sexy. Despite her name, she looked more like an NFL cheerleader—but with the best legal brain in the business. She had a disarming stare, which she used to good effect. Mason was one of the few who knew she had a glass eye. And one of the few who knew what had caused it.

Ivan Bondi, the founder of the company, looked every bit as pleased as his investors as he went over to the sideboard and pulled a bottle of Dom Pérignon from an ice bucket. "I know it's early in the day," he said, "but I'd like to thank everyone. This technology is a game changer, and your commitment is enabling us to go forward." The cork made a cheerful pop, and he poured a glass for everyone.

The investors, company officers, board members and support staff all stood and lifted a glass. Mason, who had put the deal together, savored the moment. Bondi's method of collecting solar energy had enormous potential to do a lot of good in the world. With the infusion of cash from the investor group, the potential now had a shot at being realized. The investors were equally happy to be in on the ground floor of a vibrant new enterprise and stood to make a fortune.

And Mason would collect a hefty commission for putting the deal together. He made a mental snapshot of the occasion—smiles all around from colleagues and associates. The windows of the boardroom on the sixtieth floor framed a view of

Lower Manhattan, with New York Harbor in the distance. The streaming sunlight glanced off the crystal champagne flutes, adding sparkle to the celebration.

Some days, he thought, life was just good.

"Mr. Bellamy?" His secretary came in, her normally calm, crisp demeanor agitated. "I'm sorry to interrupt, but she says it's urgent."

"What is it?" He set down his champagne flute without having enjoyed a single sip.

"She says her name is Faith McCallum."

Damn. What the hell was she doing here? He turned to his clients, who regarded him in bewilderment. "Excuse me. I need to step out for a moment." He left the conference room, shutting the door behind him. Faith was waiting in the reception area, looking wildly out of place in faded jeans and sneakers, a gray hoodie and a backpack. "I've been trying to reach you all morning," she said without preamble.

"I've been in meetings all morning. I never take my phone into meetings."

"I know. Your assistant told me that, and she refused to interrupt you unless it was an emergency."

"So there's no emergency. Thank God."

"No, but there's something urgent."

His gut twisted as he imagined all kinds of issues with his mother. Thinking of the succession of caregivers they'd gone through, he dreaded losing another one—particularly this one. "What's going on?"

She wrapped the strap of her backpack around her finger. "I don't know where to start, even though I thought about it all the way down here. I took the express train."

"Damn it, just tell me."

She hesitated, glancing at the various doors that were open to the corridor.

"This way," he said, picking up on her cue. He strode to his corner office.

Her gaze flicked over the spectacular view from the floor-to-ceiling windows, but she focused on him. "As I said, it's not an emergency, but this can't wait. Your mom is with Lena today until we get back there."

We. Had she said *we?*

"Whoa, slow down. You took the train all the way from Avalon—"

"I wanted to see you in person."

He felt a thump of panic in his chest. "Why in person? Jesus, just tell me."

"It's about your mom's fall down the stairs." She paused, and her eyes softened. "It wasn't an accident."

"What the hell was it, then?" He was annoyed now, his heart pounding with trumped-up panic. "A murder attempt?"

"No," she said, and her face turned soft with sympathy. "Mason, it was a *suicide* attempt."

Though he didn't move a muscle, he felt everything drain out of him. The feeling echoed the moment he'd gotten the call about his father's death—incomprehension, and then a rush, as if he were being scoured from the inside. After the draining, there was nothing. No thought or emotion. Just an empty, ice-cold ache.

"That's bullshit," he snapped. "You're full of shit."

She didn't even wince. It was as if she'd been expecting—maybe trying—to get a rise out of him. "I'm sorry," she said simply. "So very sorry. It's a shock, for sure, but she's safe for now, with Lena and the others."

"How the hell can you come down here, barge in and say something like this?"

"I didn't want to have this conversation over the phone."

"I'm at a loss here. This is . . . Jesus Christ." He raked a hand through his hair. "Wait a second—whoa." The words tasted like poison in his mouth. He felt a ball of ice forming in his gut. "You're saying my mother tried to kill herself."

Faith nodded, her face soft with sympathy.

"By driving her wheelchair down the stairs." His mind reeled with the news. Without thinking, he grabbed her hands and stared into her eyes for a moment. He saw nothing but genuine concern there. She was so different from any woman he'd ever known. Wise and compassionate. "You're serious."

She nodded. "I'm sorry," she said again, and gently removed her hands from his.

"What gave you the idea that she tried to kill herself? She's been getting used to her new life—finally. It makes no goddamn sense."

"No, it doesn't," she said softly. "Not for Alice. And yet . . ."

He studied her eyes, noting for no particular reason that they were a soft, misty shade of gray. And that they were filled with a sorrow that felt as deep as his own.

"Your mother needs you," Faith added. "I haven't contacted your brother and sister. I thought you'd want to do that yourself."

"Who's with her now?" he asked, feeling a thud of panic in his gut.

"Lena and Phil. I left strict orders that she wasn't to be left alone until—"

"Until what?"

"How quickly can you be ready?" she asked.

"Ready for what?"

"To go to Avalon."

"Now?" His head was spinning.

She nodded again. "Thank God she survived. But there's a lot of work to do. We have to figure out why and make sure there are no further attempts."

He mentally regrouped his day. He had a

conference call and a business lunch on the agenda, a meeting at the bank, drinks with a client, and then he was meeting Regina for sushi afterward.

But when he looked at Faith, he had only one thought. “Let’s go. I’ll drive.”

Mason’s car glided through the prepaid toll lane and then shot ahead, leaving all the other vehicles in the rearview mirror. He tried not to be that pathetic cliché, the guy who was in love with his car. But sometimes he couldn’t help himself. He deeply loved this car.

In the passenger seat beside him, Faith looked around the cockpit of the Tesla. “This car is really something,” she said. “It’s really all electric?”

“Yep. Never needs a drop of gas or oil.” He couldn’t help showing off the neck-snapping acceleration. The car leaped forward, then glided like a pat of butter across a hot skillet.

Faith gave a little squeal. “Okay, that was fun.”

“You squealed. I haven’t made a woman squeal in a long time.”

“But you have a girlfriend.”

“Regina.”

“And you’ve never made her—Never mind.” Her cheeks flushed red. “Don’t answer that. Just drive. And know that inside, I’m squealing.”

“I used to think guys who were into their cars were douchebags. Then I fell in love with this one.”

"You couldn't help yourself. One smooth ride, and you were a goner."

"Exactly. Sorry."

"Never apologize for falling in love."

"I like the way you think." He liked a lot of things about her—except the fact that she had come to deliver this nightmare news to him. He focused on navigating to the throughway. Then he set the cruise control and turned down the stereo. "Start talking," he said. "I need to know what's been going on. A suicide attempt? I can't even get my head around that."

"I can only imagine how frightening it must be for you. But there's a way through it."

"There damn well better be." His hands on the steering wheel felt cold. There was a ball of ice in his stomach, too. And in his chest, where his heart was supposed to be.

He glanced over at Faith. She was staring straight ahead, watching the road. "When did she tell you?" he asked.

"Tell me what?"

He ground his teeth together. "That she tried to kill herself."

"Oh. Well, she didn't tell me."

"Then how the hell—"

"I figured it out. And she denied it."

"Whoa, hang on for a second. She denied it?"

"She said I'm completely wrong." Her voice softened, and she slowly turned to face him. "But

I'm not. I questioned everyone and went over the EMT report."

Doubt crept in. "I don't understand. Jesus, you called me away on a *hunch?*"

"It's more than a hunch."

"Okay, assuming you know what you're talking about, why now? She got through the worst part of the accident. What made her choose this moment?" His stomach was churning.

"That's what I hope you'll talk with her about. The day she fell, did anything unusual happen?"

"My brother, sister and I were away." He still remembered the feeling of keen exhilaration they'd all felt on the mountain that day, and how the sensation had collapsed into panic. "Do you think she freaked out because we were scattering the ashes?"

"Do you?"

"I don't claim to be an expert, but it just doesn't seem like the kind of thing that would make her want to throw herself down a flight of stairs."

He glanced over at Faith, and he was struck by the soft emotion in her face. "My mother survived a damn avalanche and all the subsequent surgeries and hospitalizations, the therapies and treatments. She's finally making a new life for herself in Avalon."

"Then we need to find out why she would want to harm herself now."

"And you think a visit from me will get to the bottom of this."

"She needs more than a *visit* from you. Is there some way for you to come for a prolonged stay?"

The knot in his stomach tightened. "I want to help. I do. But my life and my work are far from Avalon."

"Are you able to commute to the city? I know it's a long way . . ."

"It's doable. You did it this morning. The problem is, I don't see how my hanging around is going to help her. My mother and I . . . we're not close." The admission stung.

"Now you have a chance to change that. Um, assuming you want to change it."

"Do you think it needs changing?"

"Could be that's exactly what's called for. You've given her everything she needs except the one thing that is going to get her through this rough time—your presence. Your emotional support."

"Okay, I get it. I can be present. But emotional support has never been my strong suit."

"It's never too late to learn."

"Sure, but having me—what? Move in? Get in her face?—is not going to magically resolve this problem."

"Of course it won't. It's just a start."

"And what makes you think she'd welcome my presence? Did she ask to see me?"

She made a sound of exasperation. “I’ve already made an appointment for her to see Dr. Rose, and you should go along, as well.”

“Dr. Rose—the psychiatrist. ‘Hey, Mom, did you really try to off yourself?’ ” The very idea of saying those words to her made his blood run cold.

“I hate that this happened,” said Faith, “but you have to get to the bottom of it. I asked the others at the house if she had any unusual visitors, upsetting news, things of that sort on the day she fell.”

“And?”

“No one could think of anything. Except . . .”

“Except what?”

She turned toward him in the passenger seat. “Have you ever heard of someone named Celeste Gauthier?”

His heart leaped when he heard the name. Everything in him wanted to say no, he had no idea who that could be. He couldn’t, though. He knew exactly who that was.

After all this time, he had thought the secret was safely buried in the past and would remain there forever. Yet somehow, it had reached his mother and, if Faith’s theory was correct, it had shattered her.

“Mason?” Faith spoke gently, as if she somehow sensed the implosion taking place inside him.

He kept the car steady on the road. Took a deep breath. Killed the music on the radio. In the few moments before he started speaking, he became strangely aware of arbitrary details—the clean laundry scent of her shirt, and the angle of her leg as she turned in the passenger seat to face him. He heard the hum of the tires on the road, and the sound of other cars swishing past. The landscape seemed to slide by in a slow-motion blur.

"Yeah," he said. "I know who Celeste Gauthier is." He kept his eyes on the road. "Did she show up at the house?"

"No. The caregiver on duty that day said a large envelope full of documents arrived from France—in French."

Mason's heart thudded in his chest. "You talked to the caregiver? The one I fired?"

"Of course. And I went over the reports from the EMTs and the hospital. Anyway, the guy said he held up each page while your mom read it. He said your mother was extremely quiet afterward, but didn't seem visibly upset. But then later that day it happened, though we've no idea if the two incidents are related. So . . . who is she?"

He ground his back teeth together, then made himself say it. "Celeste Gauthier was my father's French mistress."

"What? Oh, my God. Really?"

"Naw, just making that up. Of course *really*."

She turned on the seat to stare straight ahead.

"Well . . . wow. Do you think this is the first time your mother heard from her?"

"That would be my assumption. Celeste was a secret. That whole . . . situation. Hell, I don't even know what to call it. It was a damned secret, buried in the past." He banged the steering wheel with the heel of his hand.

"But you knew about it."

He nodded. "I was the only one. Until now, I guess."

"That's a big secret to carry around. How long have you known?"

"Since I was seventeen years old. I spent the summer in Paris that year. And that's when I found out."

Part Two

✵ ✵ ✵ ✵ ✵

"No pessimist ever discovered
the secretof the stars,
or sailed to an uncharted land,
or opened a new doorway
for the human spirit."
—Helen Keller

✵ 13 ✵

Paris, 1995

As the Air France 747 circled Charles de Gaulle Airport, Mason tried to resign himself to the fact that this summer was going to suck. He knew it was lame and ungrateful to even think such a thing. What guy in his right mind would think a summer in Paris could suck?

But damn. All of his friends were up in Montauk at the tip of Long Island, surfing and partying and getting laid.

Mason, on the other hand, would be working in an office. Never mind that the office was within spitting distance of the Eiffel Tower, and the agency he'd be working for did important work funding humanitarian missions. It was an NGO known as AIDE—*Alliance Internationale pour le Développement de l'Éducation*—originally founded by his grandfather George Bellamy, and Mason was here to fulfill a family tradition. Just like his father before him, Mason would spend the summer between his junior and senior years with a group of youths as an intern at the agency. It was the summer his parents had been promising him since he'd started high school. He tried to be excited about the weeks to come. He didn't want to be that overprivileged kid who had no clue about what real work was.

The other interns came from all over the United States, Europe, Africa and Asia. It was a rare opportunity, not to be taken lightly. All his life, Mason's parents had drummed into him that he should do good work. He was privileged. That meant he had responsibilities to those less fortunate.

Okay, thought Mason. *I get that. I still would rather be surfing.*

He had looked down the list of other interns, wondering if any of them were hot girls. Some of them had names so exotic, he couldn't even tell if they were guys or girls.

Leaning his forehead on the window, he gazed down at the inchworm-shaped loop of the Seine, which divided Paris into Rive Droite and Rive Gauche. And he tried to keep his leg from jiggling and annoying the guy in the seat next to him.

He'd hardly slept at all on the transatlantic flight. He had watched a movie called *Before Sunrise*, which had all the cuss words edited out, about an American guy and a French girl who met on a train and made out in Vienna and fell in love even though they knew they'd never see each other again. Most of it was pretty boring, but the French girl in it was hot, and when her dress slipped down one shoulder, Mason got a boner.

Just about anything related to girls had that effect on him.

Later, he had finished his John Grisham book, which made being a lawyer look way more exciting and dangerous than it probably was. He'd eaten every bite of his in-flight dinner and breakfast. People complained about airplane food, but Mason thought it was awesome.

He pretty much thought all food was awesome. And in Paris, of course, it was going to reach a new level of awesome. Or *formidable,* as the French would say. He spoke French pretty well. His dad had insisted they all learn the language, on account of the family business.

He realized his foot was jiggling again. He pressed his hand on his knee, forcing it to stop. The aircraft landed in a rumble of landing gear and wing flaps, then taxied to a halt at the gate. Mason levered himself up from his seat. He collected his backpack from the overhead bin and headed for the exit, shuffling along with yawning businessmen and sleepily blinking tourists.

He thanked the flight attendants in their native French, earning patronizing smiles because they probably thought he'd exhausted his entire French vocabulary; then he joined the stream of passengers in the Jetway. The lineup at passport control seemed impossibly long and slow. He had to piss like a racehorse. Where had that expression come from? The arbitrary thought floated through his mind. How did anyone know how bad a racehorse needed to piss?

Immigration and customs lines were a drag, but Mason gritted his teeth and shuffled along with everyone else through the lines. Kids and their short-tempered parents griped at one another. Most of the French people took out cigarettes, poised to light up the second they stepped out of the terminal. Apparently for smokers, the new ban on all in-flight smoking was torture.

The guy at passport control barely looked at him, just stamped his passport and gave him a brief nod.

The next stop was baggage claim, followed by customs, and by that time, Mason felt as though his back teeth were floating. Fortunately, the customs officials didn't think he looked too sketchy. His mom always made him dress half decently for flights, claiming you got better treatment that way. So he was wearing a polo with the Dalton School logo, twill chinos and leather slip-ons. He probably looked douchy, but at least he wasn't going to see anyone he knew. All the kids he knew were partying back home.

He finally found the men's room and nearly collapsed with relief. Then he washed up, dousing his face with water to wake himself up, and joined the swelling throng at the exit. It took him only a moment to spot his dad. They had a set rendezvous spot at Charles de Gaulle—a café that sold Trevor's favorite type of beer, Blanche de Belgique, which was served in old-fashioned pottery tankards with hinged lids. No matter what time of day it was, when Trevor came to pick someone up at the Charles de Gaulle Airport, he could always be found with a cold beer in a stein, seated at one of the café tables, looking like Falstaff with a big grin on his face.

Mason ran to him. "Dude!" he said as they man-hugged.

"Hey, son, it's good to see you. How was your flight?"

People always asked that. "It got me here."

"So I see. Glad you made it, buddy. It's going to be a great summer."

Working in an office. Woo-hoo. "That's the plan," he said, forcing cheerfulness.

"Yep. You got everything?"

He nodded, zipping his passport into his jacket pocket and grabbing the handle of his rolling duffel.

"Omar's waiting to take us home."

"Omar?"

"Mr. Hamini. New driver. Algerian guy. He's great."

They found the car in the waiting lot. It was a black Citroen, the kind a diplomat might ride around in. Mason's dad liked having a driver in the city because parking was totally impossible. Dad did have a car, though, and he'd already promised Mason they would take a couple of road trips out to the coast. Mason was totally pumped about driving in France.

He noticed someone in the passenger seat.

"Oh, forgot to tell you. Omar's daughter is in the car. She's another intern at the agency, so I told him to bring her along. There's a reception tonight, and I thought it'd be nice for you to have a friend in the group."

Mason yawned and stretched. "That's fine. Whatever."

Omar came bursting out of the car. "Welcome, welcome, we are happy to meet you at last." His French was heavily accented.

Mason shook his hand. "Thank you."

"Just remember, wherever you wish to go, I am at your service." The guy was swarthy and strapping, wearing wrinkled trousers and a wool sport coat that looked way too heavy for the heat of the day. Grinning beneath a full mustache, he hoisted the bags into the trunk.

"Thank you."

They got into the car. "My daughter, Katia," said Omar, gesturing at the passenger in the front seat. "Katia, this is Mr. Bellamy."

Mason nodded at the girl in the front seat. She wore a veil that covered her head and another that obscured the lower half of her face. Above the veil, her eyes were large and richly brown, with thick lashes. Somehow he could tell she was smiling. There was a sparkle in her eyes, and they squinted in a friendly way.

"Hello, Mr. Bellamy," she said. Her voice was nice—smooth and deep, like an actress's.

"How about you call me Mason?"

"*D'accord.*" She nodded. The eyes kept smiling.

"I think the two of you are the same age," said Mason's dad. "Seventeen, yes?"

Katia nodded again.

"School has just finished," said Omar, speeding onto the expressway that ringed the city. "She is going to spend the summer serving her family and pursuing her studies."

"Sounds awesome," Mason muttered under his breath to his dad in English.

"My father is joking," Katia said in perfect British English. "I'm going to be working at the NGO for the summer. The same one you are. And I assure you, it will be *awesome*."

Mason felt his ears turn red. "Oh, cool."

The beautiful dark eyes smiled again, and she turned toward the front. She took out a paperback novel in French and started reading. Her father said something in Algerian, and the eyes flashed. Defiance? Did girls in veils defy their fathers?

"Speaking of work," his dad said, "here's how it lays out. You'll be going into the office three or four days a week. You'll work with Thierry Rousseau. He's in charge of communications and funding initiatives."

"Sounds good." Truth be told, Mason was slightly excited about financial stuff. His dad had always been adamant that he, Adam and Ivy should learn the family business, and certain things about it were totally cool. International finance sounded classy, and more important, it sounded interesting. His dad put business deals together. He must be pretty good at it, because he made a lot of money.

"The other days are all yours," his dad said. "I want you to enjoy the city. And the countryside. I got you a student rail pass so you can take unlimited side trips."

Mason folded his hands behind his head and grinned. That sounded more like it. He was here, so he might as well make the best of the situation. It was a far cry from the way he spent most summers, though.

Most years, he and his brother and sister went to camp. And summer camp rocked. That was where he had learned to sail a boat, cast a fly, scale a sheer rock face. At camp, he had kissed his first girl, drunk his first beer and made friends from all over. At the end of the camp session, the whole family would travel to one of the places served by the NGO, and that was where the real work happened. They had built houses in Cambodia, dug wells in Ghana, helped migrant workers in Kentucky, worked in a vaccination clinic in Peru . . . He lost track of all the different places they'd been. A lot of times the conditions had sucked—raging heat, bugs, pit toilets, uncomfortable beds. But there was another side to it that wiped out all the parts that sucked.

It felt good to help. It was that simple. He didn't like talking about it or even thinking about it. He liked feeling it. And no matter how annoyed he got when his parents were dragging him all over the globe while he'd rather be hanging out with his friends, he always ended up finding that moment. The one that made all the bugs and heat worthwhile.

Mason had been twelve years old the first time he'd felt it. That was the year Ivy came down with pneumonia, and his mom had to stay home with her for weeks. Adam and Mason ended up spending the entire summer in Montauk with their grandpa George Bellamy.

Grandpa George was magic. Mason had always known it, for as long as he could remember, all the way back to when he was a tyke. That summer, he had taken Mason and his brother, Adam, to the PAWS shelter near his summer place on Long Island, where he put the two of them to work.

At first the boys had been horrified. While their friends were playing Nintendo and going to the beach, Mason and Adam were picking up dog poop and hosing out kennels. No matter how much lemon-scented cleaner was used, the place reeked. Mason was sure his formerly fun grandfather had gone senile, forcing him to work like a rented mule.

And then he'd met Sam—short for "Samuel L. Dachshund." He was a tiny, skittish wiener dog, so skinny you could count his ribs—if he would let you get close enough to count. He was mean and scrappy and funny-looking, with a pointed nose and crooked teeth and long, floppy ears.

Despite the growling and snapping, Mason felt a squeeze of love in his heart when he looked at that trembling, growling little dog, huddling in the corner of his crate, his whip of a tail curled under his bony hips. Mason approached the crate slowly. He dropped a treat just inside the door. The starving dog snapped it up, then retreated to the corner again. Mason repeated the process. Several times a day, he would place a treat into the crate. The dog would dart forward and grab it. By the end of the second day, Sam was taking treats from his hand. After another day, he let Mason stroke him a little, on his chest. Eventually, he allowed Mason to pick him up.

It felt like a little miracle, holding that trembling pup against his chest. Sam licked Mason's chin. After several days of being held, licking and playing, Sam allowed Mason to give him a bath. Mason held him while a volunteer trimmed the dog's toenails. Within three weeks, little Sam was sleek and well fed, and when a nice lady named

Mindy came to the shelter, she cradled him in her arms and said, "Okay, I'm going to take him." She adopted him on the spot, then called her husband to tell him she was bringing home a dog.

As Mason said goodbye to the little dachshund, that squeeze of sentiment in his heart felt bittersweet. Grandpa George said, "That's the way love works sometimes. You get to have someone for a while, and then you let him go. And that's okay because you did some good in the world."

"I'd rather have the kind of love I can keep."

"We all feel that way, my boy. Let's go get some ice cream."

Helping became a Bellamy summer tradition.

In his more cynical moments, Mason figured his parents' insistence on volunteer work was geared to give him a decent topic for his college application essays. Still, he could not deny the heart squeeze that happened time and time again, whether he was helping a stray dog in New York, or an old lady in Trinidad who was too frail to make her way to the village well.

When he got to his dad's apartment in Paris, he retrieved his bags and thanked Omar for the ride. As his dad explained the door code and elevator keypad, Mason kept thinking about Katia's large, dark eyes and wondering what was going on behind the veil and under all those swaths of fabric wrapping her as if she was a fragile icon being shipped somewhere far away.

"What's up with her?" he asked his dad as the car went down around the building's service alley.

His dad shrugged. "Katia? She seems like a nice kid. Keeps to herself. Omar and his wife are pretty traditional."

"You think?"

"If you need a ride, there's a call button in the apartment."

"I'll pass, thanks."

Dad nodded. "The metro is quicker, anyway. Closest station is Rivoli, but it's easier to cross the bridge to St. Michel. More connections there."

The elevator let them off right into the apartment, which was why there was a strict security code. The door glided silently open, and they walked into Dad's home away from home. His folks had bought the place years ago when Dad realized he was spending so much time working in Paris. It was way smaller than their place in Upper Manhattan. There was a kitchen and lounge room with a balcony overlooking a park with shade trees and stone fences and sandy walkways lined with benches. The spare bedroom was the size of a closet, but Mason and all his gear fit in it.

He thought he was too keyed up to sleep, but when he wheeled his luggage into the little bedroom, he did a face-plant in the middle of the bed and crashed for several hours. When he woke up, the sun was low, and for a moment he couldn't figure out if the orangish thread of light through the blinds was sunrise or sunset. He was shocked to see the time—after seven. The day was nearly gone, and he had to go to that dumb reception for the interns. Yawning, he got up and shuffled to the bathroom, then to the kitchen, because he was starving.

As he approached the fridge, he heard a noise. His dad's voice, somewhere in the apartment. He spotted his father out on the terrace, pacing as he talked on a cordless phone. Moving through the dim apartment, he could hear his father speaking in a rapid murmur, in French. "What about Cancale?" he was asking. "You've always liked the coast out there. Simon loves it out there." There was a pause. "Of course I would visit, *chère*, why would I not? It's just that with Mason here, we must . . . Yes. I understand. Me, too . . ."

Chère. Dear. An endearment. The word raised a weird prickle on Mason's neck.

He slid open the door to the terrace and stepped outside.

"*D'accord. À bientôt.*" His father ended the call.

"Who is Simon?" Mason asked.

"What's that?" Dad looked distracted as he set aside the phone.

"Simon. Who likes it in Cancale."

"Oh. A friend. The son of a friend."

Chère. What kind of friend did you talk to like that?

Mason stared at the cigarette in his father's hand. "You're smoking."

"Everyone smokes in Paris." Dad stubbed it out in a flowerpot on the enamel-top café table.

"Great." Mason picked up the light blue package of Gauloises. "I'll join you."

Dad grabbed it from him. "Don't be a smart-ass."

"I've never seen you smoke before."

"It's a nasty habit."

"Then why do it? Jeez, Dad."

"I know. Sorry. I'll lay off the Gauloises."

Mason planted his elbows on the railing and looked around the city. It was still lively at twilight, the warm summer air filled with the scent of roasting coffee and the sounds of traffic punctuated by the occasional two-toned flare of a siren.

"We should go. You've got that thing—the reception for the interns you'll be working with at the agency. You up for it?"

Mason shrugged. "I guess."

"It's not far. We can walk."

He took a quick shower and dressed in something he figured his mom would approve of—navy chinos and a collared shirt that didn't look too wrinkled. They crossed the river at the Pont Royal and walked together along the Quai d'Orsay, passing busy cafés with red awnings, strolling tourists and flower sellers, people just getting started for the night. Dad showed him the St. Michel metro station where he could catch the subway or RER—the express train—if he needed to. Near the cathedral of Notre Dame, a group of French girls was singing a close-harmony rendition of "Kiss from a Rose," their accents butchering the song but their voices nice.

All along the Seine were the *bouquinistes*—the booksellers operating out of battered, dark green metal boxes attached to the stone walls of the river embankment. The variety of books and trinkets was mind-boggling. He glimpsed everything from ancient comic books to dirty magazines to art prints and dumb stuff for tourists, like key chains, marionettes and neck scarves printed with scenes of the city.

One thing he could say for Paris—there was action and bustle. Always something to look at, like a woman dressed and made up exactly like the Mona Lisa, holding a gilt frame and cadging for tips. Old guys in flat caps were playing pétanque at a tiny park, a woman in a head scarf was bringing in her cages of birds for the night and somewhere a saxophone played a lonely melody. The air smelled of coffee and food and piss, and the traffic surged relentlessly along the main streets. Mason's dad strode through it all like a native, and they arrived at the reception only a few minutes late. The director greeted them and gave them name tags.

Then it was time to mingle. Mason hated mingling. It seemed phony and forced, but this gang would constitute his social life all summer long, so he figured he might as well make the best of it. Plus, he was starving, so the quicker he got the social niceties out of the way, the better.

The group included Taye, a Nigerian, who wore a soccer club shirt and was already piling a plate high with stuff from the buffet table. Malcolm, a Brit, was surly, copping an attitude with monosyllabic answers to all the polite questions. The other American was Lisa Dorfman, who in the first five minutes of conversation let everyone know she was a student at Andover and intended to go to Princeton, that her mother was a judge and her father a playwright. Mason found her beyond annoying. The other student, Katia Hamini, arrived with her father and glided around in her veils, quietly observing the event.

Misfits, dorks and elitists. "My favorite," he grumbled.

"Hey," his dad murmured.

"I know," Mason said, heading off the correction.

There was a quick welcome and orientation talk. They were given schedules and contact information for everyone. There would be work trips to SHAPE headquarters near Brussels, and to The Hague, where the UN convened. Awesome, Mason thought glumly. There were plenty of places in Europe he longed to explore, but those two were not on his list.

Lisa Dorfman paraded herself back and forth in front of him in an obvious ploy for attention. He supposed she was cute with her blond ponytail and varsity tennis team body, but her snooty personality obliterated the cuteness.

When he went over to the snack table for some cheese and grapes, she sidled up to him. "Try the Reblochon," she suggested. "You can't even get it in the States because it's got some kind of live culture in it that isn't FDA approved."

He put a hunk of it on his plate. "I don't know much about cheese. I'd be just as happy with some Cheez Whiz on a Ritz."

She laughed as if he'd said something hilarious. "So you go to the Dalton School, right?"

"How do you know that?"

"Didn't you read the welcome packet? It's got the scoop on all of the interns. Plus, my mother looked them all up on the internet."

"Very thorough of her." Mason didn't spend much time on the internet. It was slow, and the phone squawked annoyingly when it connected.

Lisa laughed again. Easily amused, he thought. Too easily. "Mum just wants to make sure I'm spending the summer with the right sort of people." She nodded toward the Nigerian guy.

"His dad is the minister of culture. Malcolm's mom is an MP and she's met, like, everybody. We couldn't find anything on the chick in the burka."

"It's not a burka. She's wearing a hijab and a niqab." He couldn't believe he actually remembered what the scarf and veil were called from his comparative religions course.

"Well, aren't you the smarty-pants. I think it's so weird in this day and age. *Repressive.*" She shuddered.

"Could be she has her reasons."

"Yeah, like maybe she's wicked ugly," Lisa whispered with a smirk.

Mason had had enough of this chick. "Excuse me," he said. "Looks like the party is breaking up." He went over to his dad. "Hey, the jet lag caught up to me. Can we head home?"

"Sure, buddy." They said their good-nights and decided to take the metro back to the apartment. It was late, and trains were few and far between, but at the top of the station, they could hear the gnashing and hissing of an incoming train.

"Come on, son," his dad said. "Run! We got this."

Mason let out a laugh and outran his dad, down the steps and along the tiled passageway, intent on reaching the train first. He did and turned in time to see his father racing along the platform, arm raised up, a big grin on his face. On impulse,

Mason flicked on his camera and took a shot, just as the train was pulling in. They jumped on, and he reviewed the photo in the tiny screen. It perfectly captured his dad's spirit—the energy, the laughter. In the photo, there seemed to be some kind of mysterious shadow falling across him.

"So we've got this weekend free before everything gets started," his dad said. "I thought we'd drive out to the coast. There's a great little seaside town in Brittany, and a friend of mine is loaning us a cottage for a few days."

That was more like it. "Cool," said Mason. "Can I drive?"

"A bit. You're not exactly legal. You're supposed to be eighteen to drive in France."

"I'll be cool about it." His dad reviewed the door keypad and elevator codes to make sure he knew how to get in and out of the place.

"I'm going to hit the hay, too," Dad said.

"I'm wide-awake. I just wanted to get the hell out of that place. It was totally awkward."

"Things like that always are. You were a perfect gentleman. Your mother would be proud. Want to call her and check in?"

"I will."

"Afterward, try to get some more sleep."

"Okay," he said. "I'm going to grab a bite to eat first."

Dad gave him a quick hug. " 'Night, son. See you in the morning."

"You bet."

Mason ate three small glass jars of yogurt with a box of strawberries. The only cereal was muesli, which was okay, but the only milk was that weird stuff in the shelf-stable carton. The French didn't know crap about cereal. People might rave about their haute cuisine, but they had never figured out how to create Cinnamon Toast Crunch, which was the only thing worth eating when you were starving late at night.

He ate a heel of past-its-prime baguette and a hunk of some kind of cheese, then guzzled a bottle of water. He still didn't feel sleepy at all. He tried calling his mom but got the voice mail. "I'm here," he said. "Dad said I was a gentleman at the orientation meeting and we're going to the coast this weekend. Tell Grandpa George I said hi." He felt a twinge of envy, knowing his mom, brother and sister were in Montauk with Grandpa. He reminded himself he was in Paris, for chrissake, and he'd better learn to like it.

He tried reading but got bored with that. He tried going on the internet. The dial-up modem squealed and failed to connect, no surprise. It never worked right.

Outside, the city was as wide-awake as he, the streets bathed in gold from the sodium vapor lights. He tiptoed to his dad's room, hearing snoring already.

Mason grabbed a few twenty-franc bills from

the hall table and stepped into the elevator. It glided down to the main floor, and he walked outside, not sure where he wanted to go, just wanting to be out in the world. He was still hungry. He thought about food almost as much as he thought about girls. What he really wanted was a big plate of fresh hot *pommes frites*.

He was about to cross the building's service alley when a scooter exited, nearly slamming into him.

"Hey!" he yelled, jumping back up the curb. "What the hell?"

"*Salaud*," said the driver, a girl. "Watch where you're going." She flipped up her visor to glare at him.

Those eyes. Mason staggered a little on the sidewalk. He knew those eyes. "You're Katia," he said in English.

She sniffed. "Yes."

"I'm Mason, remember? From the meeting tonight."

"So?"

He couldn't help staring because she looked totally different in tight jeans and a shirt that showed her stomach, her hair in a long black stream down her back. *Whoa.*

"*Montes*, *vite*," she said. "Get on. Hurry."

He didn't even think twice, but saddled up behind her. She smelled of spicy soap or shampoo. His feet found the footrests, and he grabbed the bar behind him. Okay, finally this night was getting interesting. "*Allons-y*," he said.

She sped away from the building and up the boulevard toward the glowing lights of the city. Mason threw back his head and grinned at the night sky. The summer was not going to suck, after all.

It didn't take a rocket scientist to deduce that Katia was sneaking out against her parents' rules. "That only makes it more fun," she explained, parking the Vespa in front of an all-night club in St. Germain.

"Yes, but suppose you get caught," Mason pointed out. "That won't be fun."

"Agreed."

"And if I get caught with you?" he continued, holding open the door for her. "What'll they do, slit my nostrils?"

"Don't be a wanker."

"Okay, sorry."

"My family—well, mainly my mom, really—is pretty conservative."

"Oh. Parents can be a problem."

The waiter came, and Katia ordered pastis called Ricard for both of them. It came in tall, skinny glasses with ice, and an angular glass pitcher of water.

"I've never tried this," he admitted. "You'll have to show me."

She added a splash of water to their drinks and

clinked her glass against his. “Cheers.”

“Cheers.” He took a sip and didn’t try to hide his grimace. “Tastes like throat lozenges.”

“I suppose it’s an acquired taste.”

He tried not to stare at her, but it was impossible. The face she hid behind the veil was as beautiful as her eyes. Smooth, creamy skin that looked soft to the touch, a pretty mouth he wanted to . . . “Do you like the movies?” he asked suddenly.

“Of course. Doesn’t everybody?”

“So I saw this one on the flight coming over, *Before Sunrise*. Have you seen it? It’s still in theaters.”

“What’s it about?”

“This guy and this girl meet on a train, and they really hit it off, but they know they only have one night to hang out together. So they get off the train in Vienna, and they hang out all night.” He laughed at himself. “I’m not making it sound as good as it is. It’s really good. It feels . . . real, I guess. Not scripted. We should see if it’s playing.”

“Everything’s playing in Paris,” she said.

“True. Then we should go.”

“Why Vienna?”

“What?”

“Why did they hang out in Vienna?”

“Dunno. Could be any city where nobody knows them, and they have the night all to themselves.”

"Oh. I see. Sounds good."

"So if you could do that, hang out with some dude in any city—"

"Some dude?"

He grinned. "Okay, me."

"And . . . ?"

"In any city. Which city would you choose?"

"That's easy. Paris. It's my favorite place in the world."

"Have you seen a lot of the world?"

"Enough. To me, this place feels like the center of everything, not just because of the usual touristy things—art, architecture, museums, restaurants. I love the energy here. Around every street corner, you can find yourself a different neighborhood. We've been here five years, and I'm certain I've only scratched the surface."

"Let's do it, then."

"What?"

"Let's hang out all night in Paris."

"We are hanging out."

"In a tourist café. Let's find something different. We can be back before sunrise."

She planted her elbows on the table, rested her chin on her hand. She had delicate fingers with nails like seashells. Her smile seemed to emanate from her eyes, lighting the rest of her face with slow deliberation.

"All right," she said.

He paid for their drinks, and then they headed

out on the scooter. He thought it was totally hot that she rode around on a scooter. His dad would freak if he knew Mason was riding behind her without a helmet, but Dad would probably approve of the girl. She was classy, smart, beautiful and fun. And Mason knew instinctively there was a lot more to discover about her.

She took him way up to the nineteenth arrondissement, a neighborhood called the Mouzaia, where they could find the best Maghrebi food. Maghrebi, she explained, was the term for people from North Africa—Tunisia, Algeria, Morocco. It was also the type of Arabic she spoke. The neighborhood was a side of Paris he'd never seen before—rough and shadowy in places, vibrant and bright in others. They snacked on chickpea cakes and strong sweet coffee, and she introduced him to mahjouba, which was like a crepe filled with spicy tomato jam.

There was something ridiculously sexy about hearing her natter on to the locals in Maghrebi. Liberally entwined with French words, it was almost comprehensible to him.

But mostly, she talked to Mason. She looked at him with those incredible dark-lashed eyes and seemed as if she wanted to be with him all night long. "You look so much like your father," she said. "Do people tell you that a lot?"

"Yeah, I guess."

"Tell me about your family's business," she

said. “Is that what you’ll do after university?”

“It’s what my parents would like me to do. I haven’t made them any promises. When I was little, I thought the family business was making money—like, literally *making* it. Other people made stuff like clothes or pipe fittings or machines or bread, but my dad would come home from work with nothing but paperwork. International finance sounds boring, but I kind of like the way it all works. My grandfather—and now my dad—is a dream maker. They find ways for people to get the money they need to go after something they want.”

“A dream maker.” That smile again. “I like how it sounds. What do you dream about, Mason?”

Girls. Sex. Food. “Lots of stuff,” he replied. “I like seeing the world. Have you ever been to the US?”

“No, but I would like to go. What’s it like?”

“Well, I live in New York—Manhattan—the busiest part. It’s a huge, awesome city. We have a place on Long Island—that’s more like a beach town. And I have relatives who live in a lake town in the Catskill Mountains. Pretty there, supercold in the winter. More snow than you’ve ever seen.”

She eyed him over the rim of her glass. “I’ve never seen the snow.”

“You’re kidding.”

“I’m from the Sahara,” she reminded him.

“Wow. Well, I’d love to show you around if you

ever come to the States. Winter in the mountains, summer at the beach. You'd love it. I could show you how to surf."

"I'm not a very good swimmer. I haven't been in the ocean since I was tiny."

"Don't you like it?"

"I don't like swimming in my clothes. Once you hit puberty, *boom,* on go the veils. You can still get in the water. But have you ever tried swimming while wearing long pants, a long-sleeved shirt and a head scarf?"

"Can't say that I have. I wouldn't make you wear all that stuff in the water."

She pressed a finger to her full lower lip, right where he wanted to start kissing her. "No, I don't suppose you would."

He couldn't stop staring at her. She was so damn pretty and cool. He was already half in love with her.

14

"Did you have a good time last night?"

Mason's heart dropped to his stomach. Crap. Had his dad caught him sneaking out already? "Um . . ." he mumbled around a mouthful of buttered tartine.

"I thought the other students seemed like an interesting bunch."

Mason looked out the window to hide his relief. It would totally suck to be found out before he had a chance to hang out with Katia some more. "Right, Dad. Interesting."

"Hey, when I did my summer at the agency, I met guys I'm still friends with today."

He could imagine staying friends with that girl forever. "That's cool." He wolfed down the rest of the tartine and put his plate in the dishwasher. "I need to go pack some stuff for the weekend."

"You don't need much. A few changes of clothes, your swim trunks. The cottage will have everything we need."

They set out after breakfast in Dad's little Renault, a hatchback the color of a wine grape, with its radio dial set on a station playing incredibly lame French pop tunes. Like a pro, Dad maneuvered the car—a stick shift, Mason noticed with some trepidation—through the twisty, crowded streets of Paris.

Dad lowered the volume of the radio. "I thought the girl was cute."

Mason's leg started to jiggle. Maybe Dad had figured it out, after all. He decided to play dumb. "What?"

"I'm just saying, you seemed to be getting along with that American girl."

"Lisa Dorfman. What a poseur." They passed through the Bois de Boulogne, heading west. He watched the city go by out the window. The Paris everyone knew and loved—the shady boulevards, the monuments and rows of restaurants, the beautiful gardens—gave way to industrial blight, same as any other city. "She said her mother looked up everybody on the internet."

"I didn't know you could do that."

"I guess you can if you've got too much time on your hands. The other kids seemed okay. So what's the story on Omar's daughter?" Mason ventured tentatively into the territory. He didn't want to rat her out.

"Omar was an ambulance driver in Algeria. Emigrated about ten years ago. He's totally reliable, keeps to himself. I've never even met his wife, and Katia's an only child. Other than that, I don't know much."

Mason suppressed the urge to dig deeper. He didn't want to seem too interested. But holy cow. He was. Katia was like two different people, one a traditional Muslim girl, swathed in veils and mystery, and the other a hot action figure, riding around on her scooter, showing off her abs.

Soon enough, the industrial blight that ringed the city subsided. Beyond the périphérique, they were out in the countryside, and once again he felt as if he was in a postcard. There were rolling hills topped by windmills, vineyards with perfectly straight rows that seemed to go on forever and châteaus just sitting casually in the middle of the vineyards, common as a garden shed. Before long, the roads turned smaller, winding through villages with old stone cottages, goats and ducks in the yard, orchards with old gnarled trees, piles of hay and gardens bursting with vegetables and flowers.

The roadside stands offered Calvados and buttery St. Michel biscuits. They stopped for lunch in a seaside resort town called Deauville, which had a boardwalk and a long, flat, sandy beach. There were boobs everywhere, because apparently French women didn't bother with bikini tops.

Mason just sat there at the boardwalk café and stared, and stared. "I'm never leaving here," he said.

His father laughed and ordered a bucket of moules with a side of frites, which came piping hot and salty in big paper cones. They each ordered a beer. It was cool that he could legally have a beer with his dad.

"There are some things the French do better than everyone else."

"Yeah," agreed Mason, staring at a topless woman, her oiled body gleaming in the summer sun.

"I was talking about the *moules frites*, you little perv."

"Sure," Mason said, bravely eating one of the fragrant steamed mussels.

His dad took a sip of his beer. "I like hanging out with you when it's just the two of us."

The statement made Mason feel a foot taller. “Same here.”

“I wish we had time to do more of this.” He leaned back in his chair. “You’re going to love Cancale,” his dad said. “Great scenery, good swimming if you don’t mind climbing down a cliff to get to the beach.”

Cancale. Mason had heard him mention it to the stranger on the phone. The afternoon drive took them past Mont St. Michel, a grand Gothic pile of history dating back to the ninth century. They didn’t stop at the historic site; Mason had been there before and it was swarming with tourists. He remembered it well because when they went there as a family, Ivy was massively cranky, and he and Adam had a great time being brats, running up and down the steep cobbled streets, begging their dad for pocket change so they could buy plastic swords and fight duels like the knights of yore.

For some reason, the memory made him sad. When he thought about it, he realized how seldom the five of them had traveled places together. Then he reminded himself again how cool it was to have his dad all to himself.

Cancale was a surprise, one of those little towns that wasn’t overrun by tourists. It was mostly locals, fishermen in flat caps, farmers and *ouvriers* in their coveralls, many with a smoldering cigarette butt glued to the lower lip. The cottage was an old stone-built structure with a tiled roof and whitewashed walls, perched on a rocky cliff above the English Channel. Flowers bloomed in window boxes, and there was a little well-tended garden surrounding it. Inside, the furniture was simple. No TV, just a CD player and shelves crammed with books in English and French.

The garden overlooked a bank of rocks. Beyond that was a craggy coastline and then the aqua-blue Atlantic. Mason felt his chest expand just looking at it. "How'd you find this place?" he asked.

"Through a friend."

"Which friend?" He didn't think about his dad having friends here. He only thought about his dad working here. Now he realized his dad had built a whole life around being in Paris and France.

"Check out the view." Dad handed him a pair of binoculars. "Those two islands out there—Jersey and Guernsey."

Mason studied the view through the lenses. "Like the cows. Cool. How far is it to the beach?"

"About a hundred meters straight down. We can go for a swim right now. Go get your trunks on."

It was an epic afternoon. He and his dad scrambled over boulders and down a ravine to a beach. Lounging on the battered rocks, they had fresh baguette, cheese and bottles of Orangina that Dad had brought in a backpack. They spent hours in the waves, laughing and paddling around, warming themselves on the grainy brown sand, poking around tide pools.

Mason liked this playful side of his dad. Usually he was so busy working or traveling he didn't have time to mess around. The next couple of days were great. He tasted some wine but didn't much like it. He ate an oyster for the first time. They listened to music and read books, and at night he dreamed about Katia.

The house felt strangely familiar, and he wasn't sure why. "Have I been here before?" he asked his dad. The brief holiday was over, and he was packing up to leave.

"No," said his dad, "but I hope we get to come back."

As he was loading things into his backpack, he knocked over a small bookcase in his room. Muttering, he set it upright and put the books back. One of the books was splayed open on the floor, revealing a photograph tucked between the pages. He picked it up and studied the image. It showed a young woman he'd never seen before, standing next to a little boy against the backdrop of the sea. There was nothing remarkable about the photo . . . except that the boy in the picture . . . there was something peculiar about him, as if Mason had seen him somewhere before. Actually, the kid looked strangely like Mason.

And that, of course, was impossible, because

Mason had never been here before, and he had no idea who the woman might be.

"Ready to roll?" asked Dad, poking his head into the room.

"Who are these people?" Mason showed him the picture.

His dad glanced briefly at the print, turned it over, then shrugged. "Dunno. Where'd you find it?"

"Fell out of a book." He picked up the book—*Le Petit Prince* by Antoine de Saint-Exupéry.

"No idea."

"The kid looks just like me as a kid," Mason said. "Check it out."

Dad shook his head. "I don't see the resemblance. Let's go, sport."

Part Three

✵ ✵ ✵ ✵ ✵

"For my part I know
nothing with any certainty,
but the sight of the stars
makes me dream."
—Vincent van Gogh

✵ 15 ✵

Mason pulled off the throughway to a charging station. As he maneuvered the car into place, Faith studied his profile, trying to picture the boy he had been. Young and earnest, determined to do good in the world. Swept up in the excitement of Paris. Falling in love for the first time. And discovering a new, hidden facet of his father.

He must have sensed a disturbance deep in the heart of the family he thought he knew. For a kid, the sensing but not-quite-knowing was a terrible feeling.

She felt an impulse to reach out to that boy. To give him a hug. To tell him everything was going to be all right. But she couldn't say that, could she? Because he hadn't told her everything yet. And she had a feeling he was leading up to the moment everything had gone terribly wrong.

"That's some summer you had," she said. "So did the seaside cottage belong to Celeste, or . . . ?"

"Yes. Her family, I think, although I didn't figure that out until much later."

"Did you ask your father for details?"

"Not at that point." He connected the car to the charging port. "This will take about fifteen minutes. Do you want a cup of coffee or something to eat?"

"No, thank you." She liked talking to him. She could listen to him all day. And she couldn't figure out why. They were so entirely different. His was a world of high finance and international travel, while hers was kids and clients. Maybe the source of the feeling was their mutual concern about Alice.

No, Faith had to admit it was more than that. This guy intrigued her on so many levels. But first and foremost, he was the key to figuring out what was going on with Alice. Faith checked her messages on the phone Alice had issued her—a smartphone that actually worked. A text message from Lena assured her that Alice was fine.

"That's probably the most exotic story of first love I've ever heard," she said, reprising the conversation with Mason. "Paris, a girl from a foreign land, sneaking around . . ."

He studied her for a moment. He had a way of looking at her that was unsettling, but not in a bad way. "Who was your first love?"

"Billy Banner, fifth grade," she said, surprised at how quickly she could recall the memory. "He had long hair down into his eyes and he rode a skateboard like he was the Silver Surfer. He took me to the movie *Hook* with Robin Williams and we held hands. Ever since, I've been a fan of comedians who are also good actors, like Robin Williams was, or Bill Hader now."

"Okay, that's puppy love," Mason said with a

laugh. "That's not the kind of love I'm talking about."

She flushed. "Oh. Then what kind of love are you talking about?"

"The real thing. I want to know the first time that crazy feeling grabbed you and wouldn't let go."

He certainly had a way with words.

"I didn't even know what it was the first time I experienced that with Katia," he went on. "She was the first person I felt completely myself with. I could let my guard down and show her exactly who I was. I wanted . . . God, everything. That feeling changed the way I looked at the world."

"Wow. That's some first love," said Faith. He had no idea how romantic he sounded. For some reason, it left her feeling flushed. "This is a really personal conversation. How did this turn into such a personal conversation?"

Mason didn't reply but simply waited, another of those comfortable silences that seemed to hover between them sometimes.

Faith leaned back against the car. "My first real love was also my last. Dennis."

Mason regarded her somberly. "I'm sorry for your loss. Really."

She studied the pavement, fissured by weather. "It's been a few years. I still miss him. Did your mother grieve hard for your father?"

"We all thought she did. Now, I guess, she's dealing with a different kind of grief."

For Alice, loss had shifted to betrayal. "We'll help her through it," said Faith. "I swear."

She noticed Mason looking at her again. Staring. Again, with oddly softened eyes. "What?"

"You're really different from other women I know, Faith."

Folding her arms, she glanced down at her washed-out jeans and sneakers. The women she'd glimpsed at his office had been like Regina—polished and sophisticated. On her best day, Faith could never be considered sophisticated. She was far too practical—and too broke—for makeup and wardrobe upgrades.

"And I mean that as a compliment," he said.

She frowned. "Different in what way?"

"You do your job like it's more than a job. I mean, you don't just show up. You bring your whole self to this work. I saw that right from the start. You connected with my mom—"

"And by 'connected,' you mean we butted heads."

"I had my doubts at first that you'd last. She tends to boss people around, play the sympathy card, and you cut right through the BS. So yeah, you're different. In my world, I see people come to work even though they don't want to be there. They leave part of themselves behind."

In his world. "We have very different jobs."

Faith wondered how he would adjust to taking a more active role with Alice. First things first. She wanted to get to the bottom of Alice's suicide attempt. "What about your mother? Do you think she and your dad were deeply in love?"

"Right up until that summer, I believed it. When I started to have my doubts, it felt like a punch in the gut. So I can only imagine how it felt to my mom."

Like a total loss of security, Faith speculated, though she didn't say so. She remembered that feeling when she'd lost her grandparents, and then her mother. A rug had been pulled out from under her. She'd lost her footing in the world.

Mason walked over to a nearby shop and returned with two frosty cobalt blue bottles. "Mineral water from Wales," he said, handing her one.

She glanced at the price sticker. Definitely the first six-dollar bottle of water she'd ever had. "You're not like anyone I've ever met, either," she said.

"In a good way, or a bad way?" he asked with a grin.

"I'm still deciding." She took a sip of the crisp, bubbly water. It was the perfect drink for a day like today. The afternoon sun dappled the parking lot, and the sky was a cloudless blue infinity. She wondered with a wave of sadness what the weather had been like on the day Alice had driven herself down the stairs. Did it matter? Did a person notice the weather when shock turned her world upside down?

"Sounds like you picked up some clues about your father when he took you to that cottage by the sea," she said to Mason.

"Sure, I guess. But remember, I was a kid. I was hot for this exotic new girl and it kind of gave me tunnel vision."

"Did you say something to your father?"

"I probably planned to at some point, but then something blew it wide-open. Literally."

"I don't understand."

"July 25, 1995."

"Is there something special about that date?"

"It probably wasn't a big deal in the news here in the US. Given what happened later, it should have been."

In the summer of 1995, Faith had been working at a part-time job and taking care of her mother. She couldn't recall any big news event. "Why should it have been?"

"Because it was a terror attack."

Part Four

✵ ✵ ✵ ✵ ✵

"The human heart is a frail craft
on which we wish to reach the stars."
—Giotto di Bondone

16

Paris, July 1995

Mason and the other interns worked long hours at the NGO. His job title was "policy assistant" but he was really just a bean counter and general office boy. He didn't mind the delivery errands because he was able to do it as a bike messenger, delivering documents from office to office. It became a high-stakes game to dodge the traffic, weaving in and out of lanes on his bike with the messenger bag on his back. Within a few weeks, he learned whole sections of the city. His French became more natural, especially *l'argot*—slang. Before long, he could curse and hurl insults like a native when a thoughtless driver cut him off or failed to yield.

The bean counter work was more tedious, but seeing Katia in the office, draped in her veils, kept him almost too revved up to think straight. They didn't talk or hang out much during the day, but the nights were theirs to meet in secret. She was a quick-change artist, throwing off the robes to reveal a lingerie-model body and a smile that was brighter than the sun. The fact that they could get in big trouble if they got caught only made it all the more enticing.

At work, crunching numbers and proofing reports opened his eyes. It took funding to do good in the world. He learned the cost of medical supplies and transport. He learned that if it didn't happen, people suffered.

Mason started to care more and more about such things. While going over some mail Thierry had asked him to read, he came across a letter with two photographs attached. The first showed a woman with an infant suffering from malnutrition. The second showed the same woman with a plump, laughing little kid. The letter was filled with gratitude for the agency. The happy kid had been the sick baby.

Mason hurried to show the pictures to his boss. Thierry studied them briefly, then smiled. "The best sort of letter to receive, no?"

"The best," said Mason.

Thierry handed it back. "Perhaps you would like to work on the quarterly bulletin. We publish it so people can see the work we do. Testimonials like this are the best way to explain our mission."

"Sure."

Thierry gave his assistant instructions.

The woman in charge of the newsletter offered him a thick file and a look of relief. "I would love to have your help with this," she declared.

That was how he found out how important this mission was. He'd come into this internship thinking it was going to be lame. Instead, he came to like going into the office, working on ways to account for every *sou* that came in or went out of the accounts.

Most of all, he liked the secret meetings with Katia. He was nearly reeling with love for her. True to her word, she showed him around the city. Whenever she was able to escape her father's vigilance, they took the scooter or the metro to go exploring. They checked out the big red rhino at the Centre Pompidou, dodging panhandlers trying to scam and pickpocket the tourists. They watched reggae bands, went to the Stade de France to see a soccer match, strolled along the Canal St. Martin and poked around the market there, went to the Musée d'Orsay to find the painting of *Whistler's Mother*. They wandered around the hills of Montmartre to the Moulin Rouge in the footsteps of Toulouse-Lautrec, stopped in bustling bistros and explored parks and gardens.

They watched street performers and gave a few francs even to the lame ones. They skipped the tourist crush at the Louvre, escaping instead to the quiet mansion and gardens of the Musée Rodin. He stared at Rodin's signature work *The Kiss* and tried to figure out the best way to get a kiss from her.

It didn't seem to matter what they did, because what was really happening was that they were exploring each other.

She teased him about his appetite. He was

hungry all the time. Instead of searching out classic French dishes like escargot and steak tartare, they ate at budget Vietnamese joints and food carts at Clignancourt, and sampled more Maghrebi dishes in Belleville.

There was a scare as they were poking around the Belleville neighborhood, looking at all the graffiti and trying to find the best place for vegetarian couscous. Katia shoved him into a doorway. "Duck," she said. "I can't let those guys over there see me."

Mason spotted two Maghrebis in cheap, tattered suits and worn-out shoes, smoking and gesticulating as they walked through a crowded market street. "Who are they? Do you know them?"

"Kind of. My father knows them—they're brothers. I don't want them to recognize me. They're trouble."

"What kind of trouble?"

"They like to stir up rallies and protests, things of that nature. They're part of a group wanting to bring the Algerian Civil War to France."

"Wait, what? What war?"

She waited until the pair disappeared around a corner. "It's been going on for a few years. The other day, some extremists killed an eighty-year-old guy, right here in Paris. It's all the talk at my house. My father says there's no chance of a peace settlement now."

"So are you saying those two guys were involved?"

"I don't know. They're agitators. And they are . . . I think the term in the US is *rat finks*. If they saw me, they would report me immediately to my parents and I'd be . . ."

"Dead meat," he said. "That's another American term."

"Exactly."

Mason felt a wave of protectiveness for her. It sucked that Katia had to sneak around, just to wear the clothes she wanted and hang out with her friends. He moved in front of her, making himself as tall as possible to shield her as the two guys passed by.

To his relief, the two brothers seemed too intent on their conversation to notice a couple of kids in the doorway.

Mason knew he had to make his move. He had never known anyone like Katia, never felt this way about a girl before. They planned a day trip to the château at Fontainebleau, out in the suburbs. He wasn't sure what she'd told her parents, but there she was at their usual meeting spot near the St. Michel metro station. She wore Western clothes, looking superhot in short shorts and a tank top, bringing along her traditional clothing in a backpack. They took a poky local train out to the town and wandered in the sunshine to the château. It was a fairyland of a place, surrounded by gardens and an impossibly beautiful forest. They bought bread and cheese and ripe cherries for lunch, and sat on a lush lawn beside a pond, eating and talking.

They savored every hour together. They talked about everything, and nothing at all—their hopes and worries. Music and movies, the progress of the soccer cup that was going on at the hippodrome, the places in the world they wanted to visit.

Everything struck them as funny, and they laughed even when there was nothing to laugh at. He reached across her for a cherry and ate it, and then gave one to her. The sight of the deep red cherry on her lips drove him crazy, and he couldn't stand it anymore. He leaned over and kissed her, a long, cherry-sweet kiss that excited him so much he felt dizzy. She kissed him back, her lips soft against his, her breath as gentle as the summer breeze.

Mason had made out with several girls before, but it had never been like this. When he finally took a break from kissing her, he couldn't keep the grin from his face. "I've been wanting to do that all summer long," he said.

"I know." She lay back in the grass and smiled up at him.

"What do you mean, you know?"

"A girl can tell such things."

"Yeah?"

"Yeah." She imitated his American accent.

"Can you tell what I want to do next?"

"Don't tell me," she said. "Show me."

Oh, boy. He nearly floated away, as if he'd chugged an entire bottle of pastis.

And then he hovered over her supine form and kissed her again, more deeply this time, nearly drowning in sensation.

This was it, he realized, with some tiny part of his brain that could still think. This was what love felt like. They made out and whispered to each other with their lips still touching. They spoke in French and English, and then she said something in Algerian that sounded as sweet as birdsong.

He repeated it, and she laughed.

"No," she said. "It goes like this." And she stated the foreign words again.

He repeated after her. "How's that?"

"Not bad, for a *ferenghi*."

"What does it mean?"

"I'm not sure I'm going to tell you."

"Fine. I'll just say it to your dad next time I see him."

That made her howl with laughter. "Go ahead, but it might get you boxed on the ears."

He pinned her wrists to the ground with his hands. "I'm not letting you go until you tell me." He leaned down and kissed her lips, her eyes, her neck, where the spicy scent of her was warm and sweet. "I'll torture it out of you."

She laughed again, but softly this time. "All right, Mason. I'll tell you."

"Good. I've broken you under torture." He kissed her for a long time, eliciting a sigh from her. Then he repeated the words and asked, "What does it mean?"

She gazed up at him with a look that melted his heart. "It means 'I want you to be my first.' "

Oh, man.

"Seriously?"

"What do you think? Of course seriously. Have you done it before?"

It was tempting to say that he had, to make himself sound like a man of the world. But when he stared into her eyes, nothing but the truth came out.

"No," he said. "Not ever."

After the day in Fontainebleau, everything in the world was brighter and clearer and more delicious. Mason thought about Katia all the time—when he was supposed to be working, when his dad took him out to dinner, when he was in the shower or riding his bike around doing errands. It wasn't like other crushes he'd had, like the time Lacey Jackson had worn a pirate wench costume that showed her great big boobs, or when Jenna Albertson slow danced with him in seventh grade and he developed a swift and humiliating boner. This was on another level entirely, like the difference between a wading pool and the ocean. He walked around with an ache in his chest that was so strong it hurt, but he wanted to feel it because it was so powerful.

And now they were going to go all the way.

"When?" he asked her. They were in the mail room together, organizing the correspondence.

"We will have to find a private place."

They couldn't use his dad's place. His father's schedule was unpredictable. He worked late a lot. Sometimes he didn't come home until the middle of the night. Other times, he showed up at random times at the apartment.

Not her place, either. No way. Even though she laughed when he brought up all the torments her overprotective parents might devise, he didn't want to tempt fate.

"A hotel?" he ventured.

"I suppose we could, but . . ." She looked around, lowered her voice. "I want to be with you the entire night."

"Yeah, me, too."

"I have an idea," she said, her eyes brightening, narrowing into arcs of amusement. It was cool how he could read her smile without even seeing her face.

"Tell me," he said.

"There's that trip we're supposed to make up to

The Hague, to observe a meeting at the UN. I will convince my parents that I should go on this trip with everyone else."

Mason couldn't breathe. He thought of holding her in an embrace like the lovers in the *Kiss* statue. He thought of being with her the entire night. The idea nearly made him explode. "Okay."

Above the veil, her eyes softened into a smile. "Okay."

Mason found condoms in his dad's bathroom, in a drawer with shaving soap and cotton swabs and those little bottles of shampoo from hotels.

If he had paused to think—but of course all he could think about was Katia and getting laid—he might've thought it was weird for his dad to have condoms at all. Because after Ivy, Mom had had her tubes tied. At least he thought she had, it was so long ago. Maybe he was remembering it wrong.

None of that mattered, or even occurred to him, because his head was spinning.

He was jittery all through dinner with his dad. He tried to keep his leg from jiggling. He tried to keep the lie simple.

"Can I go away next week?" he asked.

"Away where?" His dad seemed distracted.

"The Hague. We're invited to observe a meeting at the UN there. Some special committee . . ."

"And you'll be supervised?"

Mason was prepared. He pushed a train schedule across the table. "We're leaving on the twenty-fifth after work. And there's a youth hostel right in The Hague where we'll be staying. The last train is too late, so I'll be gone two nights."

His dad conceded without a fight. "Sure," he said. "Sounds like a good time."

Understatement.

"Stay out of trouble."

"Dad."

"Just saying. Take your time. Enjoy it."

"Thanks, Dad. So, are you going to be okay without me?"

Dad still looked distracted. "What? Oh, yeah. Sure. I'll find something to do with myself."

"Stay out of trouble," Mason said, emulating his father's voice.

His dad looked flustered for a second. Then he grinned. "Hey. That's my line." He took out his wallet, handed Mason an extra supply of francs. "Seriously, have fun up there. Keep your passport with you. You never know what could happen."

You have no idea, Mason thought.

He practically ran to the meeting place at St. Michel. He was in a fine sweat of love. He couldn't stop thinking about the night that awaited them at the end of the train trip. They would be alone, just the two of them, finally.

He wondered if Katia had had such an easy

time getting away from her parents. He would find out soon enough.

The metro commuter crush seemed even more intense than usual. He watched the flow of pedestrians streaming down the stairs and along the labyrinthine passageway, past a cacophony of performers and beggars and tourists. He and Katia had a regular meeting place at one of the subway entrances by the Brasserie St. Andre, but he hadn't spotted her yet. They would take the RER up to the Gare du Nord, and from there, they'd catch the train to Holland.

He checked his watch. It was just after six. They'd arranged to meet at six. He started feeling jittery again, and he paced back and forth. Where was she?

He walked around the square, dodging students and tourists. In the distance, the cathedral of Notre Dame loomed, its blocky towers and curved buttresses silhouetted against the clear sky of the summer evening. He spied three of his friends from the group—Lisa Dorfman, who was talking and bossing people around as usual, Malcolm and Taye, who were ignoring her as usual.

"Our first junket," Malcolm said, adjusting the strap of his red backpack. He nodded toward the metro entrance. "You coming?"

"I'm waiting for Katia," said Mason.

"Oooh, Katia," said Taye, fake-fanning himself.

“She’s not coming,” Lisa stated in her know-it-all way. “Her folks would never let her.”

Shit. Could Lisa be right? Malcolm scowled at her. “I’ll wait. See you at the Gare du Nord.”

“Fine, just remember our train’s at seven.” The three of them went down the stairs together.

Mason tracked a pair of gendarmes across the plaza. A woman walked past Mason, and the breeze snatched away her fluttery pink scarf. She didn’t seem to notice as she hurried toward the stairs. He picked it up and went after her. The pink fabric felt silky and fragile to the touch. “*Excusez-moi, Madame*,” he said. “*Votre écharpe* . . .”

She turned to him, her hand on the stair rail. “*Merci, eh*?” she said with a smile.

She was gorgeous, like, supermodel gorgeous, with shiny blond hair and long, slender legs. She was so beautiful, he felt a bit tongue-tied. “*Je vous en prie*,” he stammered.

Then she was gone, disappearing into the station, and he went back to scanning the area for Katia. She was no supermodel, but infinitely more attractive to him, because of the way he felt about her. Just when he started to worry she wouldn’t show up, he saw her coming up the tiny, high-walled Rue Suger. Just for a moment she seemed unstuck in time, her swathed figure against the sand-colored stone of the old mint. The veils covered her hair and neck, and only her face stood out, framed by the fabric like the face of a nun.

She seemed oddly ephemeral, as though the breeze that had blown the pink scarf could sweep Katia away, too.

Then she spied him, lifting her arm in a wave. As she came toward him, dodging cycles and scooters, her overnight bag bouncing against her leg, he could see the moment when all her worries and hesitations dissolved. Relief lit her eyes.

Everything was going to be fine, he thought. It was going to be amazing. Or so he hoped. He suddenly wished he wasn't such an amateur. At some point in the not-so-distant past, each of his parents had felt obliged to have "the talk" with him. Of course it had been awkward and uncomfortable and not all that helpful, but the gist of it was obvious. The key elements were safety, love and respect. It was not rocket science.

Parents didn't get into the mechanics, yet that was what guys needed to know about. For that kind of advice, there were kids at school who liked to kiss and tell. Or kiss and lie. Mason had kept his ears tuned in. Chances were, the guys on his varsity crew team were no more savvy than he was, but maybe he had gleaned something useful from their locker-room chatter.

When Katia took his hand and he slipped his arm around her waist and pulled her in for a kiss, he realized he already had all the information he needed.

"Give me a moment," she said. "It's hot under

here." With that, she pulled her black, long-sleeved tunic over her head and shoved it into the bag with her other things. "There, that's better."

"You look incredible," he said, kissing her again. He wondered what the other interns would say when they saw her in Western garb.

"You're sweet. Sorry I'm late, but there are plenty of trains at rush hour." They would need to take the B line, a fast RER link between Charles de Gaulle and Gare du Nord.

They had reached the entrance to the north-bound train when Mason heard a hoarse voice shouting Katia's name and a string of words in Algerian.

He didn't need to understand the language to know the two guys approaching them were pissed about something. They were dressed in blue workers' coveralls and black caps.

"*Merde*," said Katia, grabbing his hand. "Pre-tend we didn't hear them."

Mason felt a twinge of recognition. "Those are the guys we almost ran into in Belleville that day," he said.

The two guys quickly caught up with them. Both started talking to her at once in harsh staccato imperatives. Mason understood some of the conversation, and the rest he could glean from their gestures. "Look at you. You're a disgrace to the family." They were referring to her lack of covering.

Then one of the guys yelled and gesticulated. Her face went pale, and she quickly turned to Mason. "I have to go back home."

"What happened?"

"They said my father's taken ill."

"Oh, man." Mason had nightmare visions of a heart attack, a stroke, a car accident. "What happened? Is he going to be okay?"

The two guys babbled at her. They were sweating, and the younger of the two was practically foaming at the mouth.

"I have to go," she said.

"I'll come with you."

The older guy yammered something else.

"He's on a scooter," she said.

"Oh. Then . . ."

"I'm sorry," she said in English as one of the guys grabbed her arm and yanked her away.

A sharp protective instinct rose up in Mason. He took a step forward. "Hey—"

"I'll try to get to the Gare du Nord later." Katia warned him away with a look.

One of the guys yammered something at Katia. Her eyes grew wide, and she got on the scooter. "Mason, I'll see you later, okay?"

"No, it's not okay. I should come with—"

An elbow landed in his ribs and he was shoved to the ground. The air rushed out of him. Katia yelled something in her native tongue. The sound of the motor drowned out her words as the scooter sped away. The second guy took off on foot, walking fast at first—and then running.

It was only much later that Mason would wonder how the pair of them happened to be in the Place St. Michel that evening, and how they had managed to locate her.

He got up and brushed himself off. Now what? Should he bail on the trip or keep going? If there truly was something the matter with Katia's father, then Mason wanted to be there for her, not that her family would allow him anywhere near her.

"Yo, Mason!"

He turned to see Taye coming toward him. He was with Lisa and Malcolm, the three of them geared up with backpacks.

"Ready to roll?" asked Lisa, giving an officious pat to the dorky passport pouch hanging around her neck.

"Where's Katia?" Malcolm asked, looking around.

"She's not going to make it, after all," said Mason, his heart sinking.

"Whatever," said Lisa. "Hey, hurry up so we can grab the next train."

The three of them joined the flow of commuters down to the trains.

Undecided, exasperated, Mason swore between his teeth and then descended the stairs into the subway. Maybe Mr. Hamini's illness would turn out to be nothing, and she would meet him and the others at the train station.

The metro stop was still ridiculously busy, the RER and metro lines crossing through the noisy underground labyrinth. The ripe smells of food, sweat, burnt air and a warm rubbery aroma filled the air. His grandpa George had once told him that smoking used to be permitted in the metro. Even though it wasn't anymore, the place still smelled like smoke.

Mason was nearing the northbound platform when across the track, a southbound train pulled in, brakes grinding and gnashing. Craning his neck, he tried to spot the others. It was a typical weekday rush hour, nothing unusual going on. But then, a few seconds later, the tunnel erupted.

It started as a single beat from a bass drum. *What the . . . ?* A vibration thundered through the tunnel like a runaway train. He felt as if the train had hit him, its impact hammering his gut and jaw. His back teeth felt rammed shut by some outside force. His bones rang from the blow of a sledge-hammer being slammed down on him. A wave of pressure pummeled everything that was soft inside him.

Sharp-smelling smoke filled the station. There was a split-second pause, followed by a shock wave. Then a fireball formed, and a flare of wind sucked everything back toward the blast. He grabbed a railing that was hot to the touch, but he held on. Something hit him like a baseball bat in the back of his head while rocks and debris struck his face. A bright orange glow danced before his eyes. The air turned red with hot bits of flying metal.

Run. Run, don't die here, run-don't-die-here, run-don't-die-here, run-don't-die-here, rundontdiehere hammered through his mind. His ears felt as though skewers were being stabbed into them. He bit his tongue and felt the blood running hot and metallic-tasting down his gullet. His hearing was gone. Something was suffocating him; he felt a screaming in his throat but no sound came out. His pants were wet, not from blood but from piss.

Somehow he found his way to an exit jammed with openmouthed, horrified people emitting screams he couldn't hear. There was a guy trying to drag himself up the stairs, but one foot seemed to be backward. Mason grabbed the guy's arm and draped it over the back of his neck, helping him to the pavement. The guy fell like a sack of rocks. A gendarme rushed forward, his face veined by running blood, and bent to help, waving Mason away.

A woman nearby wandered about, acting as if nothing had happened. He couldn't hear her voice, but he could read her lips. "I need to get to the train. I should get home." She seemed completely unaware that most of her clothes had blown off, or that her face, bare stomach and breasts were covered in soot.

He looked down to see that his shirt and pants were shredded, and somehow he had lost one shoe. The Place St. Michel was a war zone now, not the heart of the Latin Quarter. The cafés, only moments ago filled with students, seethed with terrified people. Cars rammed into one another, coming to a standstill as the drivers abandoned them. It was totally surreal, seeing the faces of the crying and wounded without being able to hear a thing.

He thought of Katia and silently thanked the guy who had whisked her away on his scooter. Then he thought of the others—Taye, Malcolm, Lisa—and fear iced his veins. They'd gone to the train platform ahead of him. Christ, what if . . .

Ambulances and fire engines lined the embankments of the Seine. Bright red civil defense helicopters circled overhead. Police barricades were assembled, sealing off streets and alleyways while crews rushed to aid the wounded. He recognized the black protective clothing and Darth Vader helmets of the French antiterrorist squad, rushing toward the tunnel.

A paramedic in a bright green vest approached him and spoke. Mason pointed at his ears and shook his head. The medic spoke again, but then someone rushed forward, holding a woman in his arms. Mason's eye was caught by the smoldering end of her fluttery pink scarf. *Merci, eh?* He recalled the way she had smiled at him, the swagger in her walk. Now one of her legs was gone, the bloody bone and sinew dripping from where her knee should have been.

Mason couldn't feel his feet touching the pavement as he walked away. He could feel the vibrations of sirens and car horns and helicopters in his gut. Shards of glass and debris littered the pavement. At one point, he found a sandal in the gutter. He stuck it on his bare foot and kept going.

Beyond the immediate area of the explosion, things seemed weirdly normal. People went about their business, stopping at the boulangerie to pick up a baguette for dinner, or sitting at sidewalk cafés over a chilled glass of pastis or citron pressé. Some became aware of the mayhem, shading their eyes to look up at the helicopters and billowing smoke. Shopkeepers came out and stood on the sidewalks, scratching their heads in confusion.

Mason became aware of sound again—the muffled roar of traffic and a constant two-toned wail of sirens. He crossed the river at the Pont Royal and followed a shady boulevard to his dad's apartment building. Passersby regarded him strangely, and one woman crossed the street to avoid him.

When he reached for the keypad at the entryway, he scarcely recognized his own hand, covered in soot and flecked with bloody cuts.

As the elevator rose, his heart rate sped up so fast he thought his chest would explode. Would it feel like the explosion in St. Michel? Would his skin feel as if it were on fire, his eardrums sucked out of his head?

The elevator door swished open to the sound of a French crooner warbling about "L'amour de l'ame." His dad was in the kitchen with a dark-haired woman. She laughed as he pulled her into his arms and kissed her on the lips. A little boy sat on a bar stool, making something out of LEGO blocks.

The scene before Mason was as blindsiding and incomprehensible as the metro explosion had been, a shock that sent him reeling.

"What the hell is this?" he asked loudly.

The woman gave a little yelp of alarm and jumped back, planting herself directly in front of the little kid.

His dad's face drained of all color. "Mason? My God, what happened to you?"

"What happened to *you?*" Mason asked, his racing heart flaring into a burn of fury.

Dad murmured something in rapid French to the woman, but Mason didn't stick around to hear. He stomped to his room and slammed the door.

The sound of the slamming door shattered him into a million pieces. He fell to his hands and knees and puked all over the floor.

Part Five

✵ ✵ ✵ ✵ ✵

"What is the good of your stars and trees,
your sunrise and the wind,
if they do not enter into our daily lives?"
—E. M. Forster

17

The oxblood-red covered bridge that spanned the Schuyler River came into view as Mason's car rounded a bend in the road. Faith realized the drive up from the city had sped by, virtually unnoticed. She blinked like an awakening dreamer. The miles had ticked away while she'd been mesmerized by Mason's story.

"I'm sorry," she said quietly. "What a horrific thing to witness, especially for someone so young. You were the same age Cara is now. It must've been awful."

"It's strange, talking about it now. That was a different life for me. I was a different person," he said. "Surviving the explosion changed me completely, in ways I'm still discovering. There was nothing to do but put it in the past and move on. That's what I thought, anyway." His hands flexed and unflexed on the steering wheel.

She knew a person couldn't simply move on from the kind of trauma he'd suffered on that summer evening in Paris. Turning sideways on the seat, she studied his profile, clean and handsome and troubled. A lock of hair spilled down his brow, and she felt a sudden and surprising urge to brush it out of the way. She tucked her hand under her thigh.

"What caused the explosion?" she asked. "Did you ever find out?"

"Oh, hell, yeah. It was huge news back when it happened. It was a terror attack. The bomb was planted under a seat in the sixth carriage of the southbound train. It was a big cooking gas canister filled with explosives and shrapnel, like nails and screws."

"It sounds horrible. Who would do such a thing?"

"A fringe group of extremists. They wanted France to end its aid to Algeria. There were eight or ten deaths that night, I don't remember. A hundred or more injured—limbs blown off, burns, blunt trauma, internal injuries . . ."

"It must've been such a nightmare," she said quietly.

"Totally impossible to describe. It remade my life in about ten seconds."

"Remade your life. In what way?"

"It was a turning point for me. I was forced to see the world differently, not as a safe place anymore."

She remembered their conversation on that starlit night, when she'd told him about her grandparents' deaths. His story of shock and terror took her back to that December day when the call had come about her grandparents, killed by a plane falling out of the sky as they were sitting down to dinner. The Lockerbie horror was a different incident, but some of the images Mason had described—the terror and confusion, the injuries, the shock—seemed eerily familiar. A haunting wave of memory swept over Faith. She had survived, and Mason had survived. But they both bore the scars.

That look he'd given her that night. Now she knew why he'd been so understanding. And she understood his reaction to the motorcycle victim. The blood and mayhem that day must have awakened the Paris horror.

Every instinct she possessed compelled her to reach out to him. It was what she did—soothed people who were hurting. But she didn't touch him, because if she was being honest with herself, she wasn't sure he was the needy one.

"I hate that you had to go through that," she told him. "And then to go home with that burden . . ."

He nodded. "I was forced to see my family differently."

"It wasn't safe anymore, either."

"That's a little dramatic, but yeah. I wasn't afraid for my safety. I just stopped trusting what I thought I knew. My parents weren't the parents I knew growing up. My dad was a liar and a cheater, and my mom . . . She was someone I felt I had to protect from finding out what was going on. I found myself in a lousy position, not wanting to be the one to tell her . . . I just kept my distance after that."

A family, shattered. "Tell me more about the

woman and the boy with your father," she said.

Mason nodded, slowing the car to troll through Avalon's main square. It looked particularly peaceful and calm, a summer afternoon filled with shoppers and vacationers, people strolling through the park.

"The woman—Celeste—and the kid named Simon took off and Dad drove me to a clinic. The hospitals were jammed but he found a clinic in Neuilly, a little bit away from the city."

"You were injured."

He touched the crescent scar on his cheek. "Cuts and burns."

"Your father must have been beside himself."

"The whole city went into panic mode. There were paramilitary sweeps through the Algerian neighborhoods, security everywhere. I was supposed to give a report to the police, but I never did. I just wanted to get the hell out of there. My dad and I had it out, that very night. I yelled at him to take me straight to the airport. I didn't even know how to begin processing everything."

"Did your mother know about Celeste?"

"No. Never. Well, maybe there was a time that I wondered if she did know, but let herself be duped." His jaw bulged as he clenched his teeth. "Now it's pretty clear she was clueless about my dad's secrets until Celeste contacted her."

Faith hated secrets. Dennis had kept his

worsening health from her for far too long, thinking he was protecting her. Instead, he had robbed her of the chance to help him, maybe even save him, or at least keep him with her longer.

Mason glared over the arch of the steering wheel. Tension hardened his jaw and the grip of his hands. "Dad was full of excuses. He claimed they were just friends, he and Celeste. Of course he would say that—the standard line of a cheater. He offered some bullshit story about how she was going through some hard times and he was just comforting her."

"You said you saw them kissing."

"Yeah. Not the comforting kind of kiss. But I was just a dumb kid. I bought right into the story because it was a way to believe nothing was wrong. There was a part of me that wanted to believe him. I let him convince me that what I'd walked in on was an isolated incident. My dad . . . He had a way of knowing what a person wanted to hear, and a way of saying it just so. He used every cliché in the book, whipping them all out as if he carried them around in his wallet. Like, 'It's not what it seems. We're just friends. I swear I won't see her again. Your mom can't know because she wouldn't understand.' That sort of thing." He flexed his hands on the wheel. "And I lapped it up like a starving dog."

"It's understandable. I think a boy would want to believe the best of his parents."

"He manipulated me, and I let him." He let out a long, frustrated breath. "In the clinic that night, my father told me three lies. He said the friendship between him and Celeste was over. He said he didn't know who Simon's father was."

"And the third?"

"He said if I kept my mouth shut, nothing would have to change for the family."

"Everything changed, didn't it?" said Faith.

"From my perspective, for sure. He made me believe it would be the end of our happy family if I told my mom what I'd seen."

Her heart constricted. "That's a lot to lay on a kid."

"He didn't order me not to tell. He said he would leave it up to me."

"Even worse. It put you in a terrible position."

He nodded. "I played my part. I guess we all did. What's clear to me now is that I detached from both of my parents that night. I mean, it was going to happen anyway, since I was heading off to college." He drummed his fingers on the steering wheel. "Needless to say, my summer in Paris ended abruptly. Dad and I managed to find seats on a flight to New York. At the airport, he went to a duty-free shop and picked out a Bulgari bracelet for my mom. I don't recall saying one word to him on the flight home. I was on painkillers from the clinic, so all I remember is sleeping the whole way."

"Wow," she said. "That's some story."

He flipped down the visor to deflect the afternoon sun. "We spent the rest of the summer at my grandpa George's place in Montauk. I went surfing with my friends, just like I wanted to do all along." Mason was quiet for a bit. "Of course, after what happened in Paris, I wasn't much interested in surfing."

"What became of the girl? Katia?"

He let out a long sigh. "We'd need to drive to Chicago in order for me to finish that part of the story."

The idea of driving to Chicago with him in this car had a strange appeal to her. "Another time, maybe."

He nodded. "We still keep in touch, the five of us—Taye, Malcolm, Lisa and Katia. Lisa lost an eye in the incident and went through three marriages. Now she's single, and she's the best corporate attorney I know. My firm uses her all the time. Taye's an economic affairs officer in the UN. Malcolm designs shoes. And Katia . . . she became a trauma surgeon. Specializes in putting people back together after terror attacks."

"A trauma surgeon. Did you tell her about your mother's accident?"

"No. It wouldn't be a bad idea, though. She works for an NGO that sends surgeons to help victims of terrorism, so she's traveling constantly. I haven't talked to her directly in a couple of years."

"I appreciate you telling me all of this. I had no idea whether or not there was a connection between your mother getting a letter from Celeste Gauthier and having the accident that same night."

He flicked a glance in her direction. "You're the first person who has heard any of this."

"Seriously? You haven't confided in your fiancée?"

"Regina?" He shook his head. "It's been twenty years. To be honest, it's not something that's on my radar every day."

"It's a lot to hold in for such a long time."

"I didn't think I had a choice. And when my father swore it was over with Celeste, I decided to believe him. I feel duped, too."

"I can understand why you'd pull away from your father. But your mother?"

"She knew something major had changed for me when I got back from Paris, so I let her assume it was the bombing. But the woman . . . well, you know her by now. She's pretty damned intuitive."

"My girls and I have noticed that about her."

"I didn't want her to ask questions I wasn't prepared to answer. I've always been a lousy liar, but I'm good at keeping my mouth shut. I finished high school and went away to college, and kept hoping my dad was right about nothing changing for my family." As he turned down the driveway, he glanced over at her. "How long has my mother known?"

"You'll have to ask her."

"Awesome," he muttered.

"She needs you, Mason. She needs to not feel alone." Faith knew the comment came from a place inside herself that she rarely showed people—the place where pain hid. Every once in a while, she yearned to let someone else in there with her, to be her soft place to fall, but she had no one. Alice did, though. Alice had Mason.

"Right," he agreed. "Whatever. It'll be a relief to get it over with."

"It's easier to speak the truth than to keep a secret."

"So you say."

"Secrets have a way of sneaking out."

"Or exploding," he said.

Mason stood in the doorway of the big sunlit sitting room, observing his mother, unseen. She was staring at her hand as if it held all the secrets of the universe. Ever so slowly, almost as if stirred by a breeze, her first two fingers moved.

"Beautiful, Alice," said Deborah, the physical therapist. "You're making good progress."

Mason regarded her, this woman who used to dive off cliffs and ride a mountain bike down the slopes of volcanoes. His heart cracked apart, and he couldn't help but wonder—was her suicide attempt really due to finding out about Celeste?

"Hey, Mom," he said, striding into the room.

She lifted her eyebrows. "Well, well. This is a surprise."

"I just couldn't stay away," he said, bending to kiss her soft cheek. He shook hands with the PT. "Good to see you again."

"Your mother and I were just finishing up. The woman wears me out."

Mason grinned. "That's my mom."

Once they were alone, he sat down across from her, leaned his elbows on his knees and carefully touched the tips of his fingers together, aligning them just so. "I have no idea how to start this conversation," he said. "So I'll just dive in."

She simply waited, regarding him without expression.

"You received something in the mail from Celeste Gauthier."

Still no expression. "And?" she inquired.

"Did she say why she was contacting you?"

"I imagine it was prompted by her learning that Trevor had been killed."

Mason's mouth went dry. "What does she want?"

"I'll answer that in a moment. I take it you know Celeste Gauthier."

Faith's words went through his mind—*Is it easier to speak the truth, or to keep a secret?*

"No," he said. "I don't know her. I saw her and

the little kid, just once, twenty years ago when I was with Dad in Paris."

Her breath stopped momentarily, the first indication of surprise. "The summer of the metro bombing."

"Yes. I saw her and her little boy with him the night it happened."

Her gaze iced over. "And you didn't see fit to tell me what was going on between your father and Celeste."

"Mom, I didn't understand a damned thing that night. I mean, come on. A *bombing*. I staggered from St. Michel to the apartment, and there they were, obviously not expecting me."

"But later. Once you were back home in the States. Did it ever occur to you that I might need to be told about my husband's affair? Did it ever cross your mind that I deserved to know my husband kept a mistress and fathered a child?"

"Hell, yes, you deserved to know," he said. "But it wasn't the job of your kid to tell you."

She inhaled sharply. "I can't disagree with that," she conceded. "It was your father's job, but he said nothing. Do your brother and sister know?"

"No," he said quickly. "Listen, Dad swore to me that they were just friends. He said she was going through some stuff and needed a friend."

"And you believed him."

"It was *Dad*."

"Did he explain that the boy you saw was his?"

Mason flashed on the photo he'd found in the cottage in Cancale. "I figured it out later, I guess. Mom, I'm sorry. What he did sucks. I don't know how long it went on. Dad claimed he would never see her again, and the issue never came up between us. I wanted to trust him. You guys seemed to . . . The two of you . . . I thought everything went back to normal."

She sat in silence. Her eyes were calm and unreadable as she gazed out the window. "Normal," she said, almost as if she were speaking to herself. "I scarcely remember what *normal* feels like."

"What did Celeste Gauthier want?"

She pursed her lips and faced him again. "The Paris apartment. I said she could have it. I'll certainly never use it again."

"That's more than generous of you."

"It's not generous. Your father made no provision for her or the boy. I suppose he's a young man by now. And Lord knows, he didn't ask to be fathered by a married man."

Trevor Bellamy had a lot to answer for. But how did you get answers from a dead guy? You didn't, Mason conceded. They could be as angry as they wanted at him, but the anger had nowhere to go.

"I'm not here because of Celeste Gauthier," he said at length. "And I'm not here because of Dad and anything he did or failed to do. None of that matters now, because it would be pointless to let it matter." He resisted the urge to stare down at his hands, and instead held her gaze with his. "I'm here because of you."

She gave another quiet gasp of surprise. "Why now?"

"Because your fall down the stairs wasn't an accident. You made it happen."

Her face didn't change, but her eyes did, flaring with momentary panic. "Don't be absurd, Mason."

"I agree, it does sound absurd, saying aloud that my mother tried to kill herself." There. He'd spoken the words. Just be honest, Faith had urged him. *Speak your truth.*

"Then why would you even suggest such a thing?"

"Because that's what happened, and I didn't drive all the way up here to debate the matter with you. I'm worried, and I'm here to help."

Her cheeks turned flame red. "Faith told you this."

"Yes."

"I'm going to fire her immediately. I won't have an alarmist and a liar working for me."

"You're not going to fire her. She's the best thing that's happened to us since your accident."

"To *us?* Do I detect a Freudian slip?"

He was not even going to address that. "Listen, Mom, firing Faith is not going to solve anything. How about you take a second and quit thinking about yourself and the shitty hand you've been dealt, and start thinking of others. The woman's trying her best. She's doing a great job compared to the ones before her."

"She's intrusive. She doesn't know her place. And she jumps to wild conclusions."

"You just don't like her because she stands up to your bullying." He got up, paced back and forth, raked a hand through his hair. "I didn't come here to talk about Faith," he said. "I want to talk about you."

"Well, I don't. I'm sick of myself."

"Mom, I'm worried about you."

"Don't. I'll be fine. Go back to the city. Go back to Regina."

"No can do. I've decided to make a big change. I'm setting up an office in Avalon. I'll be living at Adam's place above the boathouse."

"And how charming to have you nearby, pointing out all my shortcomings and flaws," she said. "How did I get so lucky?"

He ignored that. "I don't intend to leave until I know you're safe."

"Fine. I'm safe."

"I need to feel sure there won't be another suicide attempt."

She sniffed. "You're being overly dramatic."

"You're minimizing and being avoidant." *Speak your truth.* "Mom, we haven't had an honest conversation since that summer. After finding out about Celeste, I didn't know how to talk to you. Not about things that mattered. We'd discuss school and politics and social issues and the weather, but we didn't ever connect again. So I can tell when someone's avoiding an issue."

"And you think *I* didn't notice this? You were a stranger when you came home that summer. I thought it was PTSD—it was, of course, but that wasn't the only thing that was bothering you."

Practically from the moment he'd stepped off the plane, she'd had him in the most aggressive therapies she could find—trauma-focused cognitive therapy, medication, group therapy, something involving eye movement, which he couldn't even remember anymore. His first days and weeks back in the United States had been crammed with appointments. He remembered thinking at one point that he wished his mother would stop rushing him from place to place and simply hug him, but it never happened. And in all the talk therapy, the writing and visualization exercises they'd put him through, he had never once mentioned what he'd seen at his father's apartment.

"I remember missing how close we used to be before that summer," his mother said, her voice barely above a whisper. "I didn't understand why you pulled away. And now I do."

The pain in her voice touched him deeply. "I'm sorry I acted like a stranger. I didn't want you to figure out there was something I wasn't telling you, something that had nothing to do with the bombing."

"I hate that his secret ruined us," she said. "Collateral damage."

Mason was surprised to see that his hands were shaking. His chest felt expansive, his limbs slack with relief. He'd held these things in for years, and it was a relief to finally let everything out. "So here we are years later, and the secret is gone. And that, I suppose, is my long-winded way of telling you that I plan to stick around and learn to talk to you again."

She regarded him with an expression he'd never seen on her face before—shock and emotion and a glimmer of happiness. "Who are you, and what have you done with my son?"

"Now who's being dramatic?"

"Mason, I truly appreciate your concern, but it's really not necessary. I don't need a keeper."

"Did it ever occur to you that I might *want* to be here?"

"You've never lived in a town with fewer than ten million people. You're going to go stir-crazy within seventy-two hours, you mark my words." She glared at him. "What about Regina?"

She'd be furious. "She'll understand."

"What do you plan to do with yourself all day, every day?"

"The same thing I do in the city. Go to work, make deals. Only instead of going back to my apartment, I'll come home to you. I can commute to the city occasionally if I need to."

"That's no life for a man like you."

"That's exactly the life I intend having."

"Until . . . ?"

"Until I know you're all right."

"I will never be all right."

"Bullshit. People live with disabilities. It's not what any of us would have chosen, but it's what we've got, and you damned well are going to be all right." He held her gaze with his. "You tried to kill yourself, Mom. It scares the hell out of me. And . . . I'm sorry. I'm sorry you were in such pain that you didn't want to live anymore."

She was silent for a long time. "You're wrong about me. Faith is an alarmist. I promise to be more careful in the future. There won't be another incident."

He wondered if he would ever get a straight answer out of his mother. "I need more than a promise. I need to *know*."

"I used to believe there were no guarantees in life, but that's not so," she said, speaking softly but with steady conviction. "The guarantee is that it will end. So what really matters is how it's spent. I would give all the years I have left of my life if I could have my mobility back. Jesus, if I could just put my own damned olive in my own damned martini, I'd be grateful, but I can't even do that."

Although she spoke with dispassion, he heard a tremor in her voice. "Mom, let me stay. You can't fix your own martini, but I sure as hell can."

Her effort to smile broke his heart. "Have I ever told you how much I hate this? How useless I feel, being such a burden on everyone?"

Okay, this was not reassuring. "You're not a burden. You give so much to the people around you. Faith was telling me on the way up here how great you've been with her girls. I mean, piano lessons? Seriously?"

"The child is rather bright. I've been able to teach her a lot, just by explaining things to her."

"Now you're talking. The accident sucks. The fact that Dad cheated sucks. But we're in the here and now, Mom. And you're still *you*."

She was crying now. "I caused it," she said, speaking so softly he could barely hear.

"Caused what?" He couldn't fathom what she was talking about. Had she caused the fall down the stairs? Or was she talking about her husband's affair?

"The avalanche," she said.

"Oh, come on—"

"It's true. Your father and I both knew the safety rules for avalanche zones. We'd been doing it all our lives. But we—I . . . yes, *I* was careless that day."

"What are you talking about?"

"The day he died. We had an argument. It was about something stupid—aren't they always? He got mad and skied away from me, straight across a runout zone where there was already some loose snow. Instead of waiting—you know you're supposed to stay off the face of the hill until your partner has gone ahead—I took off after him. I could tell the snow was unstable, but I was so determined to get in the last word that I ignored the warning signs. I yelled at him like the worst kind of nag. And that was when it happened. That was when the whole mountain came down on us."

Holy shit. Mason had no idea what to say to that. No wonder she felt guilty. Instead of speaking, he put his hands on hers and wished like hell she could feel his touch.

She stared down at their joined hands. "So there you have it. I know how to be safe in an avalanche zone, but we argued and I violated the rules and the entire thing was my fault. Then I found out he'd cheated on me, fathered a child, and I wondered why we'd never fought about *that*. And then I realized *all* of our arguments were about that, and I just didn't realize it."

The expression on her face tore Mason apart. "Mom," he said. "I'm sorry you were in such pain that you wanted to die. I'm sorry I wasn't there for you. I'm here now, and I'm staying for as long as you need me. Maybe forever."

• • •

Faith headed to the kitchen for her morning coffee. She was surprised to hear Ruby up and talking to someone.

"To tell you the truth," she was saying with crisp authority, "Cocoa Puffs are the bomb. The very essence of crunch, with *chocolate*. But I can't do any of the good cereals anymore. My mom won't let me. The added sugar sets my numbers off the charts, so I have to stick with no sugar added."

Faith walked into the kitchen to find her younger daughter and Mason Bellamy solemnly contemplating the cereal selection lined up at the breakfast bar. She felt instantly self-conscious in her discount-store nightshirt commemorating the Avalon Hornets' regional pennant win in the bush league. She was wearing flip-flops that had seen better days. And couldn't she have taken ten seconds to comb her hair?

"Good to know," Mason said, offering her a wave. He wore jeans with a black T-shirt and a blazer, looking casually elegant. His appearance made her feel even scruffier. Had she at least brushed her teeth? Yes. Yes, she had. At least she thought she had. This man had a unique way of causing her brain cells to die, one by one.

"Hi, Mom." Ruby climbed down off the bar stool and gave her a hug. "Did you know Mason is moving in? He's taking over the apartment above the boathouse. It's okay with Adam, 'cause Adam is training to be a smoke jumper."

Faith had thought he'd be more resistant. "That was fast."

"I can work fast when I know what has to be done."

"Same here," said Ruby. And with that, she took out her test kit. With a minimum of fuss, she stuck her finger, placed a drop of blood on a test strip and recorded the level on her chart. Then she primed her insulin pen and injected herself. "There. Thirty more minutes, and I get to eat."

"Hey, you're pretty slick with that stuff," said Mason.

"My daughter, the pincushion," said Faith.

"I used to freak out when I first started, but it's okay now."

"Impressive," said Mason.

To Faith's surprise, Alice came through the doorway with her morning aide. She usually didn't make an appearance until later. She offered a general nod of good morning to everyone, but her attention stayed fixed on Ruby. "Let me be certain I understand this correctly. You have no problem with blood and needles and stabbing yourself with sharp objects, and yet you claim to be afraid of dogs, water and the third grade."

Ruby admitted this with a sheepish nod, then went about putting her school lunch together.

"You forgot heights, the dark and cursive

writing," Cara added, coming into the kitchen. "Oh, and those little cotton balls stuck down inside pill bottles. She's afraid of those, too."

"Odd, how could I forget that?"

Mason looked from his mother to Ruby to Cara. "There's a saying my mother used to tell me," he said to Ruby. " 'Fear makes the wolf bigger.' Do you know what that means?"

She nodded, studying the floor. "I guess."

"I have a very smart mother," he added. "We both do."

Okay, thought Faith. He believed she was smart. At least he wasn't focused on Faith. Maybe he hadn't noticed her disreputable nightgown.

"Are the Avalon Hornets a local outfit?" he asked her suddenly.

Shoot, he'd noticed. "Bush-league baseball team. They're based right here in town."

"Can we go to a game sometime?" Ruby asked. "I like baseball games. Especially the popcorn and hot dogs."

"We'll see," Faith said.

"You always say 'we'll see' and hope I'll forget I asked," Ruby pointed out. She turned to Alice. "Will you come to a baseball game?"

Alice looked startled. Then she said, "Why, yes. I might enjoy that."

"Cool." Ruby went around the end of the counter and gave her a kiss on the cheek.

Faith's heart swelled with love for her daughter

in that moment. Ruby's natural affection was such a beautiful gift. Even Alice at her crankiest was unable to resist it.

Cara slathered a piece of bread with peanut butter. "Thank God it's the last day of school," she said, cutting off a bite and giving it to Alice. Then Ruby put the tall coffee mug on Alice's tray and angled the straw just right.

Mason looked even more astonished at the girls' familiarity with his mother.

"I thought you liked school," said Faith.

"I do, but I'm getting picky. If I had to sit through one more lecture in American Studies, my head would explode."

"I'd like to see that," Ruby said softly.

Faith turned to Alice. "We have the rehab place at ten today."

"It's on my calendar."

"The rehab place?" asked Mason.

"I'm getting more training with my driving skills," said Alice.

"Cool. Mind if I join you?"

"It's not necessary."

"I'd like to."

"Don't you have work to do?" She took another bite of Cara's toast.

"I just got here. It's going to take a few days to find office space in town and get set up."

"Grab your stuff, Rubes," said Cara. "Donno is waiting."

"I haven't had my breakfast," Ruby protested. She stuffed her lunch in her backpack, then peeled and ate a banana, dipping it into a cup of plain yogurt. "Two minutes," she mumbled around the mouthful of banana. "That's all I need. Two minutes."

"It's rude to keep the guy waiting. He's got better things to do than wait around for us."

Faith was glad for the end of school, too. No more mornings of bickering and rushing around. "Be good," she said, giving each girl a quick hug.

Alice went with the aide to get ready for the rehab center. Faith folded her arms across the front of the old nightgown, vowing to be more presentable at breakfast from now on. "Welcome to mornings at the lake," she said.

"Thanks."

"Probably not as peaceful as a typical morning at your place in the city."

"Right. I do find inner peace by checking email."

"Your mother has never shown up so early for breakfast before. Having you here . . . Maybe it motivated her."

"Sure. She's thrilled to pieces. Can't you tell?"

Faith poured two cups of coffee and slid one across the counter to him. Something very strange happened to her whenever he was around. She felt a powerful and undeniable attraction. It was stupid, of course. He was unavailable in multiple ways—emotionally, physically, socio-economically. But he was so doggone good-looking. So nice. And funny. And smart.

She wondered if the brother was anything like him. She wondered if the brother was available.

"How did your talk with her go?" she asked.

"I had to save your ass from being fired."

Faith was not surprised. "I figured she'd be mad."

"Not to worry. You're not going anywhere. It was a difficult moment in a difficult conversation."

She sensed there was a lot more he wasn't telling her, and that *difficult* was probably an understatement. "And?"

He added cream to his coffee. "And we've got a lot of ground to cover. Why are you looking at me like that?"

"I suppose I expected more resistance from you."

"Thanks."

"I didn't mean . . . Never mind. You dropped everything and came up here, and no matter what your mother says, she's grateful. What can I do to help?"

"We're going to her shrink. The two of us, together. I'm sure it's gonna be a barrel of laughs."

"Oh, boy," she said, putting her cup in the sink. "I better get ready for the day."

He stood aside, making a formal gesture at the door. “Be my guest.”

As she passed by him, he said, “You told me it’s easier to speak the truth than to keep a secret.”

“I said that? I don’t recall saying that. But generally speaking, it’s probably the case.”

“Right. Generally speaking. Just so you know, even though I’m here, this arrangement doesn’t thrill me. But—”

“This is not about you.” She bristled. Was he backpedaling already? “It’s about your mother, who is hurting and afraid and needs your support. So if you have to be pissed at me for telling you to step in, go right ahead. However—”

“Thank you,” he said.

“What?”

He gave her that funny, crooked smile again. “That’s all I was going to say, Faith, if you’d let me get a word in edgewise. Thank you.”

At the rehab facility, Mason stood on the side-lines with Faith, watching his mother work through her routine with her trainer. The place resembled a very specialized gym, with an array of equipment, mats, boards, weights and machines. Therapists were working with people of all levels of ability, from a ninety-year-old with a broken hip to a kid whose shaved and scarred head indicated a brain injury. This was a far cry from the gym he belonged to in Manhattan, where his mother had once dominated her CrossFit class.

Yet the expression on her face was familiar to him. "That's the mom I know," he said, noting the intensity in her eyes. "That focus and determination."

"Right," said Alice with a taut smile. "That's me. Grim determination."

To his amazement, she was working out on a stationary bicycle. Like a treadmill, it was powered by electricity, but the movement of the pedals would improve her muscle tone and cardiac function.

"Your progress has been remarkable," said Tim, the rehab trainer. "The fact that you're a gifted athlete is quite an advantage. All the qualities you drew on in your athletic training are still the keys to success—determination, focus, discipline, strength and consistency."

"Yay, me," she said.

"We're still working on the attitude." He grinned at Mason and Faith. "When we first started working together, this lady was about as friendly as a honey badger. Now I'm her favorite, right, Alice?"

"You've worn away my defenses," she said. "Now I'm Rebecca of Sunnybrook Farm."

"Not quite, but you should be proud of all your hard work," he said. "I've seen you figure out ways to use your arms even with your limited functionality. A few months ago, you had almost nothing on either side." Tim covered her hand on the adaptive handlebar. "Now you've figured out how to straighten your wrist and sometimes manipulate the fingers."

"How useful. All that does is make my hand open involuntarily."

"Keep working on your hand mobility, Alice. It takes a lot of hard work to make a miracle happen. I wouldn't be surprised if you found a way to make your fingers move."

"Great. Pretty soon I'll be able to flip you off."

"I live for the day." Taking care to protect her collarbone, he transferred her from the bike to her chair.

Mason studied a clear plastic model that showed the nervous system, the muscular and skeletal systems. The human body seemed intimidatingly complex to him. Faith stepped up beside him. "I've always thought it was so beautifully simple," she said.

He felt a flash of humor. "I was just thinking the opposite. I'm bewildered. It's like looking at electrical lines in Thailand."

"I feel that way about finance, and that's your specialty," she said. "I suppose we all have our areas of expertise."

"I just wish the experts could find a way to repair a spinal cord." He stared at the illustration of the C7 vertebra. When he thought about his mother's injury, it didn't look beautiful or simple at all. She had lost the use of all the nerves that connected below the injury.

"There are two parts to the nervous system," Faith said. "Central and peripheral. I've been reading about electrical stimulation treatments, but her neurologist didn't think she was a candidate."

"I keep wondering if we've really left no stone unturned in my mom's case. Did we find every expert, pursue every treatment?"

"Things change every day in this field," Faith pointed out. "What about your . . . Katia? The girl you knew in Paris."

He felt a twist in his gut. "What?"

"She's a physician now, right? A trauma surgeon. You said you kept in touch."

Then he got it. "Oh, you mean to ask her about my mom. Good idea. I'll check with her today."

"By keeping her strength up, Alice will be ready for anything. And I guess by now you've seen how her attitude plays a part."

"Oh, yeah. The trainer's good with her. So are you, Faith. I have to admit, when you first started with her, I thought you were pretty hard on her."

She raised her eyebrows. "Really?"

"I overheard the two of you butting heads. Then I realized why." He studied the model again, with its network of nerves. "Have you always been interested in neurology? Or anatomy in general?"

"I'm interested in anything that might affect my client," she said. "But yes, I love neurology and anatomy and all things medical. Which means I'm in the right profession. When I was young, I dreamed about becoming a doctor."

"You should have gone for it," he said. "I bet you'd make a good one."

Her smile turned wistful as she traced her finger along the model's arm nerves. "Life has a way of creating detours around the best-laid plans."

He found himself wondering about the path her life had taken. A hard road, based on what he knew. Becoming a mother and then a widow before the age of thirty, shouldering mountains of medical debt, dealing with Ruby's condition. Yet Faith faced every day with a positive attitude.

As the session was winding down, she grabbed Mason's arm. "Hey," she said. "Check it out."

Just her hand on his arm made every cell in his body wake up. "What's that?"

She didn't seem to notice her effect on him. "That guy over there, the one who's just finishing with the walking bars."

Mason saw a tall, muscular man gripping a set of parallel bars. One of his bare legs was terrifically scarred, and there was another long scar on his upper arm.

"Friend of yours?"

"He's the guy. The motorcycle accident guy."

Mason still got chills when he remembered that day. "You sure?"

"Yes," said his mother, gliding past in her chair.

"Tim just told me. We should go and say hello." Without hesitation, she approached the struggling man. "I'm Alice Bellamy," she said. "This is my son Mason and Faith McCallum."

He paused between parallel bars. "Rick Sanders," he said.

"You crashed your motorcycle in front of my house," said Alice.

The guy looked sheepish. "Yeah? Not my best day."

"I'm sorry it happened," she said.

"That makes two of us."

"Faith was the first one to help you after your crash."

Rick Sanders turned to her, his eyes wide. "Oh, man. Really? *Thank you.*"

He reached out to shake her hand, but Faith stepped forward and folded him into a hug, then stepped back. Mason loved how natural she was with people, even strangers. "I'm glad I was in the right place at the right time."

"You saved my life. I always meant to find out who you were, but . . ." He gestured down at himself. "It's been a long recovery."

"Are you going to be all right?" asked Mason's mom.

"If I have anything to say about it, yeah. I'm told it's going to be a long road, though." He regarded her with real warmth and interest. "So, do you come here often?"

To Mason's astonishment, his mother blushed. At least, he thought it was a blush; her cheeks turned pink, and although she didn't smile, her eyes seemed lighter. "I'm a regular," she said.

Faith motioned Mason to the lobby. "We can wait out here until she's done."

Mason's surprise must have shown, because she gave a little teasing laugh.

"What?" he said. "What's funny?"

"The expression on your face."

"Oh, yeah. Well. So was that flirting? Was she flirting with that guy?"

"You tell me."

The blush on his mother's face. The sparkling eyes. "It's not every day I see my mom flirting with some guy."

"Does it bother you?"

"Anything that makes her want to live her life is cool with me."

Faith's eyes softened. "Well said."

✵ 18 ✵

"The end of the school year means the beginning of awesome," said Cara's friend Bree. They were at the Sky River Bakery, just finishing up their shift. Jenny McKnight, the owner, had given Cara morning shifts for the summer, which worked out great, because it meant she was done by noon and had the whole day ahead of her. The whole day for hanging out, dreaming, reading books, messing around in the lake . . . and wondering what the heck she was going to do with herself after senior year. Her school counselor had spent all of five minutes telling her she had the potential to get into any college she wanted, but he stopped short of explaining how she might actually make that happen.

Just for today, she wasn't going to worry about the future. Because back at Downton Abbey, something like a miracle had occurred. Old lady Bellamy had agreed that Cara could have a friend over and they would all go swimming. It was the hottest day of the year so far, the thermometer aiming toward ninety, so the lake was the only place to be.

Cara didn't have all that many friends. She wasn't a jock or a gleek or an A-lister. Mostly, she kept her head down and flew under the radar. Bree was the closest thing Cara had to a best friend. They worked together at the bakery. They were both training this summer for a triathlon, so they were pretty pumped about spending an afternoon in the water.

They drove together in Bree's car, a secondhand Subaru. Cara watched enviously as her friend drove along the lakeshore road. She was still saving up for driver's ed.

"So is old Mrs. Bellamy, like, superweird?"

asked Bree. "I mean, I figure I'd be weird if I was stuck in a wheelchair."

"Well, she's a little weird, but it doesn't have anything to do with her being in a wheelchair. She can be cranky a lot of the time, and sometimes funny as hell. I didn't like her when we first moved in, but I do now. She's really smart, likes talking about books and movies, and she has amazing taste in music. She let me download a bunch of David Bowie songs from her computer."

"That's cool."

"She's completed several triathlons—before her accident, obviously."

"Wow. Think she'd give us some training advice?"

"Sure. Let's ask her."

Following Cara's directions, Bree turned down the tree-lined driveway to the grand entrance gate. "Are you kidding me?" Bree said, getting out of the car. "Look at this place."

"I told you it was like being on *Masterpiece Theatre*." She gestured at the house and grounds. The heat of the day kicked into high gear. The air felt like an oven, tingling across her skin.

They went into the pool house to change. Cara had to stick with last year's swimsuit, but it still looked okay, she supposed. It was a dark purple bikini with a tie-dye pattern, and even though it came from the discount store, it didn't look that way. Still, she felt a twinge of envy when her friend put on a bright new bikini, navy-and-white-striped, fresh for this season.

Whatever.

Her mom and Alice were already outside, making their way along the path down to the lake. Ruby tagged along behind, looking like a condemned prisoner on her way to the gallows. She and Alice had made a deal that they would both go swimming. It would be a first for Ruby. Normally, she squealed and ran away the moment she got in up to her knees.

Such a timid little thing. Sometimes in her darkest moments, Cara wondered if Ruby might one day get as sick as Dad. She wished her little sister had known their father the way Cara had. Years ago, he had been active, brave, always laughing. But the dad Ruby had known was a sick man, struggling through each day. *Damn diabetes.*

Cara had this crazy idea of going to medical school and becoming a doctor and helping people so they didn't have to suffer like Dad and Ruby. Maybe she'd even go into pathology and find a cure for diabetes. But medical school—so out of reach.

"Hello? Earth to Cara." Bree nudged her in the ribs. "How about you introduce me."

Cara shook herself back into the moment. "Sure," she said, and made the introductions.

"Thanks for letting us come swimming," Cara

said to Alice. "It's the perfect thing for a day like today."

"I imagine it would be," said Alice. "There's nothing like plunging into a cold lake on a hot day."

"Alice used to do competition cliff diving," Cara told her friend.

"I'll stick with jumping off the end of the dock," said Bree.

"Mom and I fixed a picnic," Ruby announced, her eyes lighting up. "Egg salad sandwiches, chips, pickles and iced tea."

"That sounds amazing," said Bree. "We brought some goodies from the bakery to pig out on. Including those sugar-free spice cookies you like."

Ruby beamed at her. "Thank you."

There was a shady picnic area by the dock with a table and lawn chairs arranged around a stone-built fire pit. Music streamed from a radio set to oldies from the '80s, and they slathered themselves with sunscreen and consumed the feast, laughing and talking. It was the start of a perfect day at the lake. Lena brought a bowl of cherries and stone fruit, and the sweet juice ran down Cara's chin as she gorged herself on peaches. She didn't worry about the mess; it would all wash off in the water.

Even Alice was in a pretty good mood, talking about how she used to train for diving on a trampoline, and travel to exotic places in the tropics to compete. It was a bummer that she couldn't do it anymore, but she seemed to like talking about it.

"Are you going in today?" Cara asked her.

"That's my plan," Alice said. "Ruby and I are *both* going swimming today."

"Maybe," said Ruby.

"There's no maybe," Alice said with her dragon lady stare. "We're doing it."

Ruby's eyes widened, but she chewed her lip and didn't protest.

"Well, I'm going in right now." Cara stood up and kicked off her flip-flops. Then, before she could let herself think about how cold the water was going to feel, she made a run for the dock and jumped off the end. Airborne for a split second, she felt utterly weightless. Then she hit the water with an enormous splash. The shock of cold engulfed her, sluicing over her scalp and freezing every square inch of her skin. It felt glorious. This day was glorious.

She surfaced in time to see Bree join in, squealing from the cold when she broke the surface. It took only a few minutes to get used to the water. Cara swam in circles with strong freestyle strokes. Dad had been a great swim coach before he became too sick to do anything. She still remembered his strong arms holding her, and the laughter in his voice as they played in the water.

Sometimes the memories were like sharp knives being stabbed into her heart. When she thought about everything he was missing—this perfect summer day, how cute and funny Ruby was, how Cara wanted to be a doctor, how good the lake water felt—she wanted to sink to the bottom and find him.

She dived down as deep as she could, exhaling all of her air, imagining he was here with her somewhere, in a secret underwater place where the two of them could meet in private.

Miss you, Dad.

When she was nearly bursting with the need for air, she scissored her legs and shot toward the sunlight. She looked toward the dock just in time to see Mom dive in. It was a pretty decent dive. Cara liked seeing her mom having a little fun for a change. Usually all she did was work and worry. She surfaced, laughing, and they paddled around together, looking up at the summer sky and enjoying the day.

"So how's it going to work?" asked Cara, treading water near her mom. "You know, getting Alice into the water."

"Mason and Donno are coming in a few minutes. They'll use the ramp, and then we'll see."

"And Ruby?"

"She claims she's going to do it. Think she will?"

At that moment, Mason and Donno arrived with a bunch of gear—floaties and foam noodles, inflatable rings, life jackets. "We're about to find out."

Mason didn't look all buttoned-down and businesslike the way he usually did. He had on board shorts and a blue T-shirt, flip-flops and a pair of Ray-Bans. Mom said he and Alice needed family time together. He seemed okay with the plan, although Cara guessed that his girlfriend, Regina, wasn't too happy, because she called him and texted him all the time. She had her own ring and text tone, so Cara could tell.

"Come on in," Bree yelled. "The water's great."

Donno waved at them. "On our way."

"Do you need some help?" Mom asked, paddling toward the ramp attached to the dock.

"We've got this," said Mason.

Donno's mother, Banni, helped Alice out of her swim cover-up. Her suit was adapted to accommodate the catheter, and Mom had gotten everything done in advance.

Donno stripped off his shirt. His body was ripped like a professional athlete's. He was naturally brown and looked amazing, like a surfer from the South Seas.

"Wow," said Bree. "Who's the guy?"

"Usually he's Alice's driver, but today I guess he's my sister's swim coach," Cara said as Donno leaned down and fitted a flotation vest on her little sister. "His name is Donno, and he comes from Bali. The whole family lives here, helping out Mrs. Bellamy."

"Eye candy," whispered Bree.

Mason said something to his mother. Then he, too, stripped off his shirt, one-handed over his head, and set his sunglasses on the table. He carefully reached down and scooped Alice into his arms, holding her like a firefighter rescuing someone. His muscles went taut as he carried her toward the ramp. Her legs looked kind of normal. They lacked muscle tone but they still looked like a woman's normal legs.

"Ready?" said Alice.

"No," said Ruby, clutching the flotation vest and Donno's hand. "I changed my mind."

"We had a deal."

"But—"

"No buts. Let's be brave."

"Brave. Yeah, okay."

"We'll go together. Donno is an expert. He used to dive for pearls in Bali."

"Are there pearls in the lake?" asked Ruby.

"No, but according to legend, there are diamonds," said Alice. "Seriously. There was a stash of them thrown into the lake at Camp Kioga one winter, or so I hear. Put these goggles on so you can look around underwater."

"Okay," Ruby said again. She clung to Donno like a monkey.

The four of them waded down the ramp and into the water. Mason still had his mother in a rescue hold, and Donno had taken Ruby by the hand.

"It's cold," Ruby wailed, tiptoeing into the shallows.

"It's supposed to be," Alice said. She let out a sigh as Mason lowered her into the lake.

"You doing all right?" he asked her.

"Yes, it's fine. Let's go all the way in."

Mason gritted his teeth comically as he got in up to his waist and then went lower. Alice floated, and she let out a laugh. "It's wonderful," she said.

"You look great," Cara told her, paddling close. "How does it feel?"

"Strange. Most of me can't feel the water, but I feel less . . . paralyzed, I suppose."

Mason had put an inflated cervical collar on her, along with some shoulder floats. "Still all right?" he asked.

"Sure," said Alice. "Ruby, you're going to love it. Donno will show you how to swim to me."

"I can't reach the bottom." She squirmed and kicked, on the verge of panic.

"Easy, little one," Donno said. "Don't fight the water. You won't win. Just let it boost you up. Come, let's go and say hi to Missy Alice."

He reminded her to practice the flutter kick they had been working on all week in the pool. When Ruby caught on to how it propelled her, she laughed with the triumph of discovery. "It's working," she said. "It feels like *flying*. Mom, look. Are you looking?"

"I sure am," said Mom.

Cara heard a slight catch in her mother's voice, and she knew why. Mom was wishing Dad could be here to see Ruby's first swim.

The kid did all right. She made it to Alice, who was floating near Mason, all by herself, with a blissful smile on her face.

"Good job, Ruby," she said.

"We're doing it, Alice. We're facing our fears! I can't touch bottom and I'm not scared."

"The key to facing fear is simply doing a thing over and over again. The first time is always the hardest."

"You doing great, Missy Alice," said Donno with a huge smile.

"We're swimming. High five." Ruby took Alice's hand and gave it a kiss. "I'm going to practice my kicking."

"That's a good plan. Practice is hard work, but it's the only way to get better at something."

"Last one in is a rotten egg!" Faith yelled the age-old challenge and ran to the end of the dock, Cara and Bree hot on her heels. Faith hit the water first and then surged to the surface with a fist pump of triumph. "First," she said to the two girls. "And therefore *not* rotten."

"We tied," Bree said. "We're both rotten."

Faith treaded water near them, watching Ruby playing in the water, with Donno never far from her side. The little girl was so proud and happy to be swimming at last. It seemed like a small step, but to Faith, it was huge. "I'll tell you what's not rotten," she said, indicating Ruby.

"I know," Cara agreed. "I'm really glad she's finally turning into a swimmer."

Alice caught Faith's eye and sent a broad wink and a smile. Faith mouthed a thank-you. Then Alice turned to Mason. It was fantastic that she could maneuver herself a little in the water. "Stop hovering," she said to her son. "I'm not helpless."

"No, Mom, you're definitely not helpless."

"Then stop hovering," she repeated.

Faith shook her head at their bickering. Then she lowered her swim goggles and said to the girls, "Ruby's in good hands. I'm going for a nice long swim." She struck out, away from shore, loving the silky feel of the water over her skin and scalp, and the momentary sense of freedom and weightlessness. She and Cara were known for their lung capacity. It was just a thing with them. Faith dived down and explored the lake bottom, watching a fish weave its way amid the sun-dappled rocks. Just for a moment, she forgot the whole world.

The moment ended when a large male hand grabbed her arm and yanked her violently to the surface. She kicked back in confusion, breaking the surface with a gasp. She found herself face-to-face with Mason Bellamy. "What the hell?" she demanded.

"You were underwater so long, I thought you were in trouble." He floated back, rubbing a livid red mark on his rib cage. "You pack a mean punch, woman."

"It was a kick."

"A mean kick, then. You're just mean. I thought you needed saving."

"You thought wrong. I was minding my own business, exploring the lake." She splashed water at him. "Sorry about your ribs."

"That makes two of us."

Removing the goggles, she said, "Let me check. I want to make sure something's not dislocated."

He folded his hands behind his head, floating back. She placed one hand under him and gently palpated the reddened area.

"Jeez," he said through gritted teeth, "you're killing me."

"Really? Does this hurt?"

"Tickles," he said. "Christ, you have to stop. Nothing's dislocated. Nothing's broken."

She put up both hands, palms out, then resumed treading water. "All right. I'm sorry for kicking you."

"You're forgiven," he said, still floating.

It was hard to take her eyes off him. He had the

best-looking abs. And somehow, floating next to him on this perfect summer day made everything even better, gilded by sunshine. The thought unnerved her, and she paddled backward, away from him.

"I was looking for the diamonds," she said, to change the subject. "The ones your mother mentioned. Did someone really throw them off a dock at Camp Kioga?"

"So they say. We should check it out."

She sighed, swirling her arms across the water. "A cache of diamonds," she breathed.

"What would you do with them?" he asked.

"God, what wouldn't I do? Send Cara to any college she wants. Get the high-tech insulin pump for Ruby—"

"You don't need diamonds for those things," he pointed out. "You need a loan."

"Right. Banks don't lend money to people with no money. Ironic, isn't it?"

"You don't need a bank. You have Bellamy Strategic Capital."

"Oh, hell, no."

"So if you find the diamonds, you'll need to spend the money on yourself." He paddled easily, smiling up at the sun.

"Finally get those red Fendi sunglasses I've been hankering for," she said.

"I get the impression you don't treat yourself enough, Faith."

"If my girls are happy, then I have everything I need. And don't look at me like that. I mean it. You'll see one of these days, when you have kids of your own."

"Big assumption there," he remarked. "Kids? Of my own?"

"Good point. That would mean you'd have to grow up yourself," she teased.

"Hey."

"Waterskiing, kiteboarding, mountain biking, rock climbing . . . and that's only the first week you were here. You play all day, Mason."

"That's it," he said, surging toward her through the water. "You're going down."

She dived to the bottom, but couldn't outswim him, and he grabbed her playfully and dragged her to the surface. They both came up laughing, their faces close. Too close. She could see every detail of his lips, his teeth. His eyelashes, and the color of the sky in his eyes. A terrible and misplaced wave of longing overtook her, and she paddled away, out of reach.

"You know I was kidding," she said. "Honestly, you've been great with your mother since you got here. I don't know if she'd admit it, but she's really grateful you came."

He held her gaze for a moment. She could tell he was about to say something and then changed his mind. "Look how far out we drifted," he said. "We'd better head back to shore."

• • •

Cara paddled around on the stand-up paddleboard. She could see her mother treading water next to Mason. They were out a ways, but they looked as if they were having a pretty intense conversation.

Oh, man. Could Mom have a crush on the guy? That would be weird, but weirder things had happened. Cara's mom had never had a boyfriend. After Dad was gone, she went out every once in a while, but the guys never stuck around. Some ran for the nearest exit when they found out Mom had two girls. But mostly, Mom just wasn't that into them. Certainly she'd never given a guy the kind of attention she gave Mason Bellamy.

It was strange to think about Mom liking some guy. Maybe the strangest thing was seeing her turn into a brainless heap of hormones like any charged-up teenager.

Of course, Mason Bellamy was off-limits. He had a girlfriend or fiancée or whatever the hell Regina was. Plus, he was a rich dude with nothing at all in common with Mom.

But still . . .

"My turn on the board," said Bree, her head popping up like an otter's.

"Get on," said Cara. "Let's try going together." It was pretty easy, but half the fun was falling in and screaming. Bree, who was something of an expert at yoga, tried some crazy poses, like a headstand while doing the splits.

Two guys on Jet Skis sped by. One of them slowed down when he saw Bree on the paddle-board. "Is there room on that for one more?" he yelled, curving back toward the girls.

"Leighton Hayes," said Bree. "Oh, my gosh, I can't believe he's stopping."

Cara couldn't believe it, either. She paddled over, treading water near the Jet Ski. A puff of exhaust made her cough.

"Hey, Leighton," she said supercasually. She tried to act as if the school's hottest guy made a practice of stopping to visit.

"Hiya." His trademark grin was as bright as the sun as he favored first Bree and then Cara with his attention. "This your crib?" he asked, indicating the house and grounds of the Bellamy place.

"Not mine, but I live here," she said.

"It doesn't suck," he said.

"No," she agreed. "It doesn't."

"Looks like you're having a party."

"I'm not."

"Which one of you wants a ride on this?"

Bree paddled backward on the board. "I'll pass, thanks."

"I'd love to," Cara said.

"Well, climb on," he said. "Let's take this for a spin."

"Cool," she said, and hoisted herself onto the back of the Jet Ski. She made a big production of donning the spare life jacket so her mom could see she was being careful. Bree lay back on the paddleboard, and they shared a conspiratorial grin.

Don't yell at me, Cara silently urged her mother. *For the love of God, don't yell.*

At which point her mother said, "Young lady, what in the world do you think you're doing?"

Cara made a face. "My mom . . ."

He grinned and waved in her direction. "Just taking a little ride, ma'am."

Her mom yelled something else, but the objection was drowned by the mad-hornet sound of the Jet Ski's gunning engine.

"Let's go check out Spruce Island," Leighton said, turning his head to the side so she could hear.

"Sounds great," she yelled back.

He twisted the throttle again and they shot forward. Cara grabbed on to him and laughed with the thrill of it. It was a total kick, speeding across the water. He made a beeline for the small green island near the north end of the lake. The whole area looked vibrant with activity, as if everyone in the world had come out to enjoy this idyllic summer day. They passed catboats and canoes and little skiffs. In the distance she could see a floatplane tethered to a dock.

The Jet Ski rounded the island, and they flew past the shoreline of Camp Kioga in all its summer glory. The resort had a swimming platform with a high dive, rows of cute wooden cottages, families playing volleyball and croquet on the lawn, people lounging in the sun and reading books.

Cara wished every day could be like this—sun-drenched, relaxing, worry-free. She felt a little self-conscious about the noise the Jet Ski made, but it was still the coolest thing ever to be skimming along, watching the scenery go by, actually hanging out with Leighton Hayes. It was like being in a dream. All too soon, they returned to the Bellamy place, and he cut the engine.

"Thanks," she said. "That was my first time on a Jet Ski. It was awesome."

"Cool," he said, turning to take the vest from her. "We'll do it again sometime. I could grab some beer from my parents' fridge. We could get fucked up and take this baby out at night."

He had to be kidding. "And we should do this . . . *why?*"

"Because it would be a kick in the ass."

Okay, so the hottest guy in the school was not necessarily the smartest. "I'm not fond of getting my ass kicked," she admitted. "Hey, we've got a picnic going on," she said, gesturing at the laden table. "There's no beer, but do you want to grab a bite to eat?"

"Sure. What's your name again?"

Seriously? "Cara McCallum."

He trolled slowly to the dock, taking in the scene at the water's edge. At that moment Milo Waxman showed up, wheeling his bike across the lawn, waving a greeting at everyone.

"What's Waxman doing here?" Leighton asked.

Cara shrugged, cursing Milo's timing. "Don't know." *Great.* She was finally about to make friends with Leighton Hayes, and Mr. Save-the-Kittens showed up. It was just her luck, she thought, her cheeks warming with a blush of embarrassment. Then she noticed the huge grin on Milo's face. He was so damned eager and harmless that her embarrassment turned to guilt.

Shading his eyes, Leighton slowly surveyed the scene from the picnic area to the ramp leading down to the lake. "Whoa, what the hell is going on here?" His narrowed gaze focused on Milo, with his awkward walk and awkward grin. Then he checked out Alice floating with her paralyzed legs behind her and roaring with laughter, Bree doing yoga poses on the paddleboard, Ruby squealing as she attempted to swim, Mom clapping and encouraging them both while Donno yelled, "Attack position, little one. You can do it!" in his thick Balinese accent.

"What's going on here?" Cara echoed. "Looks like your typical swim party to me."

"Looks like a goddamn freak show to me."

As the sarcasm rolled off his tongue, Leighton Hayes didn't look so good to her anymore. His face was hard with superiority, his sneering mouth an ugly twist.

"Hey, I changed my mind about the picnic," Cara said. "You're not invited."

And with that, she grabbed on to the dock ladder, pressed her foot against the side of the Jet Ski and gave it a shove.

"Guess you fit right in with this freak show," Leighton said, and gunned the engine. He was gone with a roar like a chain saw, leaving a rooster tail of water in his wake.

Bree paddled up beside her. "I just witnessed an act of social suicide, didn't I?"

Cara laughed, feeling oddly liberated. "Probably, yes."

"Are you nuts? He was totally into you. I bet he was going to ask you out."

"I saved him the trouble." Cara grabbed a towel. "He's not so hot." She joined the others as Mason and Donno were helping Alice out of the lake. Mom brought towels and a robe for Alice, and Cara noticed something curious. When he didn't think anyone was observing him, Mason seemed to be checking out her mom. Maybe that crush Cara had noticed earlier was mutual.

Nah. She was imagining it. Or maybe he was just being a regular guy. Mom was not exactly a fashion queen, but she had a really good figure that she never showed off, except when she went swimming.

Cara turned her attention to Milo. She wrapped a towel around her waist and walked over to him. "Hey," she said. "Are you here collecting again for kibbles?"

"Nope, just wanted to watch you flirting with Mr. Dreamboat. Or should I say Dream-ski?"

"I wasn't flirting."

"That's good, because it looked like a fail. He couldn't get out of here fast enough." Milo pushed his glasses up the bridge of his nose. "Hey, Bree."

"Hiya, Milo. Welcome to summer."

"So," said Cara, "what are you doing here, really?"

Alice was back in her chair with her French terry robe on. "I invited him," she said. "Hello, Milo. I'm guessing you have a special delivery for me."

"Yes, ma'am. Would you like to meet her now?"

What? *Her?* Cara and Bree exchanged a glance. *Her?*

Milo went over to his bike and carefully took a small dog from the carrier attached to the back.

"This," he said in a voice filled with pride, "is Bella."

No one moved. The only sound was an old Eddie Vedder song on the stereo, drifting through the stunned silence as everyone stared. Milo set down the dog, patted his leg and walked over to Alice. The little dog trotted amiably at his side. Bella then focused on Alice, sat directly in front of the wheelchair and waited with her long, floppy ears at attention like a pair of ponytails.

Like everyone else present, Cara simply gaped in astonishment. Milo Waxman had brought Alice a *dog*.

And not just any dog, but a ridiculously cute little dachshund, with startling blue eyes, a smooth brown-and-white coat and speckled highlights at her eyebrows, chest and knees.

A *dog*. Had Alice actually requested this, or was Milo feeling foolishly brave?

Ruby stepped discreetly behind Mom. She had always been pathologically afraid of dogs. Even supercute ones, like the shiny little dachshund.

"Hello, Bella," Alice said, her voice uncharacteristically soft and warm. "It's nice to meet you."

The dog shuffled her front paws on the grass and made a little sound in her throat.

"She'll sit on your lap when you invite her," Milo explained. "The command is 'up.' "

"Bella, up," said Alice.

Without a single beat of hesitation, the dog leaped up and landed light-footed in Alice's lap. Alice looked at the dog. The dog gave her chin a single lick.

Cara was shocked to see tears forming in Alice's eyes. Just for a moment the dragon lady disappeared behind the loveliest emotion Cara had ever seen on Alice's face.

"She's wonderful," Alice softly declared.

"Thank you, Milo. I have a feeling that she and I are going to get along just fine."

Mom stepped forward and dabbed Alice's cheeks with a towel, sensing probably correctly that Alice was embarrassed about her emotional display.

"What a fantastic idea," Mom said. "Is she a service dog?"

"That's right," said Milo. "She's trained as a therapy dog, a companion dog and an assistance dog." He beamed proudly at Bella.

Slinging a towel around his shoulders, Mason moved forward and offered his hand to the dog. "That's great, Mom," he said. He grinned ridiculously at the floppy-eared dachshund. "But seriously, a wiener dog?"

"Don't let her size fool you," said Milo. "She's really nimble, and smart, too. I've been training with her for six months—obedience and service tasks. ADA law states that a service dog can't ride in carts or be carried, so Bella isn't certified in that area, but she's in compliance. You're going to be amazed at what she can do."

"Like what?" asked Ruby, peeking out from behind Mom.

"She's mastered fifty tasks," Milo announced, as proud as a new papa handing out cigars. "All are meant to help someone like Mrs. B with daily living needs, safety issues and companionship." He turned to Alice. "Like, if your arm falls off the armrest and you can't get it back on, she'll put it there for you. Or if you lose your covers at night, Bella will cover you back up. She can bring a phone and pick up dropped objects, including something as small as a penny in a corner. And she can dial 911."

"No way," said Cara.

"Way. And that's just a start. You'll see. Trust me, she's got mad skills."

In that moment the expression on Milo's face made him a hundred times better-looking than Leighton Hayes.

"You did a wonderful job," said Alice. "I'm delighted that you found me a dog so quickly."

Ruby kept staring. "Tell us some other stuff, Milo."

"Well, we're going to have to make some adaptations around the house. If there are tug straps on doors and cupboards, she can open them, unload a dryer and bring clothes or a bag of medications, tug off Mrs. B's shoes and socks. She has some computer skills, too. She even knows how to get a snack from the fridge and open a beer."

"No kidding," said Mason, looking as amazed as everyone else. "In that case, I know several ex-girlfriends I'd like to refer to you."

"Don't be cheeky, Mason," said Alice. She turned her chair toward Ruby, who was still keeping her distance.

"Ruby, come and take a look at Bella."

"I'm scared."

"I realize that. But you can still come over here and take a look."

"A bad dog bit me when I was little. I still have a scar." She stuck out her skinny white leg to show a small, fading scar on her shin.

"That was unfortunate. Now, do you remember what I used to say to my kids when they were small?"

"Fear makes the wolf bigger."

"Yes. And Bella's nothing like a wolf. She's not and never has been a bad dog."

"Actually, she was, as a puppy," Milo said.

"That's not helpful." Alice scowled at him.

"Just saying. Bella was abused as a puppy. Her first five months of life were spent locked in a bathroom at an apartment complex. The neighbors called animal welfare and they found her starving and being kicked around by some guy. Dr. Shepherd, the vet, said she was so malnourished that her bones might not grow normally, but we gave her a chance at PAWS, and she's totally healthy and ready to work."

"You see," Alice said to Ruby. "Bella has been trained, and now she's very affectionate."

At the sound of her name, the dog whipped her tail and perked up her ponytail ears.

"But what if she doesn't like me? Shelley Romano says a dog can smell fear."

"Remember how you went in the water?"

Ruby rolled her eyes. "You mean like, ten minutes ago? Yes, I remember that."

"You were afraid, but you trusted Donno and you did it anyway. Now I'm asking you to trust Bella."

"Okay." She looked up at Donno. "Come with me."

"Sure thing, Ruby Tuesday."

She clung to his hand and edged toward the dog. "Did you name her Bella?" she asked Milo.

"Nope, the president of PAWS named her Miss Bella Ballou. Now that you're the owner," he said to Alice, "you can name her anything you want."

"Bella is the perfect name for her. Do you know what the name Bella means?" Alice asked Ruby.

"It means beautiful in Italian, like the Bella Luna pizza place in town," Ruby stated with authority.

"That's right. Do you think Bella is the right name for this little one?"

Ruby looked at Mom and then at Alice, and then let go of Donno's hand. She took a deep breath, stepped forward and held out her arm, holding her hand palm up. Bella gave it a polite sniff and then a quick lick with her tongue.

"I absolutely do," said Ruby.

✵ 19 ✵

"This has been some kind of day," said Mason, handing Faith a glass of wine. He'd found a bottle of sparkling blanc de noir chilling in the fridge. He'd practically had to arm wrestle Wayan for it. The chef had incredible taste in wine, but he protected the collection as if it were the crown jewels.

"Thanks," she said with a fleeting smile. "It's showing no signs of slowing down. I don't know if I will ever get Ruby to bed tonight."

They were sitting together on a peeled birch bench on the lawn facing the lake. The frogs had just started their nightly chorus, and fireflies glimmered in the bushes down by the water's edge. Below them, at the water's edge, golden flames danced upward from the fire pit. Around the fire, his mother, Milo and the new dog, Cara and her friend were swapping stories, roasting hot dogs and corn on the cob, and watching the sun go down.

"A toast," he said.

She smiled, touching the rim of her glass to his. "To what?"

"You pick."

"I don't even know where to begin," she said with a laugh. "To the end of school. To Alice and

Ruby swimming in the lake. To Bella, the world's cutest service dog."

He liked the sound of her laughter and the way her face softened when she talked about her girls. "Sure, let's drink to all that."

She tasted the blanc de noir. "Wow." The expression on her face changed to a look of complete gratification. It was the kind of look every guy wanted to see on a woman's face when they were having really great sex.

He pulled his mind away from the thought. "Good, huh?"

"Yes. Is this champagne?"

"Nope. Blanc de noir. It means white from black—a white wine made from dark grapes. If you press red grapes and then take away the skins, you end up with white wine. So this, which I practically had to arm wrestle Wayan for, is a sparkling wine made from Pinot Noir grapes."

She tasted it again. "I love it. Seems a bit fancy for a picnic by the lake, though. Shall we take a glass down to your mom?"

"In a minute," he said. "There's news."

She frowned. "What kind of news?"

"After the gym the other day, I couldn't stop thinking about our conversation. You know, about leaving no stone unturned. I took your advice and made a call to Katia Hamini. I tracked her down for a Skype call. She spoke to me from a trauma center in Amman, but she's got a trip to

New York on the calendar. In her line of work, she sees spinal cord injuries all the time. She told me about peripheral nerve restoration. Have you heard of it?"

"No. I know there's the brain and spinal cord—the central nervous system. And then there's everything else—the peripheral system. Those nerves can heal and regenerate if they're injured."

Faith's eyes grew brighter. He wondered if she had any idea how he felt when she leaned in closer, her eyes bright and her lips moist with sparkling wine, seemingly enraptured by the conversation. "Does your friend think she can help Alice?"

"I described my mother's case, and Katia brought up a procedure called nerve detour surgery. It sounds far-fetched, but it's been done." He pulled out his phone and checked his notes. Not only had he recorded the call with Katia, he'd written down the main points. "Sorry, I didn't trust myself to remember all this. The technique involves rerouting peripheral nerves in the arm, creating a detour so they attach to the spinal cord *above* the injury." He put down the phone and set aside her wineglass. "Hold out your arm."

She complied, and he could feel her pulse flutter beneath his fingers. "There's a nerve here—" he traced a finger from her hand up along her arm "—that can be rerouted. The very first time it was tried, it restored function in the patient's hand."

He looked up at Faith. “You have goose bumps.”

She took her hand away. “It’s exciting,” she said. “The possibility for your mother, I mean. And the outcome is that she’ll get some hand function back?”

“Yep.”

“Mason, that’s wonderful. So what’s the next step?”

“Katia once worked with a peripheral nerve surgeon named Dr. Cross. He works at New York Presbyterian down in the city, and when Katia described my mom’s case, he was optimistic. There’s a whole team reviewing her records, and she’ll need to undergo further tests, but it’s looking good for my mother.”

“Wow. Have you told her yet?”

“Let’s tell her tomorrow. I have a feeling she’s going to be exhausted after today.”

Ruby came speeding up the hill from the fire pit, Bella leaping along at her side. The kid had very quickly gotten over her worries about the dog. No surprise, thought Mason. The little service dog was as impossible to resist as Ruby herself. The kid was still wearing her swimsuit, her bare feet and knobby knees grass-stained from playing with the dog.

“I made you something,” she announced, setting a paper plate on the peeled birch bench where they were sitting. “Voilà. S’mores. I made them myself.”

"Oh, man," said Mason. "My favorite."

"I said she could have one tonight because she did such a good job swimming today."

"She did do a good job," he said. He was beginning to understand Faith's vigilance when it came to Ruby's sugar intake. He took a big bite of the gooey concoction, savoring the ridiculously sweet, charred marshmallow and chocolate. "That's delicious, Ruby Tuesday. Thanks."

Faith nibbled at hers. "Wonderful, kiddo."

Ruby beamed. "Okay, Bella and I are going back to Alice. Already, Bella doesn't like to get too far away from her. She's very devoted." She took off, the little dog trotting at her heels.

Faith's face was soft with love as she watched them go. "Did you know your mother was planning to adopt a service dog?" she asked, then took another bite of the s'more.

"What? Uh, no." Mason had been distracted by a small drip of melted marshmallow at the corner of her mouth. If he was being truthful with himself, he had to admit he'd been distracted by her all day. Trying not to stare at her when she'd stripped down to her bathing suit had become a herculean task.

She looked incredible in a swimsuit. From the first day he'd met her—covered in a stranger's blood, yelling orders at Mason—he had known she was a woman who downplayed her looks. But the swimsuit confirmed his suspicions. Her long, lean legs and taut abs were on full display, as was one of the best racks he'd ever seen on a woman—anywhere.

This was problematic. He was in a relationship with Regina. Unlike his late lamented father, Mason was not about to betray a commitment he'd made.

He remembered something Faith had asked him, that first night she'd moved in to take over his mother's care. *Where does your mind go when it wanders?* He had not been able to answer that challenge that night, or perhaps he'd been unwilling to.

Since he had moved to Avalon, his mind had definitely been wandering. And not just to Faith and her big gray eyes and gentle smile.

The sound of voices and laughter wafted up from the lake. Just that sound, the sweetness and simplicity of it, reminded him that a different kind of life was possible—living in a quiet place, kids and dogs . . . There was a part of him that liked it far more than he'd anticipated, this feeling of family and belonging. Being here caused him to think about things in a new way, even to think about a kind of life he'd never considered before.

It wasn't real, of course, but in this moment, it seemed very real.

"So how do you feel about it?" Faith asked.

"What? Oh, the dog? I think it's terrific. In fact, I'm sorry I didn't think of it myself."

"You can't think of everything." She finished her s'more and methodically licked her fingers, one by one.

He nearly groaned aloud. That mouth.

"Hold still," he said.

"What?"

He reached out with his thumb to brush a bit of melted marshmallow from the corner of her mouth. And with every single cell of his body, he wanted to taste her there.

She gave a soft gasp, then smiled a little, looking flustered. "Messy dessert," she said.

"I don't mind messy things," he said.

She seemed to be staring at his lips. If he just leaned forward six more inches, he would be kissing her. The expression on her face suggested she was reading his mind.

"Mason . . ."

"Hey, let's go pour a glass for my mom."

"Oh! Of course. Um, I'll run inside for another champagne flute."

As soon as she left, he snatched up his phone and sent a text message to Regina.

We need to talk. Can you come up this weekend?

Faith wondered if Mason Bellamy had almost kissed her, or if that had simply been wishful thinking on her part. Yes, she told herself—

repeatedly. The almost-kiss had never happened. Surely she'd imagined that moment of vitality and budding intimacy.

By the following weekend, she knew for certain that this was the case, because Regina came up to visit on the Friday night train. And her arrival—a stylish whirlwind, pulling gifts out of a Birkin bag like a magician pulling rabbits from a hat—was a stark reminder that Mason Bellamy could not possibly view Faith as anything but his mother's caregiver. A guy like that had a type. And the type was embodied by Regina Jeffries—beautiful and poised, groomed to the last millimeter of her ombré-polished fingernails. She was educated and charming and a pleasure to be around. Even Faith liked being around the woman, which was great, because trying to compete with her would be an exercise in futility.

"Let's go fix something special for cocktail hour," Alice said to Faith. "We can have a little welcome party for Regina. I'll explain how to make a strawberry rhubarb fence hopper." Ever since finding out about the nerve detour surgery, Alice had been in a good mood. She'd already sailed through the preliminary screenings and was optimistic about the upcoming meeting at New York Presbyterian.

"Sounds delicious," said Faith. "Lead on."

First they went to the raised kitchen garden to gather some fresh strawberries and rhubarb stalks, a few sprigs of mint and sweet woodruff. She also picked some sweet peas, which had just started to bloom. Bella, who was never far from Alice, trotted along happily, sniffing the area. Her tail ticktocked like a metronome.

"The garden is looking great," said Faith, checking out the early yield of beans and peas, cherry tomatoes, marigolds and nasturtium.

"I have your daughter to thank for that."

"Ruby?"

"I wasn't much interested in gardening, but she talked me into planting a little of everything." When she spoke of Ruby, Alice's expression softened.

"I used to love to garden with my mother," said Faith. "She wasn't well, so she did most of the planning, and I did most of the work."

"Sounds familiar."

"Did you and your kids keep a garden when they were little?" asked Faith.

"No. I was usually too busy doing something with Trevor or planning something with Trevor. Knowing what I know now, I'd kick myself if I were able-bodied."

"Alice—"

"It's true. He was my main focus, and now I wish I'd been more present for my children. When I think back through the years, it seemed I was always rushing off somewhere with Trevor, either leaving them with a sitter or dragging them along without bothering to check and see if they wanted to come." She sighed. "I was not the best mother in the world."

"Quit being so hard on yourself. I've seen the way you are with Ruby. You're a wonderful mom."

"Maybe now I am. Could be she's my second chance."

"Maybe you're hers," said Faith.

"Nice to hear, but I don't know what you mean."

"This has been our best summer in a long time, Alice, and I give you credit for that. Ruby will always have her quirks, but thanks to you, she swims in the lake and made friends with a dog. She's stopped sleeping with the lights on. We might even get her to accept third grade without a fight."

"You're very kind, you know that?"

"What a nice thing to say. If you keep talking like that, you'll never get rid of us."

Alice grinned and turned her chair toward the house. "Let's go fix some cocktails."

They went to work at a small bar area in the lounge room. The bar had a rustic beam counter outfitted with a small fridge and ice maker, a sink and an array of whiskeys, cordials and exotic ingredients. Faith recognized the bottle of Lagavulin Mason had shared with her when she'd first arrived, but found herself bewildered by the liqueurs, aromatics and simple syrups lined up like soldiers for inspection.

"You'll need the shaker and the muddler," Alice said. "That wooden thing that looks like a small baseball bat. The ingredients are fresh strawberries and rhubarb, Becherovka—that's a special liqueur from Prague—vodka and sparkling elderflower water. The sweet woodruff and mint blossoms make a nice garnish."

Within a few minutes Faith had assembled all the ingredients and concocted the most glorious-looking pitcher of cocktails she'd ever seen. She made a smaller supply, minus the alcohol, for the girls. Alice wanted to serve it on the deck to welcome Regina.

"It's nice of you to include us," Faith said as she got out the good glassware. "However, it's really not necessary."

"I'm aware of that," Alice said. "But you're still on the clock." She laughed at Faith's expression. "And besides, I'm remaking my life. Isn't that what I'm supposed to be doing? Surrounding myself with people who make me feel secure and supported."

"That makes perfect sense to me."

Bella, the service dog, whipped her tail as if she understood.

"Just so you know, I wasn't happy when you told Mason I tried to kill myself."

"I didn't think you would be."

"I'm still not happy. But I understand why you did it."

"How are you doing, Alice?" asked Faith, adding cubes to the silver ice bucket.

"Better," she said. "And not so long ago I would have choked on that word. Since then, I've learned that life can get better. Now, let's get everything set out, and I'll send Ruby to find her sister and Mason and Regina."

Outside, Faith placed some shell-pink-and-white sweet peas in a jar on the table. "I've never done much entertaining."

"I used to enjoy it quite a lot," Alice said. "Of course, it all depends on whom you're entertaining."

"That's the key, isn't it?"

Ruby came to join them, dropping down in the grass to pet Bella. "Cara's not home. She's at the PAWS shelter working on some project with Milo. Mason said he and Regina would come in a minute. They were having a serious discussion."

"How do you know it was serious?" asked Alice.

"Their faces looked really serious. Can I take Bella to play on the lawn?"

Alice nodded. "Trouble in paradise?" she asked after Ruby was out of earshot.

"I'm sure he and Regina miss each other now that he's up here," said Faith.

"I've told Mason repeatedly that there is

absolutely no need for him to stay here. He can move back to the city anytime he wants." She tasted the drink Faith had set down in front of her. "But that's not why he's staying."

Faith's heart skipped a beat. She sensed Alice was about to reveal something. But just then, Mason and Regina appeared on the path between the boathouse and the patio. As Ruby had pointed out, they looked serious. Somber, even.

"It's happy hour," Alice announced. "Look happy, you two."

Faith busied herself pouring the drinks. "It's called a strawberry rhubarb fence hopper," she said. "You'll have to ask Alice why."

Regina took a tentative sip. "Gosh, that's sweet." She set her glass aside.

Mason downed a big gulp of his. "Delicious," he exclaimed. "Good timing, too, because we've got something to tell you."

"Good Lord, are you pregnant?" Alice demanded, staring at Regina.

"Jeez, Mom," said Mason.

"We've set a date," Regina said.

"For what?"

"For the *wedding,* Mom. Third Saturday in October."

"A wedding?" Cradling the dachshund, Ruby came to join them. "I love weddings. There was one on *InStyle TV* that was filmed in Hawaii, and it was amazing. Are you going to Hawaii?"

"The Pierre," said Regina. "It's a hotel in New York." She glanced at Alice and quickly added, "We're looking at venues around here, too."

"Where's your ring?" Ruby asked.

"Don't pester Regina," Faith said.

"I just want to see the ring."

"We haven't chosen one yet," Regina said quickly.

"I'm sure you'll find something beautiful," Faith said.

"Well, then, a toast is in order," said Alice. "To my son and his bride-*soon*-to-be."

Mason lifted his glass. "Thanks, Mom."

"I'll clink your glass for everyone," Ruby said, proudly taking charge.

Regina took the smallest of sips. "Thank you, Alice."

"Congratulations," Faith said. "That's very exciting." In a way, it was a relief to hear. This took him definitively off the market, and she could definitively quit wasting her time letting her mind stray to foolish places.

Mason tried to replicate the day on the lake with Regina. He had such great feelings about that incredible afternoon. He could almost pinpoint the moment he'd fallen in love with Willow Lake, a place so different from life in the city. His mother had been swimming, using her body to the best of her ability, and actually smiling about it. Faith and the kids had been practicing their dock-jumping poses, and Milo had managed to persuade the new little dog to come down the ramp and swim around. A certain song by Eddie Vedder had been playing on the stereo, and there had been something completely perfect about that moment.

"I have a confession to make," he told Regina.

"Mmm?"

"I'm falling in love with this place."

"It's certainly scenic," she said, lying back on a chaise longue in a pose of perfect relaxation. Maybe she was starting to love Willow Lake, too. Then she asked, "How are you going to live here? Your job is in the city."

"My buddy Logan's going to share office space and an assistant."

"Logan? I didn't know you had friends here."

"He was a client. I helped him fund a resort acquisition. He took over Saddle Mountain. It's a local ski hill. He's got mountain biking and a zip-line course set up for the summer. We should check it out."

"Zip lining? Mountain biking?" She laughed. "My favorites."

"Hey, you might like it."

"So this office space . . . and assistant. You're saying you'll be able to run Bellamy Strategic Capital from here?"

"It'll be fine. It's temporary."

She took a sip of her sparkling water. "Everything is temporary with you. What about me? Am I temporary?"

"Babe, you know better than that."

"Actually, I don't."

"We just told my family about setting a date," he stated.

"We told your mother, not your family."

Everybody here felt like family, thought Mason, but he didn't try to explain. She wouldn't under-stand. "Hey," he said, taking her hand and pulling her to her feet, "last one in is a rotten egg."

"Nobody says that anymore."

"I just did. Come on." Keeping hold of her hand, he ran down to the dock with her. Donno was already in the water with Alice, and Banni was setting the picnic table with drinks and snacks.

At the end of the dock, Regina balked. "It's going to be freezing."

"Only at first. Trust me." With that, he dived in and shot to the surface. The water felt amazing, a fresh sluice of crystal-clear coolness.

Regina wore a gold-and-white designer bikini, and an expression of grim resolution on her face. She executed a crisp, clean dive, surfacing nearby.

"Welcome to Willow Lake," Mason's mother called.

Regina surfaced with a loud gasp. "I hope you have a remedy for hypothermia."

He pulled her into his arms. She was trembling

from head to foot. "That's not helping," she said, her teeth chattering.

"Swim around for a while. You'll get used to it."

"I have a better idea. A vodka tonic and a nap in the sun." She gave him a quick kiss and swam to the dock ladder.

"She didn't last long," his mother said.

"She'll come around."

But the day felt different. It just didn't have the spirit and energy he longed for Regina to share, because he wanted her to fall in love with Willow Lake the way he had. So far, not so good. Something was missing. It happened to be Faith's day off, and she was spending it with her girls, so she was around, but not on duty. Apparently, she had promised Ruby a new swimsuit if Ruby would jump off the end of the dock and swim to the ladder. With that incentive, the kid had demonstrated her new skills first thing in the morning, and they all went to town.

In the afternoon he could see the three of them out on the lake, playing on the paddleboards and kayak, their laughter drifting across the water. Mason kept his focus on Regina, intent on making this work. She was gorgeous and smart, and together they made a great team. He could easily picture them traveling the world together once Adam returned and they moved back to the city. With Regina, the transition from single to married would be seamless.

"I'm stealing Wayan," she said to him.

"What?" His mind had drifted again.

"If you weren't so busy staring at her, you would have heard me," Regina said with a teasing laugh. "I said, I'm stealing your mother's chef, Wayan. He's fantastic." She sampled a dab of hummus on a kale-and-sesame wafer. She strictly followed a gluten-free, vegan diet, and Wayan was somehow able to make it palatable.

I wasn't staring at her, thought Mason.

Except he had been.

It was nothing, he told himself. She was just so different from anyone he'd ever known. She and her girls were a breath of fresh air, and they'd turned his mother's life around. That was it. He felt a deep appreciation for her.

"It's not that you were staring at her that bothers me," Regina said as if reading his thoughts. "It's the *way* you were staring at her."

"My mother tried to commit suicide," he said, determined to ignore his fiancée's observation.

Regina nearly choked on her vodka tonic.

"That's why I have to be here. There are things she needs to work through. I want to be here to help her."

"Of course," she said. "Mason, I'm so sorry."

"Thanks, Reg. I hope like hell she's going to be all right."

"What can I do to help?" She brightened. "I bet she'd love to be in on all the wedding plans."

He had no idea. The prospect of making wedding plans had zero appeal to him, but his mother might feel differently. He took Regina's hand and smiled at her. "She might," he said. "You could ask her."

Out on the lake, a game of chicken had started up, with Donno and Ruby versus Faith and Cara. His mother bobbed nearby, cheering them on.

"I think she's preoccupied," said Regina.

20

"I have a date tonight."

Faith stared at Alice, wondering if she'd heard correctly. She hoped her surprise didn't show on her face.

"Oh," she said. "With anyone special?"

"I don't know if he's special or not. That's the point of going out with him. Rick Sanders."

"The motorcycle guy." They saw him frequently at the rehab place, doggedly working with a physical therapist. He had a ready smile and kind eyes, and always had a friendly word for Alice. "That's great," she concluded.

"Well, I certainly wouldn't know. I haven't been on a date since I was in college. Trevor Bellamy took me to the spring formal forty years ago, and I never looked at another man. So it might not be great at all."

"Let me know how I can help you get ready."

"Call the salon—you know, that cute one in the town center?"

"Twisted Scissors."

"Yes, that's the one. See if they can get us in."

"Us?"

"You don't think I'm going to do all that by myself."

"But—Okay, fine. I can wait while you get all dolled up."

"Please don't say *all dolled up*. It creeps me out."

Faith had learned weeks ago that Alice got snippy when she was nervous about something. "All right, then, I'll wait and catch up on my trashy-magazine reading. I love magazines so much, it makes my teeth ache."

"Well, that's too bad, because you are required to get dolled up right alongside me."

"What? *No.*" Faith could not remember the last time she'd had her hair done at a proper salon. The cost was prohibitive.

"Don't worry about the cost," Alice said, as if reading her mind. "This is my treat. Consider it part of your duties."

The girls at the Twisted Scissors were sisters—Tina, Leah and Maxine Dombrowski—and proprietors of the nicest salon in town. Faith knew them because one of her former clients used to have a standing weekly hair appointment here.

Faith used to like waiting around at the salon because it was her one chance in the week to sit and look at magazines. She liked the ones that took her someplace beyond her world. There was something relaxing in the act of gazing at photos of food and clothes and gardens and decor—the everyday trappings of an untroubled life. Her weekly one-hour escape.

Faith had never availed herself of the Dombrowski sisters' services. A seventy-five-dollar cut and style simply wasn't in her budget. Besides, Faith had convinced herself that getting pampered and pretty were unnecessary indulgences for a home health aide.

When she walked through the doors of the salon behind Alice, the exotic smells of hair and skin products enveloped them, and she was hit by an unexpected yearning.

"Thanks for working us in," Faith said.

"As you can see, we're in dire need," Alice added.

"She has a date tonight," Faith told the sisters.

"Excellent," said Maxine. "And how about you?"

"No date for me, thank you very much."

"Well, you are going to have to go out, because I swear to all my stars and little catfish that you'll want to show off how good you look."

"I'll settle for impressing my kids," Faith said.

"Nope, not good enough. What about a girl date? You know, out with your girlfriends."

"I suppose I could, if I can get Cara to watch Ruby."

"Ruby will be fine at the house," Alice pointed out. "She can have pizza and watch a movie with Philomena."

"All right. I suppose I could always join the Friday Night Drinking Club."

"Why am I only now hearing of this?" asked Alice.

"My friend Kim mentioned it that day she came over. It's just a silly name. A group of women friends get together at the Hilltop Tavern every Friday to hang out and gossip, listen to live music sometimes."

"Perfect," said Maxine, tying an apron on her. "I've been dying to get my hands on you." Then she turned to Alice. "And you. I hope you're prepared to lose the spinster bun."

"In case you haven't noticed," Alice said, "there's a reason I wear my hair pulled back. I have special needs."

"Honey, we all do." Maxine draped a large smock over both Alice and her wheelchair, then turned to her sisters. "I'm thinking foils for both of these ladies. Highlights are always a good look for summer."

Tina and Leah concurred, but they suggested doing more than hair. Tina insisted that they each needed a manicure and pedicure. Leah was a talented makeup artist, and she promised amazing results.

"This is a first for me," Faith said, staring at herself in the mirror. The foils lay like fish scales, overlapping on her head. "My girls won't know their own mother."

"It should become a regular thing, then," Alice declared. "Keep them guessing."

While they were under the warm lights, Tina and Leah took turns doing their makeup and nails. To Faith, it felt like an incredible indulgence, but she loved it.

"You're looking at me funny," Alice said to her. "Why are you looking at me funny?"

"I've never seen you more chatty and relaxed."

"That's the magic of a salon. It's a safe place to talk about anything, like a confessional."

"Well put," said Maxine. "Get things off your chest."

"My husband was unfaithful to me," Alice said, instantly grabbing the attention of the three stylists.

"Oh, honey," said Tina, carefully shaping Alice's nails. "Join the club."

"I suppose Mason told you all about it," Alice added, holding Faith's gaze.

Faith didn't confirm or deny it.

"I'd kill the bastard," Leah added.

Alice caught her breath, but then she said, "It's

already been done. He died in an avalanche, and I ended up in this chair."

"Oh, my gosh." Leah turned the shade of one of her designer rose blushes. "I'm sorry. I didn't mean to sound flippant."

"Don't worry, it's been more than a year. I'm adjusting to the idea."

"An avalanche." Maxine shuddered. "You must have been so brave."

"I don't consider myself brave," said Alice. "It happened very fast, like being swept into an ocean by the coldest wave you can imagine. It's hard to express the thoughts going through my head—panic, mostly. Regrets. My children's faces. The rescuers say I survived because I had a beacon and an airbag. So I can't claim to be brave." She bit her lip and her eyes shifted away. "I'm working on it."

"I'm sorry for your loss," said Tina. "Even though he cheated, I imagine it was awful to lose him."

"It was," Alice agreed. "But I struggle with feeling so betrayed by someone I'll never be able to confront. You see, I never found out about the cheating until he was gone. Sometimes I fantasize that I get to face him one more time. To ask him why. To tell him how I feel about it."

"You could tell us how you feel," Faith said, amazed at Alice's openness in the salon.

"I thought I was doing that."

"You're doing fine, honey."

"Not if you ask Faith, here."

"Hey," said Faith.

"You made my son move in with me, for heaven's sake."

"I didn't make him. He wanted to. And tell me you don't like having him around."

"I do," Alice conceded. She sighed. "I'm working on having no regrets about marrying Trevor."

"You have your three great kids," Faith pointed out.

"Excellent point. I suppose Mason, Adam and Ivy are proof that there was a reason I was with Trevor."

"Adam Bellamy's your son?" asked Tina. "The firefighter?"

"My sister's had a crush on him forever," Maxine said.

"She's actually thought about calling 911 just to get him to show up," Leah added.

"Cut it out, you two." Tina fanned Alice's nails while blushing furiously.

"Good grief, don't fall in love with my son. With either of them," said Alice.

"Why not?" Faith was startled to hear her say this. She wondered if Alice had given the same advice to Regina.

"Because I worry that my sons—and maybe Ivy, too—are damaged."

"I haven't met Adam yet," Faith said, "but Ivy and Mason are wonderful."

"You're right, but I worry about their relationships. They never saw the kind of love that lasts. My marriage was a lie. Even if I didn't realize it until recently, there must have been some sense of that in the family."

"It was real. You raised a family, traveled the world, did humanitarian work."

"But I do find myself regretting that I *stayed* with Trevor."

"Regrets are poison," Maxine said. "Do yourself a favor and don't go there."

"She's right, Alice. You have really great kids. Give them some credit for being good people. And they do know how to love. They saw your love every day."

"They—well, Mason, certainly—saw me being cheated on."

"I really doubt that's how he defines your family, or yourself, or anything else, for that matter."

As Maxine guided Alice over to the sink to rinse, Alice was quiet. She shut her eyes as Maxine sluiced water over her hair, carefully cradling her head. Then it was Faith's turn. She found the pampering to be utterly relaxing, and intimate in a way she hadn't experienced in a long time. In the course of her work, she did a lot of touching—but no one ever touched her back. She liked the simple sensation of her head being gently supported in the rinsing sink.

Leah added the final touches to their makeup, and Maxine took care of the blowing out and styling. When she swiveled the salon chair around for Faith to inspect, a stranger greeted her in the mirror. Her hair was done in long, golden-brown waves that caught the light. The makeup was subtle, giving her skin a smooth glow.

And then there was Alice.

"I need a tissue," Faith said, feeling an unexpected surge of emotion. "I might cry."

"Don't you dare ruin your makeup," Leah warned her. Then she smiled. "You both look fantastic."

Alice was beautifully groomed, the pulled-back bun gone in favor of a dramatic, short cut, a rich blond that highlighted her skin tone, graceful neck and lovely cheekbones. She looked remarkably like the young woman in the keepsake book her children had made, chronicling her adventures. And she was smiling in a way Faith had never seen her smile before—but not at her image in the mirror. At Faith.

"Look at you," she said. "You're gorgeous."

Faith blushed. To her knowledge, no one had ever called her gorgeous before. Not even Dennis. He'd loved her, but he wasn't delusional. "We both are," she said.

"We've got a problem," Alice said as she settled up the bill. She had an e-wallet on her phone, an adaptive device to help her make transactions easily.

Faith tried not to gasp at the cost of the pampering. "What, we can't afford this?"

"Don't be silly. No, the problem is our wardrobe. We need something new to wear. Let's go to Zuzu's Petals."

Faith wasn't familiar with the boutique. The only kind of shopping in her budget was window-shopping. "It's just down the street, isn't it?"

"That's right. Let's go."

They said goodbye to the Dombrowski sisters, and Faith propped open the door. Alice held her chin up and drove herself outside. "I haven't shopped here yet," she said, making her way along the sidewalk. "Ivy loves the place."

The boutique had a scalloped awning and a display of silky scarves and sundresses in the window. Faith was happy to see a wide door with a flat threshold, making it easy for Alice to navigate. Soft music and the scent of potpourri drifted through the place. There were a couple of women browsing the racks and a shopgirl dressing a mannequin.

"You must be Alice," said the woman behind the counter. She was fresh-faced and petite, all smiles. "Adam's mother."

"Does my reputation precede me?"

"He works with my husband, Jeff Bailey. I'm Suzanne."

"Nice to meet you. Is your husband away for special training, too?"

"No, he's home. We—He misses Adam." She came out from behind the counter. "How can I help you?"

"I'm looking for something to wear to the Hornets game tonight," said Alice. "Faith is going out for a girls' night, so she needs something, too."

"Oh, that's not nec—"

"Stop being tedious, Faith," said Alice.

"You came to the right place," Suzanne said, her face lighting up. "With your nice blond coloring, how about something in turquoise or royal blue? Something pretty and flowing . . ." She was a woman on a mission, showing Alice graphic tops, wrap skirts, pretty sandals to show off the pedicure. Alice was quick to decide on a gorgeous aqua silk wrap dress by a trendy Japanese designer. It had fluttery sleeves and the main selling point—it could be donned front to back and had shoulder fastenings.

"That's lovely," said Faith, holding the dress against Alice in front of the mirror. "You're going to be a knockout."

"We'll see about that. Your turn."

"But—"

The protests were futile. As she had in the salon, Alice insisted on treating her. She left the shop with the first new dress she'd had in ages, a fabulous halter sundress in a nice plum-colored print, and a pair of cork wedge sandals. They stopped at the Sky River Bakery, choosing an umbrella-shaded table where they could enjoy the breeze. As Faith had hoped, Cara came out to wait on them.

Her daughter stood there for a moment, gaping comically. "Holy crap," she said, "look at you two."

"We had makeovers," said Faith. She felt slightly self-conscious, but laughed at her daughter's expression. "Success?"

"Oh, my gosh, yes. You both look so pretty."

"We're going out tonight," Alice said.

"Alice has a date," Faith added. "With Rick, the motorcycle guy."

"No kidding. That's cool. Are you going, too, Mom?"

"On Alice's date? I don't think so. I'm just going to the Hilltop Tavern with some friends to listen to the live music."

"Nice," said Cara. She quickly brought them their favorites—Paradise iced tea and blackberry kolaches. Then she had to go wait on other tables. Faith watched her daughter with pride. Cara took her job seriously. She was just friendly enough, attentive and intuitive.

"She's doing well," Alice said, following Faith's gaze.

"Yes. Sometimes I feel guilty that she's working

rather than hanging out with her friends and having fun."

"Looks to me as if she's doing both. I don't think you need to worry about that girl, Faith. She's smart and scrappy, and she's going to do well at anything she tackles. She told me her dream is to go to medical school."

"She said that? She never told me." Faith's heart softened as she watched Cara taking down an order at another table. Cara had grown up with her father's illness, and now Ruby's. She'd always been interested in all things medical, but she hadn't told Faith her secret dream. "She knows I worry constantly about the expense of college. Now I feel guilty about putting limits on her dreams."

"Stop it. She's doing great, and she'll find a way to get what she needs, and you'll be there to help her."

"You're right, Alice. Thank you," Faith said. "And thanks for everything today."

"We both needed a lift," Alice said.

"True. But please don't make me a charity case."

"You have a problem accepting gifts, don't you?"

"No, I . . ." She didn't receive many gifts. Her favorites were homemade things from the girls —cards and napkin holders and picture frames. "Thank you," she said again.

"And thank you. This was a special kind of

therapy for me," Alice said. "It was good to talk about the things that happened in the past. I don't want to keep being haunted by them."

"Then don't allow it. Savor all those great memories of your family and the adventures you've had."

"The adventures were wonderful. It's just that I wish we—Trevor and I—had been more in love. We were partners, but there was never that deep emotional connection. Perhaps it doesn't exist. Perhaps I only dreamed it could."

"You didn't dream it, Alice," Faith said softly.

"Spoken by one who knows."

"Yes. I was very lucky to have found that with Dennis." Slightly flustered, she looked away.

Alice sighed. "I envy you those strong, clear memories of love. I don't have that, not anymore. I don't even know how to grieve for Trevor. I thought I missed him. But I missed a person I didn't even know. He was my main focus, but now I'm looking back and seeing us through a different lens."

"There doesn't really seem to be a right or wrong way to grieve," said Faith. "I used to think Dennis would be indelible, that he would stay with me forever. Lately, I worry that my memories of him are fading."

"Why do you say you're worried?"

"I've already lost Dennis once. Now I'm forgetting him in pieces—the shape of his hands, the sound of his voice. How do you hold on to someone who's been gone so long?"

"Maybe you're not meant to remember the details. Just the feelings. Just the lessons. Just the love."

Faith stared at her. "Wow."

Alice laughed. "You don't get to be as old as me without learning a thing or two." Then Alice grew thoughtful. "Perhaps it's supposed to work this way. The details fade because it's time to let them go. Time to move on to something new."

"I've moved on."

"I mean something new, as in a new relationship."

"Oh. Maybe." Her cheeks reddened. "I've dated here and there, but nothing ever comes of it."

"Clearly you're not dating the right sort of men. Listen, if I can do it, at my age and in my condition, it should be a cakewalk for you."

"Point taken. But I'm still going to stick with my girlfriends tonight."

21

"I could get used to this kind of rush-hour commute," Mason said to his buddy Logan O'Donnell. They had knocked off work early and ridden their bikes to the Hilltop Tavern for a Friday night beer.

Mason had helped Logan line up financing for the Saddle Mountain resort project, never an easy sell to investors. Both he and Logan shared a taste for extreme sports and high-risk business ventures. Now they shared office space in a vintage brick building near the Avalon Free Library.

"Completely different from the financial district in the city, eh?" Logan remarked.

"Yeah. When I ride in Manhattan, it feels like I'm in some kind of urban combat video game." They went inside, letting their eyes adjust to the dim, cool interior of the bar. The yeasty smell of beer filled the air. A chalkboard listed the specials—Dogsbody IPA and a local band called Inner Child.

Logan checked his watch.

"You need to be somewhere?"

"Naw, man. My kid's with his mom for the weekend. My wife was in the city today, but this is our usual Friday night hangout because of the good beer and live music. Nightlife around here can be limited."

"A microbrew and a basket of chips is all the nightlife I need lately."

"Sounds as if you're settling into the small-town scene," Logan said as the waitress set two cold ones on the table, along with a basket of chips and peanuts.

"It's definitely a change of pace," said Mason. "I guess I could get used to it."

"This place grows on you. I originally moved up to Avalon from the city to be near my son, and ended up staying. Now I'm dug in as if I'd been born here—new wife, new baby on the way."

"How is married life treating you?" Mason asked.

"Fantastic. And I never thought I'd hear myself saying that about being married. The fact that I got married again was totally unexpected. After my divorce, I had nothing good to say about the institution. Never saw myself going there again, not without a suit of full body armor. And then Darcy came along and exploded all the excuses and hesitation."

"That's great," Mason said. "I'm happy for you."

"Thanks. I'm not saying it was easy, but once I fell for her, it felt like something I'd been waiting for without even knowing I was waiting for it. Now I can't imagine life without her."

"To Darcy, then," said Mason, lifting his glass. "Glad it's working out for you."

"I used to think relationships were hard work. Now I know they don't have to be, not if they're right."

"My friend, the philosopher." Mason drank again. It sounded impossibly romantic. Maybe Mason had felt that way long ago, when he was a dumb, hormonal kid, crazy about his captivating foreign girlfriend . . . but that seemed like a dream, or another life. Regina sometimes told him they needed to "work" on their relationship, but Mason was never quite sure what she meant about that.

"How about yourself? Adam told me you have a girlfriend in the city. Says she looks like a super-model."

"He said that?"

"Yep."

"I hope he meant it in a good way. Regina is my fiancée now."

"Hey, congrats, buddy." He raised another salute.

"Sometimes I think about the fact that I got engaged, and I'm like, *whoa.* How'd that happen?"

Logan folded his arms and leaned forward, scrutinizing Mason. "How come I'm not getting a here-comes-the-groom vibe from you?"

Mason drummed his fingers on the table. There were things he tried not to think about, but certain thoughts kept cropping up, and he didn't really know what to do about it.

"There's a complication," he said.

"You mean another woman."

"God, *no*." He flashed on a memory of his father, kissing a strange woman in his Paris apartment. "*Never.* But . . ." He paused, frustrated with himself. How was it that he could put together complicated business deals that made people's heads spin, but he couldn't find a way to explain this weird feeling in his gut?

"Spill it, dude." Logan drilled deeper with his stare. "The doctor is in."

"Okay, I'll give it a shot. So it's all good with Regina. We work together, we like the same things, we've been dating a couple of years and we totally get each other."

"But . . . ?"

"There's this woman—Faith McCallum. No, hang on, it's not what you're thinking. She's a woman, not the *other* woman. She's in charge of my mom's care, a total impossibility for me. Nothing's happened. Nothing's *going* to happen. But I . . . We . . . I've never met anyone like her."

Logan leaned back against the seat and regarded him calmly. "Problem solved, then."

"What the hell is that supposed to mean?"

"It means you just answered your own question, dude."

"There was no question."

"Not aloud, there wasn't. But I heard you loud and clear. What you're trying to figure out is this—if I'm all in with Regina, why the hell do I keep thinking about Faith?"

"Wait, what? No, that makes no sense."

"The whole world agrees that love makes no sense." Logan shrugged philosophically.

"Bullshit. I wasn't born yesterday. Regina and I are great together. We both like to work hard, play hard, travel, go to dinner . . . It's all good. Believe me, I studied the terrain before I decided to settle down. We're a solid match, the two of us."

"Let me guess. Your families know and like each other. You share the same friends, the same social circles."

"Sure we do. She's just right for me."

"Oh, dude." Logan took a gulp of beer and set down his empty mug. "Been there," he said, "divorced that."

"How do we look?" asked Alice, waiting in the foyer for Donno to bring the van around. Ruby, Cara and Philomena regarded her and Faith with unmasked admiration. Bella skittered around, her nails clicking on the floor tiles. The little dog could read Alice's signals perfectly and knew she was being left.

"Come on," Cara said. "You know you look good."

"Beautiful color choices on both of you," Phil remarked.

Coming from her, that was high praise. The housekeeper had impeccable taste in decorating and clothes.

"You both look pretty every day," Ruby said loyally. "Today you're extra beautiful. I really like your hair like that, Mom."

"Aw. Give me a hug, sweetie. And remember, you can call me on my mobile anytime."

"No way," Ruby assured her. "Phil and I are

having pizza and movie night. *The Sound of Music*. She was shocked when I said I've never seen it."

"We were all shocked," Alice said.

"A gross oversight on my part," Faith said. "There's probably a special hell for parents who forget to make their children watch that movie."

"It's okay, Mom," Ruby said. "You can't remember everything."

"Thanks, Rubes. Anyway, you're in for a treat." She turned to Cara. "What about you? Plans?"

Cara offered her usual noncommittal shrug, but her cheeks colored a little. "I'm going to help a friend out with a project."

"Specifics, please."

"Milo needs my help with some puppies. They're too young to stay at the shelter over the weekend, so they're at his house."

So that explained the blush. Lately, Milo Waxman had been coming around, ostensibly to check on Bella, but most of the visits tended to end up with Milo and Cara going swimming or paddling together. He seemed like a great kid, dedicated to animal rescue and being eco-friendly. Still, he was a seventeen-year-old boy, and like any other boy, he probably spent most of his time thinking about sex.

"Is he home alone?"

"He's got a sister," Ruby chimed in. "Wanda Waxman. She's a real pill."

"Mom," said Cara. "Jeez."

Alice looked up at Faith. "You've had the talk?"

"Many times," Faith assured her. "All the time. Much to Cara's dismay."

Alice nodded sagely. "I've said it before—raising boys is easier than raising girls. Especially in the teenage years, when the hormones hit. With a boy, you only have to worry about one penis. With a girl, you have to worry about *all* of them."

Ruby giggled behind her hand. Philomena grabbed her and pulled her along the hallway toward the home theater.

"Oh, my God." Shouldering her backpack and bike helmet, Cara marched toward the door.

"You really have no filters," Faith said to Alice.

"I'm entitled," Alice said simply.

Cara turned back toward Faith. "All the bike lights are working, I'll check in when I get there and when I leave, and I'll be home by curfew."

"I don't like you biking at night."

"Fine, then teach me to drive."

"This very minute?" Faith shot her a look. "Sure, I'll get right on it."

Cara pressed her back against the door. "I'm fine, Mom. I've been biking in the dark to the bakery for the past two years."

Faith took a breath and let it out slowly. Her daughter was stronger, taller and smarter than

Faith had been at that age. Cara was streetwise and confident. She *would* be fine. "Call my cell when you get there."

"I will." She yanked open the door, probably in a hurry to escape before Faith came up with another objection or condition. Then she stopped in her tracks and turned back. She gave Faith a quick hug, then bent and kissed Alice on the cheek. "Later, babes," she said, and rushed away.

Alice looked after her thoughtfully. "Just a hunch, but I do believe you have nothing to worry about with that girl."

"And that's supposed to stop me from worrying?" Faith held open the door and Alice rolled out just as Donno was lowering the van's lift.

"Of course not, but make sure you have a good time tonight."

"Only if you make the same promise."

"Does anyone have a good time on a first date? I scarcely remember."

They rode to the ball field in silence. Donno turned the music to a Balinese track with soothing wind instruments and percussion, but Alice didn't look soothed at all. She looked like a woman on the way to her own execution as the ramp lowered her to the parking lot. The weather was perfect—a golden summer evening. The air was redolent of popcorn. The lighted scoreboard announced a special appearance by Yankees pitcher Bo Crutcher, who had played for the Hornets before making it to the big leagues.

"This is a bad idea," she said through her teeth. "I can't believe I agreed to do this."

"A very wise woman once said that fear makes the wolf—"

"Yes, yes, but you and I both know it's just a saying," Alice said.

"There he is. The big bad wolf himself." Faith waved at Rick, who was coming toward them very slowly, leaning on a cane. He looked fantastic with his abundant salt-and-pepper hair and a pale blue shirt, the sleeves rolled back at the cuffs. In his free hand, he held a small bouquet. "Go, Alice. Enjoy the game."

Looking grim, Alice rolled forward. Rick met her halfway and said something that instantly made her smile. Then he leaned down and hung the bouquet on the armrest of her chair.

"Let's go, Missy Faith," Donno said, leaning out the window. "She's gonna be okay, that one."

Faith felt strangely vulnerable as Donno let her off in front of the Hilltop Tavern. She was so accustomed to managing Alice and Ruby that once she was on her own, she wasn't quite certain what to do with herself. Together with the new hair and outfit, she was a stranger in her own skin.

"Hey, gorgeous."

She spun around, then grinned. "Hey, yourself. I

was just feeling as though I'm playing hooky tonight."

"And that's the point." Kim Crutcher gave her a quick hug. "I'm glad you could join us for once. You're going to love this group of gals. Some of them were beginning to think I'd made you up. I kept telling everyone, 'Wait until you meet my friend Faith . . .' and you never showed."

"I'm here now. Thanks for including me."

They went inside and found a group of women at a corner table. Kim introduced her to the gang—Maureen Haven, the town librarian, who was married to the band's lead singer, Eddie. Sophie Shepherd was the wife of the local vet, who was also the band's drummer. Kim's husband, Bo, used to play bass in the group, but since his baseball career had taken off, he'd had to quit the band. Jenny McKnight, whom Faith knew because she owned the bakery where Cara worked, waved from the far end of the table. Guinevere from the bookstore and Suzanne from the boutique joined them, as well. And then there was Claire, a Bellamy by marriage, and a fellow nurse. Faith greeted everyone, reveling in the feeling of being *out*. Childless. Clientless. She needed to do this more often.

"Just so you know," Suzanne said, "this gorgeous outfit she's wearing is from my shop."

"Such a great dress," said Sophie. "That's the perfect shade of plum on you."

Faith felt instantly at ease with these women. "Thanks. I'm really glad to be joining you."

"We're here every week," said Jenny. "Welcome to the Friday Night Drinking Club."

They all raised their glasses, and Faith sipped her sweet summer drink. Everything about the evening felt good—the music, the women's laughter, the platter of snacks delivered to the table by the good-natured waitress. It was the first time in a long time Faith had made her own social life a priority. That was the great thing about her job. There was always something to learn from a client. Alice Bellamy had a way of pushing people out of their comfort zone, and that included Faith.

She helped herself to snacks from the appetizer platter, her spirits lifted by the circle of friendly faces. She beamed at Kim. "I don't have to ask how the twins are doing. I get to follow them on your Facebook page."

"Aw, thanks," said Kim. "They're wonderful. You never post, though. What's up with that?"

Faith shrugged. "Busy," she said. "And boring, if you want to know the truth."

"Stop it," said Kim. "Look at you. You're glowing. Love the hair."

"Alice and I went to the salon today. And shopping."

"A very sophisticated form of therapy. One of my faves."

Claire Bellamy leaned in. "Good for you," she said. "Did Aunt Alice enjoy herself?"

"Immensely. She's at the Hornets game tonight."

"Nice. Glad she's getting out more. Ross and I want to drop by for a visit one of these days. And what's this I hear about the elusive cousin Mason moving to Avalon?"

"Since Adam is away, we—he—thought someone should be there for her."

"That's nice." Claire sighed. "I never had a family of my own until I married Ross. When they're not driving you crazy, they're the best thing ever."

"Mason?" asked Kim. "What's he like?"

"Drop-dead gorgeous and rich," Claire said.

"Emotionally unavailable and taken," Faith blurted out at the same time. She and Claire locked gazes, and she blushed. "He's the son of my client. And he's engaged."

"So does he have a friend?" asked Kim.

"He doesn't seem to have any friends," she said. "Not around here, anyway."

To her relief, the band started up with a cool version of "I Melt With You." There were three pitchers on the table—beer, wine and blackberry-infused lemonade. She didn't want to talk about Mason. She didn't want to think about Mason. She wondered why she couldn't seem to stop herself.

"Your husband's such a good singer," she said to Maureen. "I mean, the whole band is good, but he's amazing."

Maureen beamed with pride. "They're fun, aren't they? I'll introduce you when they take a break."

"Have you met Ray Tolley?" asked Sophie, indicating the keyboard player.

He was a tall, lanky guy in skinny jeans and a faux-vintage T-shirt with a "Willow Lake Surf Club" logo. Under a baseball cap turned backward, he had long, unruly hair and nice eyes.

"No," said Faith. "Should I?"

"Absolutely," Sophie said quickly. "He's single, and he's been checking you out since you got here."

Faith's cheeks heated. "Go on."

"He has," Maureen agreed. "And he's a big sweetheart. Very talented, too. He studied classical piano at some fancy place in Rochester. I bet the two of you would hit it off."

"Not interested." Faith's knee-jerk reaction to meeting a guy was always the same. She closed up like a clam. The only guy she didn't feel that way about was Mason. It was safe to admire him from afar, because he was unavailable. Which made him the perfect crush for her.

"How do you know you're not interested until you meet him and hang out for a while?"

"Believe me, I'm sparing the guy some

awkwardness. I've got two girls. That's almost always a deal breaker with guys." She watched him do an impressive riff on the keyboard in the middle of "Certain Girls." At the end of the riff, he looked directly at her and smiled.

"Okay," she said, blushing. "He's cute. Introduce us at the break."

Mason was picky when it came to live music. He had no patience for screechy, amateurish, poorly mixed cover bands. Inner Child was a pleasant surprise. The lead singer had a quick hand on the guitar and a soulful voice. The bass player—and the reason Logan had wanted him to hear the band—was Brandi, their shared office assistant by day. She looked totally different in her bass player getup—a plaid miniskirt and tight top that showed her bare midriff, a funny flat driving cap with a pom-pom on top.

"With looks like that, she doesn't have to be good," Logan pointed out. "But she is."

Mason was indifferent to her looks. He tried to enjoy the set, but he kept mulling over his earlier conversation with Logan. *Been there, divorced that.* How did a guy avoid making a mistake? Only by not taking a leap of faith in the first place.

Maybe his decision to move ahead with the wedding plans with Regina had been rash.

Come on, he told himself. Rash? He and Regina had been a couple for two years. They'd studied the situation from all angles. The two of them got along great. He could close his eyes and picture a future with her. A place in the city, and another on Willow Lake for weekends, once his mom was doing better and Adam returned. Trips together for business and pleasure. Maybe, just maybe, a kid. Maybe two. Regina claimed she was open to the idea, although she was quick to point out the virtues of nannies and household help.

He couldn't figure out what was making him balk. Or maybe on some level, he did know. Against his will, it seemed as if every time he pictured that future, other images intruded. Images of the life he'd been leading since coming to live at the lake, such as workdays that didn't extend through the dinner hour and into the night. Laughter around the dinner table, bonfires at the lake, the sound of little kids laughing, tomatoes ripe from the garden, music playing in the background, a sense of connection.

He was sure Regina wanted those things, too. If they worked at it hard enough, they could make it happen.

The band took a break, and music came through the speakers. A few couples got up to dance to "Wonderful Tonight."

Logan checked the screen of his phone. "I gotta bounce. Darcy had a late meeting in the city, and her train gets in at ten."

"Guess I'll call it a night, too," said Mason,

finishing his beer and eating the last of the chips. "Thanks for the pep talk."

"Is that what it was?" Logan grinned. "In that case, you might need another drink."

"No, I'm good. Preoccupied, maybe."

A burst of female laughter came from a table full of women across the room, on the other side of the pool table. "Darcy'll be sorry to miss out on that," Logan said.

"What is it, a hen party?"

"Her group of friends. They meet here on Fridays for drinks and gossip."

Mason looked at the group again, and did a double take. He felt a flash of recognition, focusing on a woman with long, shiny hair, leaning forward with her elbows on the table. *Faith.* Faith was with the group. She was laughing and talking, not taking care of his mom or her kids or planning and scheduling things. Oh, man. He'd never seen her all fixed up for a night out. She looked amazing.

"Perfect song for getting laid," Logan was saying.

Mason frowned. "What?"

"The Eric Clapton song that's playing. Women love that stuff. It's probably why he wrote it—to get laid."

"Yeah. Good to know." He was suddenly unable to think about Eric Clapton or anything else . . . except maybe getting laid. "Hey, go meet your train. I'll get this." He signaled the waitress for the check.

"Thanks, man. See you next week."

Mason nodded, but he didn't even watch his friend go. He couldn't take his eyes off Faith. He wasn't used to seeing her like this, chatting with friends, sipping a drink from a stemmed martini glass. He wondered if he should mind his own business, or go over to her and say hi.

As he was considering his options, Faith looked toward him, and a smile lit her face.

Yes. He should go and say hi.

Then he realized she hadn't seen him at all. That smile was for someone else—the band's keyboard player. The guy stepped right up to her table, bent down and said something to her. A moment later, she put her hand in his. They walked out onto the floor and started dancing to the getting-laid song, and for no reason he was willing to admit to, Mason felt a slow burn in his gut.

The waitress took forever to deliver the check. It landed on the table just as the song ended. He put some cash in the folder and stood up. No point in sticking around now. He navigated through the crowd toward the exit . . . and came face-to-face with Faith. Her dance partner went to the bar as she moved back toward the table full of women.

"Hey," she said, her smile brightening. "I didn't know you were here, Mason."

"Hey, yourself. Hazard of small-town life."

"I wouldn't call it a hazard. It's a perk."

She listed slightly to the side, and he realized she was tipsy. He'd never seen her tipsy before. Her smile was quicker, her gaze slower, as she looked up at him. She caught her lower lip with her teeth, and he noticed she was wearing lipstick. He'd never seen her wearing lipstick before, either.

"You're not driving tonight, are you?" he asked.

"What? No. I've had three cocktails."

"Okay, I'll give you a lift back to the house."

"Thanks," she said, "but I've got a ride."

Shit, the keyboard guy?

"Oh. Well." Mason knew he sounded like a lunkhead. "I'm headed home now." Home. When had he begun thinking of the lake house as home?

"I'm not." She shook back her hair and lifted it away from her neck.

He tried not to stare at her neck. "Who's with my mother?" he asked, feeling a flash of concern.

"She went to the Hornets game."

"What?"

"The Hornets game—they're the local minor-league baseball team."

"I know what the Hornets are. Who's with her?"

"Rick Sanders."

"What the hell?"

"She's on a date, Mason."

"She can't be on a date. She's—"

"She's what? In a wheelchair? Old enough to be your mother?"

"Yes. What's the deal with this guy?" He had a nightmare image of the motorcycle guy with his mom. His defenseless mom.

"The deal is, they're on a date. She's a grown woman. Dating is not reserved for the young and able-bodied, in case you haven't noticed."

"I know, but—"

"This seems to make you uncomfortable," she observed. "I wonder why that is."

"I'm not uncomfortable. Just . . . taken aback, I guess."

"He seems like a nice guy. And it's great to focus on something other than her injury and the challenges it presents." She studied him thoughtfully, moistening her lips with her tongue. "One thing I've learned in my job is that the heart wants what it wants, when it wants it."

"Yes, okay. Still—"

She touched her finger to his lips, startling him. "Hush, it will be fine. Trust me, I'm a professional." She ruined the effect with a soft hiccup.

At that moment the keyboard guy returned from the bar with two drinks. Mason offered him a curt nod and said to Faith, "See you later, then." He tried not to look as though he was in a hurry as he made a beeline for the door.

Faith wanted Ray Tolley to kiss her good-night. She didn't say so, of course, when he dropped her off at the front door. She didn't just want the kiss. She wanted to *like* the kiss. She wanted the kiss to make her forget the kiss she *really* wanted.

Stop it. Just stop.

But he didn't kiss her. And he didn't make her forget.

She let herself in, quietly shutting the door behind her. In the dim light of the foyer, she leaned back against the door and shut her eyes, letting out a sigh as she touched her fingers to her lips. She should have kissed *him*. Why hadn't she gone for it?

"It's after midnight."

She gasped, and her eyes flew open wide. "Mason. You startled me. And I know what time it is."

He was carrying Bella under one arm, probably so the dog wouldn't wake the household by barking. He set her down, then stood very close to Faith. His hair was mussed as if he'd run his fingers through it. His shirt was open at the collar, the sleeves rolled loosely back. As he planted his hands on the door frame, effectively imprisoning her, she caught a whiff of fine, smoky Scotch whiskey.

"I don't like you staying out so late," he said. "I want you here, Faith. I want you home."

It was a ridiculously possessive thing to say, even borderline appalling. Yet she found it exquisitely provocative. The fantasy part of her knew exactly where she wanted this moment to go.

"Mommy?" A faint, shaky voice whispered through the foyer. The reality part of her came crashing down.

Ruby. She stood there in her summer cotton pajamas, her Gruffalo held loosely in one hand.

Faith ducked beneath his imprisoning arms. "Hey, baby," she said, sinking to one knee and taking her daughter by the shoulders. Immediately, she felt the child's unnatural sweat, the shaking. "Is everything all—Damn it." In one movement, she scooped up the little girl and rushed with her into the great room, depositing her on the sofa.

"What's wrong?" Mason demanded, right behind her.

"Hypoglycemia," Faith said. "Honey, just relax. It's going to be okay."

"How can I help?" asked Mason.

"Stay with her. I need to grab her kit."

He knelt down beside the sofa, tucking an afghan over her and the Gruffalo. "Hey, you," he said softly.

"Hey, you," she echoed, her whisper thready and strained.

Faith raced to the kitchen and returned with the emergency kit. Ruby's symptoms were all too familiar—shaking, sweating, agitation—and they wouldn't go away on their own.

"Should I call someone?" Mason asked.

She knew he meant 911, but didn't want to say so in front of Ruby.

Faith shook her head. "We've been down this road before. Ruby's a trouper. Here, I'll let you do the fun part. You get to squirt the cake icing into her mouth."

"Seriously?"

Faith handed him the tube. "Ruby, don't fall asleep on us, okay?"

Her face was as pale as the moon, her eyes enormous and full of pain. "My head hurts."

"I know, baby," Faith murmured as she prepared the injection. She mixed the powder with the diluent and shook the tiny bottle, then filled the syringe, holding the clear tube up to the light to make sure it didn't change color.

Meanwhile, Mason fed Ruby the icing, which she was almost too weak to swallow. With quick, practiced movements, Faith tapped the syringe, pinched up an area of Ruby's thigh and injected the Glucagon. The child had so little fat that the needle had to go in at a slant to keep the medicine from going into muscle.

Ruby winced and then whimpered. Mason's face mirrored her pain. "Sorry, Ruby Tuesday. I'm really sorry," he said.

"Give her some of these pretzels," she said, dropping the syringe into the sharps disposal box. "I'm going to go make you a ham-and-cheese sandwich, Ruby. Your favorite. Be right back."

As she worked hastily in the kitchen, Faith was on adrenaline-induced autopilot, the sensation familiar, circling her heart and her mind back to incidents with her mother, with Dennis, past spells with Ruby. Every drop of alcohol Faith had consumed at the Hilltop had evaporated the moment she'd realized something was wrong with Ruby.

Suppose this was a punishment for neglecting her kid and haring off to a night at a bar? Maybe it was a punishment for craving the forbidden fruit that was Mason Bellamy.

She was just finishing up with the sandwich when she heard faint music drifting sweetly from the great room. The melody was as soft and delicate as a whisper, expertly played. Grabbing the sandwich and a tea towel, she hurried back to Ruby.

It wasn't a recording, but Mason, seated at the Steinway, gently stroking a Chopin nocturne from the instrument. He glanced up as she entered, but didn't stop playing. Ruby lay placidly on the sofa, her color already better as she munched on a pretzel. Next to her were Bella the dog and her Gruffalo, looking cozy and content. Faith sat down on the floor next to her and did a quick check of her levels, then fed her half the sandwich. At some point, Ruby drifted off to sleep.

Faith stood up, gazing down at the beautiful

child, her angel face relaxed now, and flush with color. The music trailed off into silence, and she felt Mason step up behind her, closing his hands over her shoulders. She collapsed against him, melting into his strength. It felt incredible to simply surrender, even for a few seconds, before reeling herself back in.

"Okay. It's okay, Faith." His whisper was warm in her ear.

"I know. Sorry. I'm being silly. Like I said, this is nothing new for us. But each time . . . It never gets easier."

"And it shouldn't, so don't apologize. What the hell was that, anyway? Explain to me."

"Hypoglycemia is another name for low blood sugar. Even when we're careful, it can happen if Ruby gets too much insulin, or exercises too much, or doesn't eat enough. Maybe she was excited about the movie tonight and didn't eat her dinner. Could be she was running around with the dog. Anyway, it can develop quickly in people with diabetes. She was right to come and get us . . . I mean, me. By now, she's familiar with the symptoms—weakness, sweating, shaking, headache."

"And if she hadn't come to us?" he asked softly.

"It can get bad, fast. If it goes on too long, it could cause seizure, coma or death." She nearly choked on the word as she stepped away and turned to face him.

He was gazing down at Ruby, his expression one of stark pain. "I don't know how you do it," he murmured.

"It's a lot," she said. "But I just do it. I always have. This is what it feels like to love a child more than you love your own life."

He furrowed his fingers through his hair in the familiar gesture, then looked deep into Faith's eyes. "How can we keep this from happening?"

"Keep this . . ." Did he mean *them?* Or Ruby? Faith went with the safe assumption. "There are no guarantees. It's something that can happen to someone with her condition. We're vigilant, we try to keep the levels right, but sometimes it goes off track."

"So taking her to a specialist, maybe getting different equipment . . . ?"

"There are some new technologies, like an implanted pump or even an artificial pancreas, but since they're so new and specialized, they aren't covered by my insurance program," she said. "And there's a jet injector that's more advanced, but it's not covered, either. The nozzles, jets and other parts have a high price tag, but I'm saving up for one."

"We'll get one tomorrow," he said. "And we'll find a specialist to look into the other therapies."

She bristled then. "*We* will not. I appreciate your concern, but—"

"It's not concern," he snapped. "It's just

common sense. You've heard of that, right? Common sense?"

Her eyes narrowed. "I know what you're doing. You do this a lot—you're trying to convince the world that you're a jerk. Why is that?"

"Because I *am* a jerk."

"Who rescues people."

"What? Bullshit."

"Don't look so surprised. I'm the help, remember? We talk among ourselves. I know you saved Phil from an abusive relationship, and Wayan's family from being separated. Lena said you paid for all her schooling and green card—"

"I'm always in the market for a tax write-off," he said with an arrogant wave of his hand.

"Then don't bother with us. We aren't interested in being anyone's write-off."

22

Faith was still getting used to her new image in the mirror. It was momentarily startling to get up in the morning and see her face framed by the long, styled cut and highlights. She dressed in white crop pants and a sleeveless checkered blouse, and even applied a touch of makeup, trying to emulate the technique of the salon.

Ruby had had a restful night. Unlike Faith. As

she went downstairs, she struggled to turn off the replaying reel of last night with Mason.

"Very nice," said Alice, who was in the kitchen, just finishing her breakfast.

"You, too," Faith said. "I love that haircut on you." She did a quick check of Ruby's chart to make sure her levels were all right. Next to Ruby's kit, she noticed an unopened box. Contents—a jet injector, and a supply of disposable injection chambers. "Where did this come from?"

"Donno picked that up at the twenty-four-hour pharmacy last night," Alice said.

Faith gritted her teeth, trying not to let her exasperation show. She was *not* going to let Mason play fairy godfather. Then she scanned Alice's care chart. There was another appointment with the neurologist and surgeon today to discuss the nerve transfer procedure.

"Shall we compare notes, then?" asked Alice. "How was your evening?"

Faith kept her head down, hoping to hide the flush in her cheeks. "It was great. I had a little too much to drink, and just the right amount of fun." That much was true. She'd enjoyed hanging out with the girls and listening to the local band. Her dance with Ray Tolley marked the first time she'd danced with a guy since a friend's wedding reception last year. He seemed like a nice-enough guy, a local musician. When he'd asked for her number, she'd gotten flustered. It was silly. She was thirty-four years old, far too mature to get flustered.

Seeing Mason at the bar had only made things worse. Unlike Ray, Mason wasn't simply "nice." He was . . . complicated. And *taken,* she was quick to remind herself. Last night's spat was proof that they didn't get along. She needed to remember that for those times when they seemed to be getting along too well.

"I need details," Alice said.

"What?" Faith knew a moment of panic. "Oh, about the Hilltop. Let's see. I had three cocktails—something called a blackberry fizz. Fresh blackberries, honey, lemon, vodka and seltzer. They were excellent, so I had a fourth one, without the vodka. The group playing was called Inner Child and they were fantastic, too. Lots of nineties cover songs, and some original stuff."

Alice yawned audibly. "You're boring me."

"Okay, I made some new friends. I danced with one guy. His name is Ray, and he plays keyboard with the band. I gave him my number."

Now her eyebrows shot up. "And when he calls . . . ?"

I'll wish he was someone else. "Then we'll see. Now it's your turn. I need details, too. Not the boring ones. What is Rick Sanders like?"

Alice's mouth softened into not quite a smile. "The game was far more entertaining than expected. I had a beer and a hot dog, and it wasn't weird at all that he helped me eat. After the game, we went up to Blanchard Park for ice cream."

"Now who's boring whom?" asked Faith. "You haven't told me what he's *like*."

"He had a career as a photojournalist for the Associated Press, and it turns out we've been to many of the same places. Now he's a stringer, working freelance and living in Woodstock."

Faith mimicked her exaggerated yawn. "That's his résumé, Alice."

"All right." She sighed, and her smile blossomed. "He's lovely—interesting and interested. We got along very well, and we're going to a movie next week. And he wasn't the least bit disconcerted about me being a quadriplegic. And having a man hold my ice cream cone for me was oddly . . . gratifying. How's that?"

"Much better." Faith paid as much attention to Alice's face as she did to her words. Everything about Alice seemed softer, more engaged. It could be due to her anticipation of today's appointment. Or it could be her new friendship with Rick Sanders.

"Morning, ladies." Looking impossibly put together, in khakis and a fitted shirt, Mason came into the kitchen. He bent and kissed his mother's cheek in a gesture that seemed natural and unforced—a gratifying change for them, Faith observed. Then he turned to her, and a beat passed. It was brief, just a blip, but in that moment, a thousand questions crowded into her mind. What did they do now? Pretend nothing had happened last night? Make a silent pact to avoid mentioning it? Ever?

"How's Ruby?" he asked.

Faith let out a breath she hadn't realized she was holding. "Fine. She had a restful night."

"Did something happen to Ruby?" Alice's eyes filled with fear.

"Low blood sugar," Faith said. "It happens. She bounced right back."

"Well, that's a relief." Alice looked at Mason. "There's coffee," she said. "I'll take a refill, please."

"Sure." He looked from Alice to Faith. "Did I interrupt something?"

"Your mother was just telling me about her date with Rick Sanders," Faith said. She still felt defensive about the way Mason had challenged her last night, questioning her judgment.

His eyes narrowed. "And?"

"It was perfectly fine," Alice said, "and we're going out again, so stop looking at me like that."

"Like what?"

"Like you're my keeper."

"I'm not—"

"Yes, you are."

"Excuse me for being concerned about my mother."

"I do appreciate your concern, but in this case, it's misplaced."

He gave her a fresh cup of coffee and positioned the straw. "All right, then. I'm cool with it, Mom. Really. Just . . . takes a little getting used to."

"What takes getting used to?" asked Ruby, coming into the kitchen. With practiced efficiency, she got out her kit and checked her levels.

"My mom going out on a date," said Mason.

"I know what you mean," Ruby said easily. "When my mom goes out on a date, I think it's weird."

"Yeah?" His back stiffened visibly.

"Uh-huh. Cara says she should get a regular boyfriend, but she never does."

"Excuse me," said Faith, feeling a terrible blush in her cheeks. "Since when do you go around discussing my personal life?"

"Since when do you *have* a personal life?" Cara asked, entering the kitchen with a big yawn.

"Don't you think my mom and your mom look pretty with their new hair?" Ruby asked Mason.

"They've always been pretty," Mason replied. "And I've always noticed that." Ignoring Faith's mortified expression, he asked, "How are you feeling today, Ruby Tuesday?"

"I'm good. Thank you for the music last night. You're really good on the piano."

"He played the piano?" asked Alice.

"Yes, but we shut the doors and he played very *pianissimo* until I went back to sleep."

"Goodness. That was certainly . . . paternal of you, Mason," said Alice.

He cleared his throat. "What time are we leaving for the surgeon?"

"I told Donno nine o'clock," said Faith.

He checked his watch. "That's good. And then—" His phone made a sound, and he checked the screen. Faith noticed that when he was thinking, a small single crease appeared between his brows. She noticed far too many things about him.

Mason's nerves buzzed with tension as everyone gathered for his mother's surgical consultation. This mattered to him even more than he'd imagined.

Presbyterian Hospital in Manhattan resembled a postindustrial cathedral, its twin wings and grand entryway both beautiful and forbidding. The final meeting was in a high-rise clinical annex adjacent to the hospital. Floor-to-ceiling windows framed a view of gardens and the river beyond, busy with freighters and ferryboats, the bridges delicately strung against the summer sky.

A bewildering array of neurological tests had already been done, along with psychological and social assessments to determine whether or not the nerve detour surgery would help his mother. What remained was for Dr. Cross, the peripheral nerve specialist, and the team of experts to evaluate her prospects for improvement following the neurosurgery procedure.

Mason checked his watch. Regina had planned to join him here, to be present for the final meeting about his mother's case. She was late.

"Everything all right?" asked Faith.

When he looked at her, the buzz of tension subsided a little. "Ask me once this meeting is over," he said.

She offered a soft smile. "It's been a long day for everyone."

"Mom's been a champ," he said.

"I have not." His mother moved her chair forward, Bella obediently keeping pace at her side. "I'm a wreck."

"You look fantastic," Faith said quickly.

Mason's phone vibrated with an incoming message. A quick check revealed a note from Regina.

> Wedding planner stuck in traffic, running super late. Probably not going to make it up to the hospital in time. So sorry. Good luck!

He glanced up to see his mother and Faith watching him. "Regina can't make it, after all," he said, dismissing the message with a swipe of his thumb. "She says to wish you luck."

His mother offered a tight smile; he couldn't

tell if she was expressing nervousness or disapproval. "Well, then," she said, turning her chair toward the conference room. "I suppose we can get started."

"I'll stay out here during the consultation," Faith said, scanning the nearly empty waiting room for a place to sit.

Mason looked at his mother. And she was looking at Faith. "I'd prefer it if you'd come to the meeting," she said.

"Alice, I'm no specialist—"

"We appear to have enough of those," said his mother, sweeping the room with a glance. "The surgery coordinator places a special emphasis on the patient's home environment." She swiveled to face the coordinator, an officious-looking middle-aged woman with a clipboard and a bun. "Isn't that correct?"

"Indeed it is," the woman said. "This is a major commitment, not just for the patient but for the entire family. A support system is crucial in order to get us to a successful outcome."

"There you have it," his mother told Faith. "We need you at the meeting. You're family."

Faith's smile lit the room like the sun coming through the clouds. Had she always had that effect on a room full of people, or was he only just now noticing it?

"Thanks, Alice. I'd love to join you."

Mason forgot his irritation with Regina as they

gathered in the conference room. He noticed that Faith had a way of touching his mother where she could feel it, the shoulder or the upper back. This woman was a gift, he thought, not for the first time.

"There you are, you ridiculous man."

Mason swung toward the door. He would know that low voice, that British accent, anywhere. "Katia. Thanks for coming. Why am I ridiculous?"

"Because you waited so long to call me."

Striding across the room, he pulled her into a fierce hug. So much had changed, yet so much was the same—the sandalwood scent of her skin and hair, the smooth song of her voice. She would always be the girl he'd fallen in love with when he was seventeen, the girl who had changed his world. And here they were, their youth stolen by violence and the passage of years, and yet she was still so beautiful.

It was a strange moment, a collision of the past and present. He could see Faith studying Katia. Faith was probably thinking about the story he'd related about that long-ago summer. So, apparently, was his mother.

"Katia, I've waited twenty years to meet you," she said.

"It's an honor, Alice. And I'm honored that Mason finally called me to help." Her warm brown eyes took in the team. They had moved into the conference room and were setting up charts and models. "I can already tell you're surrounded by talent."

"I like to think so." His mother regarded Katia for a moment. "I've met the others my son was with in the metro explosion—Lisa, Malcolm and Taye—but never you."

"My family moved to London that summer. Paris did not seem like a safe place for us," Katia explained. She seemed incredibly poised as she took a seat next to Mason's mother. "Is there anything you want to ask me about that day?"

"Is there anything you want to tell me about that day?"

They spoke softly, yet the moment felt tense.

"I can tell you I felt an enormous sense of guilt that people were injured in the blast," Katia said. "My father's friends made me leave the metro station shortly before the blast."

"You never told me that," Mason's mother said to him. Then she turned to Katia. "Are you saying these 'friends' had some kind of foreknowledge of the attack?"

"I'll never know for certain. After they took me home that night, we never saw them again."

Mason had unconsciously moved closer to Faith. She seemed to sense how agitated he was from this conversation, because she gave his arm a reassuring touch.

"Katia," said Faith, "you've had such a remarkable life and career. I read about you online."

"Oh, dear. Nothing terribly scandalous, I hope."

"On the contrary. Your humanitarian work is inspiring."

Mason nodded. "It makes me all the more appreciative that you made time for this."

She smiled and stood up. "We made a pact, the five of us," she told Faith. "We promised to always stay in touch, and to drop everything if one of us asked for help." Then Katia looked at Mason's mother. "This is the first time he's ever asked."

The surgical coordinator started the meeting. Everyone listened closely to the details of the procedure.

"Bottom line, Alice, your spinal cord can't be fixed," Dr. Cross explained. "We simply don't know how. What we do know how to do is reroute your peripheral nerves—the ones in the arms that connect to your spinal cord above the spot where it was injured." The doctor explained the procedure, step by step, in detail.

"There are a lot of steps to recovering," the nurse practitioner added. "The peripheral nerves we plan to reroute will have been severed and reattached to different muscles. It takes time to heal, weeks to heal and months to retrain your brain to talk to these nerves. You'll be working on strengthening your muscles, too, because they've been idle since your accident."

Mason glanced at his mother and then at Faith. Both of them listened with eyes wide and full of hope. The medical team was cautious but enthusiastic about the procedure.

"I'm ready," Alice stated. "The sooner this process can start, the better."

"You understand the hand function restored will not be immediate," said Dr. Cross. "You won't magically wake up and start mixing your own martinis."

"We'll see," said his mom. "I mix a mean martini." Then she grew serious. "Listen, I'll do whatever it takes," she told the entire team.

"My mother is a world-class athlete," Mason added with a surge of pride. "She has the mental and physical strength to go through whatever training is required."

"Good to hear," the physical therapist said. "You're going to need every resource you have. It takes time to reprogram the brain to understand the changes this surgery is going to bring about. Nerves that used to bend the elbow will now provide the ability to pinch, that sort of thing. Other patients report that this is the most difficult part of the procedure."

"I can do difficult," said his mom.

"Good. Sounds like your background as an athlete is going to help with the intensive physical therapy. There's a mental component, as well. You'll be retraining your brain to 'talk' to the new wiring system. Ultimately, you'll have the use of your hands."

Mason, his mother and Faith had already studied and read the materials they'd been given, but to hear the doc actually say the words was bone-chilling. His mother stared down at her hands for a long time. "That would be amazing after all this time."

"We can't promise you'll be playing Chopin again, but you're going to be able to do a lot more without using assistive devices. Operating your chair, writing with a pen, using utensils, combing your hair, brushing your teeth. These are all realistic goals. You'll have more use of your arms, and you'll be able to hold things precisely between your thumbs and fingers. You're going to regain control of the very thing that makes us human."

The expression on his mother's face was both beautiful and piercing. Mason realized that she had spent a year staring at her hands, unable to make them work. She must be blown away by the possibility of regaining control over them.

"You look as if you could use a hand now," Faith said quietly, and bent down next to his mother. Ever so gently, she took a tissue and blotted at his mom's cheeks, and then the two of them headed for the ladies' room.

At the end of the meeting, the conference room emptied out. Mason stood alone at the window, staring at the sky. The euphoria he felt was so powerful that it hurt his chest when he breathed. The hope in his mother's face, and the prospect that she was going to regain some of her mobility, nearly wrecked him. He was shaking, and tears blurred his vision, and his heart was about to burst.

Hearing a sound behind him, he turned to see Katia there, her large dark eyes drifting over him. "Your mother and Faith would like you to meet them downstairs," she said. "They need a bit of time."

He nodded, sharply grateful that they had Faith to look after his mom's needs.

"It's good to see you," he said.

"Likewise," she said. "Your mother . . . I'm so sorry. This will make things better."

He wondered how many I'm-sorrys she tendered in her job, treating people injured in explosions, car bombings, shootings. After the 1995 metro bombing, she had been consumed by guilt upon learning her cohorts had been injured. Maybe that had been why she had been compelled to practice medicine.

"I can't tell you how much we appreciate you referring us to Dr. Cross," Mason said.

She reached up and brushed at a stray tear on his cheek. "You just did."

"Where are you staying? Can I take you to dinner, or . . . ?"

"I'm staying at the Mercer Hotel, and I have plans for dinner—with Dr. Cross, in fact," she said. "Tomorrow, I'm off to DC for a symposium. Don't worry about entertaining me, Mason. You've got enough to think about at the moment."

She studied him with those long-lashed, probing eyes.

He grabbed a tissue from the box on the table, mopped his face. "Something wrong?"

"I'm not sure. How are you doing?"

"Great, like I said on the Skype call. Busy at work, lots of travel. Once my mother gets through this next phase, I'm going to go on a nice long trip, maybe try kiteboarding, or—"

"Stop." She smiled. "That's not what I'm asking. You showed me your heart twenty years ago, Mason. You've been trying to hide it ever since. Why is that?"

"What, you're a psychiatrist now?"

"You go all over the world on adventures, rescuing people along the way, but I've never seen you settle into your own life. I wonder what you're looking for."

"Same thing everybody else is. Looking for the life that feels right."

"I have a feeling the life you're looking for might be right in front of your nose."

He laughed. "In your medical opinion."

"I'll send you a bill."

Alice stared at herself in the mirror of the ladies' room while Faith washed her hands and reorganized the gear bag that traveled everywhere with them. *I hate that fucking bag,* thought Alice. It was filled with extra tubing, disposable gloves and drainage sacs, the sort of things no one thought about—unless they found themselves in this godforsaken situation.

Then her gaze shifted to the small, eager-eyed dog in her lap, and her mood instantly lifted. Bella knew a lot of commands, but the best thing about her was her attitude.

Take a breath, Alice reminded herself. *Look down at your hands. If this procedure goes as planned, you'll be using your hands again.* The prospect filled her with a cautious sense of joy. She had taken so much for granted before all this started. Now she finally took to heart the hardest—and the simplest—of life lessons: let every moment matter.

Faith turned to Alice with a smile. "All set?"

Alice smiled back. "Is my hair okay?"

Faith fluffed it with her fingers. "Beautiful. This new cut is working well for you." She stepped back. "Well. Exciting day, yes?"

"Yes. It's a lot to take in, but I'm hopeful."

"We all are." Faith beamed at her.

She really was a lovely young woman, thought Alice. It wasn't the sort of beauty that shouted and drew attention to itself. It emerged gradually, like a flower opening. Until she put on her bikini, of course, Alice thought, recalling the look on her son's face the day of the first swimming party. No man could ignore a figure like that.

"I need to spend some time with Mason this afternoon," Alice said, propelling her chair toward the door. It was going to be a difficult conversation, but since he had come to stay with her at the lake, she was confident they'd get through it.

"Of course," Faith said. "I could tell he was very moved by the idea of you getting some mobility back." Her cheeks flushed pink, and her eyes took on that universal brightness of a woman in love. She probably had no idea how her feelings shone. "We all were. I can't wait for you to tell my girls."

Alice studied Faith—her aide. Her friend. Someone she loved like a daughter. Yes, Alice definitely needed to have words with Mason. "I can't wait, either," she said, heading down the hallway.

The elevator car was too crowded for the chair. Oh, how Alice despised that. "You go ahead," she urged Faith. "Tell Mason that Bella and I are on our way."

Faith didn't argue. She always seized on any chance to foster Alice's independence, and Alice appreciated that more than anyone knew. Having Faith and the girls in her life had changed everything for Alice, and it was about time she discussed the situation with her son.

• • •

Downstairs, Mason stepped outside and flagged a taxi to take Katia to her hotel. Then he paced up and down on the sidewalk in front of the hospital. Here on the street, the world looked the same. None of the people hurrying by, going about their business, knew that what had taken place at the meeting was going to change his mother's life.

He raked his hand through his hair once, twice. His phone vibrated, but when he saw who the caller was, he let it go to voice mail. He was looking forward to telling Regina about the meeting, but not at this moment, when he felt so raw, when everything was so new.

"Are you okay?" asked Faith.

He hadn't heard her approaching him. When he turned to look at her, he knew his face still wore that raw expression. "Yes," he said. And then, "No. Don't worry, though. I'll deal. Where's Mom?"

"On her way down. The elevator was too crowded, so she waited for the next one."

He nodded, trying not to pace. "Damn, I didn't think it would hit me like this."

"None of this would have happened if you hadn't taken charge, called Katia and found a way to make this amazing procedure happen. It's a miracle."

"For a miracle, it's going to take a lot of work, but Mom seems excited."

"She is. I'm happy for you, Mason. More important, Alice is happy. That light in her eyes . . . We don't get to see that too often."

"True. Listen, Faith. I don't think I've ever told you . . ."

"Yes?" Her face brightened and her lips looked impossibly soft. He shouldn't keep noticing stuff like that, but he couldn't help himself.

"I just want to make sure I say this—you were right all along. I can never thank you enough for caring about my mother in the best possible way. I know she hasn't been the easiest of patients. Hell, none of this is easy, but . . . you've been great, Faith. Thank you."

"You don't have to thank me." She lowered her gaze. "It's nice that you did, though."

They didn't talk anymore, just stood together, waiting for his mom. When he was around Faith, he never felt the need to fill the silence with small talk. Sometimes it was enough just to stand and breathe the air and watch the world go by. The urge to touch her, just to take her hand or maybe put his arm around her, was way too strong, but he resisted.

A few minutes later, his mother arrived, gliding over to join them, Bella trotting at her side. "Well, now," she said, tipping back her head while Faith put on her sunglasses. "Things are looking up."

"Are they ever." He grinned. "Do you want to call Adam and Ivy, tell them the news?"

"I was going to phone Adam tonight and Ivy in the morning." She smiled up at him. "Thank you, Mason, for pursuing this. It's incredible to think the surgery will give me back some of my hand function."

"What do you want to do next?" he asked. "We could go somewhere for a bite to eat, or a drink to celebrate."

"That sounds lovely," his mother said. "Faith?"

She glanced at his mother. "Thanks, but I have a couple of errands to do while I'm in the city. Just send me a text message when you're ready to go back to Avalon."

He felt a momentary brush of nervousness as she headed for the subway station. Even after living at Willow Lake, he wasn't a hundred percent confident of looking after his mother's needs.

He felt his mom watching him. "What?" he asked.

"Nothing."

"Really?" he demanded with a twinge of irritation.

"She has a life of her own, you know."

"What's that supposed to mean?"

"Just that Faith is . . . I suppose we're so accustomed to having her close at hand that it's easy to forget she has a separate identity. She does feel like family, but she also works for us."

"For you, you mean." Discomfited by the

conversation, he took out his phone and checked his messages. "I'll be staying in the city tonight, if that's okay."

"It's absolutely fine. Is everything all right?"

"Uh, yeah. I just need to spend some time with Regina, go over some things with her."

"Such as . . . ?"

"Jeez, Mom."

"Oh, right. You get to grill me about Rick Sanders, but I can't ask about Regina?"

"You can ask," he said.

Donno moved the van into place by the wheelchair ramp and lowered the lift.

"Where to, Mom?" asked Mason. "Drinks at the Algonquin? Tea at the St. Regis?"

"I have a better idea. Let's go shopping in midtown."

"Sure, sounds good," he said. In truth, he ranked shopping right up there with rotating the tires on his car, but today was all about his mother. "Do you need anything in particular? My treat."

"A pot of Crème de la Mer from Bloomingdale's would be nice, if you're looking to spoil me."

"Always," he said. Cream of the sea? What the hell was that? He helped Donno secure the chair, and they drove toward midtown. The traffic outside surged along in fits and starts. Pedestrians streamed across intersections en masse, and delivery trucks blocked the side streets. A bike messenger nearly got nailed by a taxicab. He raised his fist and let loose with a string of epithets.

The streets were gridlocked in midtown. Donno let them out near the Pulitzer Fountain so they could walk the few blocks to Bloomingdale's. Walking around with his mother beside him was an eye-opener. Bella was at her best when she had a job to do. Even though she was short, she made her presence known, strutting forward with a confidence that belied her size. The little service dog had the ability to cut through a crowd like Moses through the Red Sea. When people spotted her neon-orange service dog vest, they tended to keep a respectful distance, even though there were lots of "awws" and "how-cutes."

Yet most passersby simply looked past his mother, though a few offered soft, sympathetic looks and made a great show of stepping aside. The world was not designed for people like his mom. A buckle in the sidewalk, a street performer or panhandler, a food cart parked too close to the curb or the ever-present towers of trash awaiting pickup forced them to take some major detours. "People don't think," he muttered, moving aside a tent sign for a nail salon.

"I imagine we were just as ignorant before this happened," his mother pointed out.

His phone vibrated, and he saw a text message from Regina.

Hope the appointment was a success. Drinks at The Ginger Man tonight? XO

"Is that Regina?" asked his mother. "Should we invite her to join us?"

"I could, but she's probably busy," he said without thinking.

"I had a nice note from her in my email the other day. Did you know she's considering Camp Kioga as a venue?"

"As . . . what?" He regarded her, distracted by the rush of the fountain and the crowd gathered there, jockeying for photo angles. "Oh. Yeah, a venue for the wedding. Works for me, I guess."

"The person it needs to work for is the bride. The groom just goes along for the ride." She looked pensive, then swung in the direction of the Plaza Hotel. "Your father and I were married at the Plaza. I can't recall making the decision. It just seemed like the thing to do. It was beautiful, of course. My mother wouldn't have it any other way. And neither would *her* mother, your great-grandma Marie."

"Granny used to love the Plaza," Mason recalled. "I remember Adam and I would hide when she came over, because she'd want to take us to high tea there. Ivy was always game, though."

"She was a good woman," his mother said. "I miss her."

She was quiet again, her mouth set in a thoughtful line.

"What's up, Mom? What's on your mind? The surgery?"

"Of course. But also . . ."

"Also what?"

"Just remembering . . . The whole time I was planning my wedding, I felt as if I'd boarded a train that wouldn't slow down, let alone stop while I took a breath. I was just swept along in all the planning and fun. No one asked me if I knew where I was headed or if I wanted to be on the train at all."

"And your point is?"

She swung her chair back toward the massive fountain and stopped near the concrete edge of the basin. "Sit," she said.

Mason sat. "Are you tired? Do you need a rest?"

She shook her head. "I'm concerned about you."

That surprised the hell out of him. With all that was going on, the last thing on her mind should be him. "Everything's fine with me. Everything's great. What's to worry about?"

"Your future," she said. "I'm going to have to be very blunt here. I'm going to have the conversation with you that I wish someone had had with me, back when I was about to be married."

"Oh, boy."

"Just listen. I know you're not a child. Quite the

opposite. You've always been mature beyond your years. But I've . . . Ah, I'll just come out and say it. You and Regina are both lovely people, but I wonder if the two of you are going to be happy together for the rest of your lives."

"That's the plan."

"Of course it is. It goes without saying that I want the best for you. I want you to succeed every bit as much as you want to. But lately, in light of all the revelations about Trevor, I've been wondering . . . and maybe you should wonder this, too. What brought you and Regina together in the first place? True love? Or your dad?"

"Mom, that's a low blow."

"This isn't a fight, Mason. I love you. I'm concerned for you. And I believe you've been on a lifelong quest to perform for your father."

The truth of her statement hit him like a punch to the gut. He was blown away that his mother had brought the topic up. The two of them rarely discussed their personal lives . . . until lately, he supposed. Until Faith had hauled him back to Willow Lake. Until they'd begun to talk about his father.

And the indisputable fact was that Trevor Bellamy had been the dominant influence—good and bad—in both their lives.

"Listen, nobody has a crystal ball," he said to his mother. "Reg and I . . . we're going to be fine. We get each other."

"My wiener dog and I *get* each other. But it doesn't mean I should marry Bella."

He laughed to cover his discomfort, because he had a feeling he wasn't going to like the point she was trying to make. "We didn't come to this decision lightly. The two of us have everything in common. We've got plans for the future. I know relationships aren't easy. Reg knows that, too. We also both know that if we work hard enough, everything will be great."

"Listen to yourself. Why does it have to be work? Why can't it be easy?"

"Because it can't, okay?"

"Yes. Yes, it can, if the relationship is the right one for you. Your father and I . . . All right, I know I'm not shattering an illusion for you when I tell you my marriage of thirty-eight years was not the fairy tale I imagined it to be. Trevor and I . . . It's hard to pinpoint what happened, but it's becoming clear to me as I watch you and Regina. Trevor and I seemed like the perfect match. Point for point, we were on the same page. Similar family and educational backgrounds. Similar life goals and tastes. By everyone's reckoning, even our own, we were going to be the ideal couple."

"But . . ." he prompted.

"Yes, there's a but. On some level—and believe me, I didn't even acknowledge it—we grew apart. The marriage was . . . I suppose 'dead' is being overly dramatic, especially now. We had a partnership. And we had the three of you, which I would not trade for anything in the world. And because I had such a wonderful family and a full life, I felt ridiculous and ungrateful for believing something was missing. What right did I have to feel that way? And so guess what I did? I worked hard. I worked my ass off to create this big happy family and this big happy life, and for the most part, I succeeded."

"Of course you did, Mom. We were all happy, and you were the reason for that. If you were unhappy, it didn't show."

"Of course it didn't show." She smiled at him. "I *was* happy with my life. I raised three fine children, and I'm proud of all of you. I found my happiness in you children, in work and travel and friends. Now I know Trevor found his happiness outside the marriage—with Celeste. I suppose that's why the news of his affair was so demoralizing. I allowed myself to tolerate a dead marriage for years. Knowing what was going on would have opened my eyes. Maybe it would have been awful to end the marriage back then. Maybe I would have been miserable. But it's also possible that I might have found someone who was more than a good match. More than a partner."

"Mom, I appreciate your candor." Mason kind of hated this conversation. Yet she clearly had something on her mind, and it was his job to listen. "But Regina and I are not you and Dad."

"Very true. Still, what kind of mother would I be if I didn't weigh in on this major life change you're about to make? You haven't listened to me in years, Mason. I want you to listen now. I'm not going to tell you what to do. No one can do that. But I'm going to ask you one thing and one thing only. Is this what you want for the rest of your life?"

"How the hell do I know? Nobody can answer that." He paused, listening to the play of water in the fountain behind him.

"I think you just did." She regarded him pointedly.

"You're still pissed at me for keeping my mouth shut about Dad's affair."

"I admit that I'm angry, but not for the reasons you think." With that, she turned her chair and glided along the crowded street, easily navigating the way to Bloomingdale's. "I'm angry with myself, angry that I poured so much emotional energy into a person who didn't deserve it. A person who was keeping secrets and living a double life. A person who didn't care about anything but the way things looked on the surface. I keep thinking about what my life would have been like if I'd realized sooner that I was married to a cheater. I was so busy keeping myself happy that maybe I didn't even realize your father and I were disconnected. Now I sit and imagine what I missed. Who knows what I would have done?"

They jockeyed for position amid a crowd waiting for the light to change. "There's no control group. You did what you did. We all did what we did. What, am I supposed to feel guilty because I didn't tell you about Dad?"

"Of course not. But I thought maybe you might have gained some insight from knowing what you know about your father and me."

"What kind of insight?"

"The kind I wish I'd had." She gazed steadily up at him. "When Faith went to tell you I tried to commit suicide, she was right."

Mason froze as he stood next to her at the final traffic light before the huge department store.

They had talked about it, but his mother had talked *around* it. The accident, she called it. The mishap. The incident. Not once had she admitted the truth, point-blank. He couldn't say it made him happy, but there was a sense of relief that she was taking ownership of what she'd done.

"Aw, Mom." He bent down, kissed her cheek.

"I just want to be clear with you," she said, blinking fast. "The past stays where it is. I was like a wounded animal, acting without thinking, but you and Faith . . . my God, everybody involved in my care . . . you've brought me back to myself. Faith's instincts about this were spot-on, and I'll forever be grateful to her for that. And your instinct to listen to her, even when I was denying it—you were spot-on, too."

And with that, she led the way to the department store. Her chair glided through the accessible entrance and she made a beeline for a slick-looking cosmetics counter. "Now, about that Crème de la Mer . . ." She spent a few minutes perusing the wares, courtesy of an eager salesgirl, offering samples.

"Jeez," he said when the girl rang up the small jar of face cream. "Really, Mom?"

She sniffed. "Some things are worth the price."

Handing over his credit card, he pretended to give a shit about the cost, but his mother knew he really didn't.

He checked his watch as Donno found them waiting at the curb. "I'll be back home tomorrow," he said.

She smiled up at him. "I like that you call it home."

He hadn't even realized the slip. "I know you'll be fine, but I'm going to ask you anyway—will you be all right on your own?"

"And by *on my own,* you mean surrounded by a staff of six? In that case, yes. I'm sure I'll be all right."

"If you think of anything else, send me a text message."

"I will. Mason, stop worrying."

As he bent to place a quick kiss on her cheek, she said, "I hope I didn't upset you. Earlier, you know. With the things I said."

"I'm not upset."

"All right, then. Give my regards to Regina."

"And by *regards,* you mean tell her you don't think we should get married."

"I never said that, Mason. And ultimately, it's your decision, of course. I will love you and stick by you, no matter what."

23

The end of summer was always a bittersweet time, in Faith's opinion. The glory days of sunshine and swimming in the lake would culminate with a Labor Day picnic by the lake. After that would come the start of school and the gradual descent through autumn and into winter. Faith had always disliked saying goodbye to summer's brilliant days and starry nights. This year she was particularly apprehensive, because it was Cara's final year of school.

Still, there was something about the fall. It was the season of crisp air and turning leaves, haystacks in the fields, boots and jeans and thick sweaters, football games, fresh apple cider . . . and memories of Dennis.

This fall would mark the sixth anniversary of his death. With each passing year, he was fading from her, and sometimes she feared she would lose him completely. Then she remembered what

Alice had said, that the love was indelible. And when Faith looked into the eyes of her daughters, she could still see Dennis there, his presence melded deeply with the spirit of her girls.

The day before the Labor Day picnic, she sat on the deck with her laptop computer. It was a new one, and it didn't actually belong to her. Alice had provided it, insisting that her caregiver needed a fast, high-quality computer.

Faith didn't miss the old secondhand clunker. The new one was slick and fast, and she actually enjoyed filling out forms for the girls' schools. By now the routine was familiar, but she felt a special poignancy at the moment. *Senior year.*

She glanced over at the garden in the sunniest corner of the yard. Both girls were there with Alice, gathering things for the picnic. Now at the end of the growing season, the oblong raised beds were exploding with tomatoes, cucumbers, berries, beans and herbs. At Ruby's insistence, there were also sunflowers, Shasta daisies and dahlias in colorful variety.

Catching Cara's attention, Faith motioned her over. "School starts the day after tomorrow," she said. "Help me fill out some of these forms."

"On my second-to-last day of freedom?" Cara scowled, but she plunked herself down next to Faith at the umbrella-shaded table. "Whatever."

Faith angled the laptop toward her. "I had to create a new log-in for the school district. The email's the same, but they wanted a new password. I picked 'BellaBallou.' "

"Everybody uses their dog's name. But it's fine. It's not like we're giving them a bunch of high-security info, right?"

"You're supposed to check off the volunteer committees you're interested in. Homecoming decorations?"

"Oh, right. Can you see me at the Homecoming dance?"

"Of course I can. You love music and dancing. You always have." Faith hadn't gone to her own Homecoming dance. She'd just discovered she was pregnant, and a school dance had been the last thing on her mind.

"Even if I wanted to go," Cara said, "I'd never get asked."

"Then go with your friends. It's more fun that way."

"In case you don't remember, Avalon High is still in the Dark Ages. You don't go to Home-coming unless you have a date."

"So find a date. I bet plenty of guys would love an invitation from you."

She twirled her fading purple hair around her index finger. "Mom. I'm a freak. Nobody wants to date me."

"Where is this coming from?" Faith asked, mystified.

"It doesn't come from anywhere. It's just a

fact. Besides, I don't have anything to wear."

"You're ridiculously creative with your clothes, and you're beautiful."

Cara patted her arm. "Spoken like a true mom."

"I bet you could come up with something incredible without killing the budget."

"Don't worry, Mom. I will survive not going to Homecoming."

"Milo Waxman would go with you."

Color surged into her cheeks. "Moving right along . . . Here's one. Cross-country and track team booster club."

"Somehow, I don't see you standing in front of Wegmans, convincing people to buy sweatbands and bumper stickers. All right, so what about this one—college night. They need help organizing speakers and programs for the fall presentation."

Cara ducked her head, but not before Faith saw the leap of yearning in her eyes. "No," she said. "Look, I'll just do peer tutoring . . ."

"Why would you shy away from college night? Come on."

"No."

"Why not?"

"College isn't on my radar, okay?"

"Yes, it is. You're not fooling anyone with that attitude," said Faith. "I know you're worried about finances, and you don't need to be."

"Right, so tuition is going to come from . . . what? The Publishers Clearing House? Why bother thinking about college until I have enough scratch to pay for it?"

"Listen, smarty-pants. I want you to dream as big as you can."

"What's the point of that if it's something that can never happen?"

"We're going to find a way. When I was in the city for that meeting about Alice's upcoming surgery, I had an appointment at the financial aid office at Columbia."

Cara frowned. "You did?"

"I want to see what's possible for you," Faith said.

"Mom, there's *possible,* and then there's *are you out of your gourd*. I know the difference."

Faith pushed aside the laptop. "I feel bad that you've had to worry about finance at your age. I want you to believe anything is possible."

"Okay, whatever. Can we finish up here?"

Between the headphones of her iPod, an ancient power ballad about building a dream together filled Cara's head. She wailed along with Grace Slick and Starship, but no matter how loudly she sang, she couldn't drown out her frustration with her mom.

Along with the singing, she scrubbed madly at the car. She had one more day of summer, and here she was all alone, pissed at her mom, ditched by her friends, with nothing to do. Bree had gone to the beach on Long Island with her family for the weekend. Milo had an annual Labor Day weekend at his grandparents' place up at Saranac Lake. Cara didn't really have any other friends, not the kind she could call just to hang out.

She might as well make use of her time. Alice had hired her to detail the lift van inside and out in anticipation of the Labor Day picnic. When the chorus came up, she aimed the hose stream straight at the windshield for a final rinse. "Nothing's gonna stop us now," she belted out.

"Good to know." A voice penetrated the noise in her head.

Startled, Cara swung around, spraying Mason Bellamy clean across his tailored white shirt. "Oh, shit," she said, tugging off the headphones. "I'm so sorry!"

He looked down at the soaking shirt, peeling it away from his chest. "Don't worry about it. No harm done."

She shut off the water. "Sorry," she said again. "I didn't hear you. I had the music on really loud."

"I know." He grinned. "Starship? Really? That's even before my time."

She dumped her wash bucket down the driveway grate. "It's my mom's iPod. She has some really old stuff on her playlist."

"Be right back," he said. "I'll help you wipe down the van."

"You don't have to—"

"True. But I'm going to."

Before she could reply, he went into the house, then came back a few minutes later wearing a plain T-shirt, shorts and flip-flops. Cara was already up on a step stool, drying the roof. "Thanks," she said, "but you should let me finish. It's my job. I'm getting paid to do this."

"Do all you McCallum women have trouble accepting help?" he asked. "I think it runs in the family."

"Nah, Ruby would let people wait on her hand and foot if she could get away with it." Cara flung a used towel as hard as she could into a laundry basket.

"Hey, what's up?" he asked.

She realized she was acting like a typical snotty teenager. Well, why the hell not? She *was* a teenager. She was supposed to be snotty. "I'm totally frustrated with my mom. On the one hand, she's all, like, 'You should follow your dreams and live the life you've always wanted.' "

"And on the other hand?"

"She's like, 'We can't afford college tuition, so you're going to have to work and go to community college at night.' "

A curious expression crossed his face, but Cara couldn't read him. Then she felt guilty. "I know I don't have any right to complain, and I just need to deal with this on my own and not expect my mom to solve everything."

"But . . ."

"I don't even know where to start," she mumbled.

The van was finished, so she climbed up into the driver's seat. "Excuse me. I told Donno I would move this back into the garage." Fortunately for her, Donno had backed the thing out and aimed it straight for the parking bay, so she just had to roll it forward. Still, she felt self-conscious with Mason standing there. Plus, she was such a dork behind the wheel. She wished she could just glide easily into the bay, but instead, she inched forward in fits and starts, taking what seemed like forever to move the van.

"Done," she said.

"Good job." He put away the bucket and carried the towels to the laundry. "Plans today?"

She shrugged. "Nah."

"I've got an idea," he said. "Come with me."

She followed him out to the circular drive in front of the house. His car was parked there. As he approached, the door handles and side mirrors popped out, even though he didn't touch the car or the key. "Get in the driver's seat. I'm giving you a driving lesson."

"Whoa." She didn't need further persuasion. She ran around to the driver's side, sank into the cushy leather and clipped on her seat belt. "This is awesome," she said. "This *rocks*."

"Wait a minute. Go tell your mom. I'll wait here."

Crap. She knew her mom would never go for it. Mom was funny about things like this. She'd want Cara to take the driver's ed class at school and do everything by the book.

Cara made a snap decision. "Okay," she said. "Be right back." She ran around the side of the house, having no intention of finding her mother. It was sneaky, but what the hell. How many chances was she going to get to drive a car like Mason's? After a moment she returned and jumped in again.

"Thanks for doing this," she said. "I'm really excited."

"So your mom said okay."

"Think how much easier it's going to be for her once I can drive," Cara said, evading the issue. She found a lever to move the seat forward. "Wow, this is really different. No ignition?"

"Nothing to ignite," he said. "The car's on. Just put your foot on the brake, and then you can put it in Drive."

"Got it." She tried to act as if she did this all the time, finding the column shifter and easing it into gear. The car made a warning sound. Embarrassed, she looked over at Mason.

"Relax," he said. "Nobody is cool when they're learning to drive. Trust me, nobody. Not even me."

She laughed and relaxed, and after that, the lesson went as smoothly as the electric car. He showed her the basics of operating the car, and then the magic happened. She put it in Drive and glided down the lane and out to the main road.

"I'm driving," she whispered. "Look at me. I'm *driving*."

"Yep, look at you."

He was a pretty good coach. He didn't nag. He let her practice smooth acceleration and braking, and once she felt okay with that, they took the back way to the high school stadium parking lot. It was deserted, the perfect spot for practicing safe turns, signaling, braking, mirrors and blind spots, avoiding distractions and watching the road. He set up a course so she could practice lane changes and intersections. Then he got out of the car and made her practice awareness of her surroundings.

That was when she discovered his acting skills. He pretended to be a clueless pedestrian staring at his phone screen, a little old man with a cane, a runaway toddler, a crazy homeless guy, complete with sound effects. His imitation of a deer sprinting across the road at night made her nearly pee her pants with laughter.

"Okay," she gasped, "I get it."

He got back in the car. "You have to expect the unexpected. Speaking of which, I spotted something interesting in the recycle bin the other day—a printout from your school. I've always known you were smart, but the report—"

"Is none of your business." Her neck and ears felt hot.

"You ought to be proud of yourself for being a straight-A student, top ranked in your class with that demanding course load. Why not share your accomplishments and make your mom proud?"

"She already knows about my test scores. And the class ranking . . . She'll feel guilty about not being able to send me to college. I know you think it's great, me getting good scores and all, but so what?"

"So you build on your strengths, even if it seems impossible."

"You don't know what it's like to be in our situation. I just need to focus on getting a job and looking out for myself."

"Whoa, hey, slow down." He laughed easily. "Do the world a favor and learn how to take a compliment. Better yet, learn how to reach out for help. Look at you, driving a car. Because you let me help you."

"It's a driving lesson, not a bachelor's degree." She was mortified by her own words. "Thank you, though. Really. Thanks. I appreciate all you've done, and it's really nice of you to encourage me, but I need to make my own way."

"That's my point. You don't need to go it alone. Talk to people. Your school counselor. Your mother. Hell, *my* mother. She could help you rock those applications."

Cara's resentment dissolved completely. Just

talking it out with him didn't really solve anything, but she felt better. She felt less alone. "Okay," she said. "I might."

"That's all I ask. And now we'd better head home."

She nodded, though she hated for the lesson to end. Mason was just the nicest guy. He was the kind of guy she imagined her dad would have been if he was alive. The thought sobered her, and she focused intently on moving smoothly from the main road to the driveway.

"You did really well," he said.

A wave of emotion rushed over her. "I wish we could do this every day."

"I'll let Adam and Donno know. They'll both take you driving."

The wave crested. The driving lesson had tapped into a sensitive spot, deep inside her. "I'd rather practice with you."

"Adam's moving back," he said. "And I'm heading to the city again. Doesn't matter who teaches you, so long as it's someone who knows what he's doing."

She looked out the window, swallowing hard, but the lump in her throat wouldn't dissolve.

"Everything okay?"

"Yeah." Her voice sounded hoarse. "Just . . . I always pictured my dad teaching me to drive. It's one of those things . . . I miss him. Even after all this time."

"Me, too," he said after a long pause. "I miss my dad, too."

It was a horrible thing to have in common, but it made her feel closer to him. "What was he like?" she asked.

"Complicated," Mason said. "When I was a little kid, he seemed like your favorite sports coach and Santa Claus and the Pied Piper all rolled into one."

She smiled. "Sounds fun."

"It was, for a kid. But then . . . after I wasn't a kid anymore, I saw his flaws. And still I miss him, flaws and all."

Cara wondered if she'd ever seen her father's flaws. He must have had them. In a way, she was glad she couldn't remember any, other than the fact that he'd had a fatal disease.

"Someone's here," she said, noticing a pickup truck in the parking area.

"Looks like my brother, Adam, has arrived."

"For a visit or for good?"

"For good. Which means I'll be leaving soon."

Alice dreamed of running. It happened nearly every night, and the experience was as vivid and bright as the sunniest autumn day. She could hear the rhythm of her feet on the pavement and feel the breeze off the lake as she sped along the waterfront trail. Her arms pumped in rhythm with her heart and lungs. Her body, mind and spirit worked in perfect synchronicity. She was soaring without wings, her senses heightened, her awareness expanding to take in the whole world.

Each morning, she hovered in the misty space between sleep and wakefulness, desperate to hold on to that sweet euphoria. Then reality would overtake her. She would open her eyes and greet the body she now had, lying exactly the way she'd been left the night before. Then she would turn toward the bedside monitor, call for help, and her day would begin.

At the sound of Alice's voice, Bella climbed onto the bed and licked Alice's chin. And the dog's bright eyes conveyed exactly the message Alice's heart needed—I love you. I'm here to help. What can I do for you?

"How did I ever get along without you, huh?" Alice asked. She was able to pat Bella with an awkward shift of one arm. "Just you wait," she said. "A few months from now, I'll be grooming you like a pro."

Lena arrived, and Alice asked her to take extra care with her hair and makeup. It wasn't often she had all three of her kids together at the same time, so this was a special day.

Shaking off the last of the running dream, Alice mentally embraced the life she had. Then she went in search of her children.

In the lounge room, she glanced at her reflection in a wall mirror before going outside. What she saw made her smile. "You're a lazy little thing, aren't you, Bella Ballou?" she said to the small dog in her lap. "You're supposed to be my service dog, but you expect me to be your chauffeur."

She stopped the chair at the French doors that opened to the patio. Bella looked up expectantly.

"Just a second," Alice said, savoring the sight of her two sons and her daughter, sitting outside, engaged in an animated discussion. Her eyes blurred with tears of happiness to see them all together again. She blinked fast, determined not to let it smear her makeup.

Adam had just returned from Montana, where he had finished his special training and survived a round of working as a smoke jumper. Alice hadn't seen Adam or Ivy since the beginning of summer, and both had changed. It reminded her of summers past, when they were kids returning from camp, inches taller, bronzed and muscled by sun and sports, dragging their disreputable duffel bags to the laundry room.

Only this time, Ivy had arrived pulling a sleek Rollaboard and Adam with a Jeep loaded with turnout gear and arson investigation equipment. Ivy had always been lovely; now, after a summer in Paris, she had that special continental *louche*, wearing a gauzy neck scarf and couture shades with negligent ease. Adam was even tougher than ever, his muscles rippling beneath a T-shirt that had seen better days. He needed a haircut, although Alice actually liked his unkempt tumble of dark curls; it reminded her of how adorable he was as a little boy.

Watching the three of them together, Alice was swept by a feeling of gratitude. Her sons and daughter were the sort of adult children everyone hoped their kids would turn into—good-hearted and interesting, accomplished, confident. Yet she felt a tiny, private flicker of worry. How was it that each one was so damned smart and attractive . . . and *alone?*

Alice thought about herself at their ages—how isolated she'd been, how alone she'd felt in her marriage. She'd forced herself to manufacture happiness for the sake of her kids and for appearances. And she'd thought she'd succeeded. But maybe not. Maybe she had failed in her dogged quest to be happy in her marriage. Maybe her children had sensed the strain she'd tried so hard to cover up. The only person she had fooled turned out to be herself. Could be that was the reason her three offspring were so cautious in their relationships.

She often thought about the conversation she'd had with Mason about Regina. *Good God, but I have a big mouth,* Alice thought. She still wasn't sure if she should have said anything at all. Most women with sons in their thirties were beyond thrilled to hear the chime of wedding bells. Most women started thinking of the expanding family, grandchildren, holidays filled with laughter and love.

Alice was not like most women, apparently. She couldn't help herself. When you saw someone about to step off a cliff, it was irresponsible not to call out a warning. So ultimately, she didn't regret bringing it up. After that day, she and Mason had never spoken of it again. He didn't seem upset with her, or put out. She had no idea if what she'd said resonated with him at all, but at least she'd spoken her mind.

When she was young and about to be married, no one had sat down with her and talked to her about the step she was about to take. Her own mother certainly hadn't. All Alice could recall her mother saying to her about Trevor was, "He's quite a catch."

Alice recalled asking, "What about me? Aren't I a catch?"

She couldn't remember whether or not her mother had answered that question.

Now Alice had to focus on her other son and daughter. Adam and Ivy didn't know anything about their father's infidelities. It was tempting to leave things be, but Alice was done with deception. Adam and Ivy were adults. They would be able to handle it.

Far better than Alice had.

The day she'd found out about Celeste Gauthier, Alice had taken a break from reality. All the endless hours of therapy and reflection had yielded. The most powerful lesson Alice had learned was that honest, loving connections to others would always save you. An able-bodied person who isolated herself was far more crippled than a quadriplegic who was deeply connected to family and friends.

"All righty, then," she said to Bella. "Let's get this party started."

Bella jumped down and pressed the plate to open the door, and led the way through with her customary prance.

"Look who's working on Labor Day," Ivy exclaimed.

Alice gave Bella her release command—*free dog*—and joined the others.

Adam bent down and gave her a kiss. "Mason was just filling us in on your surgery. We're stoked, Mom, and we'll be here to help any way we can."

"I know you will. I'm a lucky mom." Alice sighed, aiming a nervous glance at him. She still didn't look forward to telling her daughter and son about their father. "First of all, welcome back to the lake, you two," she said.

"And second of all?" Ivy could read her like a book. "What's going on?"

"I need to talk to you about something that came up this summer." She caught Mason's eye, and he offered a nod of encouragement. "It seems . . . Damn." She decided to be simple and direct. "I found out your father had an affair in Paris with a woman named Celeste Gauthier. And they had a son together twenty-three years ago."

Watching the faces of her younger son and daughter, Alice instantly realized two things—Adam already knew, and Ivy was reeling in shock.

"I'm really sorry, Mom," Adam said, giving her shoulder a squeeze. "That sucks."

"Wait, you knew? How long have you known?" Mason demanded.

Adam shrugged. "Years and years."

"And you didn't say anything?" Alice felt conspired against, but at the same time, she understood. Like Mason, Adam had been in an untenable position. Apparently, both had embraced the family tradition—head down, mouth shut. A fresh surge of anger rose in her. Damn you, Trevor.

Ivy sat down in a chair next to Alice. The disillusionment in her eyes tore at Alice's heart. "I don't know what to say, Mom," she whispered. "Dad . . . he was . . . Oh, God. There's a boy out there . . ."

"I took it hard, too," Alice said. One day she would explain everything. Not yet, though.

"Can I still love Dad?" Ivy asked. "I need to figure out if I can still love him."

"The love you and your father shared doesn't

have to change. Don't let it. Keep the good memories close."

Ivy nodded, though she still looked freaked out. "I don't want to dismiss what he did. But you're right—I don't want to forget how much I loved him, how good he was to me."

"That's all right," Alice said.

"What about you? Are *you* all right?"

"Yes. In a way, it's liberating. I'm determined to move forward with my life. It's all I can do."

Ivy nodded again. "Okay. So I have one more question."

"What's that?"

"When do I get to meet Rick Sanders?"

It was so very odd, being the parent and having to present a guy to her kids. "How about at the picnic today?"

Faith liked watching Wayan and Banni work together. As they prepared the Labor Day barbecue, they were focused and clearly in sync. Wayan's training as a chef added a special polish and flair to his natural talent. The feast included traditional fare, like grilled corn on the cob and juicy watermelon, alongside Balinese specialties—sticky rice with mango, and curried vegetables wrapped in banana leaves and steamed over the open grill.

Everyone was gathered on the patio for drinks before the feast. Banni and Wayan offered a tray of appetizers in their signature Balinese style—a banana leaf and nasturtium blossom garnish. Banni offered Wayan a spring roll dipped in coriander chili sauce, and he pretended to swoon as he took it from her.

After Dennis died, Faith used to feel a special ache whenever she saw a close affectionate couple together. Now she felt that twinge of yearning, but the first thing that came to mind was not Dennis.

"That smells incredible," said Mason, looking over Wayan's shoulder at the grill.

"You should see what I can do with a piece of meat," said Wayan. He often teased Mason good-naturedly about not eating meat.

"If anyone could tempt me, it would be you."

"We should have a toast," Alice said. "Does anyone know of a Labor Day toast?"

"The only ones I can think of are depressing—the end of summer, the start of school, setting the clocks back," said Faith.

"To coming home," said Adam. "It's good to be back, Mom."

"Here's one—to me actually making a toast." Alice's eyes were full of hope.

"That's going to be awesome, Mom." Mason touched his glass to hers.

"Where's your gorgeous fiancée, anyway?"

"Switzerland. Working."

"On Labor Day. Hmm. I was hoping she could join us."

"She'll be sorry." Ivy sneaked a sample of the berry cream dessert. "Wayan, what did you put in this? Crack?"

"Hey, Mason, if Adam's coming back, where are you going to live?" Ruby asked bluntly.

Faith caught herself holding her breath. There was a part of her—a very secret part, she hoped—that wanted him to say he wasn't going anywhere, that he would stay here forever. But now that Adam was back, Mason would return to the city and resume his life. That had been the plan from the beginning.

"I've got an apartment in Manhattan," he said. "I'll be moving back there."

"Why do you have to go?" asked Ruby, undoubtedly voicing the thoughts of several people at the gathering. "We *need* you here. You said you'd teach me to play 'Doe a Deer' with two hands on the piano. And you're teaching Cara to drive. And your mom—"

"Wait, what?" Faith whirled around to glare at him.

"He let her drive his car yesterday," Ruby said. "I saw them."

"Shut up, brat," said Cara.

Mason spread his hands, palms up. "She's eighteen. It's time she learned to drive."

"I don't disagree. But it's not okay to put a child behind the wheel of a car without checking with her mother."

"Oh. Yeah, about that—"

"It was me," Cara burst in.

"What do you mean?"

"He's trying to keep me out of trouble. I said it was okay. I kind of implied you were on board . . ."

"Lovely."

"It's cool, Mom. I have to learn, and Mason's an awesome teacher with an awesome car."

The awesome teacher and the awesome car were going away. Faith realized part of her resentment came from the fact that he was leaving. This had been their best summer since Dennis, and whether he realized it or not, Mason was a big part of that—his commitment to his mother, his humor, his ridiculously active problem-solving brain. She'd grown to love the atmosphere that had developed around the house, with the girls and Alice and the staff all working and playing together. She'd always known it would be temporary. Of course she'd known that.

Faith had borrowed some books from Mason. It turned out he was as avid a reader as she was, and they shared a taste for long, deeply involving novels about big, unwieldy families. The night before he left, she gathered up the borrowed books and took them to the boathouse.

He must not have heard her approach; he stood on the upper deck looking out at the lake. Maybe it was her imagination, but to her, he looked immeasurably sad as he faced the lake and spoke with quiet intensity on the phone. Why? He was going back to the life he loved in the city. What did he have to be sad about?

She waved to get his attention and set the books by the door. Then she tried to tiptoe away, but he finished his call.

"Hey, Faith."

"I didn't mean to interrupt."

"It's all right. I need to finish getting my stuff out of here so Adam can have his place back."

"Okay, well . . . there are your books." Feeling awkward, she moved toward the stairs.

"Wait."

She stopped and turned back.

"Come on in. I have about two fingers left of Lagavulin. Let's finish it off as a farewell to summer."

He held the door open, and she stepped inside. The boathouse quarters consisted of one big studio room, outfitted with rustic furniture made of peeled pine, hand-woven pillows and wrought-iron fixtures. There was a small kitchen bar and a study nook, and a gigantic king-size bed.

He poured two shots and put the bottle in the recycle bin. "Cheers, Faith."

"Cheers." One sip reminded her of their first drink together—the smoky taste of peat, the quiet of the starlit night and the feeling of utter relief that she'd found a safe, happy situation for her girls. "I want to thank you for everything," she said. "Except maybe taking Cara driving without talking to me first. I'm not sure I should thank you for that."

"I'm the one who should be saying thank you," he said. "You dragged me up here kicking and screaming—"

"I don't recall kicking. Or screaming. You were a good sport about it. Your mother needed you, and you came." She polished off her drink, feeling its effects warming her inside. "Wow, that's good." She looked around the apartment. There was a packed bag by the door. The sheets had been stripped off the bed. A chandelier made of a ship's flywheel hung high above the bed. A spare lightbulb lay in the middle of the mattress.

He switched on the light. "I need to change the bulb," he said. "I know, I can hear you thinking up the punch line now."

"I don't know any punch lines. Should we get a ladder?"

"I can reach." He dragged a bar stool over to the bed. "Hold this steady for me."

"Mason—"

"It's fine." He climbed up while she held the stool. She couldn't escape the sight of his long, sinewy legs. Stretching as high as he could, he managed to unscrew the old bulb. He wobbled a little. “Jeez, why would anyone put a light fixture where no one can reach it?”

She took the dead bulb from him and handed him the new one. “Don’t you dare fall,” she cautioned him.

“You’re a nurse. You’ll put me back together if I break.”

“Right.”

He replaced the bulb, and it flickered on. “Success,” he declared. “We’re a good team—*Shit*.” Even as he spoke, the bar stool wobbled, and he came crashing down on the bed.

“Mason!” She lost her balance and practically fell on top of him. They clashed together on the bed, and it was awkward and weirdly exciting, and she laughed to cover her embarrassment.

“I’m all right,” he said, and just for a moment, his arms came up and he held on to her while they righted themselves. And then . . . he didn’t let go.

The strangest sensation came over Faith. She could feel his heart beating fast—as fast as hers. And it was probably her imagination, or maybe just wishful thinking, but she could have sworn their hearts were beating at the same rate. In sync.

Totally flustered, she jumped up and grabbed the fallen stool. “Sorry,” she said. “That wasn’t very helpful of me.”

“You’re always helpful, Faith.” He stood up and took a step toward her.

She kept the stool between them. “I’d better let

you finish packing. And I've got to make sure the girls are ready for school tomorrow."

"Right," he said, sounding brisk.

"I know your mother is really going to miss you," she told him.

"She's going to be fine now that Adam's back. I'm not needed here anymore," he said.

The feeling of not being needed was like death to Faith.

She'd always known Mason's sojourn here was temporary. Now that his mother was full of life and looking forward to the surgery, now that Adam was moving back, Mason would return to the city. To Regina.

But there was no way around her own feelings.

She was going to miss him like crazy.

Part Six

✵ ✵ ✵ ✵ ✵

"It is not in the stars to hold
our destiny but in ourselves."
—William Shakespeare

✵ 24 ✵

Mason and Adam had basically swapped places, Cara observed. They were both really good guys, but everything felt different with Mason gone. True to his word, he'd enlisted both Donno and Adam to help her practice driving—this time with her mom's approval.

It wasn't the same, though. They would all just have to get used to the idea that Mason had gone back to his life in the city. Right now, he was probably dealing with wedding plans. Regina didn't seem too interested in visiting Avalon; they hadn't been up in weeks, not since Alice had finished her surgery and had been going hard at her rehab program ever since. Regina was okay, Cara supposed. Smart and really stylish, but Cara wasn't that impressed by her.

She had started her senior year of high school with mixed feelings, and now it was amazing to think she'd come to the end of school at last. Yet there was also a lot of uncertainty. She wanted to go to college, make something of herself, but figuring out how to go about it was overwhelming.

There was one thing she needed to do right now. Her mom had managed to rope her into planning fall college night, an open house to highlight college options for seniors and their families. The gala event would be held at the Avalon Meadows Country Club. A dozen colleges would be represented, each determined to attract the best and the brightest students in the district. There would be a performance by Yale's Whim 'n' Rhythm, an a cappella group. The West Point choral group would follow. There would be presentations from Skidmore, Harvard, Rochester and Columbia, featuring current students and alumni. Local students were supposed to come and hear all the great things about going to a college that cost more than the moon.

And somehow Cara had been put in charge of finding the keynote speaker.

This, at least, was a no-brainer.

She found Alice in her study with Rick Sanders. The two of them were laughing as Alice practiced her new hand ability. Thanks to the surgery she'd undergone, she was learning to grasp things with her fingers. At the moment she was grasping a dog grooming brush and attempting to brush the ever-patient Bella's coat while Rick took their picture.

"Hey, Cara," said Rick, setting down his camera. "How's it going?"

"Great," she said. "Actually, it will be great if we can talk Alice into being the keynote speaker at college night."

"I already told you," Alice said. "It's flattering to be asked, but no, thank you."

"Sounds like an exceptional gig," Rick said, cheerfully ignoring the *no*. "Can I come?"

"You've already been to college. So have I. I'll pass," said Alice.

Cara knew Alice was a sucker for a challenge. "Do you remember what you said to me once, that day we went through the college admissions letters?"

"And what was that?"

" 'Are you saying this is a legitimate roadblock, or is it an excuse to avoid doing something that scares you?' "

"Listen, I know what you're trying to do, but it's really not necessary. I don't have anything helpful or inspirational to say to a roomful of people."

"They're going to love you."

"They're going to be polite and feel sorry for me."

"Depends on what you say. It's a fifteen-minute talk. You can tell them about studying behavioral psychology. Or being on the swim team. Or reading 'The Rape of the Lock,' " Cara said.

"Sounds riveting," Rick said.

"Please. I have one job with this committee," Cara pointed out. "Don't make me fail."

Alice stared at her. Then a decisive light came into her eyes. "I'll make you a deal," she said. "If I agree to speak at your event, you have to agree to apply to three of the colleges represented that night."

Cara pursed her lips, already mentally tallying up the application fees.

"Don't worry about the application fees," Alice said, as if reading her mind. "I'll see that they're waived."

"On what basis? What makes you think I'm special?"

"My girl, if you don't believe you're special, who else will?"

Faith was seeing someone. Well, sort of. She had gone to a Friday night football game with Ray Tolley. The next weekend, he'd taken her and Ruby on a drive to look at the fall colors, pick apples and take them to a cider press, and the three of them came home with several gallons of the freshest apple cider they'd ever tasted. Faith and Ray saw a couple of movies together, and when Inner Child performed at the Shawangunks Outdoor Festival, she'd gone with a few friends for the music and dancing. The autumn colors around the Grand River Gorge had created a magical setting for the event. The beer was delicious, the music was great and it was a lovely, fun day.

So, yes. She was seeing someone. Ray was incredibly nice, very funny, a talented musician. They got along fine. After their most recent date—the town gallery walk followed by dinner at the Apple Tree Inn, they made out in the parking lot. His lips were sweet with the crème brûlée they'd shared for dessert, and she wanted sparks to fly.

It was . . . nice. But nice wasn't the same as flying sparks. She stepped back, resting her hands on his shoulders, and smiled up at him.

He smiled back, but his eyes held a quiet knowledge. "Is this where one of us says, 'It's not you, it's me'?"

"Aw, Ray." She wished she didn't see the disappointment in his eyes.

"I like you, Faith. I like you enough to level with you. We've been having some good times together, but I can tell you're not feeling it. I mean, us, together."

"And you are?"

He reached out, smoothed a lock of her hair back behind her ear. "I'm not going to lie. I'm into you. No, don't say anything. I'll get over you. These things . . . they don't work if they're one-sided."

Cara was stupidly nervous about college night. She told herself not to be. Alice was going to be awesome. She was smart, and she'd do a great job. Philomena had done her hair and makeup, and even little Bella was tricked out in school colors. Yet when Cara knocked on the door of Alice's room, Alice greeted her with a scowl.

"Is that what you're wearing?" she asked bluntly, in full-on dragon lady mode.

Cara looked down at her jeans, Doc Martens and rock-festival T-shirt. "You're the star of the show, not me."

Alice sniffed. "This way," she said. "Into the vault." Bella trotted after her. "That's what I call my closet. I'm much too fond of nice clothing. Don't give me that look. You can keep the combat boots—those are actually kind of cute . . ."

To Cara's surprise, the vault was not a bad place to shop. She found a gray canvas pleated skirt with leather closures, and it looked good with leggings and her boots. Alice picked out a navy-and-white-striped boatneck top, and a short cashmere cardigan.

"There," Alice said. "Now you look like a young woman with good prospects."

Cara couldn't deny that she felt more confident, wearing nicer clothes. "You're not so bad yourself," she said. "It's time to go. Donno's taking you in the van, and I'll come later with Mom and Ruby."

After Alice left in the van, a midnight blue sedan glided like a stealth aircraft into the driveway.

Cara's heart soared. She had sent Mason an email, inviting him to come hear his mother speak, but she'd never heard back, so she assumed he was ignoring her. She should have known better. He never ignored things that were important.

"Mason," Ruby yelled, rushing out to greet him.

"You came!" She turned to everyone else. "He's here!" Then she ran to Mason. "I can't believe you're here."

He swooped her up into his arms. "I heard a rumor that my mother was going to be the star of the show tonight. I wouldn't miss it."

Then he gave Cara a hug and turned to her mom. "Hey, Faith."

They didn't hug. Cara kind of wished they would, but that would probably be weird, because he was engaged and he probably shouldn't be hugging other women. Especially her mom, because Mom looked at him as if he was a box of Godiva chocolates.

He let Cara drive his car to the event. Ruby and Mom were in the backseat, Ruby nattering on about the fancy car, with its big-screen display and surround-sound system. "Put on 'Climb Every Mountain,' " she insisted. "You know, from *The Sound of Music*."

"Oh, my God, no," Cara begged. Ever since Philomena had turned the kid onto that movie, Ruby had memorized every single song.

"Please."

"Only if you promise you won't sing," Cara said. "Mom—"

"You're the driver. You get to pick the music," her mom said. Yay, Mom.

"But it's *my* car." Mason scrolled through the playlist and found the number. "Come on, what good is a song like this if you don't sing along?" And with that, he turned up the volume. A moment later the deep, operatic tones of Mother Superior filled the car.

Ruby joined right in, and then Mason picked up the melody, belting out the song with a fake operatic vibrato. Mom couldn't resist adding her voice, either, and finally Cara caved to the pressure. They yodeled "Climb Every Mountain" for at least three miles, until they were laughing so hard they couldn't sing anymore. When Cara got out of the car, Ruby gave her a swift, hard hug. "You look really pretty," she said.

"Thanks. That's a nice thing to say."

"After high school, are you going away?"

"Yeah. Probably."

"I'm gonna miss you. What'll I do without you, Cara?"

"Wherever I go, I'll always come back to see you, squirt."

"It won't be the same."

"Nothing ever stays the same, Ruby Tuesday," said Mason, grabbing the kid's hand and giving her a twirl until she started to giggle. "It's more interesting that way."

"How are you not the same?" Ruby asked, eyeing him up and down.

"That's a long story. Let's go inside."

A long story. Cara wondered about that. She could tell by her mom's narrowed eyes and intrigued expression that Mom was wondering, too.

At the entrance to the country club, Cara found Milo passing out flyers for the service dog training program. His committee with PAWS was dedicated to turning strays into working dogs for people who needed them. "I know one guy who is not going to have to lie about his community service on his college apps," she said.

Milo grinned. "I'll just have to lie about my athletic prowess. Think they'll believe me if I say I'm a pole-vaulting champion?"

"Pole vaulters are a dime a dozen," Cara said. "Guys who rescue puppies—it's no contest."

"From your lips to Yale's ears."

"Oh, so it's Yale now," Cara said.

"A guy can dream."

"That's what tonight is about, right?" Cara's heart skipped a beat. It was painful to want so much, to want *everything*. "Hey, listen. I want to hear more about those diabetic medical alert dogs you were telling me about."

"For Ruby?"

"Can she, like, be put on a list for a dog?"

"Sure. I'll get you all the info."

"Thanks, Milo. You're the best. I've been thinking how great it would be for Ruby and my mom to have a dog that can sniff out her blood sugar level. And after I'm gone, she'll have another dog for company."

"We'll make it happen. Let's go inside. Looks like they're getting started." Milo stepped aside with a fake-gallant bow.

After the opening remarks and a great number by the Yale group, it was time for Alice's speech. Accompanied by Bella—who wore a service dog vest in Harvard crimson colors—she glided to the podium. The crowd murmured with admiration as Bella took the mike from the host, brought it over to Alice and then settled down, as attentive as everyone else in the room.

With slow deliberation, Alice gripped the mike and fitted it into its holder. Her face glowed with pride at the simple gesture.

Cara could tell the moment Alice spied Mason. They were all sitting together in the front row. He gave his mother a thumbs-up sign, and her face lit like the sunrise.

"I'm not going to talk to you tonight about being a quadriplegic," Alice said, looking directly out at the crowd. "I'm sure as hell not expecting you to feel sorry for me, and I'm not going to tell you to follow your dreams. Dreams are what happen when you're sleeping, and I want everyone to be wide-awake."

Murmurs of laughter. Alice gave a brief overview of what it was like for her to go to college, to create a future for herself and pursue a career and family. She was witty and sharp, and not at all boring. Her concluding remarks brought the house down. “I’ve done a lot of things in my life, including the accident that landed me in this chair. You might think the accident is the worst thing that’s ever happened to me. But it’s not. The worst thing is that I stopped listening to my heart.”

She paused and took a long, steadying breath. “The hardest part of life is not a physical struggle or financial worries or anything like that. The hardest is learning to be who you are and whom to love, and to love the life you’ve made for yourself. I do not have a single regret. I’m proud of the things I did. I’m not sorry for the stupid things I did, and believe me, there were a lot of them. I’m just glad it all happened. And the best part of life started with choosing my education. So don’t tell me you can’t attend college. Don’t tell me you can’t climb a mountain or learn a language or explore outer space. Don’t tell me it can’t be done. The smallest success starts with the greatest motivation.”

The reception afterward was a crush of well-wishers and snacks served by crisply dressed waiters. Cara bent down and gave Alice a hug. “You *nailed* it,” she said. “I knew you would.”

“She’s right,” Mason said. “Way to go, Mom.”

“Thanks for coming,” said Alice. She looked around. “Where’s Regina now? Switzerland again?”

When Mason found Ruby the day after his mother’s college night speech, she was practicing

"Doe a Deer" on the piano. Ruby's obsession with *The Sound of Music* continued. She walked around in a long gray robe, with a coif and veil over her hair, and at a moment's notice she would fling it off to reveal a blue dress and an apron. She'd memorized all of the songs.

"Hey, Sister Mary Shortstuff," he said.

She spun around on the piano stool, her nun's coif flying. "Hey, yourself. Alice said you broke up with Regina."

Oh, boy. So the cat was out of the bag. "We decided not to get married, after all."

The relationship had ended several weeks before, coming to a slow, grinding halt as the realization had come over them like a storm cloud. He vacillated between a feeling of relief and one of defeat. The bottom line was, Mason had finally admitted to himself, and then to Regina, that he longed to be here, in Avalon, close to his family. Spending time with his mother—and yes, with Faith and her girls—made him realize what he really yearned for—a family. Not just for show or to entertain his mother, but to give life its deepest meaning.

Regina told him flat out that she couldn't see herself moving to a small town. She acknowledged—and not graciously—that Mason was a changed man, and she didn't like the changes.

"Why did you break up with her?" asked Ruby. "She's beautiful, and she wears designer clothes.

That black-and-white sundress she wore on the Fourth of July was Missoni."

"Someone's been watching too many style shows on TV. I didn't break up with her."

"So did she break up with you? What did you do? Did you beg her to take you back?"

"Enough with the questions, brat. You're right that she's beautiful and wears nice clothes. But we both realized that although we care about one another and share a lot in common, it wasn't enough to make a lifetime commitment."

In fact, he reflected, he and Regina had broken up the same way they'd gotten engaged—by mutual consent.

"So you didn't ever love each other."

"We liked each other and got along so well that it seemed like love. But it wasn't the kind of love that would keep us going for sixty years, like my great-uncle Charles and his wife, Jane. You'll understand when you're older."

"I understand now."

"I think maybe you do. That's pretty cool."

"Why'd you propose to her in the first place, then?"

"I didn't. We were sitting around one day and we decided that we liked doing things together and working together and we thought we'd stay together."

She pinched her lower lip, studying the songbook propped on the piano. "Maybe you're like Captain von Trapp and the Baroness. You were supposed to be in love but it kept falling flat because you were distracted by Maria."

"Who? What? Oh, *The Sound of Music*." He scarcely remembered the plot. It was about a rich Austrian widower who wanted to bang the governess, something like that. "No, we're not like that," he told Ruby. "It was just . . . a mistake. People make mistakes. Reg and I thought we'd make a good pair, but we were wrong."

"Dude," she said.

"I know," he conceded. "We didn't exactly think things through." Or maybe, he mused, they had overthought everything and convinced themselves that this was what they wanted out of life.

"Does this mean you're staying off the market?"

"What?" He gave a short laugh.

"That's what people say when they don't want to date—that they're off the market."

"I'll probably take some time," he said.

"I'm sorry," she said.

"Thanks, Ruby Tuesday."

"Does it hurt?"

"What? No. Or . . . yes. I feel bad that we got engaged and it didn't work and we had to let each other go."

"Don't feel bad for trying."

"Okay, that's good advice. Thanks." The kid was so damn sweet. In one conversation, she broke his heart more surely than Regina had.

"You're welcome. Are you off the market for good?"

"No." His reply came swiftly. "Like I said, I'll take some time."

"And then what?"

"And then you quit asking so many questions. Let's go drown our sorrows in a whole bag of Cheetos."

She grabbed his hand and planted a kiss on it. "Just so you know, I think Regina's out of her gourd for letting you go."

"Yeah?"

"You're a keeper."

"I am? Does that mean you're keeping me?"

"No, silly. I'm a kid. When the right one comes along, she'll know you're a keeper."

"I think you're the right one. My Cheetos buddy."

"Just don't tell Mom."

25

"I've invited Simon Gauthier to spend the holidays with us," Alice announced as they were finishing dinner one night shortly before Christmas. "I hope that's all right."

No one moved a muscle. No one said a word.

Mason looked at his brother and sister, who sat frozen in place.

Finally, Adam dropped his fork onto his plate. "Jesus H. Christ, Mom. Seriously?"

"Actually, I invited them both—Simon and his mother—but Celeste didn't care to come. Understandable, wouldn't you say? Simon readily accepted. I believe he would like to meet his half brothers and sister."

"Why didn't you tell us he was coming?" Ivy demanded.

"I just did."

"And why did you invite him?" asked Mason.

"He's your half brother. I'm sure the three of you have questions. And he does, too. I have nothing against this person. He didn't ask to be born into the mess your father made. I don't have any illusions that you'll become lifelong friends, but—"

Ivy jumped up and gave her mother a hug. "But maybe we will, and how cool would that be? Mom, you're amazing. Inviting Simon here was incredibly generous of you."

"I'm kind of surprised he wanted to come," Adam said. "When will he get here?"

Bella skittered over to the doorway. Her pencil-thin tail stuck straight up like an antenna, and she gave a single, sharp bark.

Alice glanced at the big antique clock on the wall. "Donno went to the airport to pick him up. Looks like he's here in time for dessert."

• • •

To Mason, Simon Gauthier was a ghost from one brief encounter twenty years before. Mason had burst into the Paris apartment after the bombing to find his father with Celeste and her little boy. The single impression had been fleeting—a kid in short pants with knobby knees and dark hair, clinging to his mother's skirt as he stared wide-eyed at the intruder.

Now in his twenties, he was tall and slender, with longish dark hair and brown eyes, a firm handshake and a direct gaze. A day or two's growth of beard shadowed his face. He wore an olive drab Utilikilt with wool socks, lace-up boots and a rough woolen sweater. His luggage consisted of an oversize backpack, battered from travel, baggage tags fluttering from the handles.

"Thank you for inviting me, Alice," he said after the round of introductions. His English was precise and fluent. "I've wondered about you and your family all my life."

"We have a lot to catch up on," she said simply. "I'm glad you accepted our invitation."

Faith and her girls came to the dining room to meet Simon. The guy was friendly, Mason observed. In no time at all, they were chatting about Simon's life in Grenoble, where he had recently finished university. He had a degree in engineering and industrial design, and he worked as a ski instructor.

To Mason, the newcomer was not the most interesting thing in the room. It took most of Mason's self-control to resist staring at Faith. He wanted to grab her and throw his arms around her. She seemed subdued, though. Standoffish. Damn, was she still seeing that keyboard player?

"We should all go for a ski day," Ivy said. "I love to ski."

"That sounds like heaven," said Mason's mom. "I used to love to ski the way most people love to breathe."

"Then you should do it again," said Ruby. She had a way of cutting to the chase.

"I concur." Simon grinned affably. "I believe we could rig something for you, Alice. You're familiar with a sit-ski, yes?"

She looked flustered. "Oh, I don't think—"

"Come on, Mom," Adam said. "He might be onto something."

She bit her lip, looking worried. Mason tried to imagine what was going through her head. The avalanche, the accident. The last time she'd been on a ski slope.

Then she smiled. "I'll make you a deal, Ruby. I'll go skiing if you and your sister come, too. And your mother."

"I'm scared." Ruby's knee-jerk reaction to anything new.

"You think I'm not?"

• • •

Faith stood at the base of the Saddle Mountain Ski Resort and regarded the network of ski trails with trepidation. There was a good dumping of powder, clear skies, and even a glimmer of sunshine. But Faith knew she was a terrible skier. She'd tried it only a few times, and that had been years ago.

"This is so cool," Cara said, clearly feeling no trepidation at all. "Did you see me on the bunny slope?"

"I did. You're a natural, kiddo. Ruby, too." Ruby was already on the beginner hill with her ski school class. She'd conquered her fear in record time, and Faith could hear her laughter across the acres of snow. The girls had gotten an early start with Ivy, who had given Cara a lesson.

"Simon told me if I can make it down the bunny slope okay a few times, he'd take me up the chairlift. Mom, you look great in that outfit."

That was something, at least. "Thanks. Ivy loaned it to me." The powder blue jacket and white pants fit perfectly. "I don't want to be one of those lame beginners who looks like a million bucks but skis like a klutz."

"Everybody's a klutz starting out," Mason said, pulling up next to them on a snowmobile. "It's kind of a rule."

Attached to the snowmobile was something called a bi-ski for Alice. The rig had two skis on a frame, a molded seat and hand controls. Two thick straps would be used by Simon to assist her down the mountain.

Donno came out of the lodge, pushing Alice in her transport chair.

"I can't believe I let you rope me into this," Faith said to her.

"It'll be fun," Alice said. "You'll see. I need you to come along because we might need more than one medic."

"Very funny."

"In case you haven't noticed, I'm trying to throw you and Mason together," Alice added.

Faith nearly choked on a cold breath of air. "Excuse me?"

"Oh, come on, you think I don't see how much you're attracted to each other?"

Faith's cheeks burned. "You're delusional."

"No. When you're together, the electricity is almost palpable, and don't pretend it's not. I have no idea what you're so afraid of, Faith. Look at me. I'm about to ski down a mountain with no arms and no legs. If that doesn't scare me, then admitting you're in love with my son shouldn't scare you."

"But I'm not—" But she was.

To her relief, Simon and Adam came over to help get Alice into the rig and up the mountain. They all met at the summit, and it was time for Alice's first run.

With Simon's assistance, she skied down the hill. It was incredible to watch. She glided as if she were on a cloud. The controls allowed her to turn and control her speed. Faith forgot her awkwardness as she skied nearby. Alice laughed and shrieked with glee the whole way down.

"She's having fun at last," Mason said, sliding to a stop next to Faith. "I love that."

Faith smiled at him. "Me, too. Your mom's an amazing woman. She's worked so hard and come so far."

Mason felt a surge of joy, seeing his mother ski again. Adam and Ivy did, too, high-fiving each other as their mother nailed the turns and figured out how to stop like a hockey player on ice. After a few runs, she pleaded fatigue, and Donno took her home with Faith and the girls. He and his brother and sister and Simon stayed to ski some more. He felt an edge of competitiveness with Simon, which was dumb, because the guy was fifteen years younger and had been working in the French Alps as a ski instructor. Still, Mason couldn't deny the urge to out-ski him.

"Last time we skied together, we were scattering Dad's ashes," Ivy said as the four of them gathered at the summit in the late afternoon. The lowering sun drew a thread of orange along the western edge of the mountains, and the lift attendants had announced that it was the final run of the day.

Simon regarded her solemnly. He flexed and unflexed his gloved hands.

"We didn't even know about you that day," Ivy added.

Simon's gaze shifted to Mason. "No? What about you, eh?"

"You know the answer to that."

"I would have liked to be there," Simon told him. "Why didn't you contact me?"

"Why the hell do you think?"

They glared at each other for about three heartbeats. Then Mason lowered his goggles and pointed his skis down the hill.

Simon attacked the final run as if it were a slalom race, trying his best to overtake Mason.

And Mason, of course, was having none of it.

They both sped toward the base, each intent on getting there first. They were nearing the bottom when a large dog shot in front of them, chasing a snowball. Both turned to avoid the running dog—but it was too late to avoid each other.

The crash felt to Mason as if he'd hit a tree. At that speed, the impact left his bones ringing. Snow powder exploded all around him; both of his skis detached from the bindings and shot up into the air. He heard a crunching sound and a rush of breath from Simon.

Within seconds, Adam and Ivy arrived. "What the hell?" Adam demanded. "Are you okay?"

Mason unstrapped his helmet, gingerly removing

it. He propped himself up on both elbows as the snow dust settled. His leg felt as if someone had taken a sledgehammer to it. "I'll be all right," he muttered, massaging his thigh. He checked on Simon, who was already sitting up, wiping snow from his face. "*Et toi*?" he asked.

"*Merde alors. Casse-toi.*" Simon spat the epithet as he dragged himself to his feet. His goggles had broken, and there was a livid bruise, already beginning to swell, on the top ridge of his cheekbone. A horizontal scratch on the bridge of his nose had started to bleed. "*Fait de l'air.*"

Ivy handed him a snowball to hold on the swelling cheek. "Welcome to sibling rivalry."

Mason and Simon resolved their differences the way any two guys would—over a bottle of hard liquor. As a peace offering, Simon bought a bottle of rare Jameson's and offered shots as soon as they got back home. They gathered around the big stone fireplace, warming themselves in front of a roaring fire and sampling the Irish whiskey. Outside, the snow was coming down in thick flakes.

His mother came in with Faith, and they both studied Simon's face, the bruise burgeoning into a proper black eye. Two butterfly bandages crisscrossed the bridge of his nose, making a white X. "When did that happen?" Alice asked. "On the slopes, or in the boxing ring?"

Simon shot a glare at Mason. "*Une petite chute.* Here, have some of this Irish whiskey. The guy at the bottle shop said it has a powerful analgesic effect." He grinned. "It appears to be working."

"In that case," she said, "I'd better try some."

"How about you, Faith?" Simon offered. "A taste of holiday cheer?"

"Thanks, but I've got to be somewhere."

Shit, thought Mason. Was she going on a date?

"My daughter Ruby's in the Christmas pageant this year. She's a lamb in the nativity scene. I need to go pick her up from rehearsals."

"You should get Donno to drive you," Mason said. "The roads are going to be terrible."

"I'll be all right," she said. "I'm used to it." She offered everyone a wave. "Have a good evening, guys."

Simon's gaze followed her with a universally recognizable male hunger. "Tell me more about Faith," he said after she'd gone. "She's a widow, no?"

"She's a widow, yes," Ivy said.

"Is she seeing someone?" Everyone knew the code beneath those four words.

Mason wanted to smack him. The kid was too young for her, still in his twenties. "Yes," he said, knocking back another shot of whiskey. "She's seeing guys who are old enough to vote."

Simon regarded him placidly for a long moment. "Ah," he said.

That French *ah*. It grated. "What's that supposed to mean?" Mason demanded.

"It means *j'ai compris*. Or as you say in America, 'I get it.' " He tapped his lowball glass against Mason's. "Does she know?"

"Know what?"

"That you like her. That you have feelings for her."

"What the hell—"

"He's right, you know," said Ivy.

"Hey, stay out of this."

"You wish. It's my job as your sister to meddle. Now, quit arguing with me and go after her."

Faith swore through her teeth at the ice-cold van, which coughed like a victim of black lung and kept dying. Finally, she got it started and sat there shivering in the cold, with the engine chugging. This was a ridiculous vehicle for her to own, but at least it was paid for. Getting a new car was one of those things that might happen "one day." But "one day" kept getting pushed back—after bills, after girls, after she figured out a way to get Cara to college.

A shadow appeared outside her window. She gasped in surprise. "Mason," she said, rolling down the window. "Is everything all right?"

"I'm driving you to town," he said.

"That's not necessary."

"I'm doing it anyway."

"You've been drinking," she observed.

"Half a highball. Give me a break. And get out of that car or we'll be late to pick up Ruby."

Sometimes, she thought, the best thing to do was to just surrender. She rolled up the window and shut off the van. The heated seat of Mason's car was undeniably comfortable. So was their silence as he drove her to the church. She kept thinking about what Alice had said earlier. There was no escaping it. Now Faith wondered if Mason knew, if he had any clue as to how much she liked him.

They arrived just as the rehearsal was wrapping up. The pageant directors, Eddie and Maureen Haven, managed to get the kids to sound like angels everyone had heard on high. The final number sounded as sweet as birdsong.

Ruby was wiped out at the end of the evening. Faith had brought along a snack for her and managed to get a few bites of food into her before Ruby fell asleep in the backseat. "She gets so fatigued," Faith explained. "Especially after the skiing today."

When they arrived back home, he picked Ruby up and carried her to the door. Ruby stirred and snuggled cozily against him. His breath caught, and the expression on his face was one of surprised tenderness, as if he couldn't believe what he was feeling. "She's light as a feather."

"I know. Sometimes she seems so fragile to me." Faith felt a familiar thrum of worry, something she lived with every day of her life. “Let’s take her straight to bed. If I know Ruby, she’s down for the count.”

Ruby didn’t wake up. They put her to bed. Across the room, Cara slept like a corpse, as wiped out as everyone else by the skiing.

Faith wasn’t tired at all. She felt like staying up all night, talking to Mason. Every nerve tingled when she was with him. They went down to the lounge room together. Outside the windows, big snowflakes wafted down. Mason added a couple of logs to the fire while Faith fixed two mugs of hot chocolate.

They settled down on the big chesterfield sofa, watched the cheery fire and sipped their hot chocolate. After a few minutes Mason set down his mug. Then he took hers and set it down, too.

“I got you a present,” he said, handing her a smallish gift bag.

She gasped in surprise. “Really? That’s so nice.”

“Open it.”

Her heart gave a wild leap when she took out an oblong case of some sort. *Jewelry?* She opened the case and gave a laugh. “Oh, my God. You got me a pair of red Fendi sunglasses.”

“Indeed I did.”

“I can’t believe you remembered.”

“You’d be surprised at what I remember about you, Faith.”

She put the glasses on. They felt chic and

luxurious, and the dancing flames in the fireplace took on a special glow. "But I didn't get anything for you."

"Oh, yeah," he said. "Yes, you did. Merry Christmas, Faith." With slow deliberation, as if he'd been thinking about this moment all his life, he took off the glasses, then slipped his arms around her and kissed her.

She softened into the kiss, holding tight, feeling their hearts beating together. It was fantastic, the kind of kiss that made her forget the whole world. When it ended, she waited for a moment with her eyes closed, wishing she never had to open them and face reality.

She forced herself to look up at him. She didn't know what to make of the kiss. Was he just lonely?

He smiled and gently brushed a lock of hair away from her cheek. "You look worried."

"Do I?"

He leaned forward to kiss her again, but she pushed herself away, drawing her knees up to her chest. "You have to stop doing this. You . . . *We* have to stop."

"I was just getting started."

"I don't want to start anything with you."

"Faith—"

"No, listen. We can't start anything because I can already tell you it's going to end badly. And it'll be a mess and people will get hurt and—"

He touched his finger to her lips. “Are you still seeing that guy? The one in the band?”

She felt powerless, mesmerized by his touch. And against all her better judgment, she said, “Right now I’m not seeing anyone but you.”

26

After the holidays Mason went back to his place in the city. It was beautiful, with a terrace and views of downtown, stylishly furnished and comfortable. There were some art pieces Regina had picked out, and they were beautiful, too, but when he looked at them, he felt nothing. The more he thought about Avalon, the less like home his apartment seemed. Still, it was a great place in a great neighborhood. He could step outside and be anywhere within a few short blocks—bars, restaurants, a gym with a climbing wall, shopping and movies and shows.

Had those things ever mattered to him?

It seemed as if everything that mattered was far away. He immersed himself in work, doing what he did best—putting together deals, making his clients happy, earning plenty of money. He took a winter trip to Nassau and tried kiteboarding, enjoying the rush of skimming along the waves, being swept along by the wind. He met people in bars, drank and danced and flirted, but it didn't fill the void inside him.

Whenever he visited Avalon, Faith managed to make herself scarce. She insisted that getting involved would be a mistake. There would be a mess—that was her term for it.

He couldn't dispute the observation. When it came to personal relationships, he had a habit of making a mess of things. He kept thinking it was different with Faith. *He* was different with Faith. He wanted things he'd never wanted before—quiet evenings at home, long, comfortable silences and conversations that had no end. He wanted to know everything about her, and to share everything about himself. He wanted forever.

The clarity of the thought resounded through him. No more overthinking or second-guessing. But the trick would be to convince Faith that he was absolutely sincere.

He decided to woo her. Court her, whatever that old-fashioned word meant. He intended to win her heart by showing her a good time.

"Come to the city," he said when she answered her phone. "We'll go to dinner and a movie."

"I beg your pardon."

"I said—"

"I heard what you said. Is this your way of asking me out?"

"That's right."

"I didn't hear any asking."

Oh. "Okay, I'll call you back."

He turned off his phone and waited a couple of minutes. Then he called her back.

"Is this Faith McCallum?" he asked.

"Speaking." There was the sound of a smile in her voice.

"Faith, it's Mason. I was wondering, would you like to go to dinner and a movie with me in the city on Friday night?"

"That sounds fun."

Yes.

"I can't, though. I have plans."

Damn. Was she seeing that guy again? Another guy? "How about Saturday?" he suggested.

"I can make that work," she said.

Faith twisted her hands together and took a deep breath, certain she was about to be fired. Alice had that dragon lady look on her face, the one she wielded like a hammer. And once Alice fired her, everything else was going to collapse like a house of cards. She'd be back to square one with the girls—homeless, searching for a way to make a living. And now it would be worse, because—

"Let me be sure I understand," Alice said in a chilly voice. "You say you intend to go to the city for a date with my son. An overnight date."

"Yes." Faith refused to apologize. She wanted this. Wanting something just for herself was a rare sensation, and she intended to pursue it. Empowered by certainty, she faced Alice head-on.

"I realize it could be problematic, me going out with my employer's son."

She had discussed the situation at length with her friend Kim. And Kim, like the good friend she was, had offered nothing but support. "The heart wants what it wants," she'd told Faith. "Everything else will fall into place."

Or not, thought Faith, regarding Alice. On the carpet beside her, Bella sat at attention, awaiting orders. To Faith, the dog looked every bit as judgmental as her owner.

"Problematic," Alice echoed. "And why would you say that?"

"Because you might regard it as crossing a line," Faith said. "And I wouldn't blame you."

"You have no idea what I think," Alice said.

"Fine, then why don't you enlighten me?" Faith just wanted to get the conversation over with.

"I think it's about bloody time, that's what I think," Alice stated. "I've watched you and Mason behaving like those little bar magnets, getting close and then breaking apart. I'm glad you're finally going to do something about it."

Faith blinked at her. "Then you don't have a problem with this."

"It's a marvelous idea. I told you that day on the ski slope that I was in favor of it." Alice glided toward her dressing room, with its racks and shelves displaying her clothes like apparel in a boutique. Bella trotted along, eager to please.

"I'm opening the vault to you," she said. "Let's figure out what you're going to wear."

"It's just dinner and a movie," Faith said, feeling giddy with relief.

"In New York. With my son. Take down that little black dress."

"I'm seeing four little black dresses."

"The one from Celine. I bought it on impulse, but it's a bit young for me and I never wore it. So many of these things are from my former life. I don't know why I kept them." Her smile was wistful. "Or maybe I do—finally. We're lucky to wear almost the same size."

Faith held the elegant dress against her, a silky whisper of pure luxury. "I can't."

"Don't start with that. It's tedious. And borrow my Missoni coat. It's chilly in the evenings, still. Grab those shoes over there." Bella trotted over, nudging each shoe with her nose until Alice rewarded her with a "Yes, good dog."

Faith picked up the glossy, red-soled pump.

"Perfect," said Alice. "Wear those."

"I couldn't," Faith said, noting that they looked brand-new.

"You can, and you will," said Alice. "You think I have any use for them?"

Mason was ridiculously nervous about the date. He wanted to impress her. He wanted to start something with her. He wanted it to go well.

He had the cleaning lady scrub every square inch of the apartment and bring in some fresh flowers and candles, because at the end of the date, he intended to bring Faith here and make such sweet love to her that she'd never want to leave.

He met her at the station, and they took a taxi to the theater. They made small talk in the cab—the chilly night, whether to go for Italian or Thai or some buzzy new restaurant they'd read about. She balked when they got out of the cab and entered an invitation-only area cordoned off by velvet ropes. "What's going on?"

"Dinner and a movie," he said. "Actually, movie first and then dinner."

She tilted back her head to check out the marquee. "Wait a second," she said. "This is your idea of dinner and a movie?"

"Yes. You said you were a fan of Bill Hader."

"You have a good memory."

It had nothing to do with his memory. It had to do with the fact that he couldn't stop thinking about her. "This is the world premiere of his new movie. One of my clients is a producer, and he got the tickets. He's going to be here tonight."

"Your client?"

"Bill Hader."

"You've got to be kidding me."

"Nope. You'll see. They'll introduce him at the

start of the movie. Oh, and over here . . ." He took her hand and led her through the jostling crowd. "Red carpet," he said.

"What?"

"We're walking the red carpet. Brace yourself."

"Forget it." She dug in her heels.

"Too late." He towed her along through a lightning storm of camera flashes. They stopped together at a backdrop screen covered in the sponsors' logos. He slid his arm around her waist and hugged her in close while more cameras went off.

She gasped and then laughed aloud. "Oh, my God. Did the paparazzi just take our picture?"

"They must think we're VIPs."

The movie was good—definitely good enough for dinner conversation afterward. He took her to Butter, because it was quiet and cave-like and romantic, and the maître d' could always find a table for Mason.

"You went to a lot of trouble," she said, resting her chin in her hand as she looked across the table at him. "I really appreciate it."

"It wasn't trouble. I want to show you a good time. It's great to see you relaxing and having fun."

"I always have fun."

"But you never let somebody else take care of you instead of always looking after others." He signaled for the check, and they walked back to his apartment. It was a cold, clear night, and despite the rushing crowds, it felt as though they were the only people in the city.

"If you're looking to impress me, it's working," she said with a smile. Her eyes grew wide as she surveyed the foyer of his building and then his apartment. "This is gorgeous. And your idea of *dinner and a movie* exceeds all expectations."

When he took her coat, he stood behind her and let his hands linger on her shoulders. Bending his head, he inhaled the scent of her hair, and the warmth of her skin wafted to him.

"What is it that we're doing, Mason?" she asked with her characteristic directness.

"I'm courting you. I'm trying to win your heart by showing you a good time."

"You showed me a good time. No, it was a great time. But that's not the way to win my heart," she said.

Damn. Really? "Then how do you suppose I go about it?"

"You don't win a woman's heart by showing her a good time," she patiently explained. "You do it by showing her who you are."

Oh. New plan.

"That's what I'm trying to do right now." He turned her in his arms and kissed her, because he would rather kiss than talk. She made a sound, something between a sigh and a moan, and her eagerness was a huge turn-on.

"Suppose we go to the bedroom."

"That sounds like an excellent idea."

Straightforward. He loved that about her, he thought as he showed her the way to the bedroom.

"The first time I saw you in a bathing suit, I got excited," he said, reaching behind her to unzip her dress.

"Really?"

"Yep. I wanted to touch you here . . ." His finger lightly ran along the curve of her waist and over her hip. "And here." He found a soft place with his lips. "And here . . ." He laid her back on the bed and took off his shirt.

A gasp escaped her, and then she stopped and pushed back against the pillows. "Wait, you're talking about the *first* time you saw me in a swimsuit? Your mom's first swim in the lake?"

"Yes. I'm getting excited again, thinking about your legs." His hand traveled along her thigh to her knee.

"So excited that you went back to Regina and set a date for the wedding," she said. "I swear, Mason, I don't get how your mind works."

"I was . . . Shit. Confused, and I know that's no excuse. But I'd been going down this road with Reg. I was committed. I wanted to make it work. I kept trying to shoehorn myself into a relationship because it seemed right." He moved over her, pressing her wrists against the mattress.

"But it never *felt* right. It never felt like this."

He kissed her, and they didn't talk anymore for a long time.

She fell asleep with her head tucked against his shoulder, and when he felt the whisper of her breath on his bare skin, he knew a moment of such exquisite happiness that it made his heart soar.

In the morning, Mason woke up smiling. He checked his messages and found his inbox full of notes about last night. "Check it out," he said, turning the screen of his phone toward Faith. "We're in *Time Out New York*."

Apparently, it was a gossip website. Their picture was posted in an article about the movie premiere. The caption read, "Finance magnate Mason Bellamy and his new squeeze."

"I'm a magnate. How about that?"

"And I'm a squeeze. A new one."

"I like squeezing you. In fact . . ."

"Hey."

He took her hand and kissed it. "That was really nice last night. And I'm not talking about the movie premiere."

"Best date I've had in years, by a mile. Maybe the best date ever."

But . . . He heard the silent but. What did she need from him? He knew she needed more. He knew how to show a girl a good time, but in all honesty, he realized much of it was artifice, pretending, just skimming the surface.

From the start, Faith had always made it clear that she valued honesty, responsibility, doing for others.

This is who I am, he thought. *What if it's not enough for her?* "Tell me about your husband," he said. Damn. Had he really just said that?

"Dennis? What is there to say about Dennis? He was my whole world, practically from the first moment I met him. Dennis was . . . ah, where do I start? He saved me. My mother died, and I was completely alone, and he came riding into my life on a motorcycle, and the world seemed to change color before my eyes. We were so young, it's incredible that we survived each other. It was one of those rare pairings that just worked, and we didn't question it. He wasn't perfect. He was reckless and not much of a planner. He forgot things, including his meds. He put things off, and he was terrible with money. But he gave me his heart, and he took care of mine. And when he left this world, my heart went with him."

She leaned back against the bank of pillows, looking tousled and beautiful and sad. "Simple as that," she said. "The only thing that kept me hanging on was the girls. For their sake, I put myself back together and carried on."

And there it was, Mason realized. It didn't matter who he was, or what he said, or what he promised. She had not—and might never—let go of her late husband.

He couldn't compete with a ghost.

Faith boarded the morning train to Avalon alone. She'd told Mason she needed time to think. That wasn't quite true. She knew exactly what she thought. She knew exactly what was happening—she was falling into a love she'd never felt before.

This overwhelming feeling was different from her love for Dennis. That had been woven of youthful hopes and dreams, the shared bond of parenthood. But this. This thing with Mason Bellamy . . . The emotions were so intense that she was afraid to let them overtake her, because she didn't want to lose this crazy, heady euphoria that infused her like a drug. It was made of a kind of passion and joy so fierce that it felt impossible. And that was a problem, because it *was* impossible. She couldn't imagine a way for it to end well.

Faith knew what she had to do. She had to shut down the sweet insanity before any real damage was done. It was the right thing to do. Back in Avalon, there was work to be done, two girls who needed her.

Not to mention Alice.

The moment she walked through the door, Alice glided toward her. These days she had such good control of her right hand and fingers that she no longer needed the breath control mechanism. “Well?” she asked bluntly.

Faith knew exactly what she was asking. Alice had survived far too much to put up with mincing words. “I had a lovely time. The movie and dinner were amazing, and Mason was the perfect gentleman.”

“Good Lord, I hope not,” Alice said.

Faith’s blush betrayed her. She tried to hide it by slipping off the borrowed shoes. “Thank you for this outfit. I felt like Cinderella.”

“In case you haven’t noticed,” Alice pointed out, “you *are* Cinderella.”

“Right. And you’re the fairy godmother. Where are the girls?”

“Ruby is helping Milo at the shelter. Milo has put her on the list for a diabetes alert dog.”

“We can’t aff—”

“Don’t start. If she qualifies, and if they find an appropriate dog, then we’ll find a way.”

“We?” Faith bristled.

“Yes. *We.* Just like we’ll find a way to help Cara go to college, and then medical school, or clown college, or whatever the hell she wants.”

“Alice, I appreciate your interest, *and* your help. But I’ve been going over the various financial aid packages for college, and they all involve me taking on even more debt. I can’t—”

“Honestly, Faith, you have a habit of taking

everything on yourself. Mason will organize the financing for you. He's very good at it."

The idea of working with him on some kind of loan made Faith feel slightly nauseous. Sleeping with a guy . . . An exchange of money . . . *No, thank you.*

"I'll figure something out," she said. "And I don't need Mason's help."

"That's true. Faith, you're as transparent as glass. Why can't you just let yourself love him?"

"Because I'm *scared,*" Faith shot back before she could stop herself.

Alice froze. She stared at Faith, looking as though she was about to explode. Then she burst out laughing, long and loud, until she gasped for breath. "Let me get this straight. You lost your mother and your husband, survived God knows what kind of poverty and eviction, raised two extraordinary girls, and you're telling me you're afraid of falling in love?"

"I'm glad you're amused," Faith said quietly. "And I'm not afraid of falling in love. I'm afraid of falling *out* of love."

"Trust me, it's not so bad." Alice made herself laugh again. "Come on. Let's go get a cup of Wayan's special coffee."

They went together to the kitchen.

"Clown college?" Faith asked.

"Just a suggestion."

✵ 27 ✵

An early heat wave came over the city, and Mason couldn't wait to get away. He craved the cool breezes of Willow Lake, and as soon as he was able to wrap up his business for the week, he headed upstate to Avalon. When he arrived, the house was quiet. Phil said his mother and Rick had taken the girls bowling.

"My mom went bowling?"

Phil smiled. "She probably just went to observe. And pass judgment."

"Did Faith go with them?"

"I don't think so."

He found her in the laundry room, singing along to a White Stripes song on the radio and folding clothes. The room was like an oven, and she'd pinned up her hair and wore a tank top and flip-flops and skimpy shorts. He stood watching her before she noticed him, feeling a warm rush of affection. She was never still. There was always some job to be done, someone who needed to be looked after—her girls, his mom, their laundry, their lives. She was a caregiver, and for Faith, it didn't seem to be just a job. It was a vocation.

"Boo," he said.

She jumped, dropping a stack of folded clothes. "You scared me," she said.

"Well, I shouldn't. Because I want you to know that I'm not a ghost."

"I can see that."

"Can you?"

She bent to pick up the dropped laundry, but he stopped her and kissed her long and deeply. "Faith, I can't stop thinking about New York."

She blushed. "It was lovely. Every moment of it."

"Then why won't you see me again?"

"Mason, I just don't see the point. That night was a beautiful fantasy. A brief escape, and I loved it, but it showed me how completely different we are, from two different worlds."

"And that's a problem?"

"No, but it's not . . . I don't think we should . . . Mason, you're getting over a breakup, and I'm just . . . broken."

"That's bullshit," he said, losing patience. "I'm not buying it. Listen, I'm sorry as hell for what happened to you. I'm sorry the man you loved so deeply is gone. Maybe you'll never have a love like that again, but he didn't use up your entire capacity to love. It doesn't work like that."

"When did you become the expert?"

"When I heard the things you whispered to me that night. Believe me, Faith, you have untapped reserves of love."

The blush spread down her neck. "But—"

"Let me finish. I look at you with your

daughters, Faith, and I thank God that guy was in the world to give you Cara and Ruby. Now that he's gone, you don't get to mourn him the rest of your life. You get to *live* the rest of your life. You're not broken. You've just put your heart on hold, and I'm telling you, you don't have to do that anymore."

She regarded him in stunned silence. At least, she looked stunned. The heat of the day wafted through the window of the laundry room.

"Let's go for a hike," he said.

"What?"

"I don't want to have this conversation in a laundry room."

"What conversation? Mason—"

"Let's go." He didn't wait for more protests, but took her by the hand and led the way along a trail that followed the lakeshore.

The trail led to the top of the lake, where a series of granite cliffs offered a commanding view of the beautiful landscape.

"How are the girls?" he asked.

"Cara's been accepted to four colleges. I'm excited for her, but I'm scared to lose her. I'm afraid of letting her down, too. The cost, even with financial aid . . ."

"She'll be fine. Give her a chance to work out her own life. You worry too much."

"It's the domain of mothers."

"You've been a mother since you were her age."

"Yeah, it's weird when I think about it that way. Sometimes I forget what it was like to be a kid, except . . ." She paused and bit her lip.

"What? What were you going to say?"

"Except when I'm with you." She offered a brief smile. "I feel like a kid when I'm with you."

"Hey, that's a good sign. I almost never see you do anything just for the fun of it."

"Life is fun enough. I don't have to *do* anything in particular to make it more fun."

"Come on. You don't think it could be fun to try kiteboarding or go off a high dive?"

"I suppose it would be fun after it was over and I realized I'd survived intact." She considered him for a moment. "We're very different, you and I. For me, life is enough. For you, there always has to be something more, something that involves danger and risk."

"Because it's fun. You challenge yourself, you push and you break through. When was the last time you took a physical risk that didn't involve helping someone out or saving a life? When was the last time you took a physical risk just for the hell of it?"

She studied him for a long time. "When was the last time you took an *emotional* risk?"

He studied her for an even longer time. "When I fell for you," he said simply, and started walking again. "Let's go jump off a cliff."

She stood stock-still, wondering if she was

hearing things. “Wait a minute, you *fell* for me?”

He stopped walking and turned back to her, holding out his hand. “Yeah. It was scary in a weird way. But I like it. I like the feeling of loving you.”

“You’re crazy. You can’t just declare something like this and then make me jump off a cliff.”

“Sure I can. It’s not as dangerous as it looks. My cousins and I used to come up to these cliffs when we were kids,” he said. The stunned expression on her face made him smile. “Listen, everything about my life got better because of you. I used to hold people at arm’s length, but I don’t want to do that anymore. It doesn’t work when it comes to you.”

She took in a breath, a gasp of surprise and pleasure. He knew that sound. He remembered it from that night in New York. And that was the moment he knew he’d won her over.

Still, she balked. “Mason. This is all really sudden.”

“It’s not. When I think back, I realize my heart knew right away. My head took longer to catch on. I think I probably knew when we took a shower together the first day we met. That’ll be a good story to tell our friends, that the first time we met, we took a shower together and then went and got tested for blood and body fluid exposure.”

Her smile wavered. “That was a long time ago.”

“It was. Because there were . . . complications.

Now there aren't." He led her to the rocky cliff edge and encompassed the area with a sweep of his arm. His heart was pounding, but his voice was steady, because he'd never been so sure of anything in his life. "That pool down there is called the Devil's Punchbowl."

She leaned slightly over the edge. "It's a long way down."

"That's what makes it fun."

"How can something that scary be fun?"

He smiled, tipping her face up to his. "You're the best thing that ever happened to me, and I never want to let you go. Ever."

Her eyes filled with tears, but she was smiling. "Then there's good news."

"Yeah?"

"I feel the same way. With every bit of my heart, I do."

He'd been waiting forever to hear those words. He turned and cupped her cheek in his hand. "Oh, baby, I hope you mean that."

"You think I'm kidding? I tried like hell to stop thinking of you, but it didn't work. You're all I think about, all I dream about. And it's kind of a miracle, because I thought . . . I didn't think love would happen to me, ever again."

His heart hammered in his chest. "You thought wrong, Faith. I'm here. And I'm not going anywhere."

She offered a shaky smile. "Okay. But I'm not

the only one in this equation. Are you sure you're ready for an instant family? Two girls who are not always the easiest people in the world to get along with?"

"I'm ready for anything, Faith. I'm so damned ready. I love you, and I love your girls, and our life together is going to be amazing."

She took a deep breath, and he could see her trembling. She swallowed hard. "I'm scared to jump."

"And I was scared to fall. But I did it anyway. And I survived. So will you." And with that, he grabbed her hand, and they jumped together.

Epilogue

The murmur of *Pomp and Circumstance* drifted through the speakers set up on the lake house lawn, echoing the iconic melody that had accompanied Cara across the stage of Columbia University that morning.

She felt a swelling of pride as she stepped through the French doors and surveyed the picnic area, where her graduation party was about to begin. Mason's cousin Daisy had volunteered to take pictures of the event, and Zach, a family friend, was making a video. The two of them were pros in the business, so Cara had taken the time to fix her hair and makeup. She'd left her high school steampunk look behind long ago, to the great relief of pretty much everyone who knew her.

No one had noticed her yet, so she paused on the deck to take in the view and savor the moment. A warm breeze stirred the new leaves in the trees and swept shimmers of sunlight over Willow Lake. The air was filled with the scent of freshly cut grass and flowers from the garden Ruby and Alice had planted that first summer. They came back every year.

It was good to be home.

The family was gathering down by the lake at the picnic area. The linens and balloons matched Columbia's signature pale blue color, and the college flag had been hoisted at the end of the dock. Folding chairs were arranged to create an aisle for Cara to reprise her graduation march. It was silly, but the least Cara could do was reenact the ceremonial march for Alice, who had not been able to attend.

After dinner, there would be a bonfire, s'mores and toasts to Cara's as-yet-undetermined future. Five years ago, if someone had told her she would end up a college graduate with an extended family numbering in the double digits, she would have thought they were high.

And yet here she was, the ink barely dry on her diploma, about to start a new chapter of her life. With so many people surrounding and supported, she was filled with confidence that it would go well.

She didn't think of the staff as "staff" anymore. Wayan, Banni and Donno, Lena and Phil—the fact that they were all still here had to mean they would be around for the long run. There were worse places to live and work than this gorgeous lakeside property.

Ruby was marching around with exaggerated movements, reenacting the processional. Her dog, a yellow lab named Fisher, obediently trotted at her side. Fisher went everywhere with Ruby. His training as a diabetes alert dog had given Ruby a new sense of freedom and courage. She was going to need it. Cara would not be the one to tell her this, but eighth grade was a bitch.

Cara thought about Milo, who had been so instrumental with both dogs. In order to finance his education, he had enlisted in the National Guard and had ended up in a military working dog detachment. He'd been deployed overseas and she rarely heard from him these days.

"I hope you're safe, wherever you are," she whispered under her breath. Then she put her cap and gown back on for photos.

Alice's dog, Bella, spotted Cara first and gave a yap of greeting. Slowly and with obvious effort, Alice raised her arm in greeting and waved, forming her fingers into an okay sign. The sight of her, using her arm and hand, brought a lump to

Cara's throat. Alice had worked so hard after the surgery.

Rick took hold of Alice's hand and gave it a kiss. "The guest of honor has arrived."

"Cara!" Ruby rushed over to the sound system and turned up the volume on *Pomp and Circumstance*. "We already started the photo shoot. Let's see you walk the walk!"

With sober dignity and perfect posture, her diploma in hand, Cara matched her pace to the music while Daisy and Zach captured shot after shot.

As she passed by all the smiling faces, Cara thought about her father, who seemed very present in her heart today. *You'd love this, Dad,* she thought. *You'd be so happy for me.*

She slowed her pace, letting the wave of emotion flow through her. Her gaze found her mother, dressed to the nines for the occasion, waiting with Mason at the end of the makeshift aisle. Mom looked so pretty and happy these days. Four years ago, she and Mason had gotten married right here in this same spot. Ever since, they'd been living out their happily-ever-after at the lake house.

Cara could still remember the anxious, stressed-out Mom of her childhood—a young widow scrambling to make ends meet. She had made sacrifices Cara was only beginning to understand, somehow making it possible for Cara and

Ruby to grow up feeling safe, secure and loved. Those hard years made Mom's current happiness all
the sweeter.

As she reached the end of the aisle and the music swelled, Cara stopped and turned to her mother. She took off her cap and angled the flat top toward the camera, showing the hand-lettered phrase she had written there this morning: *Thank you.*

✵ Acknowledgments ✵

I am so very grateful for . . .

My publishing team—Meg Ruley, Annelise Robey of the Jane Rotrosen Agency, Margaret Marbury, Lauren Smulski, Loriana Sacilotto, Craig Swinwood and all the good folks at MIRA Books.

Mindy Anderson, proud owner of the real Bella Ballou, Sam and Rocky. Thank you for your support of PAWS.

The Waterfront Bakery Brain Trust: Elsa, the comma putter-inner. Kate, the comma taker-outer. Sheila, Lois and Anjali—my first readers and best friends.

Cindy Peters, for her social networking savvy, can-do attitude and positive thinking, and Elizabeth Maas, for newsletters and just . . . everything.

Lori Cross and Jerry Gundersen—my sister and my soul mate. Every book is a challenge to complete, but this one in particular would never have materialized without their love and support during the writing of this novel.

Special thanks to Jim McMahon, a real-life caregiver who gives new meaning to "care" and "giving."

Center Point Large Print
600 Brooks Road / PO Box 1
Thorndike, ME 04986-0001 USA

(207) 568-3717

US & Canada:
1 800 929-9108
www.centerpointlargeprint.com